PETER GREEN AND THE UNLIVING ACADEMY

PETER GREEN

—— and the ——

UNLIVING ACADEMY

THIS BOOK IS FULL OF DEAD PEOPLE

The Unliving Chronicles

ANGELINA ALLSOP

TCK PUBLISHING.COM

ISBN: 978-1-63161-064-6

Published by TCK Publishing
www.TCKpublishing.com

Get discounts and special deals on books at:
www.TCKpublishing.com/bookdeals

Sign up for Angelina's VIP mailing lists for news, free books, and giveaways at:
www.aaallsop.com

For a free book from Angelina go to:
www.aaallsop.com/deadworld

For Jared Allsop, who inspired me to go for my dream.

CHAPTER ONE

HELLO, YOU'RE DEAD. PLEASE WAIT IN LINE.

OURTEEN-YEAR-OLD PETER GREEN WOKE UP knowing only three things: the proper way to put on a tie, that lemon custard was disgusting, and that he was dead. Sure, he knew a few other things like, you know, math and history—well, *some* history, just not his own. He knew his age, but couldn't tell you anything about his last few birthdays. And he couldn't tell you how he'd died. It was like he'd been reset to factory mode—a blank screen with no personal data left whatsoever.

Pete blinked groggily. *Where am I?* He winced as a bright white light shone through the blurry haze in his eyes. Slowly, color entered his vision and noises filtered through the nothingness. Voices and movements were all around him. It sounded as though he were surrounded by a bustling crowd of people.

He blinked some more, and his eyes finally focused enough for him to see that the bright white light was a chandelier. He sat up slowly, expecting pain but finding none.

He looked around, never more confused in his life—er, *after*life. He seemed to be lying in the middle of a rather busy lobby. The building was grand, nearly every inch of it covered in gleaming marble.

From the corner of his eye, a woman in a pretty red dress bent down toward him. Pete turned to her, smiling, and then yelped. "What the—?"

It wasn't a woman but a squat, ugly man with long red hair pulled back in a ponytail, wearing a sour expression.

"Whit th' whit?" the man asked in a heavy Scottish accent. He pulled a little at his white security T-shirt tucked into a navy blue kilt. The man had a large scar running across from the top of his skull down over one eye to just above his jawline. *No.* It wasn't a scar. It was an open wound!

"Are you okay?" Pete pointed a shaky finger at the man's face.

The man looked affronted. "Na, son. I'm naea'richt. C'moan, dinnaejuist lie thare," he said and poked Pete with his security baton. His red ponytail swung as he pointed to the bustling crowd. "Can't ye see how fur stowed it'sth'day?" He looked at his watch. "T'is rush hour. 9:15, 'n' we hae a train crash 'n' earthquake, 'n' you're juist lying tharelik' tis yer kip."

"My what?"

"Yer kip." He rolled his eyes and said, "Yer bed."

Pete blinked and patted the floor. *It definitely wasn't his bed.* An image of grass flashed in his mind, but the next moment it was gleaming marble again. He rubbed his eyes and tried remembering how he'd gotten here, but another sharp poke and yell from the angry guard interrupted his thoughts.

"I'm dead," Pete said blankly.

The security guard gave him a "well duh" look and pulled him up by the scruff of his neck.

"Weel, obviously. How come dae ye think yer here?" He didn't wait for Pete to answer and asked as he looked around, "You 'ere wi' anyone?"

Again, the man answered his question before Pete could even open his mouth. "Aye, a' coorse not," he said, rolling his eyes and pointing down a hall. "Listen, ye donder don thare, fill ootth' form, then they'll tak' ye whaur ye need tae be, 'kay?"

Pete turned to the man and looked him in the eye. "Uh, thanks…. Thank you, Angus."

The guard looked taken aback. He touched the white badge sewn onto his white security shirt.

"Na problem," he replied slowly.

Pete opened his mouth to ask why he couldn't remember anything, but the guard had already moved on to yell at another confused man who had been sleeping in the middle of the busy lobby floor. With a sigh, Pete looked up at the chandelier and painted ceiling and then around at the massive circular room he was in. It was about the size of a football stadium and was surrounded by marble archways all leading to different places. On one end, an archway led to a wide path to the west track subway; the opposite led to the east side tracks. There were signs for Portal Stations 1-30 to his left, and to his right were stations 31-40. He headed towards the archway the man had pointed to, with a sign that said Government Services.

As he walked, he mindlessly straightened his tie and smoothed his shirt and was shocked to find it untucked. Wait a second. He faltered and stopped walking. A woman bumped into him and cursed at him. He tried to apologize but couldn't quite make his voice work. Frankly, he was at a loss for words.

He looked down, mouth open, at his outfit. He was shoeless and dressed in blue striped pajamas with an expensive, cream-colored Battistoni silk dinner tie tied in a four-in-hand knot. Not exactly the usual clothes he'd pick from his closet. At least, as far as he could remember. A tie and pajamas? Even in reset mode, he knew that was an odd combination.

He touched the tie in wonder. What could he have possibly been doing when he died?

A sharp bump to his shoulder shook him from his thoughts. He looked up to see a man in an expensive business suit brush by. The man was loudly complaining as he wove through the crowd. "…might miss my port. Why do people always choose rush hour to die?"

Pete looked around and noticed that he had attracted the attention of another guard. Before the guard made his way over to start yelling at him, Pete quickly started walking again.

Several paces away, he paused at the back of the line he had been directed to and sighed. It was almost as long as a line at Disneyland. The man in front of Pete saw him looking around and sniffed.

"We picked a good time to die, huh?" he said dryly. The man's cheap brown suit had dark splatters on it that had to be blood. He wore a brown hat that, when he lifted it to scratch his head, revealed a fist-sized hole in his skull.

"Just like the people at Purgatory to design the DRD like a DMV—life's slowest bureaucracy. I know this is a small town and all," he added angrily, "but this is already a pretty big Port Station. They should invest in making this division even bigger. Or," he added, loudly, "they could separate the DRD from the insanely busy Portal Station," as though this should be obvious. He got several nods and amens to this from people around him.

He shook his head. "No other Port is set up this way."

He turned to Pete and added, "I mean, look at this." He pointed at the line in front of them. "This is just the line to get the ticket to wait in the real line."

"Oh," Pete said, flabbergasted.

The man chuckled. "That's how things are done in Purgatory. There are lines to wait in more lines." He hailed a boy shouting on the corner, a stack of newspapers bound at his feet. The boy ran over and gave one of the papers to the man, who tossed him some coins in return.

"Soon as my paperwork is in and I get my new ID," the man said, "I'm outta here."

Vaguely, Pete wondered where the man had gotten money from, but he asked instead, "Where are you going?"

The kid ran back over to his corner. "Paper!" he started back up. "Get your paper!"

"Got some family up north," the man said to Pete. "I'll stop there first." He shook open his newspaper. "Then, I'm not sure. I'll look for work and see how that goes." He lowered his head and became engrossed in an article, leaving Pete to contemplate his words.

Pete looked around. By then he'd gathered that he was in a transportation building set up like a train station. As the line moved forward, Pete could see from a different angle that there was a ticker hanging from the roof, constantly changing. He could hear the clatter of the letters and numbers as they changed. DEMONTON TO PURGATORY, ARRIVAL 10:10. Then, the sign switched to say: PURGATORY TO VALHALLA NONSTOP, DEPARTING 11:15. This clattered away to say PURGATORY TO NORTH POLE, 9:30 DELAYED TO 10:32 and on and on.

People rushed to work—whatever work in this world meant—carrying briefcases or purses. Occasionally, a voice would come on over a loudspeaker announcing arrivals and departures. A chorus of moans met the announcement that Portal 32 was closed due to technical difficulties.

When the line moved again, he could finally read the label printed on the glass doors: Department of Registered Deaths. A few more minutes and the line pushed him through the doors into the busy room beyond. There were about five people in front of him now. When he looked closer at the lady at the counter handing out tickets, he suppressed a gasp.

The woman behind the counter was a skeleton. Pete would have actually mistaken her for some sort of decoration had she not been arguing with a large man in a trench coat in front of her desk.

"Everyone gets a ticket. Everyone goes in line," she said, with a heavy Jersey accent. "I don't care who you were. Here, you're just dead—and you get in line." She did not seem angry, almost a little bored in fact, and shooed away the man fuming in front of her. She pulled a box of cigarettes out of the breast pocket of her dress and tapped it on the top of her desk with her left hand as she gestured lazily at the next person in her line.

The cries from two small babies held by the anxious mother before the counter made the skeleton lady turn her head slightly. Pete was surprised to see she was wearing lipstick, cat-eyed glasses, and earrings. She wore the blonde hair attached to her skull in a fifties bob. She nodded at the woman and sucked in a puff of smoke. Having no lungs to fill, the smoke escaped her ribcage and went into her dress, making it look like it was on fire.

After about five minutes, Pete stepped up to the counter and smiled at the skeleton. He wasn't sure if she smiled back, but her body language seemed a little friendlier.

"Good morning. I just died."

"Alone?" When Pete just looked at her, she repeated, "Did you die alone?"

"Yes…" he said. "I believe so."

"And are you meeting someone here?"

Pete frowned. "I don't know."

"Do you have your memories?"

"No." He was relieved that this was a common enough thing for her to ask. "You want 1A-19."

Pete stared blankly, and she tapped her pen impatiently right in front of him. "The form on the wall."

Pete looked down while she typed a couple of things. Along the wall of her counter were forms resting in clear plastic shelves labeled:

A19-2-93 (INCIDENTS ONLY), Form 14-27-B, T.H.E.R.N. form 97 (PARENTS, CHILDREN PRESENT), T.H.E.R.N. Location form P119 (PARENTS, CHILDREN PREVIOUSLY DECEASED), and finally 1A-19 (CHILDREN - 18 AND UNDER).

She finished typing, and a ticket came out of a small machine with a number on it. "Take the ticket and your form, fill it out, and then they will call your number." She nodded at him, and Pete knew he was being dismissed.

He thanked her and looked around for a vacant seat. The large room was filled with rows of occupied chairs and a line of booths, each with an attendant behind a window talking to some mangled or bloodied person holding documents of some sort or another. Pete found an empty chair next to a smiling woman with a missing eye.

He was nervous, and there was an annoying tingling in his skin, as though he were forgetting something important. He couldn't help but feel that though he seemed to be in the right place and doing the right things, there was something very wrong. Rubbing at the goosebumps on his arms, he looked at the paper in his hands. The printed instructions read:

FILL OUT THE INFORMATION BELOW AS COMPLETELY AS YOU CAN. PLEASE USE A BLACK OR BLUE PEN. ILLEGIBLE FORMS WILL NOT BE ACCEPTED. PLEASE ASK AN ATTENDANT FOR HELP IF YOU ARE MISSING YOUR ARMS OR IF YOUR HANDS ARE UNUSABLE.

Pete frowned and began filling out the form. It didn't take long, as it only asked for a few things:

Name, Last and First

Middle Initials (optional)

Age

D.O.B. (Date of Birth)

D.O.D (Date of Death)

Place of Birth

Place of Death

When he finished answering the first three questions—and staring blankly at the next four—Pete didn't know what to do to pass the time, so he began looking around again. Along the walls were signs that said things like: BLUE OR BLACK PEN ONLY. DOCUMENTS SIGNED IN BLOOD WILL NOT BE ACCEPTED.

Another sign cheerfully said: ASK ONE OF OUR FRIENDLY ATTENDANTS ABOUT WORKING IN A GOVERNMENT POSITION! GREAT BENEFITS! GREAT PAY!

A smiling…thing…was depicted on the poster. She was wearing a white blouse and her head was shaped much like an anteater, and she had a similar skin tone. She wore lipstick and had brown hair sprouting from the top of her scalp. It was pinned to the side in an attempt at an elegant side-bun.

Pete kicked his feet nervously and looked up absently at the screen. He jumped when he saw his number flashing. He jolted out of his seat, almost dropping his paper, and walked to the window to find an impatient-looking young woman.

The woman looked to be in her early twenties and had dark blue eyes, sandy blonde hair, a dimpled chin, and a large forehead covered by bangs. She wore only a small amount of makeup. Nervously smoothing his tie, he slid his papers through the slit in the window. He could smell her perfume through the glass.

She pursed her lips and picked up the paper, squinted at it for a second, and spoke into a microphone. "This is all you remember?"

"I'm missing my brown shoes," he responded without thinking. He cringed. Where had that come from?

Instead of rolling her eyes, she simply wrote it down on the paper. She then turned to her computer and began typing again. She paused and used her mouse to click several things before turning back to him. "You can keep a copy of this for your records." She pulled off a carbon copy of the form. As an old printer chugged something out, she stopped what she was doing to put on some lip balm.

The woman clicked the mouse a couple more times and then took his form and turned to a printer that was chugging out a document. "Looks like you're from New York." She scanned his paper. Her eyes flicked up to him. "Funny, you don't have an accent." She quickly pulled the paper out of the printer, tore it expertly along the perforated edges, and stapled one half to his copy of the forms. She then pulled out a map.

"How do you know that?" Pete asked. "Why can't I remember anything?"

"You'll pick up the rest of your memories later. When you turn eighteen. I wasn't supposed to even tell you where you were from."

Pick up his memories? He wanted to ask her more, but her tone and the look she gave him made it clear the subject was closed.

"You're close to where you need to be." She unfolded the map and placing it down in front of her, facing him. She pulled out a pen and circled a building. Then she pointed at it with her pen, listing out the directions turn by turn.

"You'll exit here and wait at the bus stop for the 119 line. Then, when you get off, you just walk down the dirt road. You can't miss it." She passed the carbon copy with the printed paper stapled to a single-ride bus pass, along with the map, through an opening in the bottom of the glass divider.

"Can't miss what?" Pete studied the map. "Where am I going? What do I do now that I'm dead?" Was he supposed to haunt this place circled on his map?

The girl squinted at him, like she thought he might be acting dense on purpose. She chewed her gum. "You go to school, of course."

School? He walked outside. Of course. Here, he'd thought he might get to do something cool in the afterlife. Nope. Just as lame as life.

He frowned again. He really wished he had his memories and wondered again where you picked up your memories up from. What did they look like?

Oddly enough, he still had that prick in his skin that this was somehow wrong. Like he truly was supposed to remember something important. Something he needed to know now, not when he was older.

Maybe it was just supposed to feel this way. He passed a walkway through a green area with benches. Maybe everyone felt this way when they died.

But he still couldn't shake that odd feeling.

CHAPTER 2

PLEASE DON'T FEED THE DODO BIRDS

ETE DOUBLE-CHECKED THE NUMBER SCRIBBLED on his map, verified he was in the right place, and sat down at the bus stop. He looked around, watching the people strolling by and the cars milling down the street. The tranquility outside was at odds with the hustle and bustle inside the Government Transit building. He found he really enjoyed the quiet.

He glanced down at the map and frowned, reading one of the ads printed on the side. Welcome to Purgatory! Your next memorable family vacation is here!

The soft squeal of brakes and the hiss of pistons made him lift his head, tensing. A bus was turning onto his street, heading towards him. When he saw the number 331 above the windshield, he relaxed. Several people holding suitcases exited and hurried toward the building he had just recently vacated.

Pete stood, suddenly feeling too wired to sit on the bench. The shock of everything had worn off, and his nerves were really kicking in now. What was this new school going to be like?

All of a sudden, behind him came a blood-curdling scream. Pete leaped about a foot in the air and spun around, looking wildly for what had made that noise. A woman was bending over tending to her toddler, and a couple of people were strolling in the distance, but it seemed no one else had heard the scream. Some fat, oversized birds hopped lazily about, pecking at the grass. They hadn't even been startled.

"What's going on?" Pete looked all around. Was he hearing things now? He was breathing heavily. Did he go mad when he died? A scary thought. He bit his lip.

He heard the scream again and nearly jumped out of his skin.

"What the—?" he screeched. Now he knew he had not been imagining it. It had been a bird who had screamed! The woman tending to her son looked up casually in his direction and then turned away.

Pete stared at the birds, and one looked curiously back at him, tilting its head sideways. The bird let out another small scream. The sound grated on his nerves like nails on a chalkboard.

He huffed. "Man, that's annoying."

"Tell me about it," a gravelly voice came from behind him.

Pete turned to see an elderly couple by the bench.

The woman raised a hand holding a handbag as she sat down. "Shoo! Shoo!" she said in a feeble voice. The birds ignored her, staring at Pete. There were more of them now, and they all started hopping towards him hopefully, letting out shrill shrieks as they went.

"Don't feed them." The man tucked a newspaper and umbrella under his arm and sat next to his wife. "Those darn dodo birds will follow you around till your second death." He harrumphed again. "No wonder they went extinct. Our problem now—darn pests."

Before Pete could ask him about the birds, the old man let out a howl of rage. Pete jumped back in surprise and the birds screamed in protest, fluttering their wings and running away in a wild zigzagging motion.

The man pointed in rage at a bus making its way to them. The bus stopped, brakes squealing and pistons sighing. The door opened and the man laid into the driver.

"You're four minutes early! If I were on time, you'd already be gone. I can't miss my doctor's appointment."

"I ain't early!" the bus driver yelled back. "Your watch is slow."

"If my husband wasn't early," his wife yelled in her quivery voice, "he would have missed his back appointment. Shame on you." She pointed her walker at him as she made her way onto the bus. "Shame!"

Amused, Pete climbed in behind the couple and handed his token to the driver, who nodded to him. Pete stood there and the driver raised his eyebrows.

"Um…how do I know when to get off?" he asked hesitantly.

"You a newbie, then?" the driver said. Pete nodded. "Aight, I'll tell you where to get off. Where you headed?" Pete showed him the paper, and he nodded.

"Oh, and now we're gonna be late!" the old man yelled. "All 'cause he dunno where he's going."

"Stop your complaining, Henry!" the bus driver yelled back.

"He has a back appointment to go to," Henry's wife repeated.

Pete made his way to a seat, tuning out the argument.

The drive became infinitely more enjoyable when Henry and his wife exited at the very next stop. Why didn't they just walk? He watched them hobble to Henry's back appointment.

As the bus drove onward, Pete looked out at the clean brick buildings they passed by in the beautiful town. Cheerful billboards were painted with bright, happy, yet muted colors.

Passengers got on and off, and there was a cheerful banter among them all. Everyone on the bus seemed to know one another. Pete smiled politely and nodded his head at two women dressed identically, except for the color of their outfits. They narrowed their eyes at him under their Sunday hats, but after Pete smiled, they relaxed and smiled back. He noticed that one loosened her gloved grip on her pink handbag, and soon the pair was gossiping about their neighbor and a boy named Jim.

Pete looked at their dresses and then down at his shoeless feet and sighed. He hoped they would have clothes for him at this school. He sincerely hoped he was not going to be stuck in pinstriped pajamas for the rest of his death.

They drove past a sign that read, Thanks for Visiting Town Square. The tall buildings gave way to charming little shops and then to white picket-fenced neighborhoods. One by one, the bus lost all of its passengers, save Pete.

After about ten minutes, the bus pulled to another stop. The driver looked back and said, "This is your stop, son."

Pete looked at him, startled. There wasn't a school in sight. The driver seemed to know what he was thinking. He nodded his head, hand still on the lever for the open door. "Just walk down the dirt road for a few minutes, and it's on your right." The driver looked less friendly now and more impatient and guarded.

Pete thanked him and walked out. The door shut not one half-second after he stepped off, and the bus sped off before he cleared the street. A rock kicked up and hit him on the leg.

"Ouch!" He rubbed his leg and stared at the retreating bus curiously. "What was that all about?"

He turned and swallowed, suddenly understanding why the bus driver had been so keen to leave.

Goosebumps rose on his arms and legs as he stared down the ominous dirt road, the ground barely visible through the thick, white fog.

A few leaves blew out from the white fog down the dirt street, and he swallowed. Was that the howl of the wind or an animal?

Scared, shaking, and barefoot, Pete stepped slowly into the fog.

CHAPTER 3

MRS. BATTINSWORTH'S ACADEMY AND HAVEN FOR UNLIVING BOYS AND GIRLS

T HE FOG SEEMED TO CLEAR up moments after Pete passed through, but the unsettled feeling in the pit of his stomach did not ease.

The dirt road had a brick wall on either side. To the right, the wall was made of rust-colored bricks. To the left was a short gray wall that ended after a few paces and gave way to thick woods. Pete shivered as he looked at the woods. It seemed darker outside than it should have been on such a bright, early morning, and he could have sworn there was something in those trees watching him.

Vines clung on the wall and grew wilder as he walked. About fifty paces later, the brick opened to a beautifully adorned, massive wrought-iron gate with the letters B and A woven into the handles.

A vine-covered sign to the left welcomed Pete to Mrs. Battinsworth's Academy and Home for Unliving Boys and Girls. Pete let out a small gasp as he looked past the gate to the massive green lawn and a looming mansion also covered in vines. It was very beautiful and green and had a fountain trickling water in the front of it. He squinted at the fountain. Was it shaped like a giant spider?

In spite of the odd fountain, most of his fears melted away as he looked at the building. Something about it felt...familiar.

"What ya staring at?" A voice made Pete jump. He scanned the area. He was getting tired of being startled.

"Uh...hello?" he said, a touch of impatience in his voice. No one was there. He tried the handle. The gate was unlocked and he pushed it open, cautiously, stepping through.

No one was hiding on the other side either. That was odd.

"I didn't say hello," the voice said again, higher this time. Without any other warning, a girl popped into view up on the wall, where there had not been a girl before.

Pete took an involuntary step backward, staring up at her. She looked pleased by his reaction. He wasn't sure if he were more surprised that she'd appeared out of nowhere or that she was holding her severed, pigtailed head in her arms. He didn't want to be rude, so he forced his mouth shut and smiled.

"How did you get up there?" He craned his neck. The wall had to be at least a good eight feet tall.

She flipped her head backward between both hands, hair whipping around madly, and stuck it back onto her shoulders with a practiced ease that made Pete nauseated. She grabbed onto a vine and swung down, letting go and free-falling the last three feet, until she landed in an expert roll and popped back up a few centimeters from Pete's face.

"Why? Are you asking for a lesson?"

"Um." The air had gone thick as paste. He had an odd feeling in the pit of his stomach.

"I'm Scoot," she said.

"What?" Pete blurted out.

The girl frowned. "My name is Scoot." She looked like she wanted to punch him, and suddenly Pete noticed how tall she was.

He swallowed hard, regaining his composure. "Sorry, you caught me off guard," he said, formally. "My name is Peter Green." He held out his hand. "Call me Pete."

Looking surprised, Scoot gripped his hand in a painful shake.

"Eyah"—he winced with pain—"would love to have a lesson, but...." He looked back at the school, conflicted. He did think it would be fun to climb the gate, but Pete was starting to be very curious about the school. What had spooked the bus driver so badly? He also wanted to know more about where he was and figure out if there was a way to get his memories back. "Maybe a rain check?"

She shrugged. Now that his own shock had worn off, he took in more details about her. Her pigtails were a shade of red that was actually more orange than red. She had a few freckles, but not many. She had a boyish, almost goth look about her, in spite of the pigtails. It was as though she had not decided if she wanted to look like a tomboy, dress like a schoolgirl, or dye her hair black and worship the devil.

She eyed his figure doubtfully. "What's with the outfit?"

Pete didn't know what to tell her. Anyway, her own outfit was rather interesting too. She was wearing what was clearly a school uniform, but it was obvious she'd made some modifications that reflected her personality. The pleated, gray school skirt and gray vest were dressed up with Halloween-themed knee-high socks and dark orange Converse tennis shoes that almost matched her hair. There was a patch sewn onto the breast of her vest that was a crest with a black spider in the center encircled in white—although it occurred to Pete as he looked back at the spider fountain that it might actually be the school crest. The white shirt under the gray vest was untucked but had designs drawn on it with a permanent marker. She wore dark eyeliner and lipstick and looked to be about his age, maybe a little older, around fourteen or fifteen.

"Well?" she asked again.

He realized he still hadn't answered her question. "Uhh." He shrugged his shoulders.

Thankfully, she let it go. "Well, come on, I'll show you the school. You look like a deer in headlights, you know that?"

"You didn't when you first came here?" Pete retorted. It wasn't like he'd just died or anything and shown up in this strange new world without his parents or friends or anyone he knew—let alone any memory of them.

"Fair enough," Scoot said mildly, surprising Pete because he'd expected her to argue, tell him no way, she'd been totally calm her first day dead. She noticed his reaction and smirked. "You'll get the hang of things quick enough."

Pete doubted it but followed after her anyway.

As they walked toward the school building, Pete recognized what he'd felt in the pit of his stomach when he saw her masterfully maneuvering on the wall. It had been jealousy: pure, raw envy, and it surprised him. He didn't remember anything about his past, but surely it involved climbing a wall or two…didn't it? He hated not knowing.

As they walked to the school, he wasn't sure, but he thought he might be hearing things—scrapes and sniffing sounds. But whenever he looked around, he saw nothing. He thought it had been his own uneven breath at first, but when he held his breath for a moment, there it was again—more sniffing and shuffling too. At one point he swore he heard a whine, but no one was there. After the ninth time, he looked behind him, and Scoot noticed what he was doing.

"That's Bark."

"Bark?" Pete said blankly. "What's Bark?"

"Bark is the invisible dog. He lives in the school. He will follow you around if he thinks you're up to no good. Which I usually am," she added as an afterthought. "I get followed a lot." She stared behind her at the empty lawn.

"Charlie and I have tried everything to make him visible again, but nothing works. I've been tempted to get a professor to help us, but I don't think any will."

"Why not? And who's Charlie?"

Scoot shrugged, her long orange pigtails dangling behind her. "Dunno… not a priority, I guess. And I'm about to introduce you to Charlie in a sec."

Shivers went up Pete's spine when his pant leg moved a little and he heard sniffing sounds by his leg. The sniffing sounds stopped once they entered the building, and he heard a distant bark somewhere off to their right.

Charlie Smith turned out to be a chubby, black-haired kid about Pete's age. He sat behind a desk in the administrator's office. He was speaking animatedly to a secretary with cat-eye glasses and long, red lacquered nails who was nodding her head, eyes closed. She had a pen in her hand and was sort of shaking the pen at him.

"Hmm. Absolutely," the woman said, not acknowledging Pete and Scoot's presence. "You hit it on the head, Charlie. I mean, how is Maddison supposed to find love after that?"

"She's hopeless," Charlie agreed fervently. "I know we're supposed to love her or something, but please." He rolled his eyes dramatically. "I mean, I am so over the whole damsel-in-distress act."

"Are you ladies done talking about your dumb show that doesn't matter?" Scoot asked. "I have a new kid here."

Mrs. Cat-Eyed Glasses stuck her nose up in the air and looked away from Scoot. "Hello, Samantha," she said haughtily.

"Scoot," she corrected with a scowl.

"Welcome to the UnOrphanage for all us UnOrphans!" Charlie interrupted what was sure to be an argument.

"Thanks…What's an UnOrphan?" Pete asked.

"Not a real thing," Scoot answered over Charlie. "Stop trying to invent words. It's not going to stick."

Charlie ignored her and replied cheerfully, "You know, Unliving orphans. But actually, we aren't technically orphans, 'cause we died, not our parents." He waved his hand. "I dunno. It sounded great in my head." He shrugged, unconcerned. "I'll test it on other subjects before I decide to adopt the phrase."

He turned to Scoot who rolled her eyes. "That sounds stupid."

"She thinks everything fabulous is stupid," he said, unruffled.

"No, I think things that are stupid are stupid," she responded.

The secretary sniffed loudly, still without looking at them. She held out her hand without looking up. When nothing happened, she finally lifted her eyes to Pete.

"Papers?" she said expectantly. He looked at her blankly before remembering the papers that were given to him what seemed like a lifetime ago.

"Oh, my apologies, Mrs…" he looked at her desk, "Delerie." He handed her the contents of his pockets. She handed him back the map, and he tucked that back into his pajamas.

"Quite all right," she said, much more warmly than before.

She began typing.

"I'm Charlie." He held out his hand.

"Pleased to make your acquaintance. I'm Pete." They shook hands. Charlie gave Scoot a grin. "Well, about time we got someone polite. Maybe you'll rub off on Red."

"Doubt it," Scoot answered.

The secretary sniffed again and tore a page from an old-fashioned printer. She folded and pulled off the edges. She handed the page to Pete. "Here is your schedule. You don't get to pick your electives since it's your first year here. There are maps on the walls to help you find your way."

Charlie pointed at the map and said, "We'll show you around, so you don't have to subject yourself to the unfashionable indignity of looking at a wall map."

Pete chuckled. "Okay, thanks." He studied his schedule.

PETER GREEN. HAMLET DORM. 7th YEAR. SEMESTER I. His classes were familiar and unusual at the same time: Mathematics for Unliving Souls, History of Afterlife, Personal Finance 1/Banking Systems, Introduction to Technology, Introduction to Death and Afterlife, Wood Shop.

Charlie pulled the schedule away from Pete. "Aw, we have no classes together." He sounded disappointed. "But we are both in the same dorms at least. There's no sense in taking you to your first hour class." He looked at his watch. "It's almost over. I'll give you a quick tour and then have someone walk you to your second period class. I know someone in it with you." Charlie's first hour was working in the Admin office. "I'm supposed to be there to help with morning rushes, but mostly we just talk about *The Unbeating Heart.*"

This turned out to be a very dramatic soap opera that involved a captain of a ghost pirate ship, a prison cook, a maid, a duchess, her husband, his mistress, and seven other main characters. Scoot said several times that the show was stupid and she did not watch it, but proceeded to argue in detail about the characters and plot anyway.

After about fifteen minutes of this, Charlie looked up. "First stop in orientation…our dorms!"

Pete blinked. They had somehow walked outside and to another wing of the mansion in the span of their argument.

They went into the dorms, which were large and spacious. The main room of Hamlet was full of cots. Books and bags were stored under the beds. The room had many windows, with long, thick curtains drawn to the side to let the morning light in. Straight ahead was a room that Charlie said led to a small study hall.

Charlie pointed out one of the beds with freshly folded sheets and a clean uniform lying on it. "This is yours." He smiled. "Pretty close to mine." He plopped down and grabbing something under his cot. Scoot leaned against the wall, looking bored.

Pete took the clothes gratefully, and Charlie pointed out the bathrooms large enough for a dozen people to the right of the main room where he could change.

On the way back with his crumpled-up pajamas, Pete paused in front of a mirror, fascinated by his own reflection. He hadn't seen himself since he died. He looked at his thin frame, sunken blue eyes, hollow cheeks, and dark chestnut-brown hair. He might have looked handsome if he weren't so thin and pale.

"Coming?" Charlie called from the other room. "We're running low on time."

"Y-yes." Pete pulled his gaze away from his reflection.

As the orientation continued, Pete could tell the manor had once belonged to someone very important and wealthy. The library looked as though it might have once been a ballroom and stood several stories tall. The hallways had marble floors, stone statues, carved floorboards, and chandeliers. Hidden behind the fashions of displaced boys and girls was evidence of the home's past affluence. Pete wondered vaguely whose house it might have been. Had it been the home of this Battinsworth person who started the school?

However, as beautifully as the manor was designed, it was much more confusing. The past owner must have been insane or paranoid because the house was designed as part maze, part home, and part deathtrap (no pun intended). There were secret doors and corridors and, according to Charlie, there were also trapdoors that led to dungeons and water pits. Pete and his new friends started walking on the second floor and somehow would end up on the fourth floor without walking up any steps.

There was even a hallway that led to a maze of mirrors. They tried to walk through two separate times, but kept ending up at the entrance of the hallway.

"We never get through here," Charlie admitted. "We try every day, but it never works."

Pete looked at Scoot, who was suddenly holding a knife. Alarmed, he stepped backward. "Where did that knife come from?"

He looked first at her short, thin-pleated skirt, then at her shirt with no pockets and her socks that could not have hidden so much as a tiny spoon, much less a knife the size of her whole arm.

"Don't worry about it." She glared at the entrance to the mirrored hallway.

"You can't knife the mirrors again," Charlie said in a bored voice. "We have to go to town this week. I need a new scarf—and you wanted brass knuckles, remember?"

Scoot turned her glare on him.

"The Bat said if you get detention again, you wouldn't go into town this month," Charlie continued. "You really want to wait another month?"

She dropped her hand and sighed.

Pete eyed her closely to see where she would hide the knife, but he got distracted when he noticed a little girl in the mirror's reflection, about nine or ten, with shoulder-length brown hair and big, round brown eyes looking back at him. He turned but she had vanished. He looked back at the mirror, wondering if the light was playing tricks on him, but saw nothing. He was about to shrug it off when he heard a hissing, a slurp, and the sound of something dragging across the floor. The mirrors closest to them now displayed something large and terrifying behind him.

Pete turned around, gasped, and stumbled backward. In front of him, at least nine feet tall, was a female humanoid shape. She had a neck that was at least three feet long, hunched so as not to hit the ceiling. She had scales and claws and long teeth that hung out of her shriveled mouth. She hissed again and dragged her back leg across the floor. Her clawed hands gripped a stick, and she moved slowly towards them, her mass blocking the exit.

But his new friends didn't seem to have noticed the monster. Pete's breath was ragged as he turned and grabbed them. "We have to run!" He interrupted an argument that had erupted about a mandatory accessories policy that Charlie had proposed.

Together, they ran into the hallway full of mirrors at top speed.

"What is it?" Charlie asked, breathless.

"Just run!" Pete shouted. They ran forward and around a mirror, dodged a long one that made them look both fat and skinny, jumped around one hanging at an angle, under two mirrors that created a tunnel, finally sliding down a short slide made of mirrors and ducking under a low hanging mirror… and ended up exactly where they had started.

"What?" Pete was completely flabbergasted. "How?"

He had been baffled before, when his new friends were the ones leading him through, but he thought they might've been purposefully leading him in a confusing, disorienting circle. This time when he ran through, it had definitely felt like he had been running forward. How the devil had he ended up where he started?

Charlie was wheezing. "I can't believe I just ran." He was truly in shock.

"How are we going to get away from it?" Pete panicked. The monster had moved two feet closer.

Scoot, noticing the creature for the first time, relaxed her shoulders. "Oh, that's Mrs. Warshaw, the janitor. She's not allowed to eat the schoolkids anymore." Pete looked at Scoot, thinking she must be joking, but she had a straight face.

"Did you see that?" Charlie wheezed.

"Yeah, C, I was there. I saw you run."

"Dang, I'll have to tell Pattie Millikouiz. You'll have to back me; you know she won't believe me."

As they walked down the hall toward the monster and Charlie and Scoot chatted about somebody named Sally Haworth's new haircut, Pete was having a furious internal debate. He wanted to simultaneously scream, run away, and cry, and also somehow impress his new friends. To distract himself, he looked around to see if he happened to see the little girl he'd caught in the mirrors earlier, wanting to focus on anything but Mrs. Warshaw.

He paused for a moment, suddenly aware of how rude his actions must have appeared. He suspected that this…Mrs.…Warshaw had noticed him run away and call her a monster. He did not know how a woman of her…caliber would react to such rudeness.

Pete started walking again, but when he drew even with Mrs. Warshaw, he stopped in front of her. He straightened, holding his breath to keep from shaking, and looked up at her face. "Hello."

Charlie and Scoot stopped talking and looked behind them.

"My name is…is," he faltered as her three-foot-long neck lowered her head to hover just in front of his face. Her large eyeballs protruded out of the side of her head, and her eyelids came up every thirty seconds or so to close over the large dark slits of her pupils.

"My name is Pete," he said in a small, weak voice. "It's nice to meet you, Mrs. Warshaw."

He ended in almost a whisper. Her teeth gleamed in the dim lighting and she hissed quietly.

"Um…" he said, not sure if the hiss was friendly or not, "I'll let you get back to work." Then, he added, "I just wanted to say hi." He slowly walked away and was very aware that her head followed just beside him until she could no longer reach.

"Wow," Charlie said when they were out of earshot. "I have never seen her smile before."

"That was a smile?" Pete said weakly.

The rest of what Scoot called "orientation" was filled with equally terrifying experiences. There was a giant snake just lounging on the sixth floor bathroom. "We'll have to go in another one," Scoot said. "He doesn't look like he's in a good mood." There was a human-shaped lump in its massive body.

They scurried out and continued with the tour. When Pete glanced through a beautiful window the size of a large automobile, he saw a wolf sleeping on a wooden bench outside. In the cafeteria, the workers all had scaly skin like Mrs. Warshaw, except for one who looked like someone had stuffed an octopus into a uniform. As they were walking past the cafeteria, the octopus screamed and leaped onto one of her colleagues, and they started fighting.

Pete swore he could hear bats inside some of the walls of the manor. Things that he thought were mere shadows would get up and walk away, leaving the area sunny in their wake. It was positively disconcerting—yet

Scoot and Charlie acted like none of it was any big deal. They ended the tour at the bookstore where instead of an attendant greeting them behind a cash register, books were dispensed from a slot as something growled loudly from an adjacent room, rumbling the walls.

"Honestly, I can never understand what she's saying." Charlie picked up the stack of disheveled books and handed them to Pete.

"That's a she?" Pete gulped.

When they made their way out to the back of the school, Pete learned that the playground had been replaced with a maze made out of hedges—the largest and most elaborate in all of AfterLife.

"Why?" Pete asked.

"Why not?" Scoot responded.

Orientation ended when the bell rang and the kids piled into the hallways. Charlie and Pete pushed past everyone until they met a tall kid with shaggy brownish-blond hair, tan and freckled skin, and light eyes.

"Brody, Pete. Pete, Brody." Charlie turned to Pete and pointing at Brody. "He has his next class with you, so he can walk you. I'll catch up with you before lunch."

Pete waved his goodbyes to Scoot and Charlie, and Brody said, "I'm fourteen DA. How old are you?" They made their way down the confusing corridors towards their history class.

"DA?" Pete raised his eyebrows.

Brody looked over and shook his head. "Sorry, I forget. It's slang for Death Age…I think. Whatever, it's like how old you were when you died, plus the time you've been here."

"Oh, I'm fourteen too. How long have you been here?"

"'Bout a year. It's pretty cool here. Well, most of it is."

"Do you remember anything?"

Brody shook his head and shrugged. "No, not much."

Pete rubbed his temple, annoyed. "I feel like I'm forgetting something important. It's making me mental."

Brody nodded knowingly. "That'll go away pretty quick."

"So we'll never get our memories back?" Pete didn't like this blankness in his mind.

"Oh, no, 'course we will. We pick up our memory files when we graduate from here."

"Memory files?" Pete's brow furrowed. "But why? Why not give them to us now?"

Brody shrugged. "Dunno. They explained it in one of my classes, but I forget the details. Something about the magic here making people crazy."

Pete frowned dubiously. "Where is here, exactly?" He was happy to finally be getting some answers. "I mean, I know we are in Purgatory, but where is that exactly?"

Brody tilted his head side to side as he walked, contemplating. "So, I really need to pay more attention in class, but from what I remember, AfterLife is kinda the big place—the universe—and Purgatory is just one place inside of it."

"But why am I here? Why did we come here?"

Brody shrugged again. "There aren't too many orphanages. I think this is the biggest one, so most kids come here. Glad I did, though. It's pretty cool here. So how did you die?" he asked curiously. They stopped walking to join a line outside of a classroom with the number 318 next to it.

Pete frowned deeper. "I don't know. Am I supposed to know that?"

Brody shook his head. "Oh, nah, not till graduation, like I said." He waved his hand airily. "You know, but some of us can guess."

He squinted, seemingly holding his breath, and his face changed to show a large burn on the side of it. He shrugged. "My powers of deduction say I was in a fire of some sort. What about you?"

Pete shook his head, looking himself over. "I'll double-check later, but I haven't found anything yet. I bet I died in a stupid way," he added dejectedly.

"No matter. I mean, yeah, I get to have a cool burn on my face, but that's pretty rare. Most people don't have bullet holes or arms that disappear. Most people just look like you do. I was just curious." Brody gave a friendly smile, but looked a little too happy for the situation.

Several of the girls next to him smiled and waved. Brody didn't change his face back to hide his scar.

"Who is the Bat everyone keeps mentioning?" Pete guessed who that might be, but asking anyway.

Brody's smile faltered, and Pete shivered instinctively. "Oh, she's the headmistress of the school. You'll meet her. She meets all the new students."

CHAPTER 4

THE HARVEST MOON

BRODY'S PREDICTION CAME TRUE LATER that same day. Pete was in good spirits as he made his way to lunch. His orientation may have been terrifying, but his classes so far felt closer to what he had been expecting. He was happy to find out that the school semester had barely started; he was really only a couple of weeks behind everyone else. There was a lot to learn, and much of it only led to even more questions, but at least the subjects were interesting, and except for one scare in which he thought his 700-year-old vampire instructor—who incidently could pass as a beautiful blond sixteen-year-old heiress with dark, sunken eyes and hollow cheeks—was going to eat him, everyone was pretty nice to him.

Maybe death wouldn't be so bad after all.

Charlie met Pete after third period and took him on a roundabout path to the cafeteria. "Just need to grab something really quick." As they were walking, however, Charlie suddenly paused, looking worried. "Oh no…"

"What's wrong?" Then he noticed what Charlie saw in the hallway ahead. "Why is there fog inside?"

"We should go back." Charlie grabbed Pete's arm. But before he could make another move, the door to their left slammed open.

A gust of thick fog flowed freely out of the room beyond, which looked like a dungeon. In the doorframe stood a towering, rail-thin woman. One of her boney hands rested gently on the hip that protruded sharply under her long, black dress, which reached the floor. Her eyes, a piercing black, were so dark it was difficult to see where the irises began and the pupils ended. Those bottomless eyes stared at Pete from behind dark-rimmed glasses, and her hair was tied into a knot that pulled back the skin of her pale face.

"Peter Green," she said in a sharp, starchy tone.

"Afternoon, Mrs. Ba…Battinsworth," Charlie said nervously.

"Don't you have somewhere to be?" she asked.

Charlie's stuttering died in his throat, and he just pointed behind her instead. With a jolt, Pete realized this was the office he had been in earlier. How could it have turned into a dungeon in just a few hours?

The answer was glaring at Charlie, who said weakly, "Yes, headmistress." He looked apologetically at Pete as he backed away, heading to lunch.

"Peter Green?" she asked again.

"Um. Yes, ma'am," he said politely.

"Welcome." She gave the most unfriendly scowl Pete had ever seen.

"…Sorry?" Pete asked, after a short pause.

"You are new," she said simply. "Welcome to the school."

"Oh…." Pete stared at her. "Um. Thank you."

A scream came from behind her office door. Pete swallowed. Somehow, he did not think there was a dodo bird loose in her office.

Her eyes followed his. "We sometimes have a problem with poltergeists."

"I see," he lied.

She pulled a pamphlet out of her pocket and handed it to Pete. "Be sure to familiarize yourself with the rules. Not knowing them doesn't excuse you from detention. You are dismissed."

She pivoted on her heel, leaving Pete staring openmouthed at her retreating back, the fog following eerily at her heels.

"So what did the Bat want?" Charlie asked ten minutes later as Pete set down his lunch tray on one of the rectangular benches in the outdoor area of the cafeteria. Through a set of double doors to his left was the indoor area, a windowed, circular room attached to the same wing as the library, filled with students waiting in line for food or chatting and laughing at circular tables.

"To welcome me." Pete plopped down beside his tray.

Scoot snorted. "I remember that." She chewed her food. "She does that with every new student. I hear most kids end up crying."

Pete thought of the way the headmistress had glared at him with those bottomless eyes, and he couldn't blame them. Quickly shoving the image aside, he set his tray on his lap and picked up his fork. He was happy to know that he wouldn't be eating grubs or worms now that he was dead and enjoyed some spaghetti while Scoot and Charlie had pizza.

But he was only a few bites into his meal when he felt a sudden, strange itch in his skin, and glanced down and almost dropped the meatball on his fork. "What the—?"

His school uniform, which he'd hurriedly put back on after his first class, melted away into his striped pajamas again. Bewildered, he pulled at his tie.

He glanced around at the other students sitting outside and noticed that many of them weren't wearing their uniforms anymore either, but a mixture of other clothing. Thankfully, he wasn't the only one in PJs. "What just happened?"

"Controlling what you wear is a talent you have to learn once you are dead." Scoot still had on her uniform skirt, though her top had changed to an orange shirt that said Rockstar on it in black block letters. "Some people never bother to practice and end up wearing the same bloody clothes they died in for the rest of their AfterLife." She frowned in distaste. "I'm one of the few who has mastered it in my age group," she said smugly.

"If I didn't know any better, I'd say you were a good student," Charlie said in mock-horror.

Scoot ignored him and pointed at Charlie's bright pink vest, lilac silk shirt, and tight jeans, "As I'm sure you've guessed, he's also mastered it. His outfit is different every day." Charlie stood up and curtsied.

Pete sure hoped he'd soon learn to master it too, so he wouldn't be stuck in these dumb pajamas for eternity.

Later that night, after dinner and about three hours of homework, Charlie called it quits and Pete followed soon after. Kids were climbing into bed, but it was only 9:30 and he was wide awake, itching for something to do besides reading more of his dull *History of AfterLife* textbook.

Charlie was still awake too, but he was talking animatedly with a boy Pete had not yet officially met, though he thought he might be called Henry.

Pete went back to the window and looked out on the moonlit grounds. The landscape was dark and alien, and the shadows cast strange shapes in the night. Suddenly, he caught movement out of the corner of his eye. A shadowy group of people was moving across the grounds towards the gate, walking a bit awkwardly. Pete squinted and saw they were hauling what looked like a large crate being them. Intrigued, he watched the crate's progression.

His burning curiosity surprised him. Why should he care about a big box being moved? But still, he did. He was tired of having so many unanswered questions. He still didn't understand why he couldn't pick up his memories now. Why would he go mad if he had them? Glancing over at his cot where his history book lay, he wondered if the memory thing was a clever way to control him and the other students. He frowned, not sure where the thought had come from—but like his name, his age, and his shoes, it had just popped into his mind.

If he couldn't get answers about his memories, maybe he could at least discover what was inside that crate and where those shadowy people were taking it at this late hour. The thought alone was enough to spur him on. He glanced around the dorm. No one was paying him any attention. If he could slip out…was that something he would do, even if it got him into trouble? What had he had been like before he got here?

Even as he was thinking this, a voice said, "You look lost." Pete jumped, just managing to suppress a squeak. A sleepy-looking kid in the bed next to the window chuckled. Breathing quickly, Pete managed a nonchalant shrug.

"It's Max, right?" Pete had been introduced at dinner, but then, he'd met so many people today it was hard to put names to all the faces.

Max nodded and brought out his arms from under his school blankets to run his fingers through his tousled black hair. He had small brown eyes, a narrow nose, and a small mouth.

"I was just wondering who I am." Then, realizing how dumb that sounded, he quickly added, "You know, who I was when I was alive. I don't even know what kind of a person I was." He shrugged, suddenly embarrassed.

Max just looked pensive. He sat up on his elbows.

"I think the point is not to know," he said seriously, "so that you can be whatever or whoever you want to be here. Well, that's what one of my teachers said, anyway. Most people think Purgatory is for people who don't want to change, and that is true for most of the people who live in this world." He waved toward the window. "But this place is also for people who needed time to change and just never got a chance when they were alive. They get to use this time to become whoever and whatever they want without memories getting in the way."

Pete nodded, feeling a bit lighter. He supposed that was a much less cynical explanation than the one he had been thinking. "I think I might have been afraid of the dark when I was alive." He stared through the window.

Max chuckled again. "Imagine that." Then he yawned deeply and lay back down, closing his eyes.

Smiling, Pete looked back out the window. *Well, Peter Green who do you want to be?* Without a backward glance, he walked calmly out of the front door of his dorms.

He was only a few steps outside when the dorm door burst open behind him, and a huffing wheezing sound followed. "What…are…you…doing?" Charlie asked in an angry whisper between huffs. "Get inside…you'll get into trouble. I can't believe I ran again. Twice in one day. Unbelievable."

Pete snorted and looked at the distant shadows bent over the box and turned back to Charlie. "I'm going to see what's in that box."

Charlie squinted into the darkness and then shook his head. "Come on." He dragged Pete back into the dorms and shut the door. "As your orientation… person…thingie, I'm responsible for you." He crossed his arms "Anyway, that means I'm supposed to teach you how to break the rules."

Pete's argument died in his throat and he uncrossed his arms. "Okay. I'm listening."

Charlie pointed to the window. "It's not dark yet. The moon is always bright until about ten p.m. That's when most things go to sleep here at the school. Give it thirty minutes after that and stick to the shadows, and the likelihood of getting caught goes down."

Pete nodded. "Okay." That was reasonable enough.

"Running…" Charlie muttered to himself as he waved Pete good night and went to wash up for bed.

After the longest thirty minutes ever, Pete peeked out of the study room, where he'd been trying but failing to read the history textbook. His mind was reeling. Try as he might, he couldn't shake the thought that had popped into his head earlier—and yet, what Max had said felt just as real and true to him as well. How could that be? But more real than both of those thoughts was the sense of urgency to remember.

Maybe he was overreacting. Several people had expressed that they had felt the same irritating feeling that they had forgotten something important because, well, they had. All the kids in this place had forgotten everything from their previous life, and most had learned to deal with it.

Still, this felt different. This felt dire. He made up his mind to do what he could starting tomorrow to find out more about how to get his memories back. But for tonight, he was going to explore more of where he was living.

Outside, he sprinted from shadow to shadow, enjoying the rush he got from running. The school looked even stranger out here than it had from the window. The shadows made the bushes and trees look like they had claws coming out of them. The wind hissing through the leaves made him shiver. After exploring the grounds a little, his excitement deflated a bit. The crate and the strange group of people were nowhere to be found, which wasn't all too surprising since he'd had to wait so long to leave his dorm.

With a sigh, he looked back at the dorms. He definitely did not want to go back to his bed yet. Water tinkled in the fountain to his left, and the gate in the distance clanged gently in the wind. The gate. Pete stared at it, thought about the way he'd seen Scoot climbing it earlier today, wishing he could try it.

Happy to finally have a purpose, he headed to the gate with a grin.

He grabbed one of the elegantly carved beams just above eye level with both hands and began pulling his body weight upward. It was so much harder than he thought it would be. Scoot made it look so easy.

"God, you're bad," a familiar voice said from behind, making Pete jump.

Pete dropped back down, looking around to spot Scoot. "When did you get here? I don't know how to climb."

"Well, that's obvious." Scoot snorted, and Pete's face grew hot. "One hand, one foot," she said and then rolled her eyes when he just looked at her. She walked over and put a hand on the gate and a foot on the rung. "One hand, one foot," she repeated, putting her other foot a little higher than her right and then her left hand a little higher. She continued to climb higher and higher, repeating the same words.

Pete had a few goes at it, and five minutes later, he was starting to get the hang of it. On his next climb to the top, he heard before he saw in the dim moonlight, a small group of kids heading for the school, leaving the woods, of all places.

They were out late. He was high enough and they were close enough that he wouldn't make it to the bottom in time to let them in, so he climbed the rest of the way up to perch on the brick part of the wall.

Unfortunately, this was the wrong move. He had both hands gripped on the wall to his left and was just pushing off the top of the gate with his foot, when the unlucky lead of the pack pushed open the gate he was hanging onto. Pete fell, yelling and scrambling to catch a hold of anything to stop his fall, and flattened the person directly below him.

The group and Scoot roared with laughter, but Pete, mortified, quickly rolled off the person. "I am so sorry—"

A powerful punch struck him, knocking the wind out of him, and he doubled over. "Oof." When the stars stopped flashing in his eyes and he could gasp for air, he straightened and looked at the thoroughly pissed-off person he had flattened.

"It was an accident," he said weakly, holding his stomach.

The girl towered over him, at least a head and shoulders taller and about twice as thick as Pete's own thin frame. She wasn't fat, but packed in. She had large brown eyes, thick blonde eyebrows, and her blonde hair was pulled back in a tight braid that was a bit disheveled from Pete's apparent aerial attack.

"Sure it was, you little twit." Her slightly upturned nose crinkling in rage. Her cheeks were pink, and she looked a little winded. Her gray vest and white shirt were twisted and the collar was popped up on one side. She was wearing gray school pants instead of a skirt like Scoot, and she had on muddy black work boots. On the left side of her shirt was a badge with a wolf's head sewn next to the encircled spider.

Pete looked over at the group of kids who were all but crying with laughter, wishing they would stop. They were making it worse. The rest of the group was composed of all boys, all at least her size or bigger. Pete noticed they were wearing the same wolf's-head badges.

Apparently taking offense to Pete's inattention, the girl punched him again, hard, sending him back to the ground with a grunt of pain.

Scoot, who had been laughing with the group of boys, stepped forward protectively. "Hey, the little twit said it was an accident, Grant," she said, squaring off to the taller girl. Pete did not have the breath to protest the name-calling; he could only clutch his stomach.

Grant eyed Scoot, sizing her up. In spite of the fact that she was a good six inches taller than Scoot, Grant seemed wary. After a long moment, she turned away in a huff and yelled for the boys to come along. As she walked off, she kicked the gate shut, with Pete on the outside, and threw him a filthy look as she made her way to the school.

He looked down at his pajamas in horror. He was scratched and dirty, and his clothes were terribly wrinkled. Scoot, however, grinned wide. "Well, well, Green. You just might be my new favorite person."

Pete's body had stayed stubbornly awake all night, as if to get payback for his insistence on breaking the rules. He knew he would regret it later in class. The only thing keeping him awake right now was his determination to find out more about getting his memories back.

He fought off a yawn as he threw his books into his backpack, opened the dorm room door, and was immediately blasted in the face with a stream of water.

"Blah!" Pete jumped back. He shielded his face and looked around. Kids were yelling and standing on their beds. Water was flooding in from the connecting bathrooms—every one of the twelve sinks was on full blast. The showers were on too, and the toilets had water shooting up from them. The ceiling sprinklers had all come on as well, giving the kids who had been sleeping a rude awakening.

Pete followed Charlie and the stream of shouting boys out of the building. Many of his soaked dormmates were drying themselves off in the chilly September morning air. Several adults were rushing their way, and judging by the herd of kids flooding out of other dorms, theirs had not been the only sleeping quarters to get soaked. Pete could hear shrieking girls from the other side of the courtyard.

"It's just water," a voice said behind them. Pete turned to see an absolutely dry Scoot scowling over at the girls she bunked with. "I don't see what the big deal is."

Charlie glared at her in annoyance. They left the chaos, Pete walking between Charlie and Scoot in hopes the two wouldn't start up another argument, and headed for the cafeteria.

Pete made it through breakfast, but only just. The many-tentacled lunch lady went berserk on a kid in line behind him and used every one of her six long arms to throw plates and milk boxes at anyone unfortunate enough to be in the vicinity. He got clocked pretty good by a milk carton in his right ear but managed not to drop his tray.

He and Charlie ran outside without filling their trays up. Pete looked down at his oatmeal, thinking wistfully of the hashbrowns and eggs that he had missed out on.

As he dug in, Scoot chuckled. "Oh yeah, guess what muscles over here did last night?"

Charlie raised an eyebrow. Scoot told him about climbing the school walls. "Then, he leaps on top of Shelly Grant—and flattens her!"

"I did not leap on her!" Pete was indignant, but they weren't listening. Their laughter grew louder as Scoot recounted the rest of the confrontation. At least she didn't mention how he was curled up into a ball after two punches from the giant girl.

He hoped the morning's events would be the weirdest part of his day, but that was far from true. Weird things continued to happen, but it wasn't until well into his first period class that he realized why, when the chalk started attacking his math teacher, Mrs. Lemmings.

"It's a full moon." She wiped patches of chalk off her cheeks—not seeming to realize she was only making it worse. "You get used to it, don't worry."

"It's Jinx or something," said a good-looking kid with dark skin and hair sitting next to Pete. One of the chalk pieces snapped in two and began pinching the teacher on the arm, and the boy covered his mouth, clearly trying not to laugh.

Another kid leaned over ."I heard a witch did it. Revenge on the Bat or something." He widened his eyes dramatically until he got whacked in the face with the chalkboard eraser.

"Ay!" He batted it away. Pete and the kid let out a snort of laughter. Their laughter quickly turned into squeals of pain and fear when the chalk turned rogue and started attacking the students.

They ended up abandoning the classroom, finishing the last ten minutes of the lecture in the hallway.

Pete took notes, awkwardly sitting on the floor, trying to ignore the erasers that were pelting the small window on the door. He watched his blonde-haired, blue-eyed professor as she paced up and down the hall. Her lips were painted a soft pink and she had a small, pointed nose. "For homework," she shouted above the bell and the buzz of students filing down the hallway, "you will need to complete pages sixty-five to sixty-seven, odd numbers only. Due tomorrow." The rest of her words were drowned out, and she gave up, waving goodbye.

The rest of his classes went similarly bad, and all thoughts of him finding out more about his memories soon vanished. It was all he could do to stay safely on his feet. Things broke, fell out of his hands, flew around the classroom or attacked the staff or students. He kept forgetting things and earned himself a painful punch in the arm when he called Scoot "Stacie."

By the end of the day, Pete was in a terrible mood. His eyes and ears had been twitching for the last three hours and were making him mental. He had wood shop next, which he was excited about, until he remembered how many sharp objects were in there.

He needn't have worried, however. When he got to the shop, Pete was greeted by the boy who had worked at a bench across the classroom from him the day before.

"Hey," the boy said, "we're working out back today. Teacher was gonna leave a note, but it's sure to fall down or something on account of the full moon and all. I was sent to make sure everyone got the message."

Pete nodded gratefully. "Do I have to grab anything?"

The boy shook his head vehemently. "No way you want to go in there today. You'll meet your second death." He laughed, and Pete forced a laugh too.

He followed a few of his classmates through the confusing hallways out onto the grounds at the back of the school, where he was met with an enticing afternoon breeze filled with the rustle of the trees and the hedges of the maze moving in the wind. The class was gathering by the fountain but gave it a wide berth as it was spouting water out erratically.

Mr. Johnson's deep, booming laugh sounded, and Pete relaxed for a moment—until he heard it again. He couldn't explain why it bothered him; the professor's laughter had been loud yesterday too. But today it was a bit higher-pitched than he remembered, and his teacher's movement was a bit stiff.

Mr. Johnson was handing out large pads of paper and pencils while he spoke to the class. Pete was a little too far away to hear the conversation.

"For several of you," Mr. Johnson said when they all settled in and drawing, "this is your first full moon as a student."

Pete looked around, curious as to who else was new.

"I learned years ago that shop class and the full moon hex just don't mix." Mr. Johnson shook his head, chuckling darkly. Pete smiled. The professor's good mood and high spirits were infectious. "Just because we can regrow limbs in AfterLife does not mean it's an enjoyable experience!" His booming laugh sounded a little like a bark.

He then began lecturing about the proper angles of boxes and various techniques for drawing them. After about ten minutes, he gave them instructions to sketch out a jewelry box they would be making for their first project and measure out the details. He walked around, giving notes and tips. Fortunately for Pete, he paused by Pete's desk for a little while longer than the others, pointing out areas that would be complex to build and talking about the tools Pete would be using, which was a bit difficult when they weren't in the workshop. Pete was feeling a bit overwhelmed trying to learn it all, but Mr. Johnson's voice was soothing, and his smile was kind, and Pete soon felt fully capable of mastering his project.

About halfway through the class, Pete looked up and noticed that the professor had begun sweating. Big beads ran all down his face and neck, drenching his long-sleeved shirt. It was warm outside, but Pete didn't think it was hot enough to make someone sweat like that.

Pete frowned, looking over at the professor's abandoned coat near the fountain. That must have been it. Mr. Johnson had been walking around in his suit a few minutes ago, and Pete supposed he would probably sweat too in a coat like that.

Not long after, the bell rang in the distance, followed by the telltale sounds of kids filing out of their classrooms. Pete realized that this had been his first incident-free hour in the day.

Standing, the students stretched and lazily gathered their things. Pete grabbed his sketches to pack up, but paused when he heard the professor behind him.

Pete stood and turned around. "Have a good night, Profess—" His voice faltered and alarm bells went off in his head at the sight of Mr. Johnson.

CHAPTER 5

PETER'S PROFESSOR BITES HIM

SURE, PETE HAD ONLY BEEN in school two days, but up until this point, Mr. Johnson had been quickly becoming his favorite professor. There was just something about the man you couldn't help but love.

Now, the teacher who'd been smiling and helping him with his jewelry box sketch had been replaced with a stranger wearing his skin. His eyes, which only minutes ago had been a soft, kind brown, became wide and completely black. They tracked the last of the students walking towards the school like they were hunting prey. Desperately wanting to join them but unable to escape the death-grip his professor had on his arm, Pete watched the retreating backs of his classmates get farther and farther away.

Genuinely alarmed, Pete realized that Mr. Johnson was panting. "Do… do you want me to get you some water?" The professor did not answer, and Pete grew increasingly nervous.

When the professor finally spoke, instead of his smooth deep southern voice, his words came out in a kind of growl. "Have. A. Good. Night," he said in jerky grunts.

"Um, thanks," Pete said hesitantly. The professor stood for several long moments, eyes closed, taking long deep breaths. "Do you want me to get someone?" Pete asked.

His professor took in several fiercer breaths, which began to sound steadier. Was he having a seizure or something? Mr. Johnson opened his eyes, which had changed back to their normal brown, and looked confused for a second. Then, seeming to realize how tightly he was holding Pete's arm, he straightened and released him. "I apologize."

Pete rubbed his numb arm. The professor let out a breath and sat down on the fountain. "I'm sorry. I am…a bit under the weather. Perhaps I should have called a sub today." He brushed his forehead with his hand, looking completely drained. He waved Pete off. "I'm okay. Go on. Goodnight."

Pete wanted to ask more questions, but the professor looked like he was about to pass out, so he turned around and hurried off.

He arrived at the dorms during a heated debate between Charlie and a set of twins named Matt and Mark Davis. By what little Pete caught, they were trying to decide which girls they thought were most likely to sprout horns by the end of school.

"Does that actually happen?" Pete was alarmed.

"Nah," said the one Pete thought was Matt. "It hasn't happened in four hundred years, but it's still fun to guess which ones have demon ancestry." He gave a dazzling smile. His dark skin and deep brown eyes made his pearly white teeth pop, even in the soft light of the dorms. "My money's on Gemilda. I mean, look at her. She looks demon-like already."

"Nah," said the other twin, Mark, "she's more troll than demon. Demons are supposed to be clever, and she's got no brains."

"Maybe she's being covert," Charlie suggested with a grin.

"Best dang covert mission I've ever seen," Mark said. "I'd say she could have a long acting career if that's the case."

The boys snickered, and the debate caught its second wind as others joined in and started shouting names.

They left for the cafeteria, and when dinner ended, Pete was chatting excitedly about the different school clubs and activities.

"We could get you into the horseback riding club if you wanted," Mark said.

Charlie shuddered. "I have discovered horses are terrifying creatures, so I will not be joining you guys on that endeavor."

"We like the archery lessons we have on the weekends," Matt said. "But there are a bunch of others. I know a girl who is in the Magic and Hexes club, and she really likes it."

As they walked back to the dorms talking about how the twins were kicked out of the cooking club, Pete daydreamed about the weekend coming up. He had enjoyed his classes much more than he thought he would, but he was looking forward to some free time. He wondered if he could find out where the memory files were kept.

He checked the watch the school gave him and frowned. It was broken. Even when he tapped the glass, the clock remained unmoving at 8:45 a.m.

He sighed as walked to his bunk and frowned when he neared it. There was a white envelope laying on his bed. He picked it up, curiously flipping it over. The school crest was printed on a wax seal. He broke it and pulled out a black card stock invitation written in gold leaf lettering. It read:

> *Peter Green,*
>
> *You are cordially invited to the Battinsworth Academy Night Society Club.*

"Oooh," a voice said behind him. Pete looked up to see Charlie reading over his shoulder, who snatched the letter out of his hand and said, "You're going, aren't you? How have I not been invited? They are so exclusive." He looked envious but then switched to interested. "Can you ask around and see how you were selected? Maybe I can figure out a way to get an invite…."

Pete snatched his letter back. "Let me see what it is first."

He continued reading,

> *You have been hand-selected to attend a special event beginning at 7.30 in the evening. This will be your only opportunity to attend. Should you miss it, you will not be invited back. After tonight's event, should you decline our offer to join the group, you will not have another opportunity to join. We regret that we do not have more information for you at this time. You will be further enlightened during tonight's event.*
>
> *In good favor,*
> *L.J.*

"I think I know an L.J." Charlie hovered over Pete's shoulder again.

Pete swatted him away but handed him the letter when Charlie indicated he wanted it. Pete looked in the envelope and found two other smaller cards. One was a curfew pass to walk the hallways after dark, and the other gave details of the meeting location.

"Why was I invited to this?" Pete more or less repeated Charlie's question.

Mark came over to read over Charlie shoulder. "It says someone recommended you."

"Right, but who? I know like four people." Pete shook his head. He looked at them, and they shrugged.

Charlie gave him a shrewd look. "Do you not want to go?"

Pete hesitated, thinking of his large pile of homework he had to do. He thought about how few people he knew and about how little he knew. There were things he needed to figure out and learn, and he wasn't going to learn them hiding in his dorm room. Besides, Charlie's reaction to the invitation made him curious.

He looked up at the clock. "If I'm going to make it, I'd better go."

Pete made sure that his curfew pass was tucked away in his pocket, grabbed his jacket, and slung it over his PJs—which had, sadly, appeared again.

Charlie, looking desperately jealous, walked him to the exit and waved goodbye as Pete walked off towards the school.

The walk from the dorm room to the front corridor door was a quick one. He only got turned around one time, which was impressive for him.

Just inside the school entrance, about a dozen kids stood in full tactical gear. Most of them were boys, but a few, he noticed, were girls. All of them stood a head and shoulders taller than Pete.

When he approached, several turned to look at him. Pete eyed the heavily protected uniforms they wore and said uncertainly, "So…I got this invitation…." He looked at the location one more time. It was definitely the right place.

No one replied, so he added, "To, um…" His voice faltered when he noticed one kid had a shot gun strapped to his back. "To the Night Society."

One of the girls snorted and nearly shouted, "You serious, kid?" She walked over and snatched the invitation out of Pete's hands. The girl was very tall and thin, with sharp blue eyes that had a slightly sunken look about them. She had a small mouth, a long nose, and stringy brown hair in a braid. She whistled. "Oh man, we usually only use these for, like, special events and stuff…. You know, a party or something. Not for work days." She looked back at her group. "Who would invite a twiggy little kid?" She studied Pete again. "Do you even know what we do?"

Pete frowned. He found he was liking this girl less and less. His face grew hot as he shook his head no. He glanced past the girl to the group, looking more closely at their attire, which looked like riot gear. They were wearing well-padded Kevlar suits, thick workmen's gloves, and held metal helmets with eye guards. That was, perhaps, why he had not immediately noticed the dark patches with the wolf heads sewn into the suits, nor the grinning, triumphant face of Shelly Grant in the back of the crowd.

Pete set his jaw in a snarl. Apparently, she'd decided it was his turn to be embarrassed in front of a crowd.

"You think it was Johnson? I heard he was going a little crazy today," said a boy with long brown hair swept to one side of his face who looked like he could be a football player. He was tall and muscular and had a black eye. When he smiled, he showed white but crooked teeth, and it looked like his nose had been broken at least once.

"Well," said a tall dark-skinned boy who, judging by his uniform and the respect the others gave him when he spoke, was the leader, "Jojo is out with a broken leg, so we could actually use some help. And remember, Hadford was small, but he was competent."

There were some murmured agreements to that.

"Dunno, boss. He doesn't look like a Tim Hadford to me."

"Neither did Hadford when he started, let me tell you. All right, listen, kid. Here's the deal. The invite is right. You get one invite only. If you decline now, you decline forever. We usually like to ease people into what we do, show them the fun family side, but you get to see the real down-and-dirty stuff first."

Pete stared at him. What was he getting himself into? "Okay...."

The leader looked at Pete with a serious expression. Everything about him gave off a don't-mess-with-me vibe, from his military-style haircut to the sharp angles of his dark, handsome face to the no-nonsense look of his piercing eyes. "The Night Society is a club that protects the school from werewolves during the full moon."

Pete waited for the kid to laugh, but he looked like he had never told a joke in his life.

"Um..." Pete swallowed. "So you kill werewolves?"

He got a round of laughs from the group, and he looked over at them, wondering what was so funny.

The leader didn't look amused as he shook his head. "No. The werewolves are students—and one is a teacher. We just make sure they don't hurt themselves or others. We're on guard duty." He frowned at Pete. "This is a serious job, and you could seriously get hurt. Messing around could get us"—he pointed at himself and those behind him—"seriously hurt. I'm not going to lie to you; we do need help on this one, but if you're going to freak out at the first sign of trouble or not listen to my orders, we should part ways while you still have all of your limbs."

Pete swallowed nervously, but then he caught the smug grin on Shelly's face and hardened his resolve. She was expecting him to wuss out and walk away.

"I'll listen, and I won't freak out." He sincerely hoped he'd be able to manage the not-freaking-out part. "Just tell me what I need to know."

Shelly's grin widened, the opposite of what he'd been expecting. It didn't seem a good sign, but he wasn't about to go back on his word. He swallowed and looked back at the kid in front of him.

The leader looked dubiously at Pete, but Pete pointed to his watch and raised an eyebrow.

The boy bit his lip, staring into Pete's eyes. After a moment, he nodded. "All right. I'm L.J., and I'm in charge. We'll do the rest of the intros later. You'll need to suit up." He pointed to what looked like a storage closet. Several of the others were already moving toward it.

The football player walked in and began handing gear out. Everyone got a gun, some getting several weapons.

Pete was given heavy protective gear of a different color than the other kids. When he zipped it up, he was handed a metal baton. "That's a taser." Everyone else had one strapped to their belt, so he strapped his on as well.

Pete felt like all his nerves were trying to jump out of his body at once. He had no idea what he was doing. So some girl he didn't know was going to make fun of him for quitting. Why did he care? She would probably make fun of him even more after a werewolf chewed off his arm.

He remembered the two people who had mentioned second death and wished he had asked one of them about it. Was it a real thing or just a joke?

"This is crazy, L.J.," the tall, muscular, brown-haired boy said quietly to L.J. "Not like you to take risks like this."

L.J. didn't reply, but gave Pete more protective gear—a helmet, extra pads to add on top of his suit, thick, heavy gloves, and a neck guard.

It was swelteringly hot, but not once did Pete want to take anything off. In fact, compared to his thick body suit, he felt that his neck and hands were too exposed.

L.J. saw Pete looking at the weapons and said, "It's not loaded with lethal rounds, rookie," and winked. "And that big boy is for L.J. only." He pointed at the tallest kid holding a massive gun.

Pete tried to say, "Oh," but no words came out.

Unsmiling, L.J. holstered the pistol on his right side and packed what looked like two grenades into a little pouch on the side of his belt. Pete saw that he had a large knife on his hip and another smaller one in a sheath by his foot.

"We're Alpha team," L.J. said. "Beta is—" He cut off as the radio squawked on his hip.

"10-4, this is Beta team radio for Alpha team, over."

"Go on, over," replied L.J.

"We have a situation that requires some assistance. Can you send reinforcements? Over."

"Copy. Reinforcements in two minutes thirty seconds. Over."

"10-4. Over."

L.J. made a circling motion with the speaker, and the team formed into two tight lines and began jogging in quick formation towards the sound.

Pete moved to step in behind the group, but L.J. held him back and pointed at a kid off to the side. "You're with Marcus tonight." Without another word, L.J. jogged off and caught up with the team.

Marcus watched the team run down the hallway through a hidden door in the wall, down another hallway and outside. The boy finished strapping on his gear and nodded for Pete to follow.

Pete was almost instantly out of breath, but the boy spoke as they jogged. "I'm Marcus." He held out a hand and Pete clumsily grabbed it.

"Pete."

"Turn here," Marcus said. They had reached the front doors. They made a right turn and ran along the front of the school in the direction of Pete's dorms. "Hopefully, we won't be needed for anything too dangerous. We'll be the second line of defense. Third wave."

He pulled his baton up. Pete hadn't realized it, but the baton was attached to a retractable line. Marcus pulled it up in front of him and with his other hand shined a flashlight. "This button stuns." He pushed it and a light flashed, leaving spots in Pete's eyes.

"When you hold it, it zaps. You let go, it stops. Simple, right? Turn here." He pointed with the baton, and they turned right, away from the dorms towards the back of the school. "Turn here."

At first, Pete couldn't tell where he was supposed to go. Then he saw it—there was a wall running parallel to the school. It was cleverly hidden by design and with the help of the shrubbery. They jogged down the narrow pathway.

Marcus shined the flashlight on the baton again. Pete tried to focus, breathing through a stitch in his side.

Marcus breathed easily. "If you press the button and then push upward, then it has extra zap." He demonstrated and a CRACK sounded, followed by a blinding light.

"Oh!" Pete stumbled slightly in the blinding light. He almost fell, but Marcus grabbed his arm to steady him.

"Whoops," he said bashfully. "Sorry, kid. Okay, we're here. Put your helmet on."

Slightly frazzled, Pete obeyed. He noticed his hot breath did not fog up his visor. They must've had some sort of ventilation in the helmet.

Marcus stepped forward to unlock a gate that suddenly appeared in the wall in front of them. A radio squawked in his ear, and he heard Marcus' voice play through a speaker in his helmet. "Heads up, it'll be loud." He pushed the gate open.

Pete frowned when he caught sight of the courtyard beyond. He could see large cages.

He stepped into the courtyard behind Marcus and almost fell backward. A wall of sound attacked his eardrums. Every few seconds, a roar like a car crash resonated, shaking the ground where he stood. There were barks and snarls and howls that made Pete's blood freeze. Shouts and commands from the teams as they managed the cages mingled in with the snarls and screams of wolves.

Kids in gear were running every which way. Pete was completely disoriented. "What? What is that?" He panicked.

"Get off the central line. Over," a voice squawked in his ear. Marcus walked over and turned a nob on the side of Pete's helmet.

"Adjust and focus," Marcus ordered.

Adjust and focus. Pete looked around in shock. Seconds ago, on the other side of the wall, it had been a quiet and peaceful scene, but now it was mayhem.

The iron cages were massive, towering at least six or seven feet tall and at least four feet wide. They shifted with each violent slam as the wolves threw their bodies into the cage walls.

"Magic disguises the entrance to this place," Marcus grunted into Pete's microphone as he adjusted the chains that rooted the cages to the cement floor. "Come help me with this." He strained against a chain.

"Pete! Focus!" Marcus snapped, breaking the spell the wolves had put on Pete. He jumped and grabbed the chain.

"No, grab the lever."

Pete cranked on the lever, and the nearest cage groaned as the chains pulled on it. Every time a wolf slammed against the door of its cage, the impact sent painful jolts up his arm and through his entire body. The effect was just as dizzying as the yelping screams the wolves were letting out.

Pete blinked spots out of his eyes as he worked and fought the urge to run with every fiber of his being.

He distracted himself with his tasks, which were barked at him in a steady stream. He watched the Alpha and Beta teams working like a seamless machine, each cog in perfect order. The kid's shouts and commands mingled with the snarls of the wolves.

When Pete could look at the animals without feeling like he was going to pass out, he saw that the smallest wolf was a good foot taller than him. The biggest had to crouch his head down to not hit the top of his cage, though when his rage broke, he snarled madly and slammed his head on the roof of his cage.

They didn't seem to have normal fur. It looked sleek, almost wet and slippery like a seal's, and ranged in color. Most had dark fur—gray, brown, or black—but there were a couple of light tan ones, and the smallest had a white coat. Pete was surprised to see a hard ridge running down the center of their backs, and some had hardened bones in the shape of spikes running along that ridge.

He tried to swallow, but his throat was too dry. He was drenched in sweat and could barely lift his hands. The noise was so loud and distracting, he couldn't help but shudder every time a wolf let out a yipping, yowling scream. Then, about twenty minutes into his back-breaking work, he heard what was probably the worst sound he would ever hear in his AfterLife.

Pete was in the middle of helping Marcus move some supplies when a terrible wrenching, crunching sound made them stop dead in their tracks.

Pete couldn't say what exactly had happened right away. There were shouts, and orders started squawking over the emergency line to all comms.

"Big T, zone 2! E and Kramer load the anti-ware sleeves. Spin a parameter. Green and Marcus, get the tubers ready and charge up the backup sticks. Greenstone and white."

It took Pete a second to realize that L.J. had given him a command. In fact, it took Marcus grabbing his arm, pulling on it and saying, "Hey, this way!" to get him moving at all. Marcus had to yell over the noise the wolves were making. What had been the occasional yowl was now a nearly continuous scream. The sound was freezing his blood again, and he was having trouble moving his arms and legs. He kept up, though barely, following in the footsteps of Marcus.

"I don't know what's gotten into them today. Sorry kid, but it doesn't seem like today was a good pick for your first one. They are pissed." Marcus cursed when he ran past a cage as the wolf slammed into the side. Pete was only mildly reassured that he was not the only one scared of them.

"I still don't get why you were invited." Marcus pulled out a standard military chest, opened it, and slid an entire rack of at least twenty grenades onto the ground. "It takes six months of training for this, and recruits are usually in their second-to-last year at least. You have barely…what? Fifteen minutes? I just don't know what they were thinking."

"Shelly thought it was a clever prank," Pete said flatly.

Marcus looked over, raising an eyebrow.

"See, I fell on her…."

Marcus barked a laugh. "You were the aerial attack guy?" Pete started to protest, but Marcus just continued to laugh. Why did everyone laugh at that story?

Marcus shook his head, struggling to collect himself, and then nodded to the rack below where the grenades were. There were five or six shiny black batons with little prongs on the end of them. These were, no doubt, something similar to cattle prods.

"We haven't ever had to bust these out since I came over."

Pete looked at them dubiously and then over his shoulder at the big wolves. "Will they even feel these?"

Marcus laughed and nodded. "Hell, yeah. They'll feel them. These babies would drop a herd of elephants." He picked one up and pulled a lever. Then he tossed it into the nearest cage and a loud crack sounded. Pete was temporarily blinded by a bright white light.

"Wow." The wolf was now unconscious.

"Five bars is full." Marcus handed him a grenade. "If it's not full, we need to fix that ASAP. They should all be good. Get going. We need them all hit now."

The stake Pete held had blue glowing bars on the side. "This one is still good even though you hit the button." He set it down to his right and picked up another stake to check it. Then he walked over to the cage with the largest wolf, who was making the most racket. He squared up to it, and the most bone-chilling thing happened: The sound completely stopped.

He knew this moment would give him chills for the rest of his AfterLife. He would have never guessed there would be anything scarier than the scream of a werewolf, but he had been wrong—their silence was worse.

Then in unison, every single wolf raised its head to the moon and howled. The sound sliced through the air like a knife through pudding. It seemed to grab hold of Pete's spine and sent uncontrollable shivers down it.

The sound was a predator's scream and tapped into his basic human instinct. Pete's animalistic need to survive was fighting to take over.

He began slowly backing away from the cages, towards the exit—and he wasn't the only one.

"What the…?" Clear fear laced Marcus's voice.

L.J., however, seemed relatively unperturbed. "Stand your ground, soldiers!" he yelled over the emergency line.

Marcus straightened, and without another word, he shut down his visor and moved double-time, handing out grenades.

Pete stopped moving back and straightened his spine. Scared his trembling would make him miss, he aimed his shaking hand to toss the grenade.

The largest wolf gave its hardest slam yet.

With a horrifying crack, the locks finally broke. The massive wolf blasted the door open, knocking two shocked team members to the ground, and barreled directly at Pete.

CHAPTER 6

THE KEEPER OF THE WOLVES

PETE TRIED TO MOVE OUT of the way, but it was too late. The wolf bit down on his helmet, its bottom jaw grabbing hold of his open visor, and dragged him backward as it kept running. Its jaws were so powerful, it flung his body around like a rag doll.

Pete felt the wolf slam through the gate like it was nothing. He screamed, trying to pull off his helmet. But the momentum of the animal was throwing his arms all over the place and he couldn't get a good grip. He was afraid he was going to break his neck.

He flailed his arms, yelling the entire time and trying to get some footing on the ground, but it was impossible. The wolf was simply too big.

Suddenly, the wolf gave an almighty heave from its back paws, and Pete felt temporarily weightless. Finally, he could control his arms and his fingers found the strap and he unsnapped his helmet.

The moment of weightlessness ended as he fell. A paw kicked him and Pete smacked the ground hard. Pain like he had never known racked his body. He would have screamed, had all the wind not been knocked from his lungs.

With a violent jerk, his body was whipped forward again. He yelped loudly when he hit several large rocks and narrowly missed a tree trunk. He slowed slightly, finally managed to gain control of his pounding head and injured neck, and forced himself to look up and see what was happening.

Pete saw with dread that the wolf was dragging him with some of the chains that had been used to keep the cage closed. The heavy chain was wrapped around both of his legs and the wolf's chest. He could hear his name being shouted, but the sounds were growing more distant with every leap. Pete knew they were moving too fast for anyone to help him. The wolf didn't even seem to notice it was dragging him along for a ride. The wolf was going to kill him and not even realize it.

In between impacts from objects in the grassy terrain, Pete recognized the dorm rooms off to the right and realized they were in the grassy area of the front courtyard heading to the main gate.

A few painful seconds later, the wolf burst through the wrought-iron gate with a tremendous clang, swinging the doors wide and ripping off one of its hinges off.

Then, without warning, the wolf stopped running. There was just enough time for Pete to yank his legs from the loose chain. And not a moment too soon because the wolf darted off towards the woods.

Pete lay on the dirt road, broken and panting. He was shaking uncontrollably, but he didn't know if it was from terror or pain. With trembling hands, he wiped the hair out of his eyes. His hand came away bloody, and he groaned.

The crunch of footsteps came through the night, and he looked over to see a tall, thin man walking his way. The moonlight flooded the road, but it cast a shadow over the man's face so Pete couldn't make out his expression. For some reason, he did not feel reassured by the sight.

Something about the man seemed odd. His casual, friendly gait was at odds with the severity of the situation. Surely the man had seen the giant wolf dragging a fourteen-year-old boy.

Pete was pretty sure the wolf had run into the woods, but they were both still in a great deal of danger. Pete sat up to try to warn the man. Spots darkened his vision, and he became dizzy and nauseated.

"Agh—" His voice cracked sharply, sending pain down his throat and making his head pound. Pete wheezed and went to push himself up farther, but his shaking arms wavered and his face planted back on the packed-dirt street.

He grunted in pain and struggled to get a grip on his body. He couldn't feel his limbs, his right leg had a searing pain just above his ankle, his left eye was swelling shut, and his arms would not respond to his brain.

Then, the only thing that could make his body move sounded through the air. Howls, terrible screaming howls, pierced the air once again. It hit him with heart-stopping reality—the wolves were close.

They were coming straight toward him. Him and this stranger.

Suddenly, Pete's arms would support him. His left leg took his weight but the right leg refused, making him stumble again. He caught himself and did an exaggerated limping run. The man, who was within a few short yards of him now, paused. His face was still in shadow, but his body stopped its rhythmic gate and was standing rigid with concern.

"Mnrn!" Pete croaked. "Mrrun!" He tried again and tackled the man backward into a bush neighboring the wall to the school.

"Oof!" the man grunted as he fell.

"Shh." Pete dragged them into deeper cover. Barely a second later, he heard the distinct heavy padding of paws on a packed dirt road, followed by the panting and yips of wolves. Pete could see from his hiding place the puffs of air coming from their mouths. When they reached the street, they stopped and looked around. Their movements became agitated. Yipping and whining, they sniffed the air.

Were they searching for him? Pete froze when the larger wolf stepped out of the forest and into the moonlight spilling onto the streets. The younger, smaller wolves stopped their sniffing and milling about to look at him as if they were waiting for instructions.

It was almost completely silent, so when the man who he was lying on top of Pete said, "Excuse me, young man," Pete jumped about a foot into the air and nearly screamed out loud.

The animals turned towards where they were hiding. Pete, without the pretense of a barrier between him and the wolves, stared at eight sets of glowing, angry eyes.

Pete was rigid and immobile, but the man stood up, looking annoyed. He brushed off his jacket and frowned at a small tear. He fixed Pete with a patronizing look.

"This is a new suit, you know." He used a handkerchief to wipe off his face and hands, then folded it back into his jacket pocket.

One of the smaller wolves approached the man, who casually scratched the top of its head. The man was quite tall, but still, the wolf's head came up to his breast pocket. It felt like the wind was knocked out of Pete. He watched the man, speechless.

He looked in his late fifties, with a neat white beard and tidy white hair under a sleeping cap. He had a sharp chin, hollow cheeks, and narrow eyes, though the night made it nearly impossible to tell their color.

Pete tried to calm his breathing. The wolves slowly encircled them, then stood behind the man and looked at Pete. Suddenly, he felt very alone. The man's casual indifference and jovial attitude made Pete wonder if he were not even more dangerous than the wolves.

There was still no sign of anyone coming to help him, and even if they were, it would be too late. Pete looked at the man, who was smiling mischievously now, and knew that he was going to have the wolves attack him. How the man was controlling them, Pete had no idea, but he did know that he was not going to die a second death cowering like a frightened child.

Making as small a movement as possible, he searched for a weapon of some sort. There were two fist-sized rocks near his right leg and he was kneeling on something hard. He hadn't noticed it at first because he'd been so afraid, but now that he realized it was there; it felt like it could be a metal rod broken off from the gate.

The man strolled casually towards Pete with all the cordiality of an inquisitive stranger, but the menacing look in his eyes filled Pete with dread. The man had finally moved into a position where the moonlight completely illuminated his face—and in that light his madness became apparent.

Pete didn't even hear what the man was saying to him, but with a flick of the man's finger, a wolf lunged at him. He yelped and rolled out of the way.

The man laughed wildly. He made a calming motion and the wolf backed up, snarling. The man took casual steps forward, and when he came within a striking distance, without even a second thought, Pete grabbed the rod and swung. He clocked the stranger upside the head, and as he did, he realized what the rod was.

With an exclamation he jabbed the man, who was now doubled over, and zapped him. There was a flash and a loud crack, and the man crumpled.

Immediately, the wolves stopped their snarling and let out simultaneous howls. Pete's knees locked together in fear. It was such a strange feeling, to be certain of his impending doom. He couldn't feel his limbs, and the air thickened in his lungs. It felt like he was suddenly deep underwater, and the surface was nowhere to be found.

The blackness crept in from all sides. He wondered in a detached sort of way if this was how he felt when he died the first time. As his vision tunneled, the last image was the largest wolf approaching, and then blackness swallowed him.

"Pete…I don't like this," said the girl with brown hair and big brown eyes. Now that she spoke, Pete could make out her large front teeth and chubby cheeks.

"Don't worry. Just stay here," Pete whispered back. He was excited about something but couldn't remember what it was.

"Pete, don't—" The girl sounded worried.

"Just stay here." Pete stood, but the second he took a step, the ground gave way and he fell into black emptiness. As he fell, he heard the girl screaming.

Pete woke with a violent start that sent shockwaves of pain spiraling through his body.

"Gkack!" was all he managed to say as he gasped for breath. "Wha…." He looked around, confused. His eyes were open, but he couldn't see anything and kept getting hit in the face with a wet, smelly washcloth. He registered that it was still night and several people were standing around him, talking and moving about with purpose and speed. He used one hand to block his face from whoever was doing a terrible job of wiping his face and used the other to push himself up.

But he immediately fell back down with a very unmanly squeal, his vision spotting from the pain.

"Where is she?" Pete wiped his face.

"Dreaming of saving a pretty lady?" Pete recognized the voice of Shelly and frowned. "There was no damsel in distress. That was you screaming, sweet cheeks."

A few chuckles erupted around him, but at the moment, Pete didn't care. All thoughts of the little girl were pushed out of his mind. Staring directly into his face was the massive form of the largest black wolf.

"P-Professor?" Pete asked uncertainly.

The wolf whined and licked Pete one more time.

"Yuck." Pete was too weak to push the beast away, though if he had the strength, he was not sure that he would. His professor did seem to be friendlier now, but still…he did not want to push it.

"You all right?" L.J. squatted next to Professor Johnson and studied Pete. "Anything broken?"

L.J.'s voice sounded like it was coming from a tiny radio underwater, and it took him a minute to process what he was saying. Pete stared at the boy, then mentally searched his body, cataloging injuries. He opened his mouth to say something, but when he finally did, neither L.J. nor the giant form of the wolf was in front of him anymore.

Pete strained to sit up again, but moving sent another flood of pain so sharp that his vision darkened, and he fell into blackness once again.

CHAPTER 7

DO DEAD PEOPLE DIE?

ETE WOKE A FEW MINUTES later to what sounded like a hundred people arguing directly into his ear. He inhaled sharply and was surprised that it caused merely a dull pain, instead of a pounding one.

"There is no way Smalls will let South High get more than ten yards on him," one voice said loudly. "He's too good and the defense—the defense doesn't even…" The unrecognizable voice started yelling over the voice of someone else cutting in.

Pete opened his eyes. The voices belonged to two boys about sixteen years old. One looked like a jock and had olive skin, green eyes, short black uncombed hair, and a square jaw. His companion was a lean, dark-skinned kid with black eyes, a shaved head, and a friendly smile.

Pete could tell by their body language that they were good friends. Several other voices chimed into the conversation and Pete continued looking around the room. There were about 15 people jammed into a small room he didn't recognize.

"He's up," someone said. The people stopped talking one by one, and the noise quieted down for a second. To Pete's embarrassment, every eye turned to him.

"Uh, hi." Pete's voice cracked slightly. He tugged on his tie that had reappeared during the few minutes he had fallen asleep.

The noise broke out again, and everyone began snickering and talking at once.

"Dude, kid, you are something else," the kid nearest him said. It was L.J., he realized, the leader of the Night Society

With a jolt, Pete noticed the silent professor in the corner. Mr. Johnson nodded at Pete, who smiled awkwardly back. A little dazed, he looked at the other people in the room. The Were Team, whom he had met last night, were all milling around, though they looked a little strange in their regular clothes, with some of the girls wearing makeup and their hair done up.

"You are something else, Green," L.J. repeated. "That was an epic first time for the books."

"Wasn't my fault." Pete wasn't exactly sure what he was defending himself from.

Another boy—a tall, pale kid sitting next to a Hispanic boy—snorted. "Man, look. He's embarrassed. Nothing to be embarrassed about. You got mad instincts. Being dragged across the school grounds by the professor on your second day of school and then zapping the Magics professor." He shook his head. "Crazy man."

"He was a professor?" Pete was alarmed.

"He'll be fine," L.J. waved off the question. He leaned forward in his chair. "Did you know they were under a spell?"

"No…" Pete said slowly. "I mean, not really. I could tell he was controlling them somehow."

Mr. Johnson grunted angrily in the corner.

"So you just zapped him?" asked someone else whose name he had forgotten, hooting with laughter.

Pete's cheeks flushed. "Well, he looked crazy." He shrugged. "I thought I was gonna die, so I figured, what could it hurt?"

They all laughed. Pete wanted to ask them whether it was really possible to die in AfterLife, but he didn't want to sound like a coward when they were supposedly all impressed by his quick thinking. He made a mental note to ask Charlie about it.

"Man, my first full moon, I about crapped my pants," one of the Ware Team members said with a laugh. "I got knocked over by…" He looked over at an unsmiling blonde girl with bright blue eyes, a soft, flat nose, and broad shoulders. "Was it you, Trixie?"

Trixie laughed. "No, I think that was Nibs."

The tall, pale kid, who must've been Nibs, shrugged and grinned.

"Right. Ya, maybe it was. Man, he just bowls me over, right?" He knocked one hand into the other. "And I'm lying there stunned for, like, half an hour." He shook his head, laughing.

Everyone began sharing stories about their first time. Four of the boys and two of the girls turned out to be the wolves from the night before. The rest of the kids were on the two teams that had been in charge of keeping the wolves in the cages. Pete supposed he had expected the werewolves to be bigger…and uglier. He eyed a girl L.J. introduced as Macie, whose pretty blue eyes sparkled as she laughed.

Pete realized with a jolt that he had expected them to all be like Shelly. He looked over to the corner where she was scowling and hissing the occasional rude comment. He had made an enemy, he thought. Her trick had backfired and he had ended up on top…somehow.

But as they all launched into their stories, Pete forgot she was even there. The kids didn't stop their tales until a thin, smiling woman in a nurse's uniform sauntered into the room. Her sweet perfume filled the air, and Pete noticed a few of the wolf kids sniff and then sneeze. Still, all seemed happy to see her.

She shooed L.J. off his seat. The boy jumped up with a dazzling grin. "Afternoon, Miss Mary."

"Afternoon?" Pete asked.

The nurse looked at her watch. "Nearly evening now." She smiled sweetly at L.J. "And it's Miss Gray to you." He winked mischievously. She shook her head but kept the smile.

The nurse had a small mouth. Her pinned-back hair looked like it would be about shoulder length if let loose, and the old-fashioned nurse cap tied into it looked to be made of paper. Her perfume—a hint of flowers and something else that Pete could only describe as sunlight—tickled his nose, and he thought for a second he would sneeze too.

She bent to examine his bandages and began poking and prodding.

"Ow," Pete said. "How long was I out?" The blinds were closed.

"Almost a full day. You missed all your classes today. Your friends were kind enough to bring your homework by." She nodded to the table beside Pete's bed, where some books were laid out. "They were in earlier today."

"Charlie?" Pete asked.

The nurse smiled and nodded. "Yes, and a tall girl. You weren't bitten," she said casually. Pete looked up sharply. "Bites don't turn you into a wolf—that's not how it works, but wolf bites do take a long time to heal," she said as though remembering some bad bites, and continued inspecting his wounds.

"How do you become a wolf?" Pete watched her examine his cuts.

It was L.J. who answered. "Just like almost any job here. If you weren't born a werewolf, like all of these kids were"—he pointed at the younger werewolves in the room— "you apply for the job and train for it." He pointed at the professor.

"Oh," Pete wanted to ask why anyone would need a werewolf but not wanting to sound rude.

Mr. Johnson's warm laugh sounded. "You're wondering why I would apply?" He seemed to read Pete's mind.

Pete blushed and nodded.

"Well, to help these young folks. A good Alpha can control a pack and guide them into maturity. It's needed in a school that gets so many natural-born werewolves. We didn't have a natural-born Alpha, so I volunteered for the job. The training is intense." He shook his head. "I'll have to tell you about it one day." He smiled.

"Sorry, I don't get it." Pete was confused. "What do you mean, natural-born? I thought everyone at the school was alive and died before their parents. Are you saying they can be werewolves when they are alive?"

The professor smiled. "Well, first, most come here because they have no parent or guardian in AfterLife, but that is not necessarily the case for all of our students. There is the occasional person whose parent signs their child up for our school."

He leaned forward in his chair. "But to answer your question, the process is simple enough. There are people who were born in AfterLife and choose to visit Life through a reincarnation process, and there are those born in Life who come here through natural means, like yourself. If a werewolf reincarnates into Life and has children, every one of those children becomes werewolves, and the same is true of any of their children born in AfterLife. No one is certain how the first werewolves were made," he said, answering Pete's next unspoken question, "but since then, their children have been born as Weres. Only one parent needs to be a Were for their children to become one. In Life, they never change, but when they return to AfterLife, every full moon, they become these elegant creatures." He smiled.

Pete thought elegant wasn't the right word, but returned the professor's smile.

The nurse finished poking and prodding and declared that Pete would probably be fit to leave in an hour or two. Food was on the way, and she would come back in an hour to check on him. She helped him stand up and went over a few stretches and exercises he should do to speed up the healing process.

The boys snickered as Pete awkwardly did his exercises.

Ten minutes later, she walked out just as her assistant walked in with some food. Ravenous, Pete almost seized the tray of food right out of his hands, but the boy was quick.

"Not so fast, speedy," he said. "In the bed then, go on."

Pete impatiently hopped into bed, wincing. His range of motion was almost all back, but he was still stiff and sore in spots.

The boy noticed and raised an eyebrow. "Think you're James Bond? Well, here ya go. Suppose even Bond needs to eat." He set the tray down and then to Pete's surprise, sat down on the chair the nurse vacated and propped his feet up.

"You on break, Ren?" asked Tyler, the jock standing next to L.J.

"Nah. Supposed to start my rounds, but I can't stand the howling that old man makes. Not sure what that one did to him" —he pointed a thumb at Pete—"but he's in a state."

"Hoo?" Pete's mouth was too full to even chew properly.

Ren raised an eyebrow. "Hungry much? The hoo I was referring to was Professor Medallion Alfineous Ellington the Third." He adopted a soothing pompous voice when he said this. "I'm Renfield, by the way, but everyone calls me Ren. Pleased to make your acquaintance."

Pete waved, swallowed hard, choked and coughed.

"That's Pete," Nibs said. "He electrocuted Professor Crazy."

"I heard." Ren smirked.

Pete gasped for air. When he could finally breathe without bits of bread flying down his throat, he frowned at Ren, who was completely ignoring him. He quickly realized he was too hungry to be angry anyway, though he would chew and swallow a bit more cautiously this time.

In spite of Shelly's occasional comment or glare, he felt welcome for the first time since he arrived. Though everyone had been nice enough and he was friends with Charlie and Scoot, this was the first time he felt like he had a place in the school, an "in."

To add to his happiness, Shelly seemed to be growing more and more frustrated that the others were not joining her in teasing him. She left mere minutes later in a huff, giving Pete a thrill of satisfaction.

Ren left shortly after, yelping when he looked at his watch and chastising his friends for distracting him so thoroughly. He promised to meet up with Pete later when they could talk longer.

As the group chatted, joked, and exchanged stories from the night before, Pete learned just how unusual his first night had been. The docile wolf that had licked his face was usually the one they dealt with for the majority of the night.

"We have to lock these guys up at first." Tyler gestured to the werewolves with a smirk. "They go moon-mad nearly every time, except Mr. J. But after an hour or two, we can let them out, and they roam the woods and come back."

"I've never seen you guys that bad before though." Marcus shook his head. Pete remembered him saying something to that effect the night before. "We looked at the cages this morning, and it looked like they had been tampered with."

"I haven't felt normal until this morning," Trixie said in a surprisingly feminine voice for such a husky girl. "Mr. Ellington must have been working on this spell for a while because this whole week was hazy. I was having so much trouble studying." She sighed heavily. "I don't think Mrs. Hayworth will give me an extension either, so it looks like my weekend will be full of playing catch-up."

"So," L.J. said finally, "we are dying to know, no pun intended—" A few people snorted. "—are you joining our group?"

Pete thought about it. He was having a lot of fun with them. It would be nice to belong to a group. Then he looked down at his bandages and frowned. Unbidden came the thought of the brown-eyed girl he'd dreamed about last night—how frightened she'd been. How much he'd wanted to protect her. Who was she? He shook his head slowly and was rewarded with a slap to the shoulder. "Oof," Pete said, surprised.

"No worries," Marcus said. "Told you he wouldn't want in."

"That was a rough first night," L.J. conceded. "Well, no hard feelings. Don't be a stranger around the school. I'd like—"

But what L.J. would've liked, Pete never found out. A sharp clearing of the throat silenced the room, and almost in unison, the crowd's heads turned toward the door to look at Mrs. Battinsworth's tall and freakishly skinny figure standing in the doorway.

The frown pinching the headmistress's mouth tightened as she took in all the happy faces. Every student adopted a guilty expression and slowly filed out of the room, throwing Pete the occasional apologetic glance.

Suddenly nervous, Pete said, "Hello, headmistress." She said nothing, and he added, a bit lamely, "How are you doing today?"

She squinted disapprovingly at him and stiffly made her way into the room. She stood above Pete, which gave him an unpleasant view into her nostrils.

He cleared his throat, which was suddenly very dry again, and waited nervously for the headmistress to speak. He forced his face to adopt a pleasantly curious expression, instead of the guilty one trying to bully its way onto his face, and looked her directly in the eyes.

She seemed momentarily taken aback. She sniffed and nodded at his bandages. "I assume you are healing quickly enough?"

"Yes, thank you," he said.

She sniffed again and adopted an almost business-like tone. "Well, you electrocuted the Magic and Witchcraft Professor, which is an expulsion worthy act in itself. You also managed to bruise Professor Johnson's mouth during a routine Full Moon Exercise."

Pete sputtered in indignation, losing all sense of his cordiality. "Do you mean he bruised his mouth when he bit my helmet?" he asked in complete disbelief.

The headmistress ignored his question. "However, since it was your first offense, and since Professor Johnson was driven mad with moon sickness and Professor Ellington had technically escaped from the mental institution where he was currently residing, you will not be punished. But heed my warning that exceptions will not be made in the future—and that electrocuting professors under any other circumstance is strictly forbidden."

She gave him a stern look, narrowing her eyes. When he only gave her a blank, incredulous stare, she spun around and walked out, closing the door to his sputtering.

A moment later, the door opened again, making Pete jump.

Ren reappeared, letting out a whistle. "Wow, I thought for sure you'd get detention. Maybe she gave you some slack 'cause you got scraped up."

"What? Why would I get detention? It was their fault! I thought she was going to apologize." Pete was getting very angry. Then he frowned. "Wait, I thought you left."

"I did." Ren gave a mischievous grin. "But I came back in as a nurse's assistant"—he pulled up a corner of his uniform as proof—"to assist you and stuff. I heard she came and I wanted to, you know, give you moral support."

Pete snorted, his shock from the last few minute's events worn off. "Well, thanks for your support, Ren." Pete smiled. Then his smile went away. "And what do you mean by cutting me slack? I thought she was here to apologize for her teachers attacking me."

Ren laughed and shook his head. "Nah, it's always the students' fault here. I'm surprised she didn't accuse you of not running faster."

Pete shook his head in disbelief.

Ren added, "You know Mrs. Nichols? Wait, you're new, right?" Pete nodded, and Ren sighed. "Ok, then you won't know her. You get her after you've been here a while or if you're an older kid. Well, anyways, she's ancient-looking and this poor new kid came into her classroom. She just goes nuts, right? Something about him smells like real sunlight or something weird like that, and she bites him. Of course, he freaks out, and—"

"Wait, she just bit him?"

"Yes, she bit him," he said impatiently. "Oh, right," he added, slapping his forehead. "I forgot you don't know: She's a vampire."

"Oh, like my finance professor? But she bit him?"

"Uh… Oh, yeah. Mrs. Yasmine, right?"

"Yannisburg," Pete corrected.

"I never had her, but kids say she's much older than Mrs. Nichols, and I guess older ones have better control." He paused, tilting his head to the side. "Or wait, is it that the older ones have less control?" His brow furrowed for a moment. "Honestly, I can't remember what the rules are. I took a test, but it was last semester and I forgot it all already."

He shook his head. "Anyways, so she bit this kid. Blood goes everywhere, he freaks out, of course. Poor guy dies, goes through registration, which is annoying and takes forever, and then gets here and gets bit by his teacher on his first day. I guess something about his smell. Well, this gets him detention for a week."

"What?" Pete said with indignation. "How can they justify th—"

"They don't have to." Ren checked his chart and marked something with a pen. "They run the place." He shrugged as if to say, What can you do? "All right, I really do have to bounce this time. I'll catch you later." He waved as he left the room.

Later that day, Miss Gray released him with instructions to take it easy and lie down often.

"You will heal quickly—everyone does in AfterLife, but you'll do it faster if you rest."

"Can I ask you a question?" Pete asked before she left.

"Yes?"

"Can you die another time?"

She smiled. "No, sweetie, that's just a rumor. I haven't heard of an occurrence in the eighty years I've been here. If your head pops off, though, do come here. It can be tricky to get it back on, and it'll click funny for weeks if you do it wrong."

CHAPTER 8

FOOTBALL GAMES ARE CONFUSING

PETE WALKED BACK TO THE dorm slowly, his mind contemplative. Now that it was quiet and he had some time to reflect, he thought about the previous night's events. The terrifying ordeal with the wolves, of course, but what was weighing even heavier on his mind was the little girl in his dream. Or had it been a memory? He felt the truth in his bones, like he knew his name and that he was missing shoes. He knew this girl, and she was important to him.

And she was in danger.

His stomach clenched uncomfortably at the very idea, but still the thought stayed—another unwavering fact.

He needed to figure out how to find her and help her. But he didn't have the slightest idea where to start.

The rest of the week passed without incident, and Pete used every opportunity to research how to find memories and connect with friends and family. It was mostly a frustrating affair. He couldn't explain why he hadn't mentioned the brown-eyed girl to his friends, except the fact that Max had told him about the dangers of getting memories in Purgatory. He didn't want them to discourage him from finding out more about her, nor did he want them to think that he was losing his mind.

So, alone, he tried to find anything he could on recollection. Instead, he found books like *Purgatory Done Right and Suppressing Annoying and Unwanted*

Memories for a More Relaxed AfterLife—books about the many dangers of looking into the past.

There was even more information about the dangers of improper memory retrieval. Pete read in horrified fascination of several documented cases where people were driven mad and turned into poltergeists from improper memory retrieval. Several disturbing photos accompanied these stories.

He had a temporary jolt of excitement several days after starting his research when he came upon a story about a young man who demanded his memories back, and when his request was denied, he attempted to break in and steal them. So it was possible! But Pete's excitement deflated when it detailed the disastrous results of the robbery attempt, outlining just how heavily guarded the Department of Registered Deaths was.

In spite of his lack of progress, he was starting to enjoy his AfterLife at the academy. Sure, the occasional dodo scream was alarming, and he was still rather bitter about his meeting with the headmistress, but it didn't change the fact that he was quite happy.

The classes were fascinating, and he had friends. As an unexpected perk, the incident with the wolves gave him temporary celebrity status. Though he didn't by any means forget the little brown-eyed girl, he was ashamed to admit this attention did cause her to be pushed to the back of his mind a bit.

Before he'd even pulled on his school uniform the morning after the wolf attack, he had been bombarded by about a hundred questions.

"How do they even know about it?" Pete asked Charlie as he buttoned up his shirt. "Did you tell them or something?"

Charlie looked confused. "Of course. I am people's source of news," he said proudly. "I wrote about it in the school paper."

"The school paper?"

"Well, sure. Would you want people spreading false information about you?"

Before Pete could answer, Charlie leaned forward. "Word is, Shelly Grant is out to get you. She was making it as though you were screaming the whole time, peeing your pants."

Of course, he had been screaming the entire time, but peeing his pants? He was eighty percent sure that hadn't happened.

"What's her problem?" Pete was furious.

Charlie shrugged. "Besides being ugly?" Pete snorted. "Not sure." Charlie held a shirt up against his stomach and tried to see his reflection in the bathroom mirror from twenty feet away. "But she has a bug up her butt about you."

He threw the shirt on the bed and looked at Pete with a serious expression. "You need someone like me hedging the stories. You are my friend, and I ain't gonna let a pig-nosed Goliath mess with my buddy." He nodded at Pete and turned to pull out clothes from under his bed.

Slightly stunned but grateful, Pete sat on Charlie's bunk and watched him examine his shirts and throw them down one by one. "Egh. I have nothing to wear," Charlie complained melodramatically.

Pete snorted again and raised his eyes at the fifteen shirts thrown on the bed. Charlie rolled his eyes. "I've worn them all already."

"Where did you get clothes from?" Pete frowned down at his uniform that had already changed back into the pinstriped pajamas. He groaned and set about changing into his uniform again, hoping maybe this time it would stick. "And how do you make them stick?" Maybe he needed to concentrate on it more?

"In town, mostly," Charlie said. "There's a small allowance I get for my secretary assistant job, and when we get to go in town, I pick something up from—" he made a face— "clearance." He gave a regretful shudder and pulled still more clothes out. He looked up, "And you just have to practice. The trick is to always expect that you are wearing whatever clothes you want to be wearing."

"Okay. I need to expect to be wearing the clothes I want to be wearing?" Pete shrugged. "I guess I can try that. When do we go in town?" He perked up. It would be a nice change of pace to see something other than the school. Maybe there was a library or bookstore he could check out to find out more about getting his memories back.

Charlie paused for a second, thinking. "Uh. I don't remember. Before the Halloween Ball, I think. Or maybe a few weeks after. I forget." He smiled and gave a dreamy expression. "Just you wait for Halloween. They know how to do a good one here. But I hear it's even better in other places. They have bigger parades and parties, and the whole town gets involved. They have swamps that creatures come out of, and covens of witches put on a whole show and stuff. Not like the rude ones who hang out around here and mess with the school. I mean cool ones who put on lightshows and summon ghouls and make the forests dance. I hear it's awesome."

After another painful fifteen minutes of watching Charlie sort through his ridiculous amount of clothes, Pete snapped and threatened to burn his entire wardrobe if he didn't hurry up and pick something. Charlie pretended to be shocked and reluctantly picked a pair of jeans, silver glittery shoes, and a maroon school shirt that looked like it had been bedazzled by a blind madman in a tornado.

After about twenty minutes (completely ignoring the part of the brain that was reminding him about his homework due in two days), Pete left the dorms with Charlie and Max and met Scoot and two other girls from her dorm.

That night would be the first football game of the season, and the whole school was charged with energy. Groups of kids were gathered and chatting excitedly. People's faces were painted, and many were crafting signs to cheer on their team.

"Am I supposed to be wearing gray and white?" Pete pointed to a group of people walking past. He sighed when he realized his pajamas were back again.

Scoot looked surprised by his question. "Yah. It's the first football game." She pointed at a sign that said Go ARACHNIDS! that the very pretty dark-skinned girl in his history class, who he thought was named Gracie Mae, was holding.

Scoot scowled at Gracie Mae and her friend Stacie, who were dressed in their cheerleading outfits and practicing with their squad.

"Okay," Pete said in a purposely neutral tone, eyeing Scoot.

In spite of Scoot's disdain for school spirit and apparent hatred of cheerleaders, they all had a great time. They watched the players practice for a while, ate snow cones and hotdogs, and participated in the sports debates. Pete enjoyed the look of complete confusion that Charlie got when they started talking about sports.

About an hour before the game, they followed a crowd walking out of the front courtyard and through the gate.

"Where are we going?"

"The game," Charlie said excitedly. "I don't even understand what's going on, but it's still so much fun to watch."

"It's in the woods?" Pete was startled as he watched crowds of kids disappearing into the woods. Lanterns were hung in random trees, lighting a path into the forest. Instead of reassuring Pete, the lanterns gave an eerie glow that made him pause.

Something slammed painfully into Pete's shoulder, making him stumble forward a few steps.

"Nervous, Green?" said a sly voice.

"You better watch your step, Grant!" Scoot squared up for a fight.

A group of kids moved onto the path, Shelly among them. She laughed and walked off with a group of tall, muscular boys all smirking and looking back at Pete, who felt his face redden.

"Out to get you," Charlie shook his head.

"Just shake it off," Scoot said. "She's not worth it."

After that, Pete's anger burned away any lingering fear he had about the woods. He barely noticed the way the bushes seemed to illuminate with the eyes of unknown creatures or how it felt like he was being watched closely or the rustling in the leaves when there was no wind to make the trees sway and dance.

They walked in silence under the hundreds of lanterns that formed a path leading deeper into the woods. After ten minutes of walking, they reached a giant clearing. They were at the back of one of two sets of bleachers sandwiching a full-sized football field.

"Wow." Pete was in awe as he looked around. He hadn't realized the woods were so big to hide something this massive. The nearest bleachers were crowded with students in the gray, black, and white of their school, while the farther ones held students in the maroon and gold for the opposing team. There was a concession stand to their right, and when they walked past it and up the steps to the bleachers, they could see the football field splayed out in front of them. Pete watched the players warming up for a moment and tried to spot Stacie and Gracie Mae in their cheer uniforms without any luck. They were far away and it was too bright, thanks to the giant stadium lights.

Pete, Max, and Scoot followed up the rest of the bleacher stairs a group of kids dressed in gray and white holding cardboard spider signs. They settled into their seats.

Charlie, who had veered off to get popcorn, returned and offered some to Pete.

"Wow!" Pete exclaimed, hands full of popcorn. "What—who is that?"

He was looking across the field at the base of the opposite bleachers. The man, or thing, was about twenty feet tall, had a misshapen head, hunched shoulders that looked like boulders, and arms that brushed the ground.

"He's a Secarian Giant," Max said. "Magnus-something, or Magtun, but I heard he played ninth-class Collar Ball." He picked up his drink off the seat beside him and took a sip. "I guess Collar Ball is a lot like football, but more dangerous. Did you know people in the stands die regularly while watching those games?"

Scoot grinned, like she would love to see a Collar Ball game.

Pete's pulse picked up. "Hang on, I thought you couldn't double-die." He frowned, thinking about what the nurse had told him. Had she been lying, not wanting to freak him out?

Max shrugged. "Well yeah, double-dying is super rare. But they get so hurt that they are in comas for weeks."

"Rare?" Pete asked. "Or impossible?"

Charlie looked over, very seriously. "Second death is a real thing. My uncle died a second death."

"No, he didn't." Scoot gave an eye roll. "He just didn't want to take care of you until you were eighteen."

"Not true," Charlie said angrily. "He disappeared long before I died."

"Exactly," Scoot shot back, "he disappeared. That doesn't mean he died."

Charlie ignored her. "There are all kinds of reports of people getting so injured, and this black cloud kinda gobbles them up and they are never seen again."

"A black cloud?" Scoot said sarcastically. "So now people don't need to port through the Death Transport system—they just need to get super-hurt and a black cloud will take them somewhere else?"

"Why don't they come back?" Charlie countered. "One lady disappeared, and all her family and friends said she was so happy and there was no reason she wouldn't come back."

They continued arguing until Max, who seemed not to be listening at all, said, "Many people think it's worth the risk. I mean, obviously, since they sell out at almost every game. I think I'd like to go one day. But the odds of a non-giant dying are very high. I hear they have protected areas of seating for smaller species, but I never looked into it much. I guess when I graduate and get out of Purgatory, I'll do more research. Shake more hands, you know?"

"What do you mean?" Pete asked. "Whose hands would you have to shake?"

Max moved his head from side to side, seeming to choose his words. "Those seats are hard to even buy. There are only a few of them, and they're heavily protected and expensive. But they're even more exclusive than they are expensive. I would have to know people to get those seats. Actors and actresses on the Death Net or Cable 9 Lives, famous Haunters, or mayors—they're the ones who get those seats, you know? Or people who know people like that and trade for favors or something. Anyways"—Max bit into his hotdog and raised his foam finger—"that's neither here nor there. We've got a game to win right now." He started yelling and booing in earnest at the opposing team, who had apparently ported a great distance to play here, as they were announced and ran onto the field.

Scoot and Pete joined in the booing, temporarily forgetting their argument and thoughts of second death. Charlie excused himself to raid the concession stand once more and came back with four hotdogs and pickles.

"Thanks!" Pete grinned as he chomped into his mustard-covered dog. It tasted amazing. Oddly, no familiarity came rushing to meet this new taste as it often did when he ate something in the cafeteria.

He shrugged and rejoined in the cheering and yelling with his friends.

The game started off with a confusing performance from Billy, the school's giant spider mascot, as he was led onto the field. Billy looked disoriented and more than a little hungry, and he kept crawling hopefully towards his attendant. The attendant nervously batted away the spider's legs and, after a short, two-minute display, led Billy off the field.

"Huh?" Pete watched the attendant walk slowly at first, then start running as the massive spider gave chase.

The game turned out to be much more violent than he anticipated. He thought he had a basic understanding of it, but when the third head went flying into the stands to a chorus of boos and hisses from the opposing team, he realized he didn't actually have any idea at all.

The players were all very large, even on his team. Pete watched with a shocked gasp as an opposing player, who was transparent and thus all but invisible in the waning sunlight, suddenly reappeared fully visible, a few feet in front of a kid wearing gray, black, and white, smashing him to the ground with an impressive tackle.

"Oh!" the crowd moaned.

"Illegal shielding!" shouted a kid in the front stands. "Come on, ref! Are you blind? That was blatant!"

Beside Pete, Max shook his head. "Nah, that was definitely legal. Blockers can shield for less than five seconds for defensive cover only in a first down. Everyone knows that." He looked contemptuously down at the kids shouting indignantly. "It was a good play," he said, albeit begrudgingly.

The game continued and soon had players leaping twenty feet through the air, conjuring winds to move the ball. Some were emerging from underground, and one even turned into a bat, flying across the field and landing in human form, to catch a long throw and scoring a touchdown.

Mrs. Battinsworth Academy ended up losing by a slim five points to a chorus of shocked and disappointed shouts, boos, and curses from Pete's side of the field. But in spite of being sorely disappointed at losing, Pete had to admire the plays and skill of the opposing team, who ran to their coach, yelling, and raised him on their shoulders, jumping with the crowd in ecstasy. The giants, tall and intimidating, had brains and a real skill for the sport, working as one cohesive unit. They deserved the win.

Pete walked away laughing with his friends. He went to the dorms, forgetting for a moment the horrors of his first week at school, the demands of homework, and the shadows of uneasy memories of the little girl with big, brown eyes. It was nice to feel like he'd found a place where he belonged.

He couldn't help but wonder...How long would it last?

CHAPTER 9

SUPER SECRET PAJAMA WARRIORS

THAT NIGHT IN THE DORM rooms, all the kids stayed up late talking animatedly about the game. Slowly, one by one, they headed to bed.

Like most nights, sleep remained stubbornly out of reach for Pete as he lay in the dark. But he was getting used to it. Sleep seemed like a strange, long-forgotten friend or relative, one that he thought of fondly but didn't entirely remember or miss. Moreover, he had been using the time to research on his own in the library. Tonight, however, he decided he needed a little break. He wasn't pushing the brown-eyed girl out of his mind, he assured himself, it was just that he was all wired up from the excitement of the game and he wouldn't be able to focus on reading. When his conscience gave a guilty twinge, he reasoned with himself that he wasn't making much progress in the school library, anyway.

He needed a new plan. Tonight, he would think of something. The nights were his and his alone, and he was looking forward to solitude and the darkness that surrounded him.

Before long, the last hushed whispers of his bunkmates drifted off into deep and steady snores. Pete grabbed a small satchel with his homework, a book, and a flashlight, and snuck out of the dorm rooms. Maybe a change of scenery would help him focus.

When he reached the front entrance of the school, he threw his bag over and climbed the wrought-iron gate in a quick, practiced motion. He took a moment to smile at his progress with climbing, grabbed his stuff, and jogged into the woods.

Most of the lanterns were burnt out, so it took him longer to navigate the woods and reach the bleachers. He was less immune to the sounds of the woods this time too. Twice he got the shivers so bad he almost turned back, but something pushed him forward. About ten minutes later, he set down his bag on the metal bleachers and stretched.

He lay down on the bottom most row and stared up at the moon. It was a really beautiful night. The weather was crisp and cool, and there was a light breeze. He watched the silhouette of leaves fall gently to the ground. The sound of them dancing in the wind was almost hypnotic, and he found himself relaxing.

A sudden bark in his ear caused him to jumped sky high. He was on his feet before he made the conscious decision to do so. Somehow he managed to stop himself from screaming, but it was a near thing. What came out was a sort of strangled squeal.

Heart racing, he whipped his head around frantically but could not see where the sound came from. It wasn't until he finally calmed down that he realized it must be the invisible school dog.

"Bark," he whispered, "Is that you, boy?"

He made kissing noises to the dog and leaned down to see if he could pet the dog. "Come here, boy." He heard sniffing and a happy panting sound, and suddenly his hand was full of invisible fur.

"Ha-ha, that's a good boy. How did you get out?" He petted Bark. He must have gotten locked out while all the kids were at the game. "You really gave me a scare." Pete scratched behind Bark's ear.

"Yeah, we noticed."

For the second time that night, Pete jumped in the air with a squeak.

Peals of laughter surrounded him, but he couldn't see where they were coming from.

Then, without warning, Scoot appeared out of thin air along with Max, Gracie Mae, Stacie, and two tall, athletic boys Pete had never seen before.

Pete just stood there staring, his hand hovering over now empty air.

"Been watching you the last half hour," a Hispanic boy said. He smiled, and his dark eyes crinkled and outlined a small scar on his lip. "You got over the gate pretty quick. Were you an athlete or something?"

Pete shook his head. "I don't know," he said slowly after the shock wore off enough for him to speak. "I don't remember."

"Oh, yeah, I know. No one really remembers, not yet. But sometimes, you just…know. You know?"

Pete did know, but the others laughed, and Gracie Mae smacked the boy's arm. "Nobody knows what you're talking about, idiot."

"I don't think I was an athlete," Pete said, "but I think I wanted to be." He shrugged, suddenly feeling stupid. "What are all of you doing here?"

The odd group exchanged looks. Stacie fixed Pete with a dazzling smile that made him feel dizzy. "Well, we're part of a group."

Scoot glared at him and cut in. "I sponsored you."

"After the werewolf incident, we would have all sponsored you." Stacie gave a somewhat rigid smile.

Pete was confused and was about to say so when Scoot cut across, walking in front of the group and said, "There are some requirements to even be recommended to the group. You have to be quick on your feet, physically and mentally—and you have to be a Sandman."

"A what?" Pete blinked.

"Oh," Max said, "that is just a nickname we give to someone who can't sleep."

"None of you guys sleep either? Ever?"

They all shook their heads. The brown-eyed, fair-skinned boy, who had not spoken until now, said, "Well, I slept once when I got hurt, but no, not normally." He wiped a little sweat off his large forehead and looked at Pete steadily with his sunken eyes.

"Why?" Pete was slightly peeved that he was just finding this out now. "Why do some of us not need it?"

"That, we aren't sure of," Max said. "It's a skill that can be learned, but no one knows why some can do it automatically and others can't. I suppose it is for the same reason that some people can sing and others can throw a football." He shrugged.

"So this is a club for people who can't sleep?" Pete asked.

"This is a club we can't tell you about until you are initiated," Scoot said dryly.

Pete thought about all the homework he wasn't getting done right now. "I don't know if I have time for—"

Scoot cut him off. "You will know if you have time for it when you find out what it is." Pete frowned, and she continued, "I've seen that look before."

Pete looked at her blankly. "What look?"

"The look you gave when you climbed that gate for the first time." She looked at him seriously. "You're here to learn, and this group can teach you things you won't learn at this school."

"I don't get it. What kind of things? What kind of group is this?"

She smiled wickedly. "Come on. We'll show you."

Pete hesitated for a minute, looked at his bag of homework he didn't want to do, and shrugged.

He struggled to keep up with them. The group was fast, even Max, who seemed so skinny and awkward and didn't look like he had an athletic bone in his body. They made it back to the school and over the gate in a few minutes. They paused to pick the lock to the gate to let Bark in, which annoyed Pete. Had they just done that first, they wouldn't have all needed to jump the fence.

They darted from shadow to shadow and crept along the edges towards the back of the school, pausing periodically to listen for noises, but they only heard the steady panting of Bark, who seemed quite content to trudge alongside them. When they reached the back of the school, they walked into the maze, which had always seemed a little creepy but seemed downright ominous in the middle of the night.

Scoot seemed to sense his uneasiness and walked up next to him. "Don't worry, these guys are cool." Then she glanced over at Stacie. "Well, most of them, anyway."

Pete raised an eyebrow and looked curiously between her and Stacie. Scoot responded to this gesture with a stony silence he now associated with danger, so he made a mental note to ask Charlie about the obvious grudge Scoot had for Stacie. When he was sure Scoot wasn't paying attention to him, he stole a glance at Stacie, watching how her hair shimmered in the moonlight as she walked. He swallowed and forced his eyes away from her.

They moved deeper into the maze. Pete tried to remember every twist and turn they made, but there were so many that it was impossible. He truly hoped they were not pranking him because he had no idea how to get out of here. He glanced at the hedges and wondered if he could climb straight through them, frowning doubtfully at the thorny roses plants that grew intertwined between them. A backup plan.

Finally, after about thirty minutes of twisting and turning, they came to a small clearing. Perhaps "clearing" wasn't the right word for it. The hedge walls spread wide into a circle, and the packed dirt lowered into what could only be described as a cave.

They must now be at the center.

He walked slowly into the dimly lit cave and looked around in awe. The ceiling was at least twenty-five feet above him, and the entire place was decorated like a gym of sorts. There were mats lining the floor, except for a running path around the wall. To the right was a boxing ring, and to the left against the far wall were benches and weights, and on that same side but closer to him were various targets kids were practicing on. Some were throwing various weapons at human-shaped targets, while others aimed at farther circular targets with guns or bows and arrows. Directly in front of Pete, about fifty feet away, was a hallway that led to other rooms.

When he looked closer at the walls, his eyes widened at the vast array of weapons hung up there—he hadn't known so many weapons existed. Maces, several types of javelins and axes, massive hammers, swords, knives, guns, throwing stars—and some weapons he couldn't even name.

Pete found himself sweating in spite of the cool air. He swallowed dryly. "Interesting place you've got here," he said to Scoot, who smiled. "I can see why you like it."

"Yeah, it's really awesome," Stacie cut in.

Pete turned to her, drawn by her beaming smile that made his insides turn to jelly, and flinched at the huge crowd suddenly gathered behind her. The kids who'd been hitting the targets stopped and faced him now. About forty pairs of eyes stared back at him. Where had all these people come from?

He shifted from one foot to the other. "Um, hi."

Scoot stepped forward and spread her arms wide. "Welcome to the Battinsworth Academy's Society of Assassins and Spies."

"We call our club BASA," said a kid Pete didn't know. He pronounced it bass-saw. "You don't pronounce the last *S*."

Pete frowned. "Okay."

The group looked at each other, a little confused. Stacie stepped forward and asked uncertainly, "Are you not interested in joining? Most people are pretty excited when they are invited."

"Oh, is that what this is? Recruitment? Not assassination?"

A couple of people snickered. Scoot came and slapped him on the back. "Nah, we want you to join. You need two sponsors, and Max and I will be yours."

"Out of curiosity, what if I say no?" Pete asked.

"You won't," Scoot said confidently.

"But what if I did? What's to stop me from telling everyone about your club?"

"Who said it was a secret?"

Pete twisted his mouth. "Spy implies secret."

"We have a contingency plan for recruits who…are not recruited." Scoot smiled an unpleasant smile, making Pete swallow hard. He started walking around looking at things, and the crowd of people dispersed to go back to what they were doing.

A group of pigtailed girls resumed throwing knives in the corner at a target twenty feet away. A group of very tall, thick boys started in on punching bags, and a pair of kids grabbed what Pete hoped were blunt swords and started sparring.

"So what do you guys do exactly? Assassinate people?" Pete asked doubtfully, as he toured the place. "I thought there wasn't a second death."

"There is." Scoot casually played with an orange pigtail. "It's just much harder to do."

That took Pete aback. He stopped walking and looked at her.

"But it's not just about killing people. There are other skills you learn that make it useful for all kinds of professions, not just spying and assassinating. That is just a catchy name some old guy made up." She rolled her eyes and smiled, looking around much like a connoisseur of art might in a museum.

"But who exactly do you spy on?"

"Well, for now, it's just kids," Scoot said, "but we are learning the skills—"

"But why?" Pete cut her off. "I don't get it. Accountants don't need to know how to throw knives"—he pointed at two of the boys who had stopped punching bags and were squared up to each other—"or punch people."

Her face cleared and she seemed to understand. "Sometimes, I forget you're new here," she said. "There's a large variety of jobs you can get here in AfterLife. On one end, you can get typical jobs. You have your accountants, like you said, as well as politicians, cooks, bakers, librarians…normal jobs. Then you've got your specialized, elite jobs like GHOST recon teams, reapers, or military and contract workers.

"But on the other end, you have the Community. It's an underbelly network of the black market. Sometimes there is crossover, especially with some of the contract work because most contractors won't ask too many questions, depending on the work they do. But clubs like this can help get you into some of the best black market schools available. We're lucky: BASA is famous for the quality of its graduates."

Pete thought about this for a moment. "So why work for this… community?" he asked flatly, though secretly he was starting to get excited.

Scoot shrugged. "Why not? You have your entire school life to decide who you want to be. You can decide if you want to be a polite, law-abiding citizen for the rest of your time in AfterLife, or you can give yourself some real options." She pointed to the smallest of the pigtailed girls who just landed her third bullseye.

Pete looked around the room. That same feeling of envy that had nearly overwhelmed him when he had first watched Scoot climb the wall tingled in his body, but this time, with it came a lingering doubt. He looked at the boys who were head-and-shoulders taller than him. Would he ever be that big? How quickly did someone grow when they were dead? Did they grow at all?

Scoot seemed to know what he was thinking.

"Listen, I will practice all my killing skills on you if you tell anyone this, but…" she looked around to see if anyone was listening, "I was a scrawny little no-one when I first came here. I didn't know how to do anything." Pete looked at her. "I saw what you did when the wolf attacked you. I was out that night. Trust me when I say you have the grit to be a part of this group. If you are willing to work for it, you can become something amazing." She looked down at Pete's clothes with a smirk. "We can also teach you how to keep your clothes on."

He could become something amazing. Hhe smoothed his tie. Was he finally getting the answer he had been searching for? Had he been going about it the wrong way this whole time? Getting memories was dangerous unless you did it the right way, but no book in the library was going to show him how it was done. He could feel that time was running out to help this girl he kept seeing. Could this group help him? The group was for assassins and spies. Well, he needed highly protected information—information only a spy could obtain.

Pete held her gaze until she looked away. Then he stood for a solid five minutes, watching all the people do everything he wished he could do. Deep down, he had known that he wanted to be in this group the moment he first walked into the room. Even more than solving this mystery in his memories, he wanted to be like these kids. He wanted to be able to do what they did.

His eyes wandered over to Stacie, who was pummeling a punching bag with her bare fists, the sweat on her cheeks making her sparkle in the gym's bright lights. It didn't hurt that joining BASA would mean possibly spending a lot more time with her.

So he turned to Scoot, a smile creeping onto his face. "Okay. Let's do it."

CHAPTER 10

THE OTHER SKILLS

PETE'S FIRST OFFICIAL BASA TRAINING session was nothing like he had expected. He couldn't say what exactly he had expected, but it certainly had not been what he experienced.

He arrived the next day, fifteen minutes early, in pajamas, while Max and Scoot were in black workout clothes.

"You'll just end up back in the PJs anyways," Scoot had said when Pete asked what he should wear. Now he was nervously smoothing his tie as he glanced around the BASA headquarters. There were not as many kids in yet, and the ones there were stretching and doing warm-up exercises. "Don't worry." Scoot looked at him fiddling with his tie. She slapped him hard in the back. "You'll be fine, come on."

They left Max to take a lap around the training room. Pete followed her further into the complex to the office of Coach Skinley, whom Scoot explained oversaw BASA here at the academy. "Here he is." They entered his small office. Coach looked up from an ancient computer he was tapping at and nodded for Pete to take a seat next to a small girl. "I'm gonna get warmed up," Scoot said to the coach and left.

The room was about ten-by-ten feet and felt even smaller with the amount of things piled into it. There were weapons thrown on the floor, training pads piled up, stacks of clipboards, and old gym clothes that gave off an unpleasant odor. The coach's desk was piled with papers and books and yet more weapons.

Pete sat down next to the girl, who smiled and said, "I'm Hanna."

"Pete. Nice to meet you."

She nodded, and Pete was pleased to see that she was nervous too. She had brown eyes that reminded him of the girl he kept seeing, but they were rounder than his ghost's. She had a small nose, just the slightest bit turned up, long front teeth, and long, straight hair pulled back into a ponytail.

"We are waiting on one more—ah." Coach looked at the door where a tall, muscular dark-skinned boy of about fifteen stood. "Here's Rex. Meet Peter and Hanna, the other new recruits. Come in. We have a Purgatory favorite, and by that, I mean boring paperwork." He chuckled at his own joke, his jaw moving under translucent skin. Pete's stomach churned a little when the coach blinked, and he could still see two eyeballs with dark irises underneath his lids. Pete forced a polite smile, and the coach, unfazed, handed over some documents.

Pete read and signed the papers, hoping against all hope that the non-disclosure torture clause was being exaggerated.

"Great, let's get started," Coach said when they returned the signed forms, and clapped his hands together. Pete noticed that Hanna looked a tad green and was playing with her long ponytail, nibbling on the end of it as she watched the tall coach give his instructions.

First, they did three laps around the outer running path. Pete was huffing before he even finished one, but Rex was faster with his long strides. As Pete was starting his second lap, Rex finished his third. Next, they did pushups and sit-ups and jumping jacks. Pete had a stitch in his side before fifteen minutes of his warm-up had finished.

They spent the next hour learning fighting techniques. In spite of how winded he was, he was having a lot of fun. He was thrilled the first time he was able to successfully tuck, roll, and pop back up. They all put on gloves and pounded on a dummy until Pete could no longer hold up his arms.

"Shooting lessons will start early next week," Coach said as they were taking their first break. He pushed the clipboard against his tight belly, rocking back and forth on his heels. "Other Skills—which have a capital letter—by the way, we will start today." He looked around the room for a second and then smiled. He blew two sharp bursts on his whistle and yelled, "Todd! Demonstration, please."

One of the boys who had greeted Pete yesterday looked up. He had been sparring hand to hand with another boy but he stopped, turned toward them, and then disappeared into thin air.

He reappeared a foot from where Pete stood. Pete really wished he had not screamed so loud. Hanna and Rex looked impressed.

Coach nodded and said, "Thank you, Mr. Camper. As you were."

Todd nodded, sweat dripping down his face, and disappeared again. Pete, Hanna, and Rex all turned to see Todd reappear twenty-five feet away and immediately resume sparring with his partner.

"Similar clubs in other schools such as ours," Coach Skinley explained, "teach the Other Skills as optional, elite abilities, but I am different. I say that our club is elite, and everyone in my club should be more than proficient in at least five of these Skills."

He looked at them coldly and then continued, "I believe everyone is innately capable of performing Other Skills and, therefore, you will begin training in them immediately. I do not accept excuses. I do not accept failure. If you want to give me either of those, you are welcome to leave." Then he smiled. "Just remember the exit clause in your contracts."

Pete looked into the translucent face of his coach and swallowed. He exchanged brief looks with the other recruits. Rex's eyes were brimming with excitement, but Hanna was a bit green again. Still, neither she nor Pete made a move for the exit.

Other Skills, it turned out, was a description that encompassed about a hundred different abilities and skills that were all supernatural or paranormal in nature.

"Since we are dead, these should all be natural to us. However," coach said, with exaggerated annoyance, "our government does not see it necessary to require it to be taught in schools. It is up to us to teach ourselves." He handed them sheets of paper with a long list of abilities. "If you intend to become a warlock or witch, you will likely be proficient in most of these. If not, the top twenty are ones I expect from my graduates."

Coach continued, "Your sponsors will take over from here. Typically, the second half of your training will be self-taught, in that the older kids teach the younger ones and self-organized training sessions are created. I am here for questions and tweaks to your techniques but much of the work done in the Community requires self-motivation, critical thinking, and discipline."

Max appeared suddenly at Pete's side and pointed at the list he held in his hand. "These are the most useful to spies."

Pete looked doubtfully at the list. "What is Shape Sliding?"

"It's a form of Shape Shifting. You change a feature or two—or force a feature not to change. Most kids do this automatically. Remember Brody's face? And Charlie and Scoot's clothes?"

Pete nodded, seeing how that could be useful. "But ice-making?"

Max laughed. "Well, some of them are more useful than others." He pointed to the bottom half of the list. "Most of these you will start to learn in earnest next year. It's really these top two that you should look at this semester."

"So just Sliding and Shadow Walking." He frowned, a little disappointed. The bottom of the list showed all kinds of awesome skills: Teleportation , Dream Walking, Haunting, Palmistry, Speed Healing, Future Prediction, and even Invisibility. If he was going to break into the DRD, these others would be very useful. "Next semester, you said?"

Max nodded. "Coach wasn't lying; he jumps right into it. You'll probably start learning all that in January."

Pete wondered if the brown-eyed girl could survive on her own until then. "I hope so," he said quietly to himself when Max walked away.

Over the next several weeks, Pete found himself struggling to keep up. The October exams seemed so far away, but his instructors kept piling on the projects and deadlines. In spite of Pete's lack of need for sleep, he was still struggling to keep up with all his homework, even with the extra eight hours a day and the weekends. Pete wondered how the other kids were managing to keep up, but he soon realized they, too, were in the study room burning the candles alongside him.

BASA training didn't slow down, either. The idea of a club for assassins and spies in a school for children had seemed absurd at first, and it was still surprising to see fifteen-year-olds teaching twelve-year-olds how to knife fight. But Pete quickly grew used to it and even loved it. Though Hanna ended up quitting on her second day, finding it all too strange, he never seriously considered leaving even when he wanted to throw up after a long run through the woods or after his trillionth failed attempt to Shadow Walk.

He could feel himself improving physically and mentally. He was sharper and paid better attention. Running, sit-ups, push-ups, and rope climbing were a common part of his almost nightly training. He also had to meditate for long periods, memorize stacks of cards and complicated codes, and pick out patterns in pictures flashed to him. On top of that, there was also hand-to-hand combat, knife fighting, knife-throwing, pick-pocketing, and even lockpicking. He learned to move stealthily in all kinds of situations.

After less than a week of training, Pete was given the assignment to move through a crowd of students leaving class, pick someone's pocket, exchange the item with another BASA member, who then had to replace the item in the same pocket without anyone noticing. No matter how many times he practiced in the BASA meetings, it was a challenge for him to do in real life.

On probably his fifth try, he dropped the pen he had been attempting to steal and when the girl looked at him, he floundered for a moment before bending down, grabbing it, and offering it to her.

"Hey, did you drop this?"

The girl smiled and thanked him, but his partner, a small boy named Dave, made fun of him for an hour after that.

However, after that embarrassing episode, things slowly began turning around. He learned to slide through crowds with a practiced ease. In class, he practiced his hand movements under his desk, subtly handing his eraser from one hand to the next, or in and out of his pocket without trying to move the fabric. He also carried around a lock and pick and would practice unlocking it while his instructors lectured. But he couldn't do it during finance, he learned, because his vampire instructor turned out to have excellent hearing and did not appreciate the sounds the pick made. When she moved at inhuman speed to put her face directly in front of his with a hiss, he quietly apologized and tucked the lock away in his pocket.

Pete had already started to see some progress with his clothes and managed to keep his uniform on for most of his first week of training. He was growing more and more pleased with the skills he was picking up, but there was a lot he was still struggling with.

One late September evening, he was jumping rope when Coach Skinley blew a whistle for the kids to stop their training and look over. He was holding out a clipboard.

"Results are in," he said in his grave voice. As he spoke, Pete could see the tendons and bones moving in his face under his translucent skin.

Coach hooked the clipboard onto the wall and walked away. There was a mad rush to the wall.

When Pete finally elbowed his way close enough to read, it felt like a kick to the stomach. Out of all the new recruits, Pete was in dead last. He stared dejectedly at his abysmal scores.

Fighting (hand-to-hand): 1 out of 5 Remedial

Fighting (sparring, weapons): 0 out of 5 Remedial

Aiming (throwing, weapons): 2 out of 5 Needs Improvement

Physical (climbing, acrobatics): 4 out of 5 Meets Expectations
Physical (endurance and speed): 3 out of 5 Acceptable
Aiming (shooting, weapons): N/A
Evasion tactics (stealth, lying, escape, etc.): 2 out of 5 Needs Improvement
Spy skills (pickpocket, lock picking, etc.): 2 out of 5 Needs Improvement
Other Skills: N/A
14 out of 35: Needs Improvement

Pete sighed and looked at the other kids' scores. No surprise: Scoot was near the top of the chart. She seemed to live for this sort of stuff. Then, with a jolt of realization, he saw the name right above her and suddenly understood the reason why Scoot didn't get along with Stacie.

"Don't worry," Max said to Pete. "Your scores in your first year aren't that important, just the final test. This is just to show where you are at and where you need to be."

Pete sighed. This was going to be a long journey.

It wasn't until the end of September that he really started seeing some change in his scores. He found he had a natural talent for shooting guns and, though he started off by shooting arrows directly into the ground and surrounding bushes and people, he finally hit one of his targets. Sure, it had been the leg of the target and not anywhere near the center, but it was miles better than when he had started.

To top it off, he had a minor victory in Shadow Walking. For weeks, he'd been wanting to slap his bespectacled teacher, Jack, for continually urging him to "become the shadows" over and over again during their meditations. It hadn't helped yet. Jack also made Pete do these long sessions of weird rocking motions and movements that just made him feel like an idiot.

But after being told off by Max for not trying, Pete decided to give the stupid rocking lessons a serious effort. They were in one of the smaller rooms in the back. Jack knelt down on the other side of the room and adjusted his glasses.

"You ready?"

Pete nodded. Without his typical scoffing attitude, he sat down and closed his eyes. It took some will on his part, but he blocked out all sound.

He was embarrassed at first, but he tried to let that go. He pretended he was in a room by himself and ignored the sounds of kids passing in the hallway. He tuned out Jack's annoying "become the shadows" chant and really thought about the shadows.

He thought of the mist that crept through parts of the school. He thought about the parts of the woods that were so dark and dense that the air seemed to thicken. The shadow blanketing those trees seemed to envelop him. This time, however, instead of the air becoming thicker, he became lighter. Suddenly, he couldn't feel his legs, and his hands, which were resting on them a moment ago, fell into nothingness. He jerked and fell forward on top of Jack. The spell was broken.

"Ow!" Jack said, part of Pete's pajamas going into his mouth. "Mef off." He shoved Pete away. "Watch where you are walking!" He straightened his glasses and finger combed his hair back into place.

"Sorry," Pete said, frazzled, "First time."

Jack huffed and sat back down to carry on with his boring annoying chant. Rex, who was nearby practicing too, looked impressed.

Pete, shaking slightly, looked around the otherwise empty room. He walked back to his original spot, startled that it had worked so easily once he put his mind to it. Annoyed that he had wasted so much time, he sat down on his haunches, instead of on his heels and tried again.

The shift in mindset did leaps and bounds for him; soon, he was improving across the board. It showed in his scores, which were brought out weekly and no longer included failing marks. Even his Other Skills went from N/A to Needs Improvement. His fighting abilities improved as well, though not by a significant amount until Coach changed around his fighting partners.

Pete was offended at first when coach stopped Todd, one of BASA's biggest fighters, from teaching Pete some moves and replaced him with Dave, one of the smallest. However, he quickly learned that Dave's small stature didn't hold him back.

Dave taught in a way that Pete could instantly relate to. He showed him how to neutralize large opponents and take advantage of his small size, something Pete had not thought would ever be an advantage. Things were finally looking up.

The one thing BASA did not teach was how to talk to girls. Stacie seemed to catch on early that Pete had a minor crush on her. She showed up at the most inopportune moments, and nearly every time, Pete would stumble, sputter, or drop something.

This was especially unfortunate, one late September night, when the final spar event of the night was announced.

"Stacie," Coach Skinley growled, "and Pete."

Pete did not register for a full ten seconds that his name had been called. The night always ended with a fight, and the coach was very good at choosing opponents that made for an exciting match.

"M-me?" Pete still didn't believe it, even as several other BASA members urged him to go into the boxing ring.

"We're waiting, Green." Coach fiddled with his whistle.

Still Pete hesitated, but when the coach didn't call someone else up, he made his way nervously into the ring.

"I'm…still new. I don't—I'm not that good at fighting."

"You're good at some stuff," Coach said, unhelpfully.

"What, math?" Pete grumbled, but Coach ignored him, blowing his whistle to start the match.

Pete's stomach clenched uncomfortably as he faced Stacie, who stood across from him. She looked so pretty with her hair braided behind her. He winced at the thought of hitting her, but knew what she did when she sensed weakness.

Pete's weeks of training kicked in, and he forced himself to slow his breathing. It was hard to look her in those startling blue eyes, so instead he focused on her right shoulder. He unclenched his jaw, loosened his fists, and relaxed his shoulders. He positioned his body into a façade of absolute calm, nonchalance that he didn't feel.

Unfortunately, she was doing the same thing, and he almost didn't see her attack. She leaped forward, kicking out with both feet in quick sharp succession. Pete rolled, just barely avoiding her. In a reactive movement, he popped up, preparing for another attack, but it came even quicker than he expected.

Her swing kick landed in his stomach, punching all the air out of his lungs. Even though she was lightning fast, he had been trained very well by his small instructor. He latched onto her foot and used her own momentum to pull her down as he went onto his back. He rolled, holding onto the foot, and she sprawled on top of him.

She twisted to land an elbow as she fell, but Pete parried, let go of her foot and rolled up to face her, his breath coming in rapid, painful gulps.

He didn't know why he did it, but he smiled at her. He tasted blood on his teeth. He knew he must be a sight and was rewarded by a squint of concern from Stacie. His smile widened a little when he realized that her smile was no longer paralyzing to him.

Letting his thoughts go and using the same method he used in his Shadow Walking meditation, he let all concerns about her go away. It suddenly didn't matter that she and Scoot were in competition for the spot as best in the class. It didn't matter that she had been an elite member for three years. It didn't matter that her eyes were like droplets from the bluest ocean.

She was merely his opponent.

Moving like he had no bones, he feinted right and then did a back kick with his right leg. She anticipated his move and jumped out of the way, but not quite in time.

He clipped her on the left side of her body, sending her spinning, and opened her up for his second kick, which landed squarely on her stomach.

It was her turn to go "oof!" She went sprawling backward and landed hard on her butt. The crowd went completely silent, watching a stunned-looking Stacie staring up at him.

Maybe he wasn't a rookie anymore, after all.

The crowd seemed to agree with his thoughts, judging by their impressed claps and loud comments. Unfortunately, it didn't last long.

In moments, Pete was on his back with a foot cartwheeling towards his face. He spun, managing to deflect most of the blow, but Stacie's toe still caught him.

"Mugh!" he said through a bloody nose. He spun again, missing a second stomp, and rolled unsteadily to his feet. He was met by a foot swinging towards his face. Again he managed to catch her foot on the way down. He was surprised and nearly dropped it. In his fumbling, she almost pulled it loose, but he managed to hold on. She stumbled, and he took advantage of her temporary imbalance, aiding in her fall with a spectacular leg sweep.

She screamed as she went down, not in a startled way but with utter frustration. She slapped her hand angrily on the mat when she landed. For the second time in the fight, the great Stacie was on her behind.

Pete squared himself but was thrown to the side. He looked over and was shocked to see that Coach had jumped onto the mat and pushed Pete out of the way. Coach now stood crouched in a defensive position looking at Stacie.

Pete couldn't understand what was happening until he saw the look on Stacie's face. With a yelp, he jumped backwards. Stacie, once so angelic and beautiful, now looked like…a monster. The pupils, irises, and whites of her eyes blended together into an inky black. Her face contorted with rage. Her mouth, now snarling, no longer looked like a human mouth. Teeth elongated out of a snout, and she snorted with an animal fury.

Pete, frozen with terror, barely registered that Scoot was laughing and going on about Stacie losing to a newbie.

Wide-eyed, Pete put his hand up in a placating manner and backed slowly out of the ring.

"Stalangela Carmila Jones. Calm down," Coach Skinley ordered.

"Find yourself," Pete's idiot annying meditation guide chanted.

Stacie growled and snorted, blowing puffs of smoke out of her nostril slits. When Jack approached the ring, Stacie hissed and spat at him, making him stumble and fall backward. There were several snickers, and Pete noticed that no one helped the tall boy up or helped him find his glasses.

The crowd slowly dispersed, leaving Coach to face the snarling Stacie by himself.

"What was that?" Pete asked, slightly panicked. He felt sweaty and flushed and very uneasy.

"Oh, she's part demon," Max said, conversationally.

Scoot, who looked more cheerful than Pete had ever seen her before, laughed and whooped. "Imagine that. The prissy little snot getting beat up by a newbie." She sighed happily. "Shame she's probably going to kill you tomorrow."

CHAPTER 11

DEATH WEEK...I MEAN, EXAM WEEK

BEFORE PETE KNEW IT, IT was fall. The air was crisp and chilly all the time now. The mornings brought several frosts that were so bad many small plants died, shriveling before his very eyes and vanishing into thin air.

With all the nonstop action of impending exams, tons of homework, spending time with his friends, and the demands of BASA, Pete was stunned when one late September morning something made him stop dead in his tracks.

Pete had finished an essay for a class and was heading to lunch when he was intercepted by Charlie and his on again, off again posse of girls. He had tears in his eyes, and several of the girls were crying. Pete looked awkwardly at the group.

"What's up?" Pete asked, surprised. For all the drama that Charlie was, he had never looked this upset before.

"You gotta come." Charlie sobbed. "Sam is leaving!"

"Sam?" Pete tried to remember who he knew named Sam. He followed Charlie. "And what do you mean, he's leaving? I thought you only leave when you graduate?"

One of the taller girls shook her head, swinging her long brunette ponytail and making Pete a little dizzy. What was her name? Had Charlie mentioned it? "Not if your parents come," she said, "and wanna take you someplace else."

"Oh." Pete was a little startled. He had really started to love it here. The thought of suddenly having to leave.... He frowned.

He furtively glanced at the girl. He had decided to swear off girls after what the BASA members called the Stacie incident, but he was starting to feel his resolve melting a little as he looked at the very pretty, hazel-eyed girl.

"I'm Pete, by the way," he said a little shyly.

"Alex," she said with a small smile. Pete felt all his insides become jello.

"Can't he stay? I mean…." He couldn't quite articulate what he wanted to say.

Alex fell in step beside him and said, "Most kids here are only here because their parents aren't. When their parents come, they can choose to leave their kid in school, but in Purgatory, people aren't usually great when they have all their memories."

Pete looked at her, a little confused.

She sighed and continued, "Okay. So, Purgatory has a unique kind of energy around it that makes it so things don't really change much. Well, that makes most people mental. Not everyone, of course. Some people love it. People who need to work through some stuff mentally come to stay here for a short bit as a sort of therapy session, right? But most people can't stand to live in Purgatory for longer than a couple of weeks if they have all their memories."

"But the teachers don't seem to be like that." he said.

"This school is the only exception to the rule that I know of. But the parents don't stay at the school, they stay in town, so they don't usually want to keep their kid here. Sometimes you'll find a parent who lets their kid stay and just picks them up after they graduate, but that's pretty rare. They usually miss their kid so much that they go straight to them and never want to part from them again."

"So where is Sam now?"

"Picking up his memories in the principal's office."

Pete froze in his step. "Wait." He turned to look at her. "They just have them in the headmistress's office?"

"Some." She raised her eyebrow a hair. "The rest he will have to get at the DRD."

She was distracted by the arrival of another girl with long, curly red hair and green eyes who joined in their trek towards the headmistress's office.

Pete followed them, his mind spinning with possibilities. Charlie was biting his lip nervously. They wound through the school in silence for a bit and joined a small group of people waiting outside of the office.

A door opened, and they could hear the secretary's voice from inside, "Here's his paperwork. You can take this to the portal station for a free transportation token."

A happy, crying couple walked out hugging a boy Pete recognized from his dorm room. The man's short and squat figure matched his son's, and the woman had Sam's fire-red curly hair and amber freckles.

The secretary stepped out. "Go to the AfterLife Affairs Global Relations building and ask for the Department of Registered Deaths. They can get Sam's filed memories and point you in the direction of the Port of Transit. They're in the same building here in Purgatory." She handed Sam's father some paperwork. "They have the rest of his memories there, and then you can get your passports printed and be on your way. Do you have a destination?"

"Well, Sam's aunt and uncle, Pat and Mark are here, you know," Sam's father said to his wife in a Minnesota accent. "So we'll probably meet up with them, and then we'll decide from there."

"What quadrant are they in?" The secretary pushed up her glasses.

Sam's father shrugged. "I have it in the papers somewhere. I'll check it later. Goodbye, and thank you for looking after our boy." He smiled down at Sam, who smiled awkwardly back. He looked a little confused. Had Sam gotten enough memories to recognize his own parents yet? That would be odd if he felt like he was leaving with complete strangers.

Sam took a minute to hug his friends and gather his things and headed off. He looked like he was trying not to cry as he said his goodbyes. Charlie, however, didn't hold back the sobs as he hugged him.

Pete watched the scene with fascinated horror. He would hate to have to leave so suddenly.

"I mean," Pete said later to Alex as they walked back—the craziness of the day had made him feel brave enough to talk to her without blubbering—"Wouldn't you hate that? We have friends here. I like this school. It would suck to leave."

"I never have to worry about that." She gave a self-conscious smile.

"What do you mean?"

"I'm one of the few exceptions. I was born in AfterLife, and my parents sent me here to go to this boarding school. It's a very prestigious school, you know."

Pete looked over, surprised. "So you've never been alive before?"

She smiled, looking a little embarrassed, and shook her head no. "It's more common where I'm from. Honestly, I don't see the point. The reincarnation process kinda seems awful. And there is a chance you could get stuck with an idiot for a parent—or worse." She leaned in and whispered conspiratorially. "I hear some, like, beat their kids." She shook her head again. "I know AfterLife is getting a bit crowded, but no way. They couldn't pay me to send me there."

He opened her mouth to ask her where she was from, but Charlie, needing comfort after losing a friend, came over and cried next to them. And the moment was lost.

The excitement of Sam leaving spread throughout the school, and it was all anyone could talk about for the next couple of days. Sam chose a convenient time to leave, Pete thought idly, as he studied for his Financial Systems exam. He was finding it tougher and tougher to study, even with the October exams starting in two days. Two times that week he'd seen the brown-eyed girl in the hall for a split second before she disappeared again. His unease was growing. Somehow, he didn't think this little girl could wait until next year for him to learn what he needed to know.

He walked into BASA that night thinking about her and was bowled over by another bout of bad news.

Coach made an annoucement to the entire club after practice. ""BASA exams are very important. So important, in fact, that they will be held after your school exams so you won't be tempted to study, instead of practice for my test. Some of the older kids know this, but we have enough new faces this year to warrant a recap." He scanned the room slowly. "All first and second year students will be given two missions. Your overall performance in both will be judged as though I were a Community member and this were a real mission. Your performance on said missions will determine whether you move forward to the next semester or not."

Pete swallowed hard. He had to move onto next year. He needed those next skills on the list to break into the DRD, figure out what had happened to him, and hopefully save the little girl.

He bit his lip and focused all his attention on Coach Skinley.

"One mission will be self-assigned. It needs to be relevant, purposeful, and challenging. If you are going to assign a mission to yourself to steal all the pens in the school secretary's office, you are going to have to defend why I should care about that in your mission report you turn in after." He stared stonily down at them all kneeling or sitting on the sparring mat in front of him.

"The second mission will be given to you Halloween night and will be executed that same night." There were several gasps and whispers at this announcement. "Yes, the day of," he repeated. "There are many assignments taken and given the day of in the Community and it is important for my recruits to be ready for them." He clasped his hands behind his back. "Everyone's mission will be different, and you cannot work together. However, there is an exception for BASA's first-years." He nodded to Rex and Pete, the only first-years left. "They are allowed help from their sponsors and unknowing civilians only. And I should say, it's tradition to keep your missions a secret for a very good reason. I will cut at least three of you, so you are all each other's competition."

Pete scanned the room nervously and saw several other worried faces as well.

Coach reviewed more of the rules and expectations and spoke briefly about the written portion of the exam. Pete tried to focus, but his mind kept wandering. He didn't know which he was more nervous about: the self-created mission, or the mission he wouldn't know anything about until the day of. What sort of mission could he create that would be relevant or important to Coach? And how was he supposed to prepare for something he didn't know anything about? Too much was riding on this.

Max told him, unhelpfully, that on average, seven people were cut from BASA every semester.

"How are we supposed to prepare for something when we have no clue what it will involve?" Pete asked as they exited the maze.

"The book does a good job of outlining that. That's what I used for last semester's test, and it served me well."

"Book?" Pete asked blankly.

"The book you got on your first night here. It's, like, the best preparation for a mission. Pete…!" Max was getting concerned. "Did you not even look at it?"

He had not. When he had first joined, Coach Skinley had given him a book, but he had put it under his bed and immediately forgotten about it. He vaguely remembered the title was *Tactical Training Guide* or something.

"I…I forgot," said Pete.

Max looked at him seriously. "Dude. I'm telling you, that book was my saving grace. I was doing the worst on all my scores up until the exam, worse than you, even, and I passed my missions and upped my scores within a few weeks of reading this book. Trust me, he cut thirteen people that semester, but I wasn't one of them because I was prepared and they were not. Go get that book."

Pete was panicking slightly by the time he found *The Art of the Spy: A Tactical Guide for the New Recruit,* written by Magdalena de la Grasso. He looked at the plain cover and sighed when he thought about everything he needed to do that month. He plopped the book down along with the large stack of others he had to read.

After the announcement of the BASA exam, Coach announced that the meetings would change slightly. "Instruction time is all but over for this semester. If you need help with something, you can ask, but now we will just have open practice hours. This will give you time to prepare for your missions."

In spite of this, Pete found himself spending much of his extra time in the next several days reading and preparing for his other school exams. When he found a break, he dove into the BASA book. De la Grasso turned out to be one of the author's many aliases. Pete looked her up in the library when he went to turn in a book. He learned that she was one of AfterLife's most notorious spies and was still active in the Community. Although the outside of her book was dull and unappealing, the inside was full of fascinating information—much like a real spy, Pete supposed.

The book was divided into practical sections. Mission prep, avoiding detection, poisons, fighting, weapons, and careers.

"What are the three properties of midnight flower?" Pete read out loud one night, fighting back a yawn. He glanced at his watch and balked at how late it was.

Max looked up and squinted with concentration, biting the end of his pen. They were the only ones in the study hall. After a few moments, Max said, "The midnight flower has combustible properties. It can also affect depth perception, but most people use it for its effect on the drinker's dreams. The drink makes it easier for others to enter their dreams."

Pete was impressed by Max's memory.

He flipped through a few other pages and read, "The seven secrets to avoiding detection. How to change your face. How to make a smoke bomb and other diversionary tactics. This is crazy."

De la Grasso explained things in ways that his teenage instructors and even his battle-tested coach had not been able to. He could have kicked himself for not opening this book until now. Surely, something in here would help him with his upcoming missions and maybe even with recovering his memories.

But before he could truly focus his attention on that, he had to get through the exams in all his other classes. He didn't think he'd ever go through a week so difficult again in his AfterLife. Even studying as much as he did, keeping up with all of his homework and not sleeping one wink, he came out of every test dazed and delirious, wondering if he would pass a single one.

Even his wood shop midterm didn't go as well as he'd hoped. His jewelry box turned out looking more like a coffin, with a lid that wouldn't open. Mr. Johnson tried his best not to laugh when he examined the box.

"How do you think it turned out?" Mr. Johnson asked in a neutral tone, a twinkle shinning in his eye.

In spite of himself, Pete gave an embarrassed smile. "Could use a little work." It was hard not to like Mr. Johnson. He was still his favorite teacher, even after he'd dragged Pete across the courtyard in wolf form.

But as the professor moved on to examine the other student's work, Pete's smile fell away. Another full moon was coming. He was relieved he'd decided not to officially join the Werewolf Club, but even so, the full moon remained a source of stress. He found himself more and more nervous thinking of a changed Mr. Johnson—and then, of course, there was also the strange jinx on the school that would likely make everything in his life go haywire.

Because the full moon occurred during the middle of exam week, the exams were paused and so were classes. Pete tried, but studying was all but impossible. Would either of the missions for BASA fall on a full moon? What that would mean for everyone participating?

He paused his studying just as the sprinklers came on overhead. As he packed up to meet his friends outside, a thought came to him. Could he somehow incorporate the full moon in one of his missions? He made a mental note to find out more information. Spurred on by his first real idea, he continued studying with a lighter heart.

His good mood only lasted a short while.

"I can't believe they make us start doing the math for Portal Configurations this early," Pete complained to Scoot that afternoon. They were lounging in a clearing in the maze on a couple small benches, which some kids had nicknamed the Kissing Place.

He had arrived a little after her and Charlie. Charlie was lying lazily on the grass, smiling up at the sky and watching a deformed butterfly flutter awkwardly across his field of vision.

"Well, lucky for us, they do," Scoot said, surprising him.

Pete, who had just dumped his bag on the grass next to Charlie, paused in the act of plopping down and stared at her with a raised eyebrow.

She shrugged. "Just in case we need a break into a portal and use it. Now, I know how to configure one."

Pete frowned, sincerely hoping this was only theoretical and that BASA did not have future plans to break into portals for assignments.

"What would you need to break into a portal for?" Charlie asked, mid-yawn.

"Oh, I dunno," Scoot said airily. "If I ever ditch this school later this semester and break out of Purgatory, I'll need to hack the system."

"Sounds like a lot of trouble. I say finish school then just get out like a normal citizen."

She grimaced and put her head back into her book. Pete was curious about what Scoot was reading, but the dizzying relief that he would be finishing his last exam tomorrow made it impossible for him to care enough to ask. Pete studied Charlie and wondered how Max and Scoot had managed to hide the fact that they were in BASA this whole time. But the kid seemed to have no idea.

Charlie, who had finished his last exam the day before, lounged for at least a couple of hours before heading off to dinner. "It's getting chilly."

"No, it's not," Scoot shot back. "You just want to show off your stupid jacket."

"Can't hear you," Charlie sang several yards away in the direction of the dorms.

Scoot snorted, twirling one of her orange pigtails. "He loves the wintertime. It's the only time we can wear stuff besides our uniform to school. Well, except situations like this." She touched the arm of his pajamas.

"Oh, dang it." Pete closed his eyes and concentrated on the school uniform. His pajamas melted into trousers and a tunic, and his expensive white tie morphed into the cheaper polyester blend of the school uniform.

He sighed, and Scoot, seeming to misread his general stress for something more specific, said, "Don't worry. It's been a long time since anyone has died during the missions."

With the tests finally over and the general buzz of excitement of Halloween in the air, Pete found it harder to focus on his missions. During exam week, there'd been a manic panic that was infectious, but now he was just ready to be done. And it seemed everyone else was too. He noticed a definite lack of attendance in the BASA gym now that the meetings were not enforced and had changed to an open gym setup.

Fortunately, there were two things that changed his attitude: choosing a mission and the BASA career fair.

The Saturday after exams, the gym was closed to workouts for the night. Tons of booths were set up, manned by all types of men, women, and creatures. It turned out that the Community was a bit more vast and complicated than Pete had initially understood. It wasn't just comprised of the underbelly of society, and it certainly wasn't just pure evil. Sure, evil was a major demand for work requested within the Community and nearly every job requested was illegal, but not everyone within the Community was evil or even considered a bad person.

This did add some complications. At one point, a light witch and dark witch got into an argument that turned into sparks flying before a frazzled-looking attendant with a clipboard ran at them and sent workers to separate their booths.

Pete learned that not only were there both light and dark witches (and warlocks), but there were also common criminals—who just didn't want to file their taxes properly or something—who would do work for you under the table. There were mob guys who would provide muscle and private investigators who wouldn't ask too many questions and would skirt the law to get you answers. And, of course, there were assassins you could hire to torture victims for you before making them disappear.

Pete was surprised by the demand for assassins. They were the highest paid and in the highest demand, but were in the shortest supply, likely because it was the hardest job.

It was quite an accomplishment to kill someone who was already dead.

Pete walked through the booths with fascination. There were skeletons at least ten feet tall behind some of the tables. He talked for twenty minutes with an Ice Hunter from New Wales District 10 who was contracted to catch dragons and sea lizards in the Arctic Tundra and oceans of the area.

Pete didn't get a chance to talk to the rep, but there was a trainer from an elite branch of a military group called Government Haunt and Operations Specialists though the group was more commonly known by their acronym, GHOST. This team was responsible for training new recruits stationed in Portal Seven, one of the most haunted and prestigious posts a recruit could go to.

He listened as the man lectured the crowd on the importance of the tests. "Groups like this are not just for criminals," said the clean-cut, no-nonsense trainer. "Recruiters look at tests scores to determine who we even allow to apply. Remember, GHOST Academy and Training is by invite only. Rarely do we look at a recruit who is not a part of groups such as these, and never do we invite a recruit who has not performed well on a mission or test."

"No pressure, huh?" Gracie Mae said to Stacie with a smirk, but Stacie seemed interested in what the man had to say. After several minutes, however, they made their way to a different booth to talk to a creature with scales and gills who had to periodically stick her head into a large bowl of water to breathe.

About an hour into the fair, a guest speaker spoke for about five minutes on the joys of becoming a reaper and then another fifteen on politics until someone politely ushered him away from the microphone.

After that, Pete met about a half dozen vampires and a translucent woman with white pupils. He chose not to speak to the dark black mass that few people would walk near.

He talked for twenty minutes with a stocky, seven-foot-tall boar named Boagon Felts with thick gray-white tusks and spider-thin, greasy black hair, not because he was particularly interested in black market goat hunting, but because his stories were completely captivating.

There was a whole world of opportunities at his fingertips. He collected pamphlets from all the guest speakers and stopped at several booths, talking to their occupants about career choices. By the end of the career fair, Pete's head was spinning with possibilities. It had sparked something that no other thing had. It had made him think about his future outside of the school, even beyond his mission to help his mysterious ghost.

A pang of guilt shot through him at the thought of how much time he had wasted. He had not seriously put any effort into learning what it took to get his memories back, and it had been over a month since he started. But keeping at this would help him, he just knew it. Even more than that, he wanted to stay in BASA because *he* wanted it. He loved the person he was becoming. He was smarter, stronger, more alert, and more confident than he had been a month ago, and he now saw what his future could be like. Perhaps, he could be a private detective, or a dragon hunter, or a member of the GHOST RECON team.

Unfortunately, he was informed by no less than eighteen people that his performance in his BASA exams would affect which Community-approved schools he could go to, which types of jobs he could get afterward, and his ILA (Industry Level Alignment), which in turn would affect how much pay he could get for said jobs.

He had a lot riding on his missions. It was time to get to work.

CHAPTER 12

THE HUNTER AND THE WITCH

"HOW CAN I GET MORE information for my mission?" Pete asked Max the next day. "I can't find anything useful in the library."

He'd learned from his BASA book that he should be studying the written documents of other spies to learn their techniques to help him reach their level. This had given him the idea that finding such documents could help him not only figure out what to do for his mission, but also with his quest to recover his memories. Of course, he'd long since reached the limits of the school library's abysmal collection.

"Which library?" Max fingered a book he had been reading. "Are you talking about the main one?" He slipped a piece of paper in the book and set it to the side. "Or did you check BASA's?"

BASA's library turned about to be even more pathetic than the school's main library—just the stacks of books in Coach's office. Pete had to shove through piles of dirty clothes and weapons to sift through them all, but it was worth the effort. These books had boring covers with boring names, written in dry to-the-point language, but they were jam-packed with gold.

As Pete walked back to his dorm, he glanced over at the gate where he had been attacked by Mr. Johnson. He held four promising books under his arm. As he studied the gate, the beginnings of a plan started to form. But first, he needed to gather more intelligence.

"Hey, so what is the deal with this witch's curse?" Pete asked Charlie, setting one of the books down on his bed a few hours later.

"Hmm?" Charlie was using a hand mirror to primp his eyebrows. "Which one?"

"Hang on. There's more than one witch's curse on the school?" Pete was stunned.

Charlie paused and glanced over. "Oh. Sorry, I wasn't paying attention. I think so, actually, but are you talking about the monthly one?"

Pete stared for a second, then nodded slowly. "But what other ones are you talking about?"

Charlie set the mirror down. "Well, there's a rumor that every seven hundred years or so, a witch comes and steals people. In fact, there were a couple of people that went missing in town a few months ago. It was a huge deal and actually started a bit of a panic." He turned toward Pete and grinned. "But I find it a bit suspicious that the two who disappeared were spotted on many occasions flirting." His eyes were alight with a brightness that only great gossip could produce.

"I can't believe their spouses decided to go with the maybe-they-were-eaten-by-an-invisible-witch-monster story." He sniggered. "Monster...." He scoffed. "Yeah, maybe in his pants." He laughed at his own joke.

Pete chuckled too. "Ok, so what about this monthly thing? Is it really a curse?"

Charlie nodded and went back to plucking his eyebrows. "Yah, supposedly she was a student here, and she was kicked out for something. I think it was some forbidden-love thing. I dunno, the rules were different back then. Turns out she was a very powerful witch. You know, like a natural-born one who didn't need a whole lot of training to use a lot of her powers." He shrugged. "Not many people really remember. It was like fifty or sixty years ago."

"What?" Pete was aghast. "And no one's been able to remove the curse in all that time?"

Charlie shrugged. "Sally, you know, the secretary? She said that they hired a few Curse Removers, but none were able to do the job. According to them, they needed the original witch to undo it. It was too strong or something like that." He stopped his plucking again. "Can you believe they still charged the school even though they couldn't do anything?" He shook his head and put away his primping tools. "You ready?" He grabbed his bag and stood.

Charlie had given Pete something to think about as he headed to class. Later that afternoon, he visited the library to do a little bit of research. Finding information on the witch turned out to be surprisingly easy. Purgatory was a town that liked to change as little as possible, and when a newcomer, as the newspaper defined most of the residents of the school, came and threw their quiet town into disarray, it became big news.

Pete rolled through the newspapers in the library's microfilm. From what he gathered, a girl named Alexandria DeKempt cursed the entire town. It took two months for the town's natural magic to wear down and counteract the witch's magic, which seemed unprecedented. He read one of the articles:

> Witch expert Hans Endelfaan commented after last Tuesday's assessment of the town's curse, "Our town has a unique magic of its own, and no young Wielder, even one as powerful as Miss DeKempt, can affect it for very long."
>
> When asked why the school was continuing to experience effects, Endelfaan replied, "The school is an unfortunate exception to our town's quiet norm. Special regulations were made to allow the school to stay in our district to protect the influx of youth to our Port Station. The school has a unique magical signature of its own, making it especially susceptible to Miss DeKempt's curse."
>
> Several Curse Breakers, including the government's own Curse Investigatory Department head and chairman Kenneth Brown, were called to the school to reverse the effects with no success.

Another article made him gasp out loud.

> Local townsmen will gather today, outraged, to protest the opening of the small Potions and Hexes shop of Sorceress Alexandra DeKempt. Townsmen were reminded of the incident five years earlier when DeKempt was involved in a town-wide hex that, still to this day, affects Battinsworth Academy of Unliving Boys and Girls.
>
> Local politician and father of three, Mayor Horrison commented, "When I learned that Miss DeKempt started a shop in our quiet town, I knew that something needed to be done. I urge the townsmen to stand together against this outrage."
>
> The protest is scheduled to begin early this morning and end at 4 p.m, with a break for lunch. Mayor Horrison invites all townsmen to sign up for a protest shift on the bulletin on his door.

DeKempt graduated, with honors, in June from the Kensington University of Witches and Warlocks, an elite Hex and Potions school in Portal 732. DeKempt herself was not available for comment.

Why in AfterLife the witch would choose to set up shop here was beyond him. Nevertheless excited, Pete looked up the address of the shop and was thrilled to find that it was still up and running. He continued to read some general background information on witches and searched the stash of books from the BASA library as well.

Pete knew that breaking the curse wouldn't be as simple as finding the witch and asking her nicely to stop cursing the school, but talking to her had to be the first step. He knew she would want something in return. But what? He had no idea, but he knew if it was possible, he needed to find a way to make it happen. Mind spinning, Pete began making a plan.

Pete's plan started off beautifully. This, oddly enough, was thanks to Charlie. Pete had known since he met him that his friend was a charming person, but never fully realized just how good he was at getting what he wanted. He was just so clever and smooth, and now that Pete noticed and saw the results of it, he was determined to add that skill to his own list of talents.

This was rather simple, actually, according to Charlie. It merely involved laughing at her jokes, asking her questions about her favorite soap opera, and "flashing your beautiful blue eyes," Charlie said, making Pete blush.

Before he knew it, he had the secretary, Sally Delerie, laughing and telling stories about her sneaking into movie sets to get autographs. A half hour later, he was walking back from the office with a permission slip to visit the town for a "research project," an extra slip for Charlie to "guide" him, and a voucher for a free taxi ride there and back.

The only minor hiccup he had on the way was running headlong into Shelly Grant.

"Watch it." She shoved him to the ground. Then she smiled. "You were trying to leave. That's against the rules." She looked regretful, but Pete knew it was fake. "As an official hall monitor, I'll have to report you."

"Back off, troll." Charlie waved the permission slip in front of her face. "Why don't you go wrestle one of your friends?" He sidestepped her, and they walked away to hail their cab, laughing at the stunned look on her face.

Now it was a little before sunset, and Pete was the one stunned. He stood in front of the witch's shop, shocked that his plan had worked so well.

He watched the back of a woman with an apron tied around her waist talking to a middle-aged woman with a crying child through the window of the shop. Charlie was out shopping and the taxi voucher expired in a couple of hours. Pete didn't know how long this would take, so when the woman and her child left, he turned the knob of the shop door and pushed his way in as a soft ding sounded.

The woman in the apron turned around, and Pete couldn't help but let out a gasp. He wasn't sure what he had been expecting. He supposed a wizened old lady dressed in black rags with a wicked grin. The grin was the only thing that would have been accurate.

Before him stood a stunningly beautiful woman with dark olive skin, hazel eyes, and pouty pink lips, currently smirking in a half-smile. She wore a long black evening gown with a small train trailing behind her. Her apron held several wands and a few different bottles.

"Your outfit is…fabulous," he said quickly, thinking of what Charlie would say.

She looked taken aback and glanced down at her clothes. Then, smiling wider, she removed her apron and twirled a little as if to show him from all angles. Her fitted black dress had an elaborate pattern of red triangles on each side. It made her look a little too much like a black widow spider for Pete's liking.

"The design…" Pete struggled to think of something. "I've never seen it before." Then after a short pause, he added, "Love it."

She beamed and stepped backwards. "Come in," she said with a hint of an accent. Was it Romanian?

He stepped into the small shop. Man, Charlie was a genius.

He perused the store and was surprised by what he saw. The space was… pleasant. There was no other description for it. It smelled like gingerbread and spices. Soft music tinkled in the background, and the waning light trickling through the window reflected off hundreds of different potion bottles.

"Is DeKempt a family name?" Pete tried for the flattering kind curiosity his friend was so good at. "I've often heard that sorceresses of your status are given an opportunity to change their names."

She quirked in eyebrow in surprise. "Why, yes, they are usually. I was asked, but I decided to keep my original name because I thought it suited me.

I thought at first about naming myself 'Lilith,' but then, I thought, no. Too common." She made a face. "Tea?"

"Please." Pete smiled. He strolled around looking at the bottles while she fussed with a pot on a small stove in the back.

"You know," she said conversationally as she poured water into the kettle, "it's fortunate I decided to go with a different name than 'Lilith.' I heard that the demoness gets offended if witches take her name. Something about brand saturation or something. Anyway, she started cursing them and their businesses. A friend of mine had to change her name and all but start over with the marketing strategy for her business." She tsked and shrugged.

"Oh…that's unfortunate." Pete didn't know what else to say.

The witch offered him a seat at a small table with cushy, high-backed chairs. She scooped up tarot cards and set down two cups, saucers, milk, and sugar, and poured the hot water. Pete picked from a handful of tea options and ten minutes later they were sipping contentedly.

"I know that you did not come all the way from that little school to chat about names and dresses, little boy. What is it that you want?"

Pete brushed away the surge of annoyance of being called a little boy and smiled his most charming smile. He pretended that he was addressing one of his professors or the headmistress.

"Well, besides finding an opportunity to spend time with a beautiful woman, yes, I did want to talk to you about something."

The witch Alexandria smirked. "My, you have quite the silver tongue." She sipped her tea and asked playfully, "What is it that you want?"

"You." When her smile went flat, he realized how that had sounded and amended quickly. "I-I mean, I want to know your story. I'm from the school and—"

"And you want to know about the curse."

Hating how red he knew he must be, he nodded.

"Why do you think I put the curse on this town?"

Pete looked at the witch steadily, hoping his nerves would not show. "Because of Dadson."

The witch looked taken aback. Whatever she had expected him to say, it had not been that. Pete didn't blame her; the name had been rather difficult to find. In fact, he had not been able to find any information on her supposed forbidden lover in the papers or from the secretary. What he had done was compile a list of all the kids who had left the school about the same time that Alexandria had and accounted for them all. The only two that he could not find information on were the witch sitting before him and a mysterious Dadson.

She looked at him for a long time, and he started to get nervous. Had he overstepped?

For a split-second, her controlled demeanor slipped, her eyes glazed over, and she had a faraway, haunted look.

"Dadson," she said shortly, and Pete realized with dismay that she was angry. "Why do you want to know about him?" She sounded bitter.

"Why does anyone want to know the truth?" She gave him a level look. "All right," he said quickly. "I want to get the curse lifted. I had something special planned for the Hunter's Moon, and it got messed up." This was a lie, but he figured she wouldn't inquire too much into it. "I rescheduled it for November's full moon, and I need things to go smoothly."

He shrugged. "But…I do also want to know the truth. What happened?"

She looked at him suspiciously, and then, fingers drumming the table, she nodded. Something told Pete that she had wanted to tell the story for a while.

Her entire demeanor changed. Her shoulders lowered a little, and she looked out the front window of her shop as if checking to see if anyone was watching them. Then she began to speak:

"I was at that school for three years when I met him. He was a weird kid, Dadson, a little younger than me. He had been there for a while, but because I was in a different grade than him, I hadn't seen him. I met him during a miss— uh, during a project for school."

Pete held his face still. Was she about to say mission? So she was a BASA member. Interesting.

"I didn't think anything of it. Then, I started seeing him around more and more. I would randomly run into him. He was a nice kid, I guess. I didn't really pay too much attention to him. I was busy. Witching Universities and specialized schools for my talents were already starting to headhunt me." She shrugged. "I was good, really good."

"I was ahead of the curve on everything, including regular school subjects, which I was told was uncommon. Witches and warlocks tend to be average or even below average in school because most of their energy or concentration goes to magic-wielding." She wiggled her fingers casually, and white cracking sparks danced around them.

"But even though I was doing well in school, I wasn't…happy. I was bored and ready to move on right then, but every school has this stupid age restriction. I was sixteen at the time, and I needed to be eighteen to apply."

She sniffed angrily. "I could've out-witched anyone there, including the head hunters who came to see how good I was." She threw up her hand in annoyance. "Or at least, that's what I thought." She shook her head and smiled a bitter little smile.

Alexandria stopped talking, looking suddenly embarrassed. She shot Pete a sideways glance. Noticing her hesitation, he made his face carefully neutral, showing only polite curiosity.

After a moment, she continued, "In school...let's just say, I had a hard time."

She looked at Pete quickly to see if he was going to make fun of her, but Pete remained completely still, the polite smile frozen on his face.

"I had a crush on this guy, Brandon Kotowski. I looked him up by the way. He's a cop now." She smiled. "He's fat and bald and makes no money." She giggled. "But back then, he was a dream, and I was in love. The thing is, back then, I wasn't nearly as pretty as I am now, and I was a bit nerdy, always studying and working on this spell or that project. Obviously, it was worth it, but at the time, it was just plain uncool.

"Then my best friend, who knew I was madly in love with him too, got a prom date with Brandon." She balled her fists. "That she-devil...literally. Now, I see that she had no choice. It's in the nature of a devil to do something like that. But back then, I was devastated and furious.

"I cried all night. I didn't go to the prom—no one asked me." She looked down at her hands folded on her lap. There was a look of vulnerability in her eyes that Pete had never anticipated he would see on this woman.

"His loss," Pete said.

She looked up at him, her hazel eyes meeting his. A bit of the confidence and smugness that he had first seen washed some of the shadows of her sixteen-year-old self away.

"Indeed." A dangerous glint lit her eyes. She scratched lazily at a black cat that suddenly jumped up on the table, purring. She stopped and grabbed the mug of tea with both hands and sipped it slowly. When she finally put the mug back, she said, "Prom sucked, but the situation left me without a best friend. All I did was study. But I was good, and I learned so quickly that the school books ran out of things to teach me.

"So I found myself looking outside of the school for things to learn. I wanted to do something impressive so the universities would have to let me in early. And at the same time, all I could think about was my troubles at school. I didn't have any friends, and the boy I really liked wasn't into me. I was lonely." She gave an embarrassed shrug. "The solution to my problem seemed simple at the time."

Pete looked curiously at her.

"I made a love spell." She looked up at Pete. "How much do you know about spells?"

Pete was startled at being asked a question, and he shook his head. "Honestly, not much. Nothing, actually."

Alexandria shrugged as if this were of no consequence. "Well, some spells are simple and easy. So easy that sometimes an average human with even a slight sensitivity to magic can cast a spell without even knowing it. They chalk it up to coincidence or good luck or an answered prayer." She sipped her drink. "But other spells are extremely complicated. Anything to do with love falls into that category. I didn't think it would be, but the more I researched, the more I saw how tough it was going to be. But honestly, I wasn't disappointed." Her eyes lit up, and she stared past her front window, though Pete knew she wasn't really seeing it.

"I finally had something that was actually challenging and at the same time would solve all my problems. What was even more exciting was the fact that it was completely illegal." She grinned.

"Why is it illegal? And how would that help you get into schools if you did something against the law?"

"Oh, that was a plus with the type of schools I was applying to—and, well, it's illegal for a good reason. It tampers with free will. I was trying to force Brandon to love me."

"I see," Pete said politely. What did this have to do with Dadson? He waited patiently.

"Clever little Dadson." she said, as though she could read his mind. "On the night I was going to perform it, that little weasel switched some things around." She paused and bit her lip. "And I fell in love with him instead."

"Really?" Pete blurted. The witch looked at him steadily. "I mean, I'm sorry, I was just surprised. How did a kid learn how to do that?"

The witch was quiet for a long time, and Pete thought she wasn't going to say anything. When he was about to apologize again for his outburst, she replied, "Turns out he was much cleverer than he led people to believe. A few teachers had noticed, sure. One in particular was the headmistress. She teaches...." She paused and looked up from her mug at Pete. "Well, she did teach advanced witchcraft, but I'm not sure if she still does."

Pete kept his astonishment to himself this time and nodded for her to continue.

"It was a private class, only a few people in it, and she didn't talk about other students. You never really knew who else had the class unless you were in it or knew someone else taking it. Since I didn't have any friends besides Elly, I had no idea that Dadson was one of her best students. Dadson was brilliant, but he pretended to be average so he was underestimated and ignored. Then, he would cut you down. I thought I could out-witch anyone, but I learned a hard lesson that day."

She leaned back in her chair with her mug and smiled, lost in memory again. "It was a wonderful feeling at first. A new lightness. Everything was beautiful because I was in love. We were happy together. Blissful, really, but like most dark curses, it had a bad side. He got distant, or perhaps I just thought he did. Then, it changed from happiness to obsession.

"I found out later," she continued, "that a weaker mind might have lasted longer in that euphoric state. If the person already liked or was at least friendly to the person, then it made the love a little more genuine. But with Dadson, I barely even knew him. I didn't feel anything toward him. So the curse twisted and morphed inside me, turning into something evil and vicious."

Alexandria laughed at that, sending a trickle of fear down Pete's spine. "He underestimated me as well." Her eyes sparkled. "He thought he was brilliant—and he was, don't get me wrong. But he didn't get people, really. He didn't see me as a threat. He knew the curse was turning, but he didn't worry about it. He found too much enjoyment in watching me obsess over him. He may have been cleverer or a little stronger than me, but that didn't mean I wasn't dangerous. He never saw it coming." She sighed and shook her head regretfully.

"I couldn't stop thinking that I was going to lose him. I was desperate to keep him for myself. I began studying a lot of dark magic. I had a tendency towards the darker side of magic even before the curse—all wielders do, I think, but the curse made me..." She searched for a word. "...it helped me see it in a way others couldn't." She took another sip of her tea and frowned. "Cold." She set her cup down. "Oddly enough, what I did to him did piqued the interest of many schools, and I was accepted into a very elite school—for dark warlocks, devils, demons, witches, and so on."

Pete swallowed, his throat dry.

"Did you know that the root of most hate is love?" she asked casually.

"Um, no, I was not aware," Pete said in a small voice.

"I started off small, using spells and rituals to keep him near me, to stop him from talking to other people, but then I started punishing him if I felt he wasn't showing me enough affection. He was strong enough to counteract most of those spells, but I started to get stronger at a rate that I know surprised him. I think he thought I had hit a peak or something, but he had helped me tap into a part of my powers I had no idea I possessed."

She chuckled to herself. "Honestly, I should send him a thank-you card one of these days." Her hazel eyes sparkled darkly.

Pete was really starting to sweat.

"Some people call it the seven-hundred-year witch."

Pete looked up sharply at that and leaned forward.

"It's kinda like—she whirled her hand around casually—"a black hole that can move and think on its own. Mine wasn't nearly as big as the original one is rumored to be. It was made by a whole coven of witches, controlled by a group in one of the border worlds somewhere." She peered at the side of her shop as though she could see worlds away to where the coven lived. "From what I read, they created this black hole to trap and torture souls. By this time, the curse had morphed my feelings for Dadson into a tight ball of rage and hatred. I hated him with a power that nearly controlled everything that I did. I wanted him to feel pain. I wanted him to die over and over again. So I made a curse, small of course, but still very powerful."

Pete stared open-mouthed at the stunning witch in front of him and calculated how long it would take him to run out the door if things went south.

"This was unheard of." Alexandria looked at Pete, who forced his shoulders to relax. "Not just because I was so young. Dark witches had been trying for ages to do it, and it finally took a whole coven to make one. But me, a pimpled little sixteen-year-old nerd had made one in her dorm room." She went quiet for a short while. "They said that the curse had transformed into something more." A shadow crossed her eyes, making Pete shiver again.

"It…was alive?" he asked, and Alexandria shrugged.

"I don't think so really. It…well, I should say, it helped transform me, kind of like a cocoon transforms a caterpillar."

Almost afraid to ask, Pete said, "What happened to Dadson?"

She waved a casual hand. "Oh, after a few days, the girls complained about someone invisible screaming nonstop inside the building. A few days later they rescued him. Like I said, I was only sixteen. The spell faded. He took about a month to heal…physically." She barked a laugh. "But he would never forget."

Pete stared at her. He could see the truth on her face, but there was something that wasn't adding up. Something that didn't make sense to him, though he couldn't quite put his finger on it.

"I don't get it. Why curse the school?"

Her smile faded and she tapped her cold mug, pensively. "Well, obviously, torturing kids is frowned upon, so I got detention."

Pete, who had made the mistake of taking a sip of his tea, spat it out. "You—detention!" he exclaimed.

She frowned as she delicately patted her gown free of tea spray.

"Sorry, I mean. That is…I would have expected something more severe."

She sniffed. "Well, part of it was his fault. I mean…technically, it was mostly my fault, since I was planning on doing the same thing to Brandon Kotowski."

"Where is he now?" he asked.

"Brandon? I told you—"

"No, Dadson."

"Oh, he's very successful. He owns an important business empire a few Worlds away. Well, anyway, I got detention, and Dadson was sent to a secret location. The love potion I created was a powerful one, but location dulls the edge. I searched the grounds of the school for him, then I searched for his file, but it was kept in a very safe place. I never found it. The curse needed something to be obsessed with, so when it couldn't find Dadson, it turned on the school itself. And it festered into hatred as it had for him."

She looked in the direction of the school. "Fortunately, for the academy, I was recruited by universities shortly after and taken away. I only got the one good curse in, but what I had planned for it…" She shook her head wistfully.

Pete stared at her. His hopes were sinking. If she hated the school, there wouldn't be any chance of her reversing the curse. Still, he had come this far.

"So… what now?" he asked awkwardly. She turned her almond-shaped eyes towards him. "I mean, this was fifty years ago. Plus, you were gone, far away from the school." He threw caution to the wind. "Hasn't the anger faded by now?"

"It has," she said, indifferent. "Well, mostly."

"So why not remove the curse?"

She picked at her nails. "I do not work for free."

Pete's heart lightened a little. "How much do you charge?"

The witch smiled and he braced himself. He might be able to convince the headmistress to pay it even if it was a lot.

"My price…is Dadson," she said, and Pete frowned. "Or, at least a piece of him."

"Piece?" Pete asked, not sure he was hearing her right.

"You have to realize that this curse is still here, with me. I feel it. There is still a lingering remnant of it. I forget it's there until I think about him and then it flares up. I am not entirely…in control."

She clasped her hands together and looked at Pete. "Because of the way the potion was created and later tampered with, I would either need him to remove the curse or need a piece of him to remove the curse myself. And he doesn't dare get close enough to me to remove the curse."

Pete shrugged in a way to say, who can blame him?

She nodded. "It's with good reason, I'll admit. But that means I need a piece of him." She looked at Pete.

He leaned back in his seat and said dejectedly, "A piece of him? You want me to go to the most protected and powerful warlock, a hundred Portals away and ask for a…piece of him?"

She chuckled at his expression. "A strand of hair will do."

"Okay…"

"They keep that with the files," she said pointedly. "The student files."

Pete looked at her, his heartbeat quickening, and she said, "I wouldn't bother asking the Bat for it. She won't budge. She doesn't trust me either and"—she smiled—"A strand of his hair in a witch's hands could be… unfortunate for him.

A dark thought occurred to Pete. "Are you…." He sighed and plunged on recklessly, "Are you going to hurt him?"

The witch considered for a moment. "I don't think so. I don't want to make the curse stronger, and feeding into the hatred will do that." She looked Pete in the eyes. "You get me the file I need, and I will lift the curse. That is my fee."

A feeling of excitement jumped in his stomach. All he had to do was steal a file from the school? This mission might end up being much simpler than he thought. Simple…if not easy. He ignored the guilty uncertainty he had about what could happen to Dadson. Pete hadn't like her maybe, but he forced it out of his mind. Maybe he could kill two birds with one stone.

They shook hands and made arrangements to meet again, but as he was walking out, he realized what had been bothering him earlier.

He turned. "Why are you here?" She raised an eyebrow. "No offense, but as powerful a witch as you are, why a small shop in Purgatory? Aren't there more… well, different things you could be doing than curing warts and stuff?"

She smiled, and suddenly Pete felt nervous again.

All she said was, "There are things to learn in this quiet little town," and closed the door in his face.

CHAPTER 13

THE ROOM WITH ALL THE FILES

ON THE WAY HOME, PETE'S mind was racing. He tried to listen to Charlie babble on about his new shirts, but he couldn't focus on what his friend was saying. He was in awe that he had gotten the beautiful and powerful witch to open up to him. He always became a stuttering mess when it came to talking to pretty girls. He winced when he thought of how awkward he'd been around both Stacie and Alex.

Charlie's gift of gossip and flattery was so effective and easy, it was unreal. He looked at his friend holding up a horribly small, yellow top and thought how underrated and talented he was. He might want to bring him in on what he would be doing. But first, he had some recon work to do.

He had not had a whole lot of practice with this. He could pick a pocket or a lock fairly well and could weave through a crowd, but maneuvering unseen down a secure hallway without tripping any security measures was another matter altogether.

Pete rubbed his head. He was getting ahead of himself. He needed to focus and list out everything he needed to do. He pulled out a pad of paper. He would destroy the paper, of course, but writing it out would help get his mind organized.

He started writing. First, he needed to figure out how and where the memory files were stored, how to get them, and what kind of security he was looking at. Then, he needed to retrieve them without the Bat or any teachers finding out. And finally, he had to get back to the witch.

That was a heck of a tall order, especially considering it had only been a month since he had been at the school, and he still hadn't learned a whole lot about how to find or extract his memories. How was he supposed to get this all done in less than a month? He frowned, pulling out his calendar.

Hang on. BASA missions were due the first week of November, right before the next full moon. Would Coach dock him for them not being able to tell if his mission had actually worked until after the assignment was due? He made a note to ask that night before he got too much further.

He sighed, feeling a pressure building behind his eyes. He decided to start with something he knew. He decided he would visit Charlie during his first period in the office. His excuse would be to talk about Alex, something he wanted to do anyway, and then somehow tie that into getting information about the files.

However, the plan went south almost immediately. The pace of his classes hadn't picked back up since the exams, but that didn't mean Mrs. Lemmings was appreciative of his thin excuse to leave class early.

"Your stomach hurts?" She raised an eyebrow. Pete held her gaze, clutching his stomach. Then, when it looked like she was about to say no, he cracked a rotten egg he had concealed in his pocket in a partially closed baggie and pretended to look embarrassed.

"I think if I use the bathroom, I might be okay," he whispered as she tried and failed to hide her disgust.

He quickly left the room, amid snickers and whispers from his classmates. His face hot, he pushed open the door and walked into the secretary's office.

"Pete!" Charlie said. "What are you doing here?"

Mrs. Delerie looked up and pulled down her cat-eye glasses. She waved a hand of red-lacquered fingernails at him.

"Pleasure to see you again." Pete smiled.

Mrs. Delerie smiled and blushed.

"Oh, what is that smell?" Charlie asked, and Pete pulled out the baggie and sealed it shut.

"Sorry, my lunch." he said lamely.

Charlie raised an eyebrow. "Well, well, well." He smirked. "Playing hooky, huh?"

Pete frowned, his face heating. He was learning that he was not a very good liar. He was not good at improvising either. Something he would need to fix if he decided to go the spy route in his AfterLife career.

"Can I talk to you?" he said quickly.

Charlie's smile faded, and he nodded and got up to follow Pete out of the office. He looked at his friend, and all of his plans flew out the window.

"I need your help, but I can't tell you why," he blurted out. Charlie's mouth was hanging open slightly and Pete realized he couldn't just leave it at that. "I have this…uh experiment…kinda. I need help with it, but I'm not supposed to give too many details."

Pete wasn't exactly out of bounds as he told Charlie that he needed the file to try and break the curse. He purposely left out BASA and the fact that it was a mission, making it seem like extracurricular work. Charlie didn't seem convinced until he mentioned offhandedly that he thought maybe Alex might be impressed.

"Oh, yes!" Charlie's whole attitude changed. "She would be very impressed. I told her that you liked her, and I think she might like you back."

"Wait." Pete felt slightly panicked. "Wait, why? Why did you tell her that?"

"Oh," Charlie said blankly. "Were you trying to keep that a secret?"

Pete's mouth moved, but no words came out. After a minute of this, he just decided to abandon ship and pretend he hadn't heard anything. "About the experiment…"

Preparation for the mission slowly started gaining more momentum. Coach gave him the go ahead, and Charlie turned out to be invaluable in intelligence-gathering. Not only did he find out exactly where the files were kept, but he also managed to get a copy of the school blueprints. This solved a lot of Pete's worries about getting around unseen at night. There were many corridors and rooms normally hidden from the students that would allow him to move unseen throughout much of the school.

For the next couple nights, Pete wandered those secret corridors, memorizing the location of their hidden entrances, where each hallway led, and documenting each person that walked through the halls at night, exactly where and when. He located the file room and tracked the guards and the times they passed the room. He only ran into one problem he didn't quite know how to solve, but as long as he found the file he was looking for and got out of there before midnight, he shouldn't have to worry about it.

Two days before he planned to attempt the first part of his self-assigned mission, Pete convinced both of his BASA sponsors to help him. Max was uncertain at first, but Scoot took no convincing at all. However, both were quiet for a long while when he mentioned that Charlie would also be coming.

"Um…interesting choice," Max said slowly.

"What, just because he's not part of BASA?" Pete said defensively. "That doesn't mean he won't be helpful. Trust me, he'll be useful."

Scoot snorted. "I guess we'll find out."

"I am the hunter, so October will be good for this sort of stuff," Pete reasoned with himself as he looked in the mirror. It was true that October fifth had brought them the Hunter's Moon, but it was now October seventeenth. It was, at least, still in the same month.

"I'm cracking," he said out loud again. He was a lot more nervous than he thought he would be.

He walked out of the bathroom with an unpleasant tightness in his stomach. The plan was set. He had recruited his sponsors to help him on the mission. He had covered every aspect he could think of. After a week of surveillance and reconnaissance, he had timed everything down to the second. So why was he so nervous?

"I'm not ready," he said to himself. Mark Davis gave him a funny look from a couple of bunks over, but Pete ignored him and sighed.

True, he had been training for a month, but now, on the night of his first self-created mission, it all felt wholly inadequate.

He walked to his bed to look through his rucksack for the millionth time. He went down his list:

Knife? Check.

Lock-pick tools? Check.

Map? Check.

Dadson Greenwich. Pete had researched him and learned quite a lot. The sly boy had grown into a wildly successful adult. He'd reached celebrity status in his local world, and his company supplied materials to nearly every construction company in the entire AfterLife.

Pete had thought his business would have had something to do with magic—but maybe after what happened to him, he didn't want anything to do with it.

"What's up?" a voice said to his left, making him jump. Pete looked over at a curious-looking Max propped up on his bed two rows away.

"Oh, uh…nervous," he admitted.

Max nodded, combing his fingers through his short, thick black hair. "Yah. First one is scary—well, all mine have been, but especially that first one."

Pete opened his mouth to ask him about his friend's old missions, wondering why he had not asked him sooner, but the words died in his mouth when he saw Charlie walk into the room.

Charlie was dressed in tight, unflattering black spandex with a black turtleneck and was putting dark eyeliner around his eyes.

"What are you doing?" Pete asked in an angry hiss.

"Getting ready to break—"

"Shut up!" Pete interrupted.

"What? Wait, is this a secret?" Charlie suddenly looked guilty.

"Of course it's a secret!" Pete hissed, in shock.

"Okay, here's the thing." Charlie held the eyeliner in his right hand. "I might have told a couple people."

"Hey, good luck tonight, you guys!" a tall, green-eyed boy with strawberry blond hair said on the way to his bunk.

Max looked like he was trying not to laugh. When Charlie went to the bathroom to finish putting on his spy makeup, as he called it, Max said in a forced-casual way, "I was wondering why you invited him."

Pete sat there blinking spots out of his eyes. "He…he's good at talking his way out of tight situations."

Max nodded. "True, he usually talks himself into those tight spots first though." Max grinned and slapped Pete on the back. "I'm sure it'll be fine, though."

Pete opened his mouth, then closed it, letting Max walk away to get ready.

"So, what are you guys doing exactly?" asked the red-haired boy, whose bed was nearby.

Charlie poked his head out of the bathroom, no doubt prepared to give every single detail of their plan, but Pete cut him off. "We want to see the monster they take out in the cages every night."

"There's another night monster? What kind? I thought the last one ran away after it bit one of the first graders," another boy, Pat, chimed in from his bed next to Red. Pat pulled on his pajama shirt, covering a large gash across his belly.

"Nah," Red answered, "you're thinking of the lunch lady who tried to eat the substitute science teacher. She didn't run away, she just went on a rampage through the school for a few hours, but she was back the next day."

"Oh, yeah, that's right." Pat started to look uninterested.

Pete let out a quiet sigh of relief. Charlie glanced questioningly at him, but thankfully he stayed quiet and walked over to lace up his boots.

When it was truly dark, the three of them headed out. Pete noticed the shades draw back from the front window, and he saw the beady eyes of a curious student.

"You guys took forever." Scoot's voice sounded in Pete's ear, making him jump a mile in the air.

"Wha—?" Pete whirled around, heart thumping, but there was no one there. Then slowly, Scoot materialized with her orange-pigtailed head resting casually on her hip, supported by one arm.

Pete, still gripping his chest hissed angrily. "You were supposed to announce yourself."

"What do you think I just did?" She raised an eyebrow. "By the way. We had about twenty volunteers in Patra's dorm if you need help. You're becoming quite popular among the ladies."

"How do they know?" Pete asked indignantly.

Charlie made a guilty sound.

Pete groaned. "Is there anyone you didn't tell?"

"Well, let's hope none of the teachers." Scoot sounded unconcerned.

Pete slowed, turning dagger eyes on Charlie. "Did you, Charlie?"

"Just in case," Scoot said, before Charlie could answer, "how much of the plan did you tell him?"

A twinge of hope sparked in Pete. "Actually, not much."

"Guys, stop talking about me like I'm not here."

Pete shushed him and waved them forward. "Come on, and keep your voices down."

Together, they melted into the shadows and halted at the corner of the school's entrance to the front courtyard behind some hydrangea bushes. Pete looked at his watch and let out a hiss of frustration. Dead again. Scoot held out her arm for Pete to read her watch. 10:15. Right on schedule.

Pete heard quiet sniffing in the distance, the telltale sign that Bark was near. The dog sniffed happily, moving the occasional leaf or stick as he wandered around the courtyard, smelling and peeing on things. Then, as had been his custom for the last week, he went silent. The front doors opened and eight men heaved a massive wrought-iron cage outside toward the gate.

The rattling and snarling coming from the cages sent shivers down Pete's spine, and he shuddered involuntarily. The snarling was nothing like he had ever heard before. It was unworldly, unnatural. The wolves were always terrifying, but these sounds were somehow worse.

"Man, Mrs. Stupenstien looks grumpy," Charlie whispered, looking at the cage.

"What? Wait! That thing is a teacher?" Pete asked incredulously.

Charlie looked over, "Oh. Ya. She teaches the younger kids."

"Why?" Pete hissed, astonished. "Why do they keep a monster like that in the school?"

Charlie shrugged. "Dunno. I think she was highly qualified. Won some award for the best teacher or something."

"But…but…what if she attacks a kid?"

"Most terrain-bound monsters on this side of the Portal sphere only hunt at night," Scoot answered.

"Okay…so what if a kid gets hunted at night?"

"Well, that's why there are curfews, of course," Max said reasonably.

"So break curfew, you get eaten?" Pete asked, stunned.

"Yes." Scoot looked at Pete with an expression that suggested she didn't see what was so hard for him to understand.

Pete shook his head, suddenly feeling exposed, and waved for them to keep going.

Getting into the school was always pretty easy. The doors were never locked, and the entrance hall was usually empty of people. Still, Pete used all the evasion tactics his coach and book had taught him, wincing when he heard Charlie trip behind him.

Now that his plan was in motion, how he could have thought that bringing Charlie on a mission like this was a good idea? Sure, if he needed to talk someone out of something, but this? He winced again as he heard Charlie stub his toe.

Even with the noises Charlie was making, they managed to stay unseen by using the hidden dimly lit hallways and corridors Pete had spent the past week learning, leading to the room with all the files. A couple of them Max and Scoot had told him about, and one Charlie had showed him. It was this last one that they were going through when they hit their first obstacle.

Pete was opening the door to leave the hallway when he heard voices. His stomach dropped violently: Mrs. Battinsworth's sharp words echoed through the hallway.

"There's no way we can be ready by then," she said.

Pete backed up slowly through the doorway, waving frantically at his friends to back up. As quietly as he could, he shut the door.

He looked around to check if there was a hiding place, but found none. The hallway they were in was just as well lit as the others, and he felt exposed. He motioned for them to take the other doorway. Charlie was the first to go through, with the others right on his heels. Peter quietly shut the door and was happy he'd made the decision when he heard the door they'd been standing behind a moment ago swing wide and slam into the wall.

"Hmmm," Mrs. Battinsworth said on the other side of the door.

"What is it?" came the unmistakable dry crackle of Coach Skinley.

"Thought I heard something," came Mrs. Battinsworth's reply.

"Was it Lizzy?" Coach Skinley asked.

"Of course it wasn't," the headmistress snapped. Her voice got quieter, and Pete soon heard the door shut, muffling her voice completely. She had exited the hallway again. He breathed out in relief.

"We have to go around," he mouthed to his friends.

Following his book's recommendations, he had mapped out several alternative routes as backup options. The detour he took them on only cost them about four minutes, and that was because Pete didn't want to risk Charlie freaking out if they started running. He had planned in some wiggle room for time and decided to leave that option as a last resort.

Pete bit his lip. He was getting to the part of the plan he felt nervous about. The part where he would really need his friends' help.

They moved to the back part of the school through a maintenance door and down a service hallway. They needed to go down to the basement. When they got to the old elevator, Pete took the key that hung on the wall and turned it in the slot. As the others piled in behind him, Max shut the gate. The ancient elevator clunked and shuddered before moving slowly down. When it stopped, Max opened the gate and Pete hung the key on the wall. They walked quickly through the empty hallway.

They made two turns and finally made it to the place they were looking for. In front of them, perhaps ten feet tall, was a solid steel vault door, which had a combination lock instead of a keyhole.

Scoot tilted her head and looked at the door. It was the first time he had ever seen her look unsure about something. "This is pretty advanced," she admitted.

Max looked guiltily at Pete. "I don't know," he said slowly, "I can't believe the academy invested in a Millington 3000. Those are pretty pricey."

Scoot shook her head. "These models have anti-Porting spells built into them so you can't go through."

"Oh!" Max looked suddenly inspired. "You can't go through, but maybe if I could see how it worked inside." He took off his jacket, and handed Pete his tools. "Let me try something."

All three of them watched him curiously as he walked to the very edge of the door and stood beside it. He started swaying his body side to side.

Scoot gasped, and before she could stop herself, said, "Oh, brilliant!"

Max's body started to flicker and before Pete understood what he was doing, the top half of Max's body melted into the shadows.

"Oh," Pete said out loud, holding Max's tools limply in his hands, entirely forgotten.

The bottom half of Max tilted forward and Pete knew that Max's head was inside the thick vault door. The vault dial started to turn of its own accord. Clink. It spun again. Clink. And again.Clink. Thunk! The dial stopped suddenly.

Max's head reappeared, and Pete whispered, "Good thinking!" He rushed over to help pull the door open. He waited for them to follow him in and closed the door.

Scoot found a light and flipped it on. They stood looking around in awed silence for a moment. The massive room was several stories high and completely full of filing cabinets.

"Whoa," said Charlie. "How are we going to find the file you're looking for?"

Before Pete could answer, something whooshed down in front of his face, causing him to squeak in surprise and fall back onto his butt.

"Pete, it's a…it's a GHOST!" Charlie said, completely stunned. "In Purgatory!"

The four of them looked up at the man, arms crossed, dressed in a security outfit, floating several feet off the floor.

"I thought you guys only worked in Life?" Pete asked the floating man.

"A GHOST can work wherever he pleases," he sniffed, looking very offended.

"Of course," Pete said quickly, "I…I was just surprised to see you."

The GHOST narrowed his eyes suspiciously. "Why? Are you not supposed to be here? Having a GHOST guard is standard security. Anyone who is allowed to be in here would have known that." He emphasized the word allowed.

"Oh, yes, we are supposed to be here. They just didn't specify that there would be a security GHOST, that's all. I just got confused."

The man smiled unpleasantly, and Pete felt his own fake smile faulter.

"Well then," he said reasonably, "you should be able to tell me what the password is."

Pete opened his mouth to say something but nothing came out. Then, to everyone's surprise including his own, Charlie said, "Lizzy."

The guard frowned, looking thoroughly disappointed. He threw up his hands, rolled his eyes, and then floated away to the wall.

"So I guess we got the password right," Scoot said sarcastically to the wall. She giggled, a strange sound coming from her mouth, and they looked back at the room with all the files.

Pete and Max turned to Charlie as they walked into the room. "How did you know what the password was?" Max asked.

Charlie shrugged. "Just a hunch."

"Who is Lizzy anyway?" Pete asked.

Charlie's face lit up. "She's the Bat's daughter."

"She has kids?" Pete asked, stunned.

"Yup," Charlie said with a grin. "But something happened, and Lizzy went, well, insane. She turned into a poltergeist before they could get her help. A real tragedy."

Pete was surprised by this news. There was something so rigid and unfriendly about the headmistress. She didn't seem to have a single motherly instinct, let alone be sentimental enough to use her daughter's name as a password.

"Okay, first things first, we have to see how these memory files are organized."

Scoot looked at Pete. "And how do you propose that?"

Pete walked over to the closest filing cabinet and opened a file:

> Penny Tollinsworth
> DA 16
> Graduation date 7.14.503 BC
> Last Known Location: 756 Port, Valhalla, section 6
> He replaced the file and pulled out the next one.
> Tom Center
> DA 9
> Graduation date 6.8.1902 AD
> Last Known Location: Birmingham, Purgatory

"They don't seem to be in any particular order." Scoot flipped through a few files in the nearby cabinet.

"So I'm noticing," Pete said, disappointed.

"Hey, what about that?" Charlie pointed to a large box in the far left corner of the room. Pete replaced the file he was holding, closed the cabinet, and walked over to what Charlie was pointing at.

Pete uncovered it, and there stood a giant computer that looked to be the same age as the elevator they had descended in.

"Well, you would think," Charlie said, disgusted, "that since Steve Jobs died, there would be better computers in AfterLife."

"This is Purgatory," Scoot reminded him.

Pete snorted. "Does anyone know how to work it?"

Max flipped on the switch and they impatiently waited for ten minutes for the computer to power on and then stared at the blank screen with the blinking cursor. No Start menu or anything.

"Well, now what?" Charlie asked.

"Does anyone know how to use this?" Pete repeated.

All of them shook their heads, staring at the giant box someone once called a computer.

They heard a sniff behind them and they turned around. "Insolence of children these days."

Charlie brightened. "You're back!" he said to the GHOST hovering in the background. The guard looked taken aback.

"Why, yes. I guard this place." He looked like he was deciding whether to be offended by Charlie's comment or not.

"Good! I wanted to ask you how you became a GHOST guard. I was thinking about becoming one. I don't know." a distressed look crossed his face. "I read that there are like a million requirements. I'm not sure I can score high enough on the SGR exam to get into a good program." He looked genuinely disappointed.

"Oh. Well." The GHOST smiled and floated down.

Scoot huffed impatiently. "Listen, Charlie, we all want to hear about this, but it may not be the time." She frowned apologetically at the GHOST. "We've got to get back in"—she looked down at her watch and gasped—"*five* minutes." She looked hopelessly back at Pete whose shoulders slumped.

The GHOST waived his hands impatiently. "Aren't you kids all supposed to be wizards at computers these days?" Without waiting for a reply, he glided smoothly over to the computer and hit the F2 button on the top. Then he typed in F < Name < First and said over his shoulder, "Name?"

Pete quickly gave him the information.

"Second floor, Aisle 7, Row 9, Column 27, bottom drawer." Then as they looked around, he squinted suspiciously.

Charlie, however, distracted him by saying, "Sorry, what were you saying before you were rudely interrupted?"

Pete thanked the GHOST as he floated over to talk to Charlie. Max and Scoot ran up the steps, but Pete hung back and looked up one more name, writing down the location.

He ran to catch up and, less than two minutes later, Pete had both files tucked in the elastic band of his pajama bottoms, which had reappeared. Pete didn't bother with changing back into his uniform, and swung his tie around behind him.

They came back down to see Charlie and the guard rolling in laughter. The guard was literally pounding an invisible ground.

"Sorry to interrupt," Pete said, genuinely meaning it.

"Oh, it's all right." The GHOST wiped translucent tears from his eyes and righted himself. "Oh, I haven't had this much fun in years. You're right— it's an elite job, but man, guard duty is boring." He turned to Charlie. "But if you're really interested, let me know and I can help you."

They thanked him and made their way back.

Pete grabbed Scoot's wrist and yelped when he read the time. "Okay, we might have a problem."

"What's the problem?" Max said.

Pete looked over at him. "Well, there is the issue of the giant snake that comes out at midnight."

CHAPTER 14

THE SNAKE IN THE TEA

"WHAT?" MAX ASKED, STARTLED. "WHAT do you mean? What snake?" Max glanced over at Scoot, who looked back blankly.

"Neither of you know about the snake?" Pete asked in disbelief. "You guys have been here longer than I have!"

"It must be a new thing. Did they hire a new teacher or something?" Scoot chewed on her lip. Her face was turning a bit pale.

"Oh," Charlie said, "That's right...they hired the new substitute, Mrs. Pennyfeather. I heard she—"

"It doesn't matter," Pete cut him off. "We need to find a way out of here. I couldn't figure out a pattern to her roaming the halls, and it almost always seemed like she knew where I was."

Charlie nodded, looking a bit disappointed he couldn't spread some new gossip. "Okay, you're probably right. Word is that her snake form is gold-colored like her hair, and she has green eyes."

"Disregarding how you found out that information, Charlie, please tell us how that helps us?" Scoot said, exasperated. "We don't need to pick her out of a lineup of snakes. If we see a giant snake in the hallway, I think it's safe to assume that it's the new teacher."

Charlie look affronted. "I wasn't done." He pouted. "She's also twenty feet long."

"Twenty?" Max squeaked. "Lead with that next time," he huffed. "Anything else useful you know about her?"

Charlie frowned. "I know she eats late at night, but only like once a month or so. I know they let her wander the halls, but Sally says she's never seen her." He shrugged. "Hopefully she doesn't wander much?"

"She does." Pete was sweating. The snake was actually much bigger than Charlie described, but his friends knowing that would not help their situation.

They walked over to the elevator, and he stuck the key in. As Max closed the gate, Pete was thinking of the first time he had seen her slither by. He had been about ten feet above the ground, up on a hidden ledge near a pillar, in the corner of a seldom used hallway. The pure shock when he first laid eyes on the snake had been unbearable. It hadn't just been her sheer size or even the shock of seeing a random snake wandering through the school. It was the fact she came out of nowhere. He had been vigilantly watching for people coming, on full alert, yet she had slithered so quickly beneath his feet that he almost shouted out loud.

Pete pressed the button to go up, swallowing hard. "She moves quickly, and she's virtually silent." He set his back-up plan in motion. "Even if she smells you, she rarely looks up."

"So how will I fit?" Charlie stared dubiously at the entrance to the vent opening in the wall. They were inside a utility closet just outside the elevator. Pete was not about to risk being out in the open. The vent was close to the ground, so no one had to climb up.

"It's wide enough, I promise. It'll just be tight. Just remember to breathe," Pete whispered. "Scoot and Max made it in there just fine."

Charlie looked at him and then back at the vent opening. "I thought you said she didn't look up. Isn't the idea to be high above the ground?"

"I also said that she moves fast and silently, so maybe keep your voice down so you don't attract her to us? Come on, get going." Pete gave Charlie a gentle push. "There's a spot where you can climb to a higher floor."

"Hurry up," Scoot whispered fiercely from several feet inside the vent.

Pete gave Charlie another gentle push, and reluctantly his friend climbed into the oversized vent.

He honestly didn't know if this plan would work. Tight, dark, enclosed spaces seemed like an ideal place for a snake to crawl, but so far, night after night in the last week, he had seen the giant golden snake only slithering out in the open corridors. Moving somewhere not in the open seemed their best chance to avoid getting caught.

"I can't see anything," Charlie complained as Pete climbed into the vent after him.

Pete punched the back of his foot and shushed him. "Your voice carries in the vents. Keep it down."

Turning around—which was difficult, as it was a tight squeeze in here— Pete carefully closed the vent behind him. Should he have gone in first, since he knew the way? He didn't think Max or Scoot did. A loud crack broke the silence and his concentration.

Pete's heart leaped into his throat. The vent shook violently, and he could hear Max and Scoot's alarmed voices several feet ahead of them. He knew right away what was happening, even before he heard a loud hiss, and another crack, followed by a second savage rattle. The way the vents were echoing and with all the turns they were making, it was hard to pinpoint where the sounds were coming from. But Pete thought was pretty sure it was coming from somewhere behind him on the other side of the vent cover.

"She's coming!" Pete yelled. "Go!" Thankfully, the others obeyed. They half-ran, half-squeezed their way through the tight passageway as quickly as they could go.

In a sort of disjointed way, he was completely aware of the situation at hand, but in another part of his brain, he was analyzing just about everything that had gone wrong, that led to them being trapped outside their dorms after midnight.

He shook himself. He couldn't worry about that now. He needed to figure out what to do.

He looked up, and he realized where he was. "Charlie, turn right!" he commanded. He worried for a second that Charlie, who sounded out of breath and panicked, hadn't heard him, but to his relief, he turned right at the last moment.

Pete could hear Charlie panting and shaking. In spite of all this, he was moving faster than Pete had ever seen him move, even on two feet.

"Did it get through?" Charlie asked him in a quaking voice.

A mighty crash sounded behind them, and they felt the biggest quake yet. "My guess is yes," Pete hissed. "Go! Go! Go!"

They picked up the pace, but even as fast as Charlie was moving, Pete was nearly on top of him.

Every few feet, he hissed out commands. "Right, right, left, straight, straight, left, left!" Then, finally, seeing pins of light, he said, "Okay, we should be able to get out here."

They should be right on the terrace that overlooked their dorm rooms. There was a ladder they could climb down. With any luck, this Mrs. Pennyfeather wouldn't follow them. But somehow, he doubted that would be the case, and unbidden memories of seeing snakes climbing trees on the Discovery Channel jumped into his brain.

Together, Charlie and Pete pushed open the vent cover, piled through, and then fell with a yelp of surprise onto the ground three feet below.

"Oof!"

Pete looked up and then wildly around. It seemed they were in a storage closet, but it was too dark to tell.

"I don't understand." Pete was huffing. "We should be on the terrace. We should be close to the dorms. Where are Max and Scoot? They were right in front of you, weren't they?"

Charlie was completely out of breath and didn't answer, but the look on his face was answer enough.

Pete cursed and pushed the vent cover on—though knowing it hadn't held the snake back the first time, he wasn't sure how useful it would be now. He scanned the area and shoved a large bookshelf in front of the vent. He doubted it would throw off the snake for long, but maybe it would give them a second or two head start. Pete dragged Charlie upright and pulled him to the door.

"Do. You. Think," Charlie wheezed, "they're all right?"

Pete nodded with more confidence than he felt. "They're better at this sort of stuff than we are," he whispered.

"How do you know?"

Pete winced, forgetting that Charlie didn't know about BASA.

"I just know," he said. "I'm sure they will be okay. We just need to find our way back. They'll be waiting for us at the dorms, I'm sure."

He stuck his head through the doorway and searched both ways. He had no idea where they were. How was it possible to be this lost after all that preparation? He eased out of the closet and walked to a nearby window in the hallway. Out the small window, he glimpsed the edge of a building, and a shimmer of hope flared up.

He waved for Charlie to tiptoe over and look out the window. "Is that the maze and the annex building?"

Charlie, who was taller than Pete by half a head, peeked through the window. "Oh yeah!" He sounded relieved as well. "There should be a window we can open and get through." He glanced behind them at the closed storage closet, and Pete knew he was thinking about the substitute teacher.

Pete nodded and followed Charlie into a classroom, shutting the door behind them.

Charlie walked up to a window. "All of them stick, except this back one."

"How do you know that?" Pete asked curiously as he helped Charlie pushed the stubborn window open.

"Scoot and I would always cut through this way during lunch to get to the Kissing Spot."

Pete nodded and followed after him. "Feel for the ledge," Charlie instructed. Pete swung his leg through and felt the ledge. When he had solid footing, he slid the rest of the way through and pulled the window shut.

"Step down one more notch." Charlie grabbed Pete's leg in the dim light. There was quite a bit of light, but the moon was casting strange shadows, and he had trouble telling what was what.

Pete's foot slipped, and he almost gasped, but Charlie whispered, "You're all right, the ledge is right there." Charlie, who had climbed down and was at a level with Pete's foot, grabbed it and guided it back to the ledge.

Pete's heart was thumping. "See?" Charlie said with a smile. "If I can do it, then anyone can." Pete laughed nervously and followed Charlie. They made it to the ground in a few minutes, landing just under the terrace balcony.

When Pete heard voices, he froze and pulled Charlie into the shadows of the building.

"What?" Charlie whispered.

"Did you hear that?"

Charlie shook his head and together they stood stock-still. Then, when Pete heard the muffled voices again, Charlie's face told Pete that he had heard them too. It was too garbled to tell what they were saying, but there were definitely people directly above them.

"How can we get to the dorms without being noticed?" Charlie gazed yearningly at the entrance to the boy's dorms about ten feet away.

Before Pete could answer, the sound of the whine of an opening gate and the hum of a truck pulled his attention. Headlights flooded the courtyard, and Pete groaned. That was the last thing they needed.

Although Pete knew that the people in the truck would not be able to see them where they were, he also knew they were very close to the loading docks.

Charlie suddenly grabbed Pete's arm. "I think I heard them. I mean, it kinda sounded like Scoot's voice just now."

"What?" Pete asked, startled. He had not been listening to the sounds above him, but watching the truck and the workers who were starting to unload boxes from the bed of the truck.

Charlie repeated himself. "Do you think those voices were Max and Scoot's?"

Pete's eyes widened. "Maybe." He studied the solid floor of the terrace above him. "Stay here," he told Charlie. Then, thinking better of it: "Actually, no. I'll check to see if that's Max and Scoot and see if they need help. Do you think you can get to the dorms without being spotted?"

Charlie nodded, then pointed. "There's a ladder to the terrace right over there. It is a little out of the way, but it's completely hidden."

Pete nodded. "If that is Max and Scoot, I'll get them and meet you at the dorms."

Charlie looked relieved and nodded. Pete watched him dart through the shadows, trip, get up, and continue running towards the dorm. Pete sighed, but at least if the workers did spot him, they wouldn't be able to tell who he was.

Sprinting over to the ladder, Pete scampered up. When he reached the lip of the edge of the balcony floor, he paused and slowly peeked his head over it.

Immediately, he recoiled, nearly falling off the ladder as the hissing form of a snake snapped in his direction. She struck the guard rail with just her head and the force of her strike shook the entire balcony. Pete nearly slipped again.

"Pete!" Scoot said, from about fifteen feet above him.

Pete heard another loud hiss. He realized with horror that the snake had climbed over the ledge and was poised to strike. Without testing his balance, he sprung from his spot to cling onto vines growing on the building a few feet to the right. His right foot ripped some out when he landed, but he managed to hold on and stop himself from dropping all the way to the ground, a good twenty-five feet below.

He grunted, grinding his teeth. His mind was starting to go numb with fear, but he forced himself to slow down his breathing.

Fortunately, the massive snake was having trouble getting leverage. She was too big. If she leaned over too much, the force of her strike would cause her to fall off the balcony, and her body was too thick to wrap around the guard rail for purchase. After a few seconds, she drew back and focused on the two victims closer to her.

Pete finally saw where his friends were. He could see two shadowy figures, wedged in between one of the window's guard rails. He didn't understand what he was seeing. How could they be there? Then, he realized what had happened.

It wasn't a window guard, but a miniature wrought-iron balcony that had been smashed upward to the window above it. They must have climbed through the window onto the balcony, and before they could climb over and onto the terrace, the snake attacked from below, smashing the iron bars, forming an impromptu prison and pinning them tight to the window.

Pete could tell that Scoot was trying to open the window, but she was trapped too tightly to move.

Stomach clenching, he watched the snake rear up to strike. The snake hissed again, a sound that sent unbidden shivers through his spine. She reared up and struck their iron prison. The window was just high enough to be inconvenient, but it was low enough for the snake to do damage with every strike.

Panting, Pete began climbing frantically up the vines. Distantly, he could hear sounds from the workers behind and realized they must have caught on to all the ruckus he and his friends were causing.

After the last hiss and crack of the snake slamming its face into the bars, Pete saw that his time was up. The last strike broke their prison/protective barrier. Pete watched in horror as Scoot grabbed wildly onto the bars that were barely holding on, and Max fell right on top of the snake's massive head.

His only stroke of luck was that he caught the snake off-guard and as he landed, he rolled away from her. Max jumped over the side as the snake sent her body smashing towards him, and he barely missed being pancaked in between the terrace wall and the substitute teacher.

Pete saw the snake rear up to strike at the hanging Scoot. Without thinking, Pete leaped onto the head of the snake, just as she struck. The force of his weight pushed her head down, and she just missed Scoot. Scoot let go and landed on Pete.

Their combined weight drove the snake back to the floor of the terrace, and Scoot expertly rolled off. Pete, not being an expert, gripped the snake's head and did not let go. He watched his friend slip over the side of the entrance as the snake started whipping its head around wildly like Pete weighed nothing.

He was still clinging to its head, but also flying through the air. He was going to be sick. She shook him left and right so violently that he thought his arms were going to rip out of their sockets.

Then, as though he had planned it, the feeling of weightlessness flowed through his body, then slipped away. He thought about the mist and the shadows. And as though someone turned on a light in his brain, he knew exactly what he needed to do.

He looked wildly around. First, he needed a place. He craned his neck and a jolt of excitement ran through him. He could see the truck in the courtyard near the open gate. Two men were still unloading it. He didn't care how they hadn't noticed the snake. The truck door was open, and one man was pushing a button that started a loud beeping noise and a loading ramp lowered.

As if the snake could tell what was about to happen, she started thrashing harder. Pete closed his eyes and focused on the snake and then on the truck. The rocking of the snake was helping him now, and he slipped back into weightlessness. With one last wild thrash, Pete and the snake toppled over the top of the balcony and fell into nothingness.

As he fell, Pete let go of the snake and twisted in midair. It was a bizarre feeling, kind of like somersaulting through runny pudding. His shoulder slammed into the ground. His training kicked in, and he turned his fall into a roll and popped back up onto his feet.

The adrenaline helped him ignore the raging pain in his shoulder.

His aim had been off. He had hoped to push the snake inside the truck, while he landed on top. He thought he might be able to roll off the top of the truck and hopefully close the truck door in time, but he hadn't been that lucky.

The snake landed on top of the truck and smashed the windshield. The men shrieked and dropped their packages.

In the back of his mind, Pete should've been proud of himself for Shadow Walking, even if he was off his mark. But somehow the massive, pissed-off snake that landed just to his left rendered that tiny fact moot.

"Run!" Pete shouted. The men didn't need him to tell them again. A white-haired man in a blue uniform jumped inside the cab of the truck. Pete wondered if that had been the wisest of choices, but the man gunned the motor and whipped the truck in a U-turn. The snake, hissing, flew off the truck and hit a nearby tree, splintering it. The driver paused just long enough to pick up his fluently cursing coworker, and they drove off madly together, spreading the contents of their truck across the courtyard and down the street.

The driver sped off without a backward glance at him. Sure, he had thrown a giant snake onto their car, but still, they should have done something to help him. Incredulous, Pete scanned and paused, ice creeping into his veins. The snake was suddenly nowhere to be found.

He swiveled one way and then the other, but the moonlight cast strange shadows, and everywhere seemed to house the angry snake. A bulky figure of a girl watched him, the faraway sounds of her laughter carrying all the way to Pete's position White hot fury shot through him, Shelly!

He swore and promised himself he would get her back for this. That meddling behemoth probably tipped off the teacher. But he shook himself. Now was not the time to focus on that.

Rustling made him whip his head to the right. He gasped. The snake was only a few feet from him, but for some reason, had not attacked him yet. Moving instinctively, Pete ran backward, his feet scuffing the dirt courtyard as he went. The snake whipped its head in his direction and licked the air, but didn't lunge like he thought it would.

Oddly, the snake moved like it was still searching for him. Could this snake be blind? Or was something else stopping it from attacking him? It certainly had not looked blind when it was attacking Max and Scoot.

Pete heard something and froze. Max was running towards him. The snake was hidden from Max's sight, but the snake—if it could in fact see— could see Max just fine.

"Pete!" Max hissed in a harsh, carrying whisper. "Pete, where are you?"

The snake hissed and slithered toward him. Max, oblivious to the snake, stood squinting in the dark.

"Get out of here!" Pete yelled to his friend. "The snake is right here!" But the voice coming out of his mouth sounded small and far away. He finally realized what was happening. He glanced down and saw that his hands were translucent.

He couldn't believe it. He was still in the middle of Shadow Walking. Pete concentrated and his hands become more and more solid. He felt the ground beneath him and realized that he had been hovering, much like the GHOST had been earlier that night.

"Pete! Duck, you idiot!" someone shouted. Stunned and frozen, Pete looked up to see the snake rear its head and strike directly at him.

CHAPTER 15

THE OTHER FILE

PART OF PETE REGISTERED THAT there was no way he could get out of the way in time. He watched, in a detached sort of way, as his very short second life came to a violent and abrupt end.

Then, he felt a solid thing ram into his body, slamming him hard to the ground and knocking all the air out of his lungs. Though he was stunned and dazed, the impact had snapped him out of his frozen state.

He rolled clumsily to the side and jumped up, his knees knocking slightly. Then he stopped moving, swaying a little, and stared in confusion. The snake was on the other side of the closed gate. The snake, furious and hissing, struck at the wrought-iron gate over and over again.

Pete stared, his brain refusing to process what had just happened. Both Max and Scoot stood huffing beside him. The snake, too thick to pass through the bars of the gate, slammed its body into it, making Pete, Max, and Scoot jump involuntarily at the ferocity of their substitute teacher.

"Time to go?" Max asked as they watched the snake look up to see if she could climb over the gate.

Pete, whose mouth was bone dry, nodded. It took several seconds for his brain to catch up.

"How did you Teleport out of the way?" he asked Scoot.

Scoot nodded and pointed at Max. "And he closed the gate. I figured it was quicker to Teleport than try to find some shadows to Shadow Walk. Come on. Max, can you get us near the dorms?"

Max got them outside the dorm room. Having Max Teleport them there had been a weird feeling. It was strange having the nothingness pushed onto him. Pete thought Shadow Walking felt easier and more natural. He was merely blending into something that was there, but Teleporting—traveling without the use of shadows—was much more useful and less restrictive. He needed to practice it more. But first, he needed to sit down. The lingering effects made Pete nauseated, or perhaps that was the aftermath of the adrenaline.

As soon as they landed, the three of them ran inside, slamming the door behind them. A couple of kids jumped in their sleep, and one cursed and yelled for them to keep it down.

Scoot collapsed in a seat in the study room, slightly out of breath, and said in an annoyed voice, "Wish I had thought about Porting when we were trapped behind that window ledge."

"Yah, good thinking, Pete," Max said. "But I must say, you were crazy for doing what you did." He sounded thoroughly impressed.

Pete smiled and wiped his sweaty face with his sleeve. "I'm honestly not sure how I did it. I'm still not very good at it."

They all stopped talking when they heard a muffled howling from the courtyard.

"Yeah, I think I'm gonna hang out here tonight," Scoot said, and they both nodded.

Charlie met them a few minutes later, and whispering, they caught him up to speed.

Pete pulled out Dadson's file, keeping the other one hidden under his pajamas. Together, they bent over it. Pete frowned. He was very nervous at first and couldn't seem to find the lock of hair.

"That's weird." Charlie suddenly pulled it out. Pete snatched it out of his hands, and he raised an eyebrow.

"You're going to lose it." Pete held onto the lock of hair.

"So what is so special about this file?" Charlie asked. He read out loud, "Dadson Christopher Greenwich. He's boring. He was boring in Life, and he was boring in AfterLife. He's average-looking, average grades. Honestly, I don't know what the point of all this was."

Pete took the file from Charlie and held it protectively. He hadn't told them the details of his overall mission as part of the rules of his midterm exam.

The theory was that if Pete was going to work for the Community, there would be times that he would need help with part of a mission but would still have to keep the overall objective a secret.

Of course, Scoot and Max knew this, but Charlie, inquisitive by nature, was expecting an answer.

Pete took a breath. He had actually been expecting Charlie to ask long before this and had an answer prepared. He signaled for Charlie to wait and went out to his bed. He pulled a slip of paper from his bed and replaced it with the second file. He returned and handed Charlie the paper.

Charlie opened the folded newspaper clipping curiously.

"I got that from the library when I was studying," Pete explained. Charlie read it, and then his eyebrows shot up as he looked at Pete. He set the paper down and grabbed Dadson's file with renewed interest.

"This is the same guy?" Charlie looked doubtfully at the picture of the boy and the newspaper image of a successful businessman.

"I think so." Pete said slowly.

"So what did you think you could do with this?" Charlie held up the folder.

Pete shrugged and pretended to look bashful. "Well, he's pretty famous. He's dating that actress...I thought...well." He paused. "If there were something embarrassing, maybe the papers would want to know?"

Charlie snorted. "Dang, Green. You're cold. Well, too bad it's all boring stuff." He glanced at the file again and yawned loudly. "I thought you might have needed it for BASA. Well, I'm off to bed."

Max, Scoot and Pete all exchanged glances.

"Hang on," Scoot said, making Charlie pause. "You told him?" she asked Pete indignantly.

Pete opened his mouth to say no, but Charlie beat him to it. "What? Him? No, I found out about BASA my first year here."

They all looked at him, surprised, and he frowned. "I assumed that was why you picked me to join in this file stealing thingy."

"How did you find out?" Max asked.

Charlie looked at him crossly. "Oh, come on. No one sneaks out of the dorms without me knowing. I need to know if someone is sneaking off to make out. People need to know about things like that."

"No one needs to know about that," Scoot said as Charlie turned away again and headed for his bed.

Once Charlie was gone, Scoot said, thoughtfully, "You know, blackmailing Greenwich might have been a pretty good mission idea."

Pete laughed, and they stayed up talking until the sun started to rise. Pete told them his theory about Shelly, and they all enjoyed their time plotting revenge against her. Scoot finally excused herself.

Max yawned. "Man, might be the second time this year I need a nap."

Pete nodded and followed Max into the dorm room. It was still early, and every bunk except theirs was filled.

Pete lay down with a sigh. His entire body felt wrecked from the night's adventure; his heart was even still pounding. Truthfully, he had serious doubts about whether he wanted to continue with BASA. He could've gotten killed. He could've gotten his friends killed. But then he thought about what his life would be like without BASA. He thought about what he wanted to do after school.

Did he want to be an accountant? No. Most definitely not.

A lot had gone wrong tonight—but then, a lot had gone right too. It had been, what, a month? A month and a half, and he had Teleported a massive snake across the lawn of his new school. He could climb walls and gates. He knew how to fight—well, sort of. The point was that he was becoming the type of person he wanted to be. He wanted to be strong, not like he was when he was alive.

Do I want to know what happened to me?

He frowned, remembering the other file under his bed. He knew, somehow that it would say that he was a weakling and a coward. Boring in Life, boring in AfterLife, just like Dadson.

But did it even matter? He knew he needed to remember something important. It was what he had been training to do all year. Resolute, Pete knew that would not be his story and he pushed quitting BASA out of his mind.

Pete got ready for his day before even the first of the early risers started waking up. He brushed his teeth and washed his face and snuck into the study room, his file stuck in between the pages of a textbook.

He was ready to read it. He opened the file and looked at the black-and-white picture of a small, mousy boy with a version of his face. He was stunned to see that he barely recognized himself.

He studied his picture for a long time. The boy had hollow cheeks and dark-rimmed eyes. He was skinny, underfed. He wouldn't call himself muscular now, but he certainly wasn't so skinny anymore. Lean, he decided was a good word for him. He smiled a little when he compared his arms, so used to climbing and sparring, to the arms of his picture self.

Somewhat satisfied, Pete flipped through the rest of the file. It was very small, with only a few documents in it, including copies of his Death 1A-19 registration form, his school admissions paperwork, and discharge paperwork. But it was the cover document with all of his family's names that he found the most fascinating.

Father: Edwin Green, 54 at time. Mother: Evelyn Green, 46 at time. Sister: Lilly Anne Green, 9 at time.

Pete looked at the pictures of them, and he was hit with an intense feeling that he was forgetting something important. Stare as he might, he couldn't remember his parents or put their faces to any particular memories. Lilly, however, was a different story. He stared at the black-and-white photo knowing that he was staring at the same girl he'd dreamed about and seen around the school, with big brown eyes and shoulder-length brown hair.

Goosebumps crawled up his arms. His sister's life was in danger.

He blinked and there was a flash. *Running—he was running through the woods. He turned to see the little girl running next to him, her pigtails flopping as she ran. She squealed as she tripped on a tree root. Her squeal turned into a scream, and she vanished as her little hands touched the forest floor.*

Another blink and the vision was gone. He sat there breathing heavily, as if he had truly been racing through those woods a second ago. He wiped sweat away from his brow and took a deep breath that, for a moment, smelled like pine needles, moss, and dirt. Pete looked down at his file again.

Cause of Death: Violence.

He read those words over and over again, starting to feel panicked. He thought that reading the file would trigger a useful memory. Something he could use to save her. Instead, he only had more questions, and felt more frustrated than ever. *What am I forgetting?* Death by violence was so vague. Was his sister doomed to his same fate? He looked back at the scrawny boy and wondered what violence he could possibly have been involved in.

Interested parties:

Kenneth Tingsly, 32 at time. Gregory Kraig, 42 at time. Mr. Alan Woodstock, 73 at time.

Interested parties? Pete looked at the names and wondered if they were the ones that led to his violent death. He tried to muster some anger, and when none came, he tried simply to remember them. The name Tingsly did sound vaguely familiar.

He flipped to the next page. There was a short bit about his family's fortune—apparently his parents were quite wealthy. A few paragraphs down held some interesting information on his family history and family tree. Several of his old family members were grayed out with the words Not Located written in free hand. Next to his most recent relative, his father's brother, were the words Not Available. He wondered what would make a person not available. Maybe that meant they had found his uncle, but his uncle did not want to watch over him. Pete found that didn't bother him; in fact, he was happy he'd ended up at this academy.

He shut his file, unsatisfied. He opened it back up to stare one more time at the pictures of his parents and sister for a long while before closing it again.

After a few minutes of staring at the closed brown folder, the edges of his memory produced the profile of a smiling man with pronounced cheekbones and a small mouth decorated by a trim mustache and beard speaking animatedly about stocks. He was talking with a stout man whose face was hidden in shadows. The profile of a beautiful woman stepped into view. When the smiling man whispered something into the woman's ear, the woman laughed melodically. She then turned to look directly at Pete and the memory instantly faded away, but not before he saw her brilliant blue eyes. Eyes like his.

He was surprised at the lurch in his stomach when he saw those eyes. Sadness? Pete didn't think so. Nostalgia was a better word for the feeling. He looked idly at his lock of hair, wondering what the point of it all was. He tucked it back into the small pouch in the folder and closed it.

With a heavy sigh, Pete went into the dorm room to put the file back under his mattress. He paused. A small newspaper clipping was resting on the floor by his foot. He bent to pick it up, unfolding it to a picture of his own smiling face. Heart thudding faster, he sat on his bed, and read:

> Greensburg's own prominent family endured a devastating loss this Saturday. Peter Green, heir to both the Green-Tech Mobile Industries and TGI Inc., was declared dead last Tuesday morning at St. Mary's Pediatric Hospital.
>
> The family, too devastated for further comment, said this was due to of a mysterious illness that had plagued the boy for several months.
>
> "He was too sick to play outside with his friends," the Green's housekeeper shared with *Daily Shade's* reporters.

"He was starting to show signs of recovery," Dr. Sing, the Green's pediatrician for three generations, reported, "but he took a turn for the worse."

Green was declared dead upon arrival Tuesday morning after the Greens' daughter and only remaining child found the boy collapsed on the lawn of their family manor in upstate New York.

Doctors are still baffled by the exact nature of the boy's illness. The family prays for answers in the upcoming autopsy.

Green is survived by his father, Edwin, his mother, Evelyn and younger sister, Lilly.

Pete stared at the article for a long while, feeling a buzzing in his head. Those words hit him like nothing else in his file had.

"Pete, wanna get food?" a voice said. Pete looked up, still holding the clipping, and Charlie paused, frowning.

"Are you crying?" he asked, astonished.

"Something in my eyes." Pete waved away Charlie's concerns and tucked the clipping into one of his school books. "Ready for breakfast?"

Pete followed Charlie to the cafeteria, all the while thinking of his lost family and the big, scared, brown eyes of his sister. *Hang on, Lilly. Hang on.*

CHAPTER 16

THE WITCH'S EXCHANGE

PETE WALKED THROUGH THE HALLWAYS, barely hearing the morning announcements on the overhead speakers.

"Just a friendly reminder," the school announcer chirped cheerfully, "please do not let the lunch ladies outside the school grounds. One ate all of Mr. Timberland's prize chickens and bit the farmer's wife. Thank you and happy Wednesday."

Happy Wednesday, indeed. The classes were dragging, and by midday, Pete was moody and stressed. He just wanted the evening to hurry and come so he could meet the witch. He had this terrible feeling something was going to stop him from getting Dadson's file to her right before it happened.

To top it off, he kept thinking he could see someone or something out of the corner of his eye. Whenever he turned, there was nothing. But every time he was left with a pang of sadness, as though he had lost something important to him, like a child who'd lost a favorite toy.

Finally, after thinking about it all day, Pete realized what was really making him anxious. At lunch, he went to the dorm room and grabbed the book he'd left the newspaper clipping in, along with his file. He still had that nagging itch that there was something he needed to remember, something he'd overlooked. His brain would do the same thing when he was researching for a paper and he had skipped over something important. It would feel like tiny alarm bells going off in his brain until he would go back and reread the whole page. Maybe that was what was happening now?

He pulled out the slip of paper but then, hearing approaching footsteps, he quickly folded the newspaper clipping and put it in his pocket. He then shoved the rest of the file back into one of his textbooks and put the book in his bag. He turned just as a group of his dorm mates walked past him into the bathrooms. Pete decided to find a more private spot to look through the newspaper clipping.

"Where were you?" Charlie asked, his mouth full of food, when Pete caught up to his friends at lunch a few minutes later. Then, not letting him answer, Charlie said, "You're missing my latest war with the Gossip Queens."

"The what?" Pete set his lunch tray down.

Charlie looked hurt and Scoot groaned. "How do you not know about the newspaper article I write?"

"Gossip column, not newspaper article," Scoot corrected.

"Sorry." Pete racked his brain for a time when he'd heard about it. "Not sure I remember you mentioning it. Hey, want my 'slaw?" He offered it to Max.

"What's this?" Scoot picked up a slip of paper from the floor.

Before Pete could stop her, she opened it and frowned. In her hand was the newspaper clipping.

He was not sure why he hadn't wanted his friends to know about the file. He supposed he found it embarrassing. He grabbed for it, but Scoot was too quick. She was looking at him, not like she would tease him, but as though she were worried.

Scoot handed the paper silently to Max, who took it curiously. As his eyes darted across the page, his expression darkened.

Charlie, who could smell an intriguing bit of gossip a mile away, trembled with anticipation.

"I'm a different person now," Pete said defensively when Max didn't say anything.

"Why didn't you tell us about this?" Max asked.

Charlie, unable to wait one second longer, reached over and snatched the paper out of Max's limp hands.

Pete's face was heating. "I didn't want you guys to think that I'm this wuss."

Max looked at Scoot and Pete frowned. Charlie was holding a hand over his mouth. "Did you get the whole file?" he asked in a hushed voice.

"What's the big deal?" Pete was a little nervous now.

"Pete, these are part of your memories."

"Did you touch your hair? Where's the rest of it?" Charlie sounded panicked.

"Yeah." Pete pulled out the boo,k and Charlie grabbed it from him and took out the file. He read it quickly.

Charlie's face paled with worry. "Ooooh. This might be bad."

"I can't believe you did that!" Charlie said for the ten millionth time, twenty minutes later, as they walked back to class.

"I don't get what the big deal is," Pete said, exasperatedly.

"It's historically dangerous." Max looked serious.

"Well, too late." Pete shrugged, though his heart was quickening the more his friends acted so fearful. "I already read my file, so it is done."

Scoot sniffed. "I don't know that I believe all that."

Pete looked over at her, hopefully. She had started off reproachfully when Charlie described how he dramatically burst in on Pete weeping hysterically over the memories of his long lost family. But after Pete had recounted a truer version of the events, her expression had changed to a more thoughtful one.

"What do you mean, you don't believe it? You don't believe in the Howling Dame?" Charlie shot back.

"Elizabeth," Max corrected.

"No one knows who you're talking about when you say that," Charlie retorted.

Max turned to Pete and said in a significant tone, "Lizzy."

Pete looked up. "The Bat's daughter? Wait…is that how she went insane?"

"They teach the Poltergeist Syndrome in my grade," Scoot said. "It seems like more of a scare tactic, though."

"Poltergeists are real. I know you believe in those. So what do you propose makes them go crazy?" Charlie asked.

Max stopped walking and raised a hand. "Pete, there's no denying that getting your memories without a government official present is dangerous, but Scoot is right. It doesn't necessarily mean that you'll go crazy right away. There are a bunch of ways to get turned into a poltergeist—and yes, messing with your memories is one way, but it's more complicated than that."

Scoot said, "Since it's too late and you already read it…."

Max shrugged. "I would say put that away." He pointed to Pete's backpack where the file was hidden. "And if you feel yourself going nuts, then say something. It's not just getting your memories that does it. It's getting your memories and staying here—he pointed around himself—"in Purgatory. This place isn't meant for people to stay here very long. People are supposed to deal with whatever issue they're dealing with and then move on. People who stay longer than that go mad."

"There are people who have lived here for years," Pete shot back.

Max nodded. "Yeah. Sure, some people never deal with their issues. They ignore them, and pretend they're fine."

"The only exceptions are the teachers here," Scott said. "But sometimes not even them. You see how crazy some of them can get. Look at the substitute. She tried to eat you."

Pete frowned but said nothing.

The rest of the school day snailed by. Pete couldn't focus and kept watching the clock. He didn't hear his Death 100 professor asking him a question and earned himself a scolding in front of the entire class.

After his final class, he rushed over to the dorm room to get ready to meet Alexandria that evening. To his surprise, he found that Max and Scoot were coming too.

Charlie held out a new permission slip. "I got them added." Pete nodded and they headed out to meet the cab they had called.

Alexandria was twenty minutes late, which is something that Pete had not expected in spite of Charlie's predictions.

Charlie peered through the darkened shop window. "Hair that beautiful is not sprouted from nothing, not even for a witch. Women need even more hair products than I do." He indicated his thick, wavy hair.

Then, seeing Scoot, he amended, "Well, some women." He turned to her. "You know, a little leave-in conditioner never hurt anyone."

"Is that a challenge?" Scoot asked cheerfully. "I feel like I could hurt someone with a bottle of conditioner."

Charlie tsked, and Max and Pete laughed.

The door opened and the witch, beautiful as ever, stood framed in the doorway. Pete's mouth went dry, and suddenly his tongue wasn't working properly.

"Good morn—good evening," he managed, then added, "Alexandria."

The witch raised a sculpted eyebrow, and Pete felt a little awkward standing on the doorstep. "I have what you asked for."

The witch's eyes widened for a split second, so quickly Pete thought he had imagined it. "We had an agreement." Pete suddenly felt nervous.

The witch held out her hand, and Pete reluctantly handed her Dadson's file. Suddenly, a million doubts crowded his brain. Alexandria had a cold, calculating look that he did not like.

"I must admit, I didn't expect you to find it." The witch smirked a little. There was greed in her eyes as she fingered the pages of the file. "You are a surprising child."

She flipped through the pages for what felt like a long time, and Pete kept waiting, sweat dripping down the back of his neck. Was she going to follow through with her end of the deal? Or would she just screw him over?

He opened his mouth, but Max cut in first. "Thank you for honoring your agreement. This will go lengths toward strengthening your reputation in the Community." The witch looked up at him, her expression unreadable, and Max held her gaze steadily.

When she finally broke the silence, she put on a smile and nodded. "Yes, that was what I was hoping for." Her tone bordered on sarcastic, but still. She walked outside her shop, and the four of them followed, perplexed, as she sat cross-legged in the middle of the street.

They paused when they got within ten feet of her, feeling the air thicken around the seated witch. Pete glanced up and down the street nervously. This would look odd to a passing pedestrian.

Alexandria saw him and scoffed. "This is Purgatory," she said. "No one is awake past nine."

Pete and Max exchanged a look and then looked back at the witch, whose beautiful chestnut hair had begun swirling around her in the windless night. Pete swallowed and took a small step back, his friends doing the same.

He could feel a pressure building in the air around his midsection. The space around the witch started to sizzle and crackle, and soon small sparks were flying around them. The street lamp above them flickered and went out. The lights above the neighboring coffee shop started flickering as well. Pete stared at the witch as she began jerking and twitching from right to left. Her hair started to lengthen and grow weightless, her voice slowly getting louder and louder. He couldn't tell if her eyes were closed because shadows enveloped her face.

Pete actually jumped with a short yelp when he realized what he was seeing. Her face wasn't cast in shadows made by the moonlight or the flashes of her magic, but shadows and things darker than the night were actually moving towards the witch. With each jerk and sway, she absorbed the shadows, pulling them inside her body. With a final shout and twitch, the witch went stock still, and the lights of the coffee shop suddenly flared to life, making them all jump. Toppled cafe tables and chairs lay in a heap behind them.

Alexandria sat stone still for a minute, and they all stood awkwardly a good distance from her on the sidewalk. Pete was about to ask what they should do when the witch slowly turned her head toward them. Pete had a sudden urge to run away but forced himself to stay put.

If that was the kind of magic required to reverse minor inconvenient accidents and small curses, Pete wondered what real dark magic would look like. The witch's eyes were black, irises and all, and she wore a smile that made him wonder if she was considering cutting open his stomach so she could play with his organs.

Charlie broke the silence. "Well. I will need the names of the hair products you use."

The witch snorted and stood to walk back to her shop. "Good night, children." Her husky voice made Pete blush.

He forced himself to peel his gaze away from the retreating figure of the hazel-eyed woman, feeling Scoot's eyes boring into the side of his head.

"Well, hopefully we didn't just double-curse the school," Pete murmured so Charlie couldn't hear.

Max shook his head. "I'm no expert, but it looked like things were flying away from the school." He turned. "Wait, where did our cab go?"

CHAPTER 17

ALL HALLOWS' EVE

UMMER HAD LONG SINCE ABANDONED them. The days had gotten colder, shorter, and windier, and several nights it snowed and melted as soon as the sun rose. But nothing quite convinced Pete that it was fall like the wild anticipation of Halloween.

Pete had far from forgotten about the second part of his mission, but it was just so easy to get swept up in the buzz. The school had been elaborately decorated. There were all the usual things, like jack-o'-lanterns and skeletons and black cats. But there was also the Hall of a Hundred Pumpkins, which was exactly what the name suggested—rows and rows of pumpkins of all shapes and sizes that had been expertly carved or painted and stuffed in the entrance of the school.

Every night, starting on the twenty-first of October, hundreds of bats swarmed the sky, and each morning thousands of black crows swirled and landed in the trees of the school and the woods across the street. Oddly enough, fairies, too, started congregating nearby.

Pete had gotten a shock one night, heading to his BASA practice when he was suddenly swarmed by hundreds of tiny, noisy lights. One had stayed still long enough for Pete to make out its tiny humanoid shape before another bit him hard on the ear.

"Ouch!" He swiped at his ear. The fairies had not liked that at all. The swarm had turned nasty, and suddenly, he was being bitten by all of those tiny lights.

He had made it to practice a few minutes late with about a hundred tiny cuts all over his body. Fortunately, the fairies preferred the tops of the trees, and he didn't have too many problems with them again. He even started to appreciate how nice they looked, but it took several days before he could look at them without flinching.

Ghouls were invited to the school and roamed the halls along with live skeletons and even a couple of giants. Typically, it was only for a few hours and usually only during the weekends, but it was enough to make the students mad with anticipation.

"A couple of years ago, they brought in Polynesian Demon Dancers." Charlie was practically jumping as he said this. "I hope they bring them back. They were unbelievable."

The Demon Dancers, Pete learned, were a group of four-legged Silo-Demons that spit fire while they danced.

Unsurprisingly, Halloween at the academy was a huge holiday where the children enjoyed a long period free of school and homework, beginning on Friday the twenty-fourth. Pete cheered along with his classmates when his final class ended. However, his celebration was cut short when he realized how much more he needed to prepare for his final mission.

He used his free week to train harder than ever. The closer to Halloween it got, the more his nerves heightened. He pinpointed all the mistakes during his first mission and how very wrong things could have gone had he not been so lucky.

Charlie entered the study room of the dorms and huffed. "There you are. I've been looking all over for you. It's bad enough I can't spend Halloween with you, Scoot, or Max, but I can't spend the week with you either?"

Scoot, Max, and Peter had let Charlie know they all had mission assignments Halloween night and would be occupied for the most part. They had promised to check in on him. Charlie had been upset at first, but being a very popular boy, he had made arrangements to hang out with other people that very same night.

Pete set down with a sigh the book he was holding . "I'm sorry, Charlie. I'm just so behind." He found he was clenching his jaw and relaxed it.

"On what?" And then not waiting for an answer, he said with a sly look, "Well, that is too bad." He paused artfully and then added, in a forced casual sort of way, "Alex was asking about you."

That made Pete pause. Alex. His face grew hot. "Oh?" He tried to sound casual. "Really?" He picked at his jeans. "What did she say?" He cursed when he realized his jeans had morphed into his striped pajamas.

Charlie held back his laugh. "You can ask her yourself if you come to one of the activities. Ah, come on. You've practiced enough. You need a break."

Halloween was three days away, but against his better judgment, Pete allowed Charlie to drag him away from his book and out to the bustling school. It was fortunate too. Pete learned a lot as he munched on caramel popcorn. For instance, he learned that he was required to have a suit and needed to reserve it for the masquerade ball after the Halloween Parade. Charlie got his measurements and helped him reserve the suit, and then immediately made him get a caramel apple with him.

"There's always a parade," Charlie said, excited, "and before that, there are a ton of activities."

As Pete chatted with Charlie, he started to understand what Coach Skinley had told everyone a few weeks earlier when he warned them not to get too focused honing their skills and forget to be a part of life.

"There is nothing more obvious," Coach had said, "than a spy who forgets what it's like to be a normal citizen. The job requires you to blend in. You can't do that if you forget how normal people live their lives."

Pete spent the rest of the day both awkwardly attempting to talk to Alex and her red-headed friend Alice and learning all he could about the activities of the thirty-first.

A couple of days later, he picked up his suit and spent that evening tailoring it to his needs. His sewing skills were minimal, and he was genuinely worried that he might lose something out of the shabby hidden pockets he had constructed. He made a note to give this skill more effort in the future, but for now, it would have to do. Tomorrow was the big day.

He walked outside Halloween morning before the sun rose, standing in the chilly wind. Though the cold was muted just like everything else there, he still found himself shivering. He suspected the shiver was more from nerves.

He looked up at the moon. If Pete weren't mistaken, there seemed to be a bit of an orange tint to it. Fog lingered on the ground around the courtyard trees. A small breeze rustled their leaves.

Overall, it was a beautiful Tuesday morning. He sat down on a nearby bench and watched the sun rise. It had become a favorite tradition of his of late. When he found the time to sit and watch the sunrise, his days seemed to go a little better.

He smiled when the first rays of the sun touched his face. He let them warm his cheeks, though it didn't do much against the chill of the morning. He let a breath out and watched the puff of air form and immediately dissipate. Then, with a quick stretch, he got up to prepare for his day.

That turned out to be a bit more difficult than he anticipated. Pete couldn't remember having so much fun. People awoke and immediately started setting off fireworks.

This woke up Charlie. Pete tried to convince him to come find breakfast with him, but Charlie, thick with sleep, insisted upon primping for the day. So Pete left him and went to get some food.

The celebration had started well before everyone was awake. Men walked around on stilts, their faces painted, dressed up in pinstriped suits and juggling pins. Others blew fire, and clowns walked around doing magic and playing silly tricks on people. Max nearly got squirted in the face by a flower button on a tall, skinny clown with blue shoes, but Scoot moved him out of the way in time.

"I didn't want to hear him crying about his face being wet," she explained as she, Max, and Pete all made their way across the grounds to get breakfast. Pete laughed, then almost immediately tripped over something firm and small. Luckily, he looked down just in time to see the tiny creature standing there.

"Wow!" He stopped short and swung his arms wildly.

His face came down to meet the creature's face as he rocked on his heels and toes until he steadied himself. It was no more than a foot tall, standing squat and scowling. The creature didn't move any part of its body. It had no neck, a very large head, as wide as the rest of his squat body, and was wearing a black suit with a red lapel. Its long, thin nose curled under its chin, and its nostrils were thin slits.

When Pete leaned over the creature, he saw that it had long gray hairs clustered just over its thin worm-like lips. It had no eyelids or irises, only large black pupils.

Those pupils turned towards Pete and the creature's scowl seemed to deepen. The only indication that it even noticed him.

"Um, uh, excuse me." Pete frowned.

It said nothing.

"Okay. Have a good one," he said lamely and moved to catch up to where Max was waiting for him.

"What was that?" Pete asked quietly as they continued to the cafeteria.

Max screwed up his face in thought. "Well, I forget the tribe and precise species, but they are kin to Mountain Ghouls. They tend to like the fog, which is probably why this is still hanging around." He nodded, indicating the thickening fog around the trees.

"Oh." Pete eyed another unmoving creature in the courtyard.

Max looked over at the other ghouls they were passing. "Actually, I bet they were hired to help with the magic for the parade."

"I see," Pete lied.

Later that morning, the air exploded with bright bursts of light. Even though it was sunny outside, the colors lit up the sky with bursts of orange, purple, and blue. They didn't look like fireworks but like snakes of light. Pete had never seen anything like it before.

The lights danced and exploded in the sky for a good ten minutes and ended with several orange lights shaped like a pumpkin. Appreciative hoots and whistles went out from the kids who had stopped to watch the display.

Around ten in the morning, trucks pulled through the wrought-iron gate and began parking. Men in uniforms pulled out tents and began setting up. On the dirt road, policemen and workers set road blocks. Pete didn't know why they bothered; hardly any cars ever went down that road. Still, the men worked away and a small group of kids gathered, watching their progress and talking excitedly.

Pete had never seen so many kids outside before. They were gathered in clusters, laughing, eating, and gesturing around at the different displays, which had multiplied overnight.

Pete noticed something climbing on the wall of the school and jumpted. It took him less than three seconds to notice that the *thing* was not alone.

"What is that?" Pete asked Max, as he squinted at the wall.

"Hm?" Max looked around, at Pete, then up at the school. "Huh." There were about a dozen six-legged creatures shaped like giant green scorpions.

Nearly camouflaged by the green vines, they scuttled along the face of the building, pausing every once in a while, just to continue once more.

"Oh." Recognition laced Max's voice. "That's so cool. I think those are... what are they called?" He closed his eyes and tilted his head back. "I can't even think; I'm so distracted about tonight."

Pete almost gasped. For a solid hour, he had not thought one time about the mission he would be doing later that night. He swallowed and nodded, a sudden knot forming in his stomach.

"I can't remember what they are officially called, but people call them Crawlers. There are a ton of them in the Port District next to Purgatory, and they are very cheap laborers because the exchange rate is so good."

Pete looked blankly at Max who said, "Exchange rate. You know, with money?"

"Oh, yes, of course. So what are they doing? You said they're workers?"

Max nodded. "Usually. I mean, that's broad to say of an entire species, but they're, like, crazy strong and crazy fast and they're known for being excellent builders. But I can't imagine what they would be doing to the school."

He watched them curiously. "I'd like to visit their world. They are famous for having crazy cool architecture. It's insane. There are all these intricate buildings—I saw a picture once. It looked like all the buildings were carved out of bones." Max bit into a sticky-sweet bun that he had picked up from a Sweets and Treats table in the courtyard.

Charlie was still busy getting ready. When Pete went to check on him, he found him surrounded by at least seven girls. Pete blushed and waved shyly at Alex, not looking directly at her. He was surprised to learn that Scoot had been bullied into helping Charlie get ready. Apparently, she and Alex were the only two girls who were strong enough to clasp his costume together.

Max and Pete left a scowling Scoot to go walk around and see all the attractions. Carnival rides had been erected the night before. A massive Ferris wheel spun on the far side by the girl's dorm, near where the brick wall and the wrought-iron wall met. On the side of the spider-shaped fountain where they were standing, workers were manning a bungee-type ride. Pete could hear screaming behind them as they made their way to the back of the school.

A small roller coaster was set up by their dorms. They paused to watch six kids whip around the twists and turns, screaming in terrified delight.

Grinning, they continued past, wanting to see everything there was to do before settling on which line they wanted to stand in first. The line for the roller coaster wrapped around the back of the school.

They cut through the line and walked towards the maze. Pete whistled as he glimpsed the heads of men on stilts going through the maze and even the tops of different animals wandering around, occasionally sprinting forward. A banner hung over the entrance: ENTER AT YOUR OWN RISK!

As he walked away, he heard the unmistakable trumpet of an elephant from deep inside the maze.

Mr. Shashea was supervising rides being given on Billy, the massive spider mascot, but it didn't seem to be going well. Mr. Shashea kept screaming and throwing the lead rope, and it looked like Billy was confused as to what to do. After about five minutes, the spider just scuttled up the wall of the school and disappeared behind a balcony. The kids riding him were dumped unceremoniously to the grassy ground.

When Coach Skinley came to yell at Pete's history teacher for losing the mascot, Max and Pete, laughing, turned to explore the rest of the fairgrounds.

"I could read it in his eyes, Greg," Mr. Shashea yelled back. "He wanted to eat me!"

A Haunted Hayride was set up just past the entrance to the maze and looked to wrap around to the back of it, taking up the better part of the grassy area behind the school. It was hard to tell because the stacks of hay made a makeshift wall, barring any sight of what was behind it.

Signs that said, Be a Human Again! Spooky Ghosts, and Ghouls! and Scariest Haunted Hayride in Purgatory! hung on the hay wall.

"Well, that's not saying much," Max observed, reading the last sign. He turned to Pete and shrugged. "Still, could be fun."

Pete studied the rest of the rides and other attractions. Booths were set up all over. Kids and workers alike were dressed in costumes. There was a ton to do, and Pete shrugged and grinned. "Sure, why not." He moved to stand in the short line.

As soon as they walked through the entrance of the hayride's makeshift wall, the sun, already dim, suddenly darkened even more.

"What the…?" Pete scanned the area. Outside, the ride had been bright and cheerful. Inside, however, with the lack of light and the thick fog, the ride felt remarkably spooky. All the chatter and laughter of the mingling kids and the shouts of glee from other rides were snuffed out. Instead, Pete could hear odd slithering noises and the skittering of insects and the caw of an occasional crow.

It looked like they had stumbled into a swampland. Max and Pete grinned nervously at each other and climbed aboard the back of the trailer hitched to the tractor. The trailer looked custom made with wooden benches built along its perimeter.

The driver, a portly man in overalls with no shirt, scowled at them. He chewed on a wheat stem and his shockingly high-pitched voice did not match his six-foot-five stature. "All right now, kids. No dawdling. Mind the steps."

Max had to stifle a snicker, and Pete thought his ribs would crack from the effort of suppressing his laughter. They sat down on one side of the trailer, next to four giggling girls. Five boys sat on the other side, all trying to look nonchalant.

"It's supposed to be super-scary," said a girl with braces to no one in particular.

"Yeah," agreed a chubby girl with red hair and freckles. "Maddy said she peed herself."

"I said," corrected the ponytailed girl on the other side of Braces with a lisp—she paused and pulled out her retainer, drooling slightly. "I said I almost peed myself. Oh hi, Pete." She blushed.

"Wha—uh, oh hi," he sputtered. "How are you? Happy Halloween." He was alarmed at being recognized. He tried not to stare blankly at the girl, trying to figure out how he knew her.

One of her friends snorted. "Maddy is such a brat. You don't actually know her," the girl with braces said. Pete sighed with relief and laughed.

"She learns random people's names and then pretends to know them to see how long they'll pretend to know her back."

Maddy snickered. "With the polite kids, it lasts a while." She shrugged. "That's how I met some of these guys." She grinned mischievously, playing with the retainer in her mouth. She was a tall, pretty brunette, wearing white shorts and a T-shirt even with the cold.

The boys on the other side of the ride began laughing and telling stories. The subject of the stories, a short boy with a pointed chin and short, brown hair, dark eyes and a few freckles on his cheeks, grinned with embarrassment.

He shrugged. "She got so much information about me and kept talking about science class. I sit in the front so, I dunno, she might sit in the back. How was I supposed to know?"

Maddy laughed. "We've been friends ever since."

Pete laughed along, enjoying the friendly atmosphere. A few exchanged names, which he immediately forgot.

The laughing and joking broke momentarily when the roar of the tractor started up again and the high-pitched voice of their host called out, "Now, now, kids. Don't be scared."

That was it. The combination of his squealing voice, the relaxed mood, and the funny stories was enough to send Pete and Max into hysterics. The rest joined in, not able to help it. As the tractor moved them along, the laughter turned into a yelp from Max, and to Pete's dismay, a high-pitched squeal from himself.

A ghost flew through the bottom of the trailer floor and shook it wildly. Fortunately, his girly scream was drowned out by the screams of their four female companions, and a couple of shouts from the boys.

The vibration of the trailer caused the tractor to swerve violently, sending some of the girls sprawling on the opposite side of the trailer. Some of the boys looked rather pleased by this sudden turn of events, especially the boy who caught Maddy.

Pete, who had been a little envious of the boy, was quickly distracted when a massive snake slammed into the side of the tractor, hissing and spitting. The jolt seemed to stall the tractor, which started whining and whirling. The huge snake took advantage of the impaired tractor and reared and slammed its pale yellow face repeatedly into the door of the tractor, trying to get at the driver. The driver yelled and swatted at the air in the direction of the snake.

"How did you get in here?" the driver squealed. "Jimmy? Jimmy! Come help me!"

"Go, you idiot!" Pete yelled. The snake turned towards him, and Pete was suddenly ready to throw all the girls in front of the snake to keep it away from him. He fell backward on the floor of the trailer, scrambling to get away, knocking over two bales of hay.

Max followed, waving his arms in a wild panic, smacking Pete hard in the face by accident.

Had Mrs. Pennyfeather found out Pete was the one wandering the halls late that night? How had he been so stupid? The snake reared back for another strike, but the screams coming from the trailer drew her attention, and she hissed and spat and lunged for the trailer. Suddenly, the trailer gave a violent lurch forward, and the snake delivered a glancing blow to the trailer, making it tip wildly.

The screams were cut short by an ear-shattering howl, and Pete's nightmare became complete. Werewolves. There was no way Pete would ever forget that sound.

Max, who was hyperventilating next to him, was saying over and over again, "How do the teachers know? How did they find out?"

Pete watched in horrified fascination as the snake, who had geared up to chase the tractor, was pummeled by a massive black wolf. The loud hissing was cut short. The angry snake wrapped herself around the thrashing form of the wolf. She squeezed and struck and struck again. The howls and snarls turned to yelps and cries.

"No!" Pete yelled. He lunged forward to jump out of the trailer, but Max grabbed him.

"No! Are you crazy?" Max shouted over the screams of the wolf.

"She's gonna kill him!" Pete desperately slapped at Max to let him go. But before he could make a move, the tractor sped on, and then suddenly they were completely drenched in darkness. Just as quickly as the dark had come, the bright light of day and the sounds of the festival filled his ears. Pete blinked at the sun in shocked confusion.

"Well, now you can say you've been spooked at the hayride," the driver said cheerfully. "It was good, huh?" He grinned down at the eleven shell-shocked teenagers.

"Wha—?" Maddy trembled. "No. No, that was different from last time."

The driver climbed out of his seat in the tractor. "It's different every time you go. You get nearly twenty different experiences."

He walked around to the back of the trailer as he spoke and opened the back for them to dismount. Pete realized he had tears running down his face and wiped them away hastily.

He stepped shakily down from the trailer and looked at Max. They just stood there looking at each other for a long moment and then simultaneously burst into wild, hysterical laughter. The rest of the kids joined in with their own shaky laughs.

One of the kids was hunched over, pointing at his friend. "Dude, you were so scared!"

"You screamed louder than I did!" he shot back.

One of the girls even poked fun at Pete. "Did you see him fall to the floor?"

Pete laughed until his sides hurt and walked through the landing space towards the exit signs, still wiping his eyes. There were other kids, all looking similarly frazzled and exchanging stories as they walked under a concrete overpass with an exit sign above it.

As he passed through the tunnel-like exit, Pete overheard a worker dressed in a uniform, the word Manager clearly imprinted over her breast pocket, lecturing a small creature with a row of massive, sharp teeth. She held a clipboard and used it to gesture angrily. "You are not actually supposed to eat any of the kids—just pretend. How many times am I supposed to tell you that? That girl you bit had to go to the nurse's office. Who knows if the nurse is even in today?"

Pete frowned slightly as he walked past the growling creature. He wondered if that was part of the ride still. By Max's look of apprehension, he must be wondering the same thing.

They waved their goodbyes to their companions and walked out of the hayride. As Pete stepped out of the vicinity of the hayride, something bright orange dropped down in front of him so fast it was a blur. He threw out his hands on instinct and caught it.

"Egh!" Pete exclaimed when he realized what he was holding. The lanky form of a girl dropped down in front of him, and Scoot grabbed her head from Pete's hands and wedged it onto her shoulders, turning it to face Pete.

"That's quite a scream you have." She smirked.

"Where did you come from?" Pete turned and looked up at empty air. "Wait. what happened to the tunnel?"

"It's a glamour." Scoot indicated he should take a couple steps backward.

He did and gasped. The open concrete exit appeared with straw-strewn ground. It looked like the wide opening that football players ran through to get onto the field.

"Did you think it was really made of straw?" she teased.

"I've seen weirder things," Pete said flatly.

Scoot nodded. "Fair enough. Charlie wants to make his grand appearance."

Pete examined the glamour on the building, stepping in and out of it, watching in fascination as the building appeared and disappeared. "Wow."

She pinched him hard and he yelped. "Ouch! What was that for?"

"Charlie. Costume. Big entrance. Come on, let's get this over with." She indicated they should follow. "He can only walk about ten feet in the thing, so he needs you to stand closer to the dorms."

Both Max and Pete laughed. "Okay, yeah." Max shrugged. "I could use my jacket."

They made their way back to the dorms, the shock of the ride already fading from their minds.

Pete grabbed a caramel apple from a smiling woman with realistic wings that fluttered every once in a while. He bit into the apple, and strange flavors exploded in his mouth.

Max noticed his expression and opened his mouth in excitement. "Hey, where did you get that? I love angel apples!" He turned back and ran after the woman, who was now floating a few feet above the ground.

"Is that a real angel?" Pete asked when Max returned, biting into his apple. He shook his head side to side as if to say *kinda*.

"She looks like she is only half-angel." Max looked back. "The full ones are...uh...scary-looking."

Scoot nodded. "Yeah, they're pretty vicious. Most are warriors or avengers. A few are non-violent...ish."

Pete glanced nervously back at the stunningly pretty woman with the sweet smile and wondered if she was one of the "non-violent-ish" ones.

CHAPTER 18

THE DEAD PARADE

THEY REACHED THE DORM ROOM, and Scoot ordered them to wait outside as she ran in. Max, shivering, told her to hurry up. When the door opened again, Pete yelled out loud.

Fortunately, that was precisely the reaction Charlie had been looking for, and he grinned triumphantly. Max's mouth fell open.

"How is it that every year you manage to shock and surprise me?" Max asked.

Pete asked, "How are you even standing upright?"

An angry grunt from somewhere behind Charlie's big costume said, "He's not!"

Both Pete and Max walked around the side of Charlie's costume and looked at a sweaty and straining Scoot. She was pushing against Charlie, trying to hold him upright. Both boys knew better than to offer to help her, nodded their hellos, and walked back around to admire the front.

Charlie stood in a ten-foot tall costume that was about a foot thick. The gleaming metal was bedazzled by about a million fake gemstones. All of the gems were clear except those in the center, which were purple and formed the letter C. It was difficult to look directly at Charlie, because of the reflection of the sun, making its slow descent in the sky and gleaming blindingly off his suit. A thousand laserbeams shot directly from the costume into Pete's eyes.

Pete suspected that had been planned. He glanced over at Max, who had produced sunglasses from nowhere.

Charlie was wearing a box-shaped helmet. He looked like a glammed-up Transformer.

"Well, Charlie," Max said, "per usual, you did not disappoint."

Charlie blushed and giggled. "It is epic, isn't it?"

"No," Scoot growled unhappily from behind.

"She kids." Charlie waved his hands airily. "But seriously, it's amazing, right?"

They assured him that it was until there was a grunt of annoyance and then Scoot ninja-rolled from behind Charlie. They watched Charlie's face comically morph in slow motion from triumphant to confused to concerned, and finally to terrified as he toppled backward.

Scoot stood up, brushing grass off her pants as the other six girls rushed over and fretted over Charlie.

"So that's enough of that." She rubbed the dirt off her hands.

Pete tried not to laugh, knowing Charlie would probably try to murder him if he did, and looked over the shoulder of one of the girls. "You need help?"

Two of the girls shooed Pete away.

"Okay, okay." He put his hands up. "Catch you later."

A couple of hours later, they met up with Charlie, still shockingly bedazzled, but now in a normal-sized maroon suit.

"You look…bright," Pete said.

Charlie nodded. "Well, sometimes you have to sacrifice fabulousity for practicality." He sounded like a martyr. Pete doubted that he would have called wearing a suit to a festival practical, but he knew better than to say anything.

They hung outside all day, only taking breaks to run inside for an extra coat or to use the restroom. He was surprised by how much Charlie's girlfriends had to use the bathroom, and they all seemed to move together in one cohesive pack.

After about the fourth time, Pete asked, "So, do they all go at the same time? Or do they just hang out inside the bathroom when only one of them has to use it?"

"Who knows?" Max said, fascinated.

"You should learn about girls during your historical research missions. I think they qualify as an interesting species."

The day continued, and they rode all the rides, the hayride getting several repeat visits, each one scarier than the last. The good times lasted well into the dark. They enjoyed several corndogs and a couple more Angel Apples and some pie. Before Peter knew it, it was almost time for the parade to start.

"We only have an hour to get ready!" Charlie exclaimed. Pete looked at him in the moonlight, not sure if he was being serious, but several of the girls frantically checked their watches.

"What do you mean? Aren't you ready already?" Pete asked.

Charlie scoffed. "One does not wear *this* to the masquerade." He was deadly serious.

Pete looked at his watch and sighed. Why did his wristwatches keep breaking? He was annoyed. This was the sixth one he had replaced in as many weeks.

Charlie waddled anxiously inside the dorms. Max stood next to Pete and they looked at each other.

"We could use this time to get ready," Pete said slowly.

Max nodded. "Yeah, well…good luck," he said.

Pete opened his mouth to reply but found his throat was suddenly too dry to respond. Scoot nodded at them and Max nodded back, and Pete knew that they understood exactly how he was feeling.

He watched them leave, standing outside the dorms for a long while before heading inside. It took him about three minutes to get ready. He did not understand how it could possibly take Charlie much longer.

"What is he even doing?" Pete asked no one in particular.

Charlie had charmed two of his girlfriends back into the dorms to help him assess his evening garb. They fussed over him, both of them dressed in long, elegant ball gowns.

"I still have to get ready, you know," the blonde one in yellow complained.

"Honestly," Pete said. "What more does she need to do? What does *he* still need to be doing?"

Red, nearby tying his shoes, considered for a moment, then answered as though Pete had not just asked a rhetorical question. "Analyzing."

Pete paused and looked at Red, puzzled. "What?"

Red put down his shoe, then pulled up his other shoe and began pulling his laces together. "Analyzing." He looped the laces together. "It takes about two to three hours to pick an outfit. There is a lot of analysis required for said outfit. Then, from what I understand, it takes about five to eleven girls to reanalyze it from there. Then it takes about ten minutes of distracted dressing, then another two to three hours of analysis once the outfit is on. I know because I had to try to sleep through it."

Pete snorted and Red chuckled, shaking his head. He went back to his shoes.

It felt good to laugh like that. It made Pete feel brave, and it was a good distraction from thinking about his upcoming mission.

He looked at his watch and nodded to himself. He set his shoulders. It was time to go. He had hoped to walk with Charlie, but he supposed it was better this way. He had never been to the parade or the ball and didn't know what to expect. Plus, things went a little different every year. But for the most part, certain areas were always blocked off from students, and it was in one of these areas that he needed to get his mission orders.

He looked at Charlie and called out to him, "I'm heading over now. I'll meet up with you when you're done.

"How will I find—" Charlie began, pouting.

"Charlie." Pete looked at the ridiculous thing Charlie was wearing. "You are wearing a white glow-in-the-dark suit equipped with functioning lights. I will find you."

With that, he turned and walked out of the dorms with a snickering Red at his heels. Red waved his goodbyes and ran to meet a small group of people hanging out in the courtyard.

The sun, long gone, had been replaced by the large, orange moon. That, coupled with thousands of fairies lights and hundreds of lanterns hanging from trees, made it so that Pete had no problem finding his way to the crowded street.

The lanterns cast an eerie glow in the thick fog gathering by the base of the tree trunks, which Pete was careful to avoid. Though there were still the noises of the fair going on and Pete could see the roller coaster chugging along with screaming kids, he could also hear distinct sounds of workers breaking down their stations.

Pete looked down at his three-piece suit and then at the crowd of very casual dressers. He frowned. Red had changed into his suit as well, but they both seemed to be some of the few. Had Pete changed too early? He didn't want to stand out.

Still, the parade was about to start. He didn't have time to go back and change. The brick part of the wall blocked his view of the street. As he moved closer, he understood why the parade was at night—to make the bright lights of the floats that much more mesmerizing.

"Wow!"

Loud music was playing, and Pete jumped when he recognized the tune of the old marching ballad that Coach Skinley would occasionally play while they were sparring.

Pete knew this was his window. He looked around. He needed to find the handoff spot. The instructions he'd been given said to "meet the masked man at the marching place with the water."

Pete walked quickly, almost running. Maddy and some of her friends were gathered around a bench by the entrance to the school. The gates were opened wide and adorned with orange and purple string lights. Bats perching upside down on the wrought-iron fence occasionally opened and closed their wings.

"Hey!" Maddy yelled out, making the boy who was resting his head in her lap jolt up. Annoyed, he glared at Pete as though it was his fault.

"Uh, hey! Hi!" He waved, not slowing down.

"It's just the intro stuff, the real parade doesn't start for another twenty minutes. You don't have to run."

Pete ran past her. He yelled over his shoulder, "Gotta meet someone," before diving into the crowd.

The entire town had made it out to watch the parade. Men, women, boys, and girls of all ages were standing and sitting or resting on shoulders of their parents, all trying to get a good view of the dirt road where the floats were making their way down.

Okay, he'd found the marching song. This song, painfully long and annoying during sparring practice, seemed to be playing at a much faster pace now. It was probably the same pace, Pete reckoned, but since it was a ticking timer, it felt like it might end at any moment.

He shouldered his way through the crowd to the edge of the street. The entire road, as far as Pete could see, was lit. There were massive torches erected, lining the borders of the school. The trees of the neighboring woods were full of twinkling lights that darted and moved around. Hundreds of thousands of fairies gathered, thickly swarming the trees and bushes, watching the festivities.

Ghouls in suits lined both sides of the street, standing still and emanating a soft, peach-colored glow of their own. Occasionally a ribbon of misty light would flutter from the creatures and dissipate into the night sky.

Then, there was the parade itself. If this was the warm-up act, the main parade would be something to behold. There were fire jugglers and trapeze artists on massive, twenty-foot floats. The first float was adorned with thousands of twinkling lights. They changed colors, reflecting off the shiny suits of the trapeze artists. The float on its heels had a giant balloon jester, and behind that a massive balloon king. The gentle breeze seemed to be doing a number on the workers, who strained to manage the huge balloons.

A part of Pete's mind registered how cool it all was. But the bigger, anxious part of his mind only saw the huge crowd. Never, since he had first come here a few months back, had he seen this many people. There had to be more people here than lived in the entire town. He wondered in sheer annoyance where they had all come from, as he wove and darted through spectators, occasionally standing on tip toes to look over their heads. The floats were making their way slowly past the school. He swept his gaze past them and then jerked his head sharply.

There! That had to be it. He doubled back the way he had come. The float he needed had already passed the school! He cursed and began running through the crowd. He got some yells of protest as he wove frantically through the crowd. He caught up to the float, panting, and looked around.

Okay... now what?

The float, a giant blue thing with fake waves automated to move in a repetitive circle, had human-sized balloons of fish lazily floating in front of the waves. A few attendants in black spandex wore bright orange, blue, and yellow fish costumes. One of them wore a costume of an orange fish with black markings around its eyes.

He squinted at it. Could that be the mask? The fishes danced around in a pattern, and Pete positioned himself to stand within touching distance of the masked fish. He crossed his arms over his chest and looked directly at it.

He tried to slow down his breathing, but his heart remained pounding out of his chest. It wasn't because he was out of breath. He was in good shape from his BASA training over the last couple of months. It was his nerves that were the problem. He was taking a risk that might cost him the entire mission. But his time was running out. The last few chords of the song were playing and he was standing here, still waiting for an oversized fish to hand him his orders.

The fish spun expertly, swinging his back fin so that it nearly swiped Pete off his feet. He ducked with a yelp at the last second. The fin swished over his hair and when Pete was down he felt something land on his hands. Without pausing, Pete tucked it inside his jacket pocket. He was helped up by some of the laughing crowd.

"Wow, careful there, sonny." A laughing man grabbed Pete's shoulders and helped him to stand. "You were standing a bit close to the rope, huh." He laughed heartily, slapping Pete's back.

Pete forced a laugh. "Thanks!" He pushed back through the crowd and scanned the area. When he was sure no one was watching him, he pulled the package out of his coat pocket.

It was small, about the size of a fist. Inside were only two things: a rock and a slip of paper. He was relieved that he didn't have to decode anything or solve a riddle. It was a straightforward mission—and yet he found himself staring at the typed words as though they were an unsolvable riddle. The slip of paper had only one short sentence: To GET THE NEXT PACKAGE, POP THE JESTER.

Pop the jester? Was his coach mad? Pop the jester! Of course that crazy skeleton would think of that. How on earth was he supposed to do that without getting caught? The man had given him no time either. The balloon was only a few floats back.

He stared up as the doomed balloon made its way towards his position. His mind went stubbornly blank. His months of training and preparing were for naught as he stared, his brain unresponsive.

Annoyance and frustration coursed through him, and he could feel the sweat forming on his face. This jacket was weighing him down—he wanted to take it off. He cursed himself for bringing so much stuff but then paused, feeling his heart lighten slightly.

He laughed out loud. He brought his stuff! Duh. Of course. He patted his jacket and touched the hard spot where one of his knives was resting.

Pete's hands shook slightly and his mouth went dry. He studied the balloon and traced a path to where it would be when the float reached his spot. Then he spotted Shelly across the road, staring directly at him.

What had she seen? Pete did not like the look she was giving him. She was staring at him like she was expecting him to do something.

Pete could have kicked himself. In his rush to meet his first mark, he had forgotten all his evasion techniques. He was now on the radar of a known enemy. Everything he had done up until this point must've seemed suspicious.

He bit his lip, thinking. She was on the opposite side of the parade. There wasn't much she could do to him right now. If she chose to give him issues later, he would have to deal with that then. Right now, he needed to keep moving forward with the mission.

Okay. How to do this? He watched the balloon coming. He had to make it so that, when he did what he needed to do, she wouldn't have a clear view. She could guess, but it would only be a guess.

He judged the distance the balloon would be once it moved in front of him. Missing at that distance was not a concern. Thanks to his training, he was highly skilled with his knives.

Part one was easy. Pop the balloon. But how was he supposed to dart into the street and pick up his package? Who knew where it would land. And how could he do that without being noticed? He sighed. He would just have to try. He couldn't see any other way around it.

As the jester balloon made its way slowly to him, Pete stayed light on his feet. If he did decide to do this for a living, he would need to make special shoes that looked fancy but were actually made for running and climbing. These were starting to give him blisters.

Studying the swelling crowd, he frowned. There were thousands of people around him, all laughing and pointing. Men and women on stilts walked through the crowd handing out candy. Families, some with small children riding on the shoulders of their mothers and fathers, watched the parade with excitement. He felt the knife in his pocket and couldn't help but feel guilty at disappointing the laughing kids.

Would popping the jester ruin the parade for them? And for what? What good would it do?

Pete thought about what would happen if he didn't pop it. He would get kicked out of BASA next semester. He thought of nights without sparring lessons. He thought about how it felt to belong to the club. He looked back at the school, at the wrought-iron gates. He thought of how proud he had been to climb the fence and how far he had come since then.

Setting his jaw, he turned to watch the jester move in front of him. With swift and well-practiced hands, he grabbed the knife and sent it flying directly at the balloon.

The jester didn't just pop—it exploded. A massive confetti bomb went off in the middle of the parade. Shouts of surprise rang from both the crowd and the staff when hundreds of small candies and confetti pieces dropped from where the balloon had been floating only moments before.

Pete's mouth opened in fascination as the crowd surged forward to grab the candy from the streets. Hidden in the storm of confetti and dim light, Pete saw a small package floating to the ground under a black parachute. Grinning, he ran with the crowd to rush in and grab it.

Pete had a moment of panic when the wind pushed the parachute away from him. He elbowed his way through and leaped to grab the package. His fingers closed around it—and suddenly all of the breath was knocked from his lungs by something very hard and solid.

He crumpled in on himself and slammed onto the dirt road. Over the swelling of the crowd, he could hear whistles of policemen trying to corral the crowd. Pete felt at least twenty pairs of feet kick and step on him.

Thick hands closed around the package, and Pete looked up in horror as Shelly Grant grabbed the small box out of his hands.

Without thinking, without even grabbing so much as a breath of air, Pete kicked his leg out and cleanly swept Shelly's legs from under her. Her triumphant grin changed to stunned surprise as she fell hard on her back.

Shelly was a boulder of a girl, built like a linebacker. She was not made to do gymnastics in a crowd of candy-grabbing maniacs. Pete, however, was built to do just that. He leaped nimbly back to his feet, snatched up the box and disappeared into the crowd.

But, Pete had been rocked by her punch. He felt dizzy and had trouble standing up straight. Had she chosen to hit him in the face, he would have been out of commission for the night. That could have been disastrous. But he had been lucky. He doubted he would be lucky again.

Still, he was excited. He was halfway done already. There were only two more achievements to complete, and then this mission would be over.

The last two would be completed during the ball, he knew, which started in an hour and a half and ended at midnight. He needed to hide. He headed back towards the dorms and stopped, thinking of his book. Hadn't he read that the best place to hide was in the middle of a crowd of people? He smiled and dove deeper, glad for an excuse to watch the parade.

Indian music played, and a woman in a colorful sari danced and jumped and spun as men played foreign-looking instruments and banged on drums. Their float was being pulled by the biggest elephant he had ever seen. It towered at least twenty feet tall and had massive tusks, one broken in half. The tusks swept easily from one edge of the street to the other with a lazy wave of the animal's head. It nearly toppled some trees when one of its tusks hit their tops. People darted away as the trees swayed from side to side.

Pink-colored bats swarmed around one float that looked like a cave. A New Orleans themed team of floats paraded down the street after it, with a loud jazz band playing enthusiastically as people danced in pairs. They wore 1950s garb and swung their partners around wildly, dipping and catching them.

Gypsies and fortune tellers sat on neon-colored floats and witches did small tricks, causing things to float or making small explosions. The men on stilts walked down the street, their colorful pinstripes glowing in the black light of a nearby float.

There were floats with zombies, others with skeletons, and even one with small dragon-like creatures. Pete could feel the heat from their fire blasts even from a distance. There was a cool float with translucent GHOSTs that would go invisible and reappear in front of the faces of the crowd. Squeals of fear and delight ran through the crowd like waves. Their float hosted a sign that read, DUTY, HONOR, STRENGTH. WE ARE THE ELITE. WE ARE THE FEW. WE ARE GHOST STRONG! VISIT WWW.BECOMEAGHOST.COM FOR INFORMATION ON BECOMING PART OF THIS PRESTIGIOUS FORCE.

When Pete saw the last float move past, he was as disappointed as the crowd around him sounded. Suddenly, he felt the weight of the small package in his pocket. He couldn't believe he had forgotten it. One eye on the crowd watching for Shelly, he opened the box and stared in absolute amazement at the object inside.

He thought back to his mission instructions.

Get to the exchange location, get your first mission orders. Done.

Follow mission orders to get next target. Done.

Use target in next mission.

He blinked a few times to clear his thoughts and shrugged staring down at a small, cheap, plastic spider. How in Purgatory was he supposed to use this to complete a mission? He pulled it out to reveal a small slip of paper beneath it. Pete read it and smiled as a plan slowly began to form in his brain.

CHAPTER 19

THE MASQUERADE BALL

PETE TRIED NOT TO GET trampled as the crowd dispersed in all different directions. It was like they'd all had enough excitement and wanted to get back to normal as quickly as possible.

The police were herding the onlookers as best they could, but for the most part, the crowd was completely ignoring their whistles and shouts. One giant simply stepped over one of them.

Pete pushed against the crowd. They were all moving toward the main road, no doubt to where they parked their cars, but he needed to move in the opposite direction to get back to the school. He paused to let a family move past him and overheard them speaking in a foreign language. Pete watched them walk by, listening curiously.

Finally, he was able to dart inside the perimeter of the school. He walked past groups of chatting students, all in their finest clothing. There was not a single person in costume or regular clothes. He tried to remember who had told him wearing a tux was optional and was grateful that Charlie had insisted he rent one.

The tux he picked looked quite sharp, Pete had to admit. His tie, a bright blue one Charlie had recommended to "draw out his eyes," was impeccably tied. Pete walked past one kid who had his tie like a shoelace around his neck and smiled. He had to hand it to Charlie—he had taste.

One thing that alarmed him was that almost everyone had a date. He frowned. Was going to hurt his mission? Would he stand out? At the same time, how would he be able to accomplish a mission while he was on a date without his date noticing that something was up? There were only so many times Pete could pretend to get a girl a drink or run to the bathroom.

Well, it was a little too late to worry about it, though he was annoyed.

He shook the thought away and paused for a moment to admire the school. He was finally able to see what the scorpion-like creatures had been making all day.

The school looked completely different. They had erected temporary—at least Pete assumed they were—walls and towers. The effect was that the school had been transformed from a large manor into a massive castle. Long, dark-maroon ribbons hung all along the length of the castle, making it look festive, like it was coronation day or a prince's birthday.

Pete looked around the courtyard. It too had been transformed in the short time that the parade was going on. The spider-shaped fountain had lights draped across its back, and the water shone with an ethereal glow. The fairies had moved from the woods to nest in the trees and balconies of the school. Several violins played on their own, floating in midair at the entrance of the school, and a long, thick red carpet had been rolled out to drape across the front lawn's circular driveway in front of the fountain.

The orange glow of the moon, along with the many thousands of lights, cast the school in a picturesque scene that even Pete, nervous about the next steps of his mission, couldn't help but admire.

His admiration was interrupted when a spotlight shone across the courtyard. One of the violins faltered slightly, and Pete looked around for the source. Concerned, he walked closer to see what was going on and almost yelled out loud when he realized what he was seeing.

Of course. He walked over to Charlie, whose suit was beaming with lights so bright he was blinding passersby. "Unbelievable." Pete laughed and shook his head.

"Oh, hey, Pete." Charlie squinted at his watch through his powerfully lit suit. "Huh. Wait. Did I miss the parade?" His face fell.

"Did you miss— ? Yes. Yes, Charlie. You missed the parade." Pete stared in utter disbelief. "You almost missed the ball. What in AfterLife were you doing? Did you add more lights?" He squinted at his friend.

"Duh," Charlie said. "It needed more."

"It didn't need any," Pete corrected.

Charlie ignored him. "Well, the ball is more important anyway." He strutted a bit, angling this way and that so Pete could get a full view of his ridiculous attire.

"So, I added lights," he said. "Whatcha think?"

"Well, you will be noticed," Pete said after a moment's hesitation.

He hadn't exactly meant it as a compliment, but it was clear that Charlie took it as one. He nodded in satisfaction and gestured to his friends to come.

"So we protested dates this year and decided to go as a group," he announced.

"How is it that I am best friends with the lead Gossip Queen, and I didn't know that the biggest event of the year required a date?" Pete said, frustrated.

Charlie looked at him flatly. "Because, my dear Pete, you tune me out sometimes."

Pete frowned, but he did feel a bit guilty. He made a noncommittal noise, and Charlie snorted. "So, you can join our group if you want," Charlie said in a generous tone.

He thought about the slip of paper in his pocket and thought about what it had said. Use the spider to take the diamond.

Pete thought there might be diamonds in the fountain and the plastic spider was merely a distraction, but that had not been the case. There were only lights in the fountain.

He unconsciously patted the pocket where the plastic spider was sitting.

"Hi," a shy voice said beside him. He turned and his mouth fell open. A stunningly beautiful girl smiled at him. She wore a green gown that made her eyes look like emeralds. Her hair tumbled in elegant waves past her shoulders, and her makeup, though light, made her look both mature and breathtakingly gorgeous. Alex was always very pretty, but since she played a lot of sports, Pete had only ever seen her in her volleyball uniform or shorts and a T-shirt, always with her hair pulled up.

Pete stared and the girl's smile faltered. "Alex," he said in a small voice, "you…you look especially nice." His brain was not working, and he seemed to have forgotten his name.

She blushed and smiled. "So do you."

Pete looked down and nodded at Charlie. "He helped. Though if I let him choose, I bet my outfit would have looked a little…well, different."

Alex laughed.

He wanted to say something witty, but he found that his mind had gone infuriatingly blank. He stood like this in a painfully awkward silence that stretched out for about twelve years until, blessedly, her friend came and rescued her with a weak "check makeup" excuse.

The group of giggling girls disappeared into Cleopatra's dorm, and Pete was left behind, feeling a little shell-shocked and embarrassed. He really needed to learn how to talk to girls. He looked over and saw that Charlie looked like he was going to have an aneurysm from forcing down a laugh.

"Oh, shut up," said Pete, as Charlie, the illuminated Gossip Queen, doubled over laughing.

Pete, blushing furiously, punched Charlie in the arm, knocking out one of his lights.

"Well," Charlie said when he got a hold of himself, "you can't be good at everything right off the bat."

Pete grunted and vowed to spend the rest of the ball avoiding Alex.

"Ah come on," Charlie said coaxingly. "You're very handsome—and she likes you."

Pete saw the girls heading back and panicked. "Uh, I'll meet you inside, okay?"

Charlie waved goodbye as Pete went through the open entrance of the school, though only a few moments later Pete heard him and the girls chattering as they followed him. But he was distracted from his panic as he looked around, wide-eyed.

The inside had also been completely transformed.

"Wow!"

The entrance had always been wide and open, but now it was absolutely massive. How did they do that? He stood in the middle of the red carpet that ran from the spider fountain through the front doors, down a very long hallway, and into an enormous ballroom. The ceiling of the corridor, now at least thirty-five or forty feet high, had flying buttresses and a giant crystal chandelier swinging from its center.

Pete was jostled from behind, and he moved forward out of the hallway toward the entrance to the ballroom. Two attendants dressed like butlers used clean, white gloves to simultaneously open the doors.

He let out another gasp and could hear girls behind him do the same. He walked into what turned out to be the upper floor of the marble-covered ballroom. Multiple chandeliers hung along the length of the room. Where Pete stood, the floor jutted out a little. Two curved staircases on either side of him led to the level below. At the base of the stairs, a pair of well-dressed men in suits were handing out masks to smiling kids as they stepped onto the dance floor.

If he were to stay on this level and walk along it, to the right were several tall French doors that led out to terraces. Pete recognized, with a tinge of surprise, that one of them was where his friends had been attacked by a large snake.

He moved slowly to the side and looked down. Kids were mingling, chatting, and dancing to a remarkable orchestra set up on one end of the room.

A man offered to take their coats. Pete declined, but thankfully, Pete saw Charlie hand his over. The man raised one well-manicured eyebrow, but that was all the reaction he had to the flamboyant coat. The girls also gave their fur coats and jackets to the attendant.

Pete waited for the group, feeling his anxiety return. They were given their coat tickets, and they made their way toward where Pete was waiting.

He turned to walk down the steps and was met with a face full of Shelly. Instinctively, he ducked. It was a good call because one of her large fists came out of nowhere and grazed Pete along his side. In a detached part of his brain, he heard the gasps of the girls behind him, but the rest of him was back on the training mat at BASA.

Pete spun into the punch, grabbing her arm with both of his hands, pulling her into the momentum of the swing and throwing her off balance. He then slammed his body into hers, folding in half and pulling her feet over her head and over his body.

She landed with a loud cry that Pete knew was more of shock than pain. He rolled away from her and popped back up onto his feet, spinning defensively to block any future blows.

But none came.

A hush spread over the crowd and Pete, realizing what he had just done, looked around at the stunned spectators.

Shelly, in a clunky white dress, lay sprawled on the ground looking stunned. Granted, to Pete she still looked very dangerous, but in the end he had still body-slammed a girl during an elegant ballroom dance.

Without wanting to, he looked over at Alex. She stared back, eyes wide with shock. Before he could think or say anything, large hands grabbed him and dragged him out into the hallway. He saw someone else picking up Shelly and dragging her out.

They were escorted quickly to the library, which was the closest room. His escort was a tall, muscular dark-skinned man with a crew cut. He wore a well-tailored suit and had a clear, spiraled wire connected from his ear to his lapel, labeling him as security.

The reality of Pete's situation slowly sunk in. He had blown it. Why hadn't he just ducked?

He knew in his gut that he was moments away from getting kicked out of the masquerade. Had he just ruined his chances to complete his mission? The air went out of the room, and he watched with detached hatred as Shelly, stunned, was marched into the room.

The doors to the library slammed open and in walked the looming figure of Mrs. Battinsworth. Pete's stomach dropped at the look she gave him. He pinched his mouth shut.

It was hard not to shrink away from her. She rose to her full height, which made her skeleton-thin figure that much more noticeable. Her hair was pulled into a severe bun, though her usual headmistress garb was replaced by an elegantly flowing, full-length, long-sleeved black gown that covered her throat with a lacy design at the neck.

The gown moved of its own accord as though she were walking underwater, and it continued to sway lazily even when she stopped moving. Over the lace, she had on a necklace made of bone; the center was a massive boney spider. Her earrings were…were those teeth?

Pete tried not to appear nauseated. He focused on her dress to avoid looking at her earrings. The dress contined to sway languidly, and then with a shock of understanding, he realized it was made of shadows. He stared at it in amazement until the sound of Mrs. Battinsworth's sharp cough brought his attention back to the more pressing matter.

"What happened?" she asked in what Pete thought was a surprisingly reasonable tone coming from such any angry face.

Pete opened his mouth, then closed it. Something didn't feel right. It felt…he knew this was so dumb, so stupid, but it felt like tattling.

When he pictured himself blaming Shelly and going back to the ball, he cringed. He didn't have a perfect word for it, but he felt cheap. He also didn't want her to have the satisfaction of having something against him. He looked at the girl who'd given him so much grief this year and forced his face blank. Painfully, annoyingly, and he was sure, regretfully, he kept his mouth shut.

Mrs. Battinsworth stiffened after a few moments and said sharply, "Fine. I don't need to know what happened."

Pete looked sideways at Shelly, who was stony-faced. He was curious as to why she hadn't taken advantage of the opportunity to get him in trouble. "I know that I saw both of you fighting." She eyed both of them sternly. "You will both be escorted to your dorms."

Pete felt his mouth drop open. "No, I need to—"

"You need to do nothing," Mrs. Battinsworth snapped. "I am utterly disgusted with the two of you. Complete embarrassments," she hissed. "You make the school look bad."

Pete felt that was a bit much, but then thought back to the memory of him body-slamming a girl in an ugly prom dress during the middle of an elegant ball. As delightfully satisfying as that memory was, he had to admit, it did lack a certain finesse. He closed his mouth on his protests.

Pete found himself staring in disbelief as he was led like a criminal on death row back to his dorm room.

Months of training, two successful—no, three successful missions. And for what? All to fail at the very end and get kicked out of BASA. Tears were forming in the corners of his eyes. He couldn't help it.

Shame and anger with himself welled up. Yes, he was mad at Shelly, but he was angrier with himself. He should have forced himself to deal with her sooner. Instead of planning for her, he had tried to ignore her like he always did.

Could he persuade Coach to give him another chance with a make-up session or something? Or maybe he could get partial credit for getting the first part of the mission done. Even as he thought this, he remembered Coach's most recent lecture about half a mission equaling no mission, and the importance of being prepared for a real-life test.

Was it all bad? Him getting kicked out wasn't the end of the world, he told himself.

But he liked the kid he was becoming.

The guards must have sensed his mood. "Hey cheer up, kid," one of them said kindly. Pete looked up and saw the guard's "It's never as bad as you think" look.

The other one scoffed and said sarcastically, "Yeah, maybe you can make your own dance in your dorms." He snickered stupidly to himself and then stopped when he realized he was laughing alone. The man looked old school, and the guy probably didn't like boys who body-slammed girls, even if said girl was scary ginormous.

But the man had sparked a crazy idea in Pete's brain. He forced his face neutral as his mind raced.

Pete had been kicked out of the dance, sure, but that didn't mean that he couldn't finish the mission. It was just an added complication. This was not over yet.

After all, he was a spy, and a spy didn't have to follow rules.

CHAPTER 20

THE QUITTERS CAN QUIT

H E WAITED UNTIL THE CLOMP of the guards' footsteps faded away before he darted to the window to watch the two dense shadows disappearing in the direction of the school.

This was going to be tricky. True, it was a masquerade ball, but he had not been given his mask yet. He had seen where they were being handed out, but he wasn't sure how he could get to the man.

His plan had to be foolproof. He trudged toward his bed, then paused, staring at Charlie's pile of clothes. He didn't remember seeing Charlie holding a mask, but knowing Charlie, he'd have several to spare. Pete began sifting through Charlie's things.

"Are you going through my stuff?" a voice from the doorway said.

Pete jumped, cursed, and spun around. "You scared me. Yeah, I was looking for a mask. Do you have an extra one?"

Charlie stood there, jacket-less, with a mask hanging limply around his neck. Alex and her friend were on either side of him like bodyguards. They smiled at Pete weakly, visibly nervous.

"Hey, what are you doing here?" Pete still rifled through Charlie's things. "You're missing the dance."

Charlie raised an eyebrow. "What am I...? Are you serious?" He stared at Pete, an incredulous look on his face. "You kick the Wicked Witch of the West's butt in the middle of a school dance without a lick of hesitation, and you are wondering what I am doing?" He shook his head, astonished. "You are a weird one, Peter Green."

Alex studied Pete with renewed interest, but Alice just seemed nervous. "I saw her about to hit you," Alice said shakily, "but I couldn't warn you in time. She just did it out of nowhere. Just like that." She snapped her fingers.

Alex grinned. "Bet she regretted it though. I saw her face." She snorted her laughter.

Pete couldn't help but grin, embarrassed. "Yeah, well. We've both been kicked out of the dance."

"So why do you want a mask?" Alex watched him go through Charlie's things.

Pete flicked his eyes to Charlie and back to Alex in the flash of a second and then said the first thing in his brain. "I want to go anyway." It was the truth. He wasn't especially fond of dancing, but it still looked like a lot of fun.

Alex frowned, but before she could go on, Charlie interjected, "And he does what he wants." He somehow managed to flourish his hips in a way that made the girls jump out of harm's way. "Okay!" Charlie clapped his hands together. "Let's get to work. You are going to need a new outfit."

Pete frowned. "Why? What's wrong with this one?"

"You were wearing it before. They'll recognize you even with the mask on."

"I have the same suit on as all the other kids," Pete said flatly, and before Charlie could protest further, he added, "If I look different from the other kids, that will draw their attention, which I don't want right now." He raised his own eyebrows at Charlie's unspoken protest. After a short moment, Charlie closed his mouth and nodded reluctantly.

"Thank you for the offer though," Pete said. Charlie seemed satisfied, and the topic changed.

"How are you going to get in?" Alex asked.

Alice and Charlie suddenly looked nervous. Pete realized they were worried he would ask them to help, and they'd get kicked out of the ball as a result. This was the social event of the year, after all. Pete knew that even just missing the dance for this short a time would affect Charlie's ability to gossip. He and his full team of queens no doubt were watching what people were wearing, how they were wearing it, and who they were with—or not with. What if he missed something important?

Pete smiled at them. "Thanks for checking up on me. I appreciate it, honestly. But I don't want to tell you how I'm getting in so that you won't be held responsible if I get caught.

Alex twisted her mouth. "But won't you need help?"

Pete thought about it, looking down at the mask Charlie had handed him. Right when he came up with the decision to sneak back into the ball, he knew he would likely have to Port inside. There were too many eyes near the entrance. If Coach had been in charge of arranging security, which he suspected he had been, there would be a lot of watchful eyes at the dance.

He was trying to figure out where would be the best place to Travel. The crowd of students, though excellent for blending in, did add complications. He didn't want to land on someone's head or upset anyone by materializing from thin air.

The image of the terrace came into his mind. He walked over to the windows and looked at the people on the balcony, gathered around chatting in small groups or pairs. He might be able to Travel to one of the shadows and then Shadow Walk to his destination. He turned back to his friend and was surprised to see Charlie shaking his head no.

"What? I didn't even say anything."

"The terrace has too many teachers. You'll want to go back using the back way."

"What do you know about a back way?"

Charlie rolled his eyes, clearly offended. "Any good investigator"—Alex snorted at that—"needs to know the back entrances to every venue because that's where couples will try to sneak off to make out." He said this as though it should be obvious. "I mean, you'll have to come in separately, so we're not so obvious—"

Pete held up a hand in a placating manner, an amused expression on his face. "That sounds perfect, but won't there be teachers there too?"

Charlie shook his head. "No, they try and keep that space clear because waiters dash in and out with plates of drinks and orders. They would just be in the way. Most of the kids avoid it too, for the same reason. You'll have to be sly when moving from the back kitchen area to the ballroom, but once you get past there, as long as you have your mask on, it shouldn't be too hard to blend in." He heaved a regretful sigh. "You do look just like everyone else."

Unconsciously, Pete adjusted his tie and straightened his suit.

"Why are you smiling?" Alex grinned.

Pete hadn't noticed he was smiling, but now his grin widened. "Oh, because I think tonight is going to be a lot of fun."

She glanced at the school, and when she turned back to him, she was blushing.

Pete tried to focus. "How do I get to this back entrance? Can I get there from outside?"

A few minutes later, Pete had Traveled to the back entrance of the ballroom near the kitchen. He wasn't very familiar with this area, as it was usually far away from where he needed to be, but he'd been through here during his reconnaissance for his first mission.

He followed Charlie's directions, melting from shadow to shadow the way he'd learned in BASA. Pete was sure it was just in his head, but he found it easier to Shadow Walk in his mostly black suit.

He found the entrance to the west wing kitchen easily enough. Before he could talk himself out of it, he slipped inside. In the harsh glow of the fluorescent lights, there were no shadows for him to use. Throwing caution to the wind, he slid his mask on and walked in with a confidence he did not feel.

Nothing to see here. Cooks yelled and shouted at each other. He belonged here as he expertly swerved and dodged a half dozen people. He moved through the kitchen to where a line of waiters stood refilling their trays.

One waved and called out, "Oh, hey, Pete." Pete started, but the waiter was already spinning around on his way outside.

He really was going to kill Charlie. One time. One time he wanted Charlie not to announce his arrival when he was trying to be covert. And how did he even get down there so fast? It was like Charlie had a superpower for ruining Pete's missions.

Annoyed, he stepped out of the kitchen in between two waiters. They were dressed similarly to him, and it made it easier to feel inconspicuous. He walked past a shadow and casually stepped sideways, melting into the wall.

The waiter behind him did a small double take, but a small crowd of people was walking past just then. The waiter seemed to think that Pete must have joined their group.

From this angle, he could see almost the entire lower level of the ballroom and a little of the level above. He looked up at the guardrail. Kids leaned on it as they socialized, cups of punch in their hands.

He noticed a huge creature nearby and started. His limbs suddenly felt heavy. He focused, and the weightless feeling of blending with the shadows overtook his body again. He looked at the creature that had surprised him. It was about twelve feet tall, shaped much like a giant praying mantis and dressed in a pristine black tailored suit. The creature paused and bent low, offering a tray of something, then straightening again, stepped over several students and bent down to someone else. It took a full minute for Pete to realize that it was another waiter.

Pete shook himself and tried to focus, but another distraction came almost immediately when a girl's dress suddenly morphed into a bloody T-shirt and jeans. Her friend gasped and pointed at her wardrobe, and the girl squealed and burst into tears. "I was trying so hard to focus." She sobbed as she was hustled in the direction of the dorms by her small group of friends.

Frowning, Pete shook himself again. *Snap out of it.* He couldn't let himself get distracted. He pulled out the slip of paper and reread it. Diamonds? He didn't see any diamonds. And how would he use a spider to get one?

He bit his lip. He needed a better angle. He started to move and then immediately froze, his stomach contracting in fear. In front of him was none other than the tall, skeletal form of Mrs. Battinsworth. As she stalked through the ballroom, she parted the crowd like a sharp knife. The shadows of her dress licked the feet of the students she was passing, who flinched away from her.

She glanced around the room, eyes glaring and mistrustful, her mouth pressed into a deep frown. Pete stiffened when her eyes roamed across his corner, but he let out a breath when they continued onward without pausing.

When she started forward again, he took a deep breath and stepped out of the shadows. He walked slowly at first and then with more confidence when he confirmed that no one around him was paying him any mind.

He slipped casually through the crowd, looking for a diamond necklace or diamond-shaped decorations, anything. Several times something shimmered or sparkled, and he got excited, but it turned out to merely be someone's watch or glass.

This was dumb. Why did the note have to be so vague?

He rolled his eyes, then looked back suddenly. A small sliver of light had caught his eye. He scanned the room again. From this angle, he could see the long maroon ribbons that adorned the length of the school had also been added to the ballroom. Acrobats swung from the ribbons and leaped from one to the other, sometimes catching one another and spinning around in midair.

Had one of them caught the light? They did have sparkly bits in their costumes. No. The sparkle had been lower, closer to his eye level.

He scanned the area, and his heart sank. He had found the diamond. He stepped out of the way of a line of moving kids trying to get to the dance floor. Out there on the floor, Mrs. Battinsworth was gliding gracefully with her partner, Mr. Shashea, who was a full head and shoulders shorter than her.

On her necklace, in the middle of the spider's black body, rested a massive, gleaming diamond.

Pete's mind went blank. How had he not noticed it when she was admonishing him?

"I must be insane." He was actually trying to figure out how to do this instead of immediately calling it off. How in AfterLife was he going to get that necklace?

His stomach tightened, and he looked around as discreetly as he could. He was still worried about being recognized. Of course, the masks helped—with the exception, Pete noticed, of a chubby boy in a light-up suit and peacock-feathered mask. He snickered in spite of his nerves. Still, the longer he waited, the greater the chances were of him getting caught and thrown out.

Think, think. He could always try cloaking for the first time. He thought he understood the concept. It was described as sort of wearing a shadow. But that might be even more apparent. A shadow moving towards you, even in dim candlelight, would be noticeable and alarming.

He eyed Mrs. Battinsworth's dress thoughtfully, a truly insane thought taking root, and racked his mind. He knew Shadow Walking gave him the ability to walk from shadow to shadow. When he was in that state, he was light and the shadows always enveloped him, no matter their size. Though, he'd only ever tried to walk in shadows his size. But he was certain Coach had said it didn't matter the size, just the mindset. If he believed he would fit, he would.

Of course, he had also never tried to walk in shadows that were moving. He watched her twirl gracefully around, considering.

"What are you going to do?" said a voice behind him, making him jump.

"Wha—? Oh, oh, hey Alex. That…that is you, right?" She giggled and nodded. It sounded odd hearing a giggle from her. She didn't look like a girl who giggled.

"You need help?" she asked. "You know…with your mission?"

He didn't even bother getting annoyed with Charlie for blabbing again. He sighed and opened his mouth to tell her no, but he changed his mind halfway through. "Na—yah."

"Na—yah?" Her mouth quirked upward, sending shivers down his spine. Her light freckles outlining her mask were dazzling him, and he shook his head to focus.

"Yes, please." It was the second time she had offered, and he realized it was silly of him not to take her help.

She brightened. "This stuff is cool. I wanted to join BASA, you know."

Did everyone know about the club? He'd been under the impression it was a big secret.

"But my dad is weird," she said. "He and the Community had a falling out. I dunno the whole story, but he said it wasn't a good idea."

Pete realized he was standing there with his mouth open, and he closed it. "Oh." He had so many questions.

"I know you don't want to hear about that right now." She looked embarrassed.

"I do," he said sincerely. Then he remembered his mission and shook his head again. "But yes, you're right. I do have a…thing. Maybe you could tell me about it on a different day?"

She nodded. "Sure. So what do you need?"

Five minutes later, the plan was in action. In spite of his terror, Pete was feeling optimistic.

As he made his way through the crowd, he was grateful that the BASA members all had different missions. The fact that he didn't have to rush to grab the diamond before anyone else did simplify things. He occasionally spotted someone he knew in spite of the masks. He passed L.J. and Ren talking to a few people who looked like they might be from the Ware Team. He tilted his head down and away so they wouldn't recognize him. He passed a few of Shelly's friends as well, whom he definitely wanted to avoid.

Minutes later, he stood in the shadows of the terrace, watching Mrs. Battinsworth and Alex walking up the stairs and out to the terrace entrance. He was surprised by how relaxed Alex looked. The headmistress was smiling down at Alex, who seemed to be telling a story. She pointed at the terrace rail, near where he was waiting, and together they walked over and looked over the side. Pete couldn't hear what they were saying. The shadows made everything muffled like he was underwater. Pete saw the headmistress laugh, something he thought he would never see. Why was she never so pleasant with him?

An involuntary shiver ran down his spine when he looked at her dress. He told himself for the hundredth time he would not see what was beneath the dress. He held his breath, closed his eyes, and envisioned the moving shadows surrounding the tall woman.

Then, he stepped forward.

It was nothing like he had expected. These were not ordinary shadows. He almost cried out loud as he was whipped violently from left to right. It was like the shadows were trying to buck him off.

It felt as though he were swimming in powerful rapids. He found it getting harder and harder to breathe. The shadowy current spun him around in circles, making him dizzy and disoriented. But finally Pete could make out blurry figures whirling by and hear their muffled voices.

For a moment he could tell Alex was right in front of him, but he was quickly whipped away, tumbling head over heels in a circular motion. He needed to stop moving and right himself. There was no way he could keep this up for long.

Pete jerked his hand out and closed it around the space in front of him. It was an instinctual movement; nothing in his conscious mind said that this would work. But amazingly enough, it did. Instead of grabbing thin air, he wrapped his hand around what felt like cloth. He was careful not to tug it, in case the headmistress felt the movement, instead holding it firm.

The result was instantaneous. His vision still spun for several moments after his body stopped tumbling, but after a little while, he could see a bit more clearly. He managed to orient himself. It looked like Pete was at the back of the dress.

It was such a strange scene he was looking at. Blurred figures moved all around him and he could hear the muffled conversations of people. Unbelievable.

He had drifted to her right side and could make out the shape of the necklace resting at the headmistress's throat.

He pulled the shadow experimentally. The blurry shape of her head did not look down and he continued to hear muffled sounds resonating from above him, presumably from his headmistress. He moved carefully; he could feel the shadow tugging to get away from his grip, but he held it firm. He climbed.

This was just weird. He could feel the vibration that Mrs. B's voice made through the shadows.

He moved slowly, hand over hand, climbing ever higher. He was much lighter than normal, but he still felt heavy, and it was awkward work without a foothold for his feet. Mental note: Practice climbing with only his arm strength. He was making progress, but he was running out of time.

After a few pulls, he had a stroke of genius and pushed his feet together, trapping a part of the shadow in between and giving him purchase.

He could see Alex's facial features a little more clearly now that the shadows were not writhing so much. When he reached his hand out to grab the necklace, her eyes widened for a second. The spider unclipped, seemingly with a life of its own, and he pulled his hand quickly out of the cool air and into the warmth of the dark hiding place.

Mrs. Battinsworth's voice did not falter, and he tucked the spider into his jacket, pulling out the other. He replaced it on her necklace, flinching when he felt the small click of the spider popping into place. He pulled his hand back right before his headmistress's hand reached up to feel her throat absentmindedly.

Her voice wavered slightly, and he froze. She turned to look behind her to the right. It was a weird sensation. He felt like he was inside a glass of water that had suddenly turned. The water didn't move directly with her, but the shadows sloshed all around him, and he continued spinning with the ones he was hanging onto. When the headmistress turned back to face Alex, he rocked wildly in the opposite direction for several seconds before calming back down.

He was nauseated, but relieved to hear her talk to Alex again. He still couldn't tell what she was saying, but her tone seemed friendly enough. Pete decided that was his cue to leave.

He waited until the rocking watery sensation subsided completely, concentrated, and stepped forward, at the same time letting the dress's shadows go. However, as though the shadowy dress were being purposefully vindictive, Pete felt something sharp whip across the back of his legs, and the earth seemed to move sideways. The violent spinning and swirling started again, and he caught his arms and spun wildly as he fell forward into the wall where he had Shadow Walked.

"Mhoof!" He slammed face first into the unyielding terrace wall.

A couple of kids glanced around, startled, but their eyes moved right over where he was sprawled upside down. He righted himself, careful to stay within the limits of the shadows.

Pete cricked his neck and rubbed his face. He had a bloody nose, and he could feel his cheek puffing up. He'd have a bruise there tomorrow. But in spite of his ungraceful landing, a smile spread across his face.

Patting the bulge in his jacket pocket, he buttoned his jacket back up and hopped from shadow to shadow until he could Port from a secluded part of the kitchen.

From there he walked to the drop point, tucking the spider into the package where the other items had been held. He placed the box in the designated spot and waited in the shadows for a half hour before he saw a shadowy figure move and swipe it up.

He sat for a few more minutes, stunned, and let out a sigh of relief.

"I'm done." Grinning like a madman, he got up to walk to the dorms.

CHAPTER 21

THE FIELD TRIP

T O TOP OFF THE INSANE night, Pete spent a good twenty minutes chatting on the rooftop with Alex, who had apparently excused herself from the headmistress and come straight to the dorms. They had walked to the rooftop, laughing and talking about what happened. Pete was thrilled to find out it was actually pretty easy to talk to her.

"I almost screamed when I saw your hand." She doubled over with laughter. "Oh my god, you have to tell me how you did that."

Pete blushed and waved it off. "I kinda winged it. So what did you talk to the Bat about?"

"My potential future career," Alex said. "I told her I visited a career fair recently and was worried that my dad would just insist on me running the family business. Funny thing is, it was true. All of it. And if you hadn't needed my help, I would have never thought to talk to her about it, but she was actually helpful."

"Really?" Pete was unable to hide his surprise.

"Yeah." Alex grinned. "I know most people don't, uh, talk to her much, but I like it."

"That's because she's terrifying."

Alex laughed. "She only looks scary. Okay, well, I guess she is pretty scary." She shrugged, and Pete laughed. "But her and my dad go way back, so she's not so scary to me."

"Did they go to school here or something?"

"Uh, no. They were in business together years and years ago. My dad is in construction, and she needed another dorm built." She pointed to one of the girls' dormitories. "He Ports a lot of large equipment through Purgatory because they have a big enough Porting station—and it's a major hub, so he comes here a lot for work. I actually just saw him last week. He came and said hi, and we had lunch."

"Really? He can just come visit like that?"

"Oh yeah, Mrs. B was cool about it. He got stuck here because a rancher was moving a whole bunch of cattle through and needed the large pods, so my dad had to wait. He would have been angry, but he said he wanted to see me." She smiled. "I think he misses me."

After what seemed like no time to Pete at all, she announced she had to go find her friend. She looked guilty. "Alice is probably furious that I abandoned her for so long already."

Pete thanked her over and over for her help as he walked her downstairs to the door. She smiled awkwardly as she waved goodbye and headed back to the dance. He watched her walk back to the dance from back on his perch on the roof, and he couldn't stop grinning.

Pete jolted awake and breathed heavily. He was sweating and looked around as though he had been running from a wild animal. He chalked it up to residual excitement from the night before. He grinned again and leaned back with a sigh, reminiscing and watching the sun slowly rise.

"One heck of a night," he told the first rays of sunlight.

Pete got up, deciding to get on with the essay portion of his assignment. By the time he had finished proofing his essay, Charlie walked up, zombie-eyed and crazy-haired.

"Ugh!" he complained at the sunlight spilling through the windows.

Pete chuckled and followed his disheveled mess of a friend out of the study room and back inside their dorm. It was normally almost empty by this time, but so many people had stayed up late the night before that most of his bunkmates were asleep or lying drowsily in their beds, hiding their faces from the sun. Pete walked over and adjusted the curtains and received a couple of grateful grunts.

He waited patiently as Charlie tied his shoes on the wrong feet and then swapped them over. The entire process seemed to take an hour, but Pete, euphoric from completing his BASA assignments, just watched in amusement, trying not to laugh and wake up his roommates.

Charlie glared at Pete's glee. "It's unnatural to be so happy this early in the morning." He grumbled as he followed Pete to breakfast.

They found Max and Scoot deep in a debate on the best way to catch a Sea Lizard, which, upon asking, Pete learned was a crossbreed between a type of giant eel and a water dragon.

"They have subspecies depending on the breed of dragon and the size of the sea snake," said Max, "but no matter the breed, a small carver's knife will not penetrate the thick skin of a sea lizard, not even a newborn. The skin is half a foot thick when they're babies, Scoot. That's not efficient."

Even though Pete was eager to hear how his friends' missions went, he listened to the debate in fascination until a loud whistling whoop interrupted it. He turned to see Red and a couple of his football buddies beelining straight for their table. Pete waved, turned back to his food, and had the fork jostled right out of his hand by a sharp resounding slap on the back.

"Oof." Pete spit a bit of egg onto his lip.

"Well, dang, Green!" Red said brightly "You sure know how to make an entrance." Pete stared at him and looked around in confusion.

Red snorted. "Last night, dummy! You walk in with a human spotlight," he said, waving his hand at a grumpy looking Charlie, "and then body slam a giant angry chick five seconds into the dance."

"It wasn't like that," Pete protested, but Red heard none of it as he was roaring with laughter.

Pete didn't want a reputation for beating up girls and he said as much, but that only made Red laugh even louder. "Dude, that chick can take on most of the football team. Don't worry about it. The fact that it was Shelly Grant makes you an icon." He slapped Pete's shoulder and walked away laughing, leaving Pete red-faced.

Charlie wore a guilty expression, which meant that he or one of his Gossip Queens had written about it in their column. He sighed.

By lunchtime, people were swearing on their undead lives that they had seen it firsthand: Shelly had pulled a knife on Pete, and after a fifteen-minute brawl, Pete had barely survived and Shelly was wheeled out of the masquerade to the nurse's office.

Some hours later, annoyed and wanting to be alone, Pete took the opportunity to slip away. He would drop off his mission debrief letter early to Coach. As he slipped through the entrance to the maze undetected, Pete wondered idly whether he would spot Alex if he hung out with Charlie that afternoon. The thought cheered him up, and by the time he found Coach leaning back on a chair, reading a slip of paper, he was in a much better mood.

An amused expression sliding onto Coach Skinley's face. "You look cheerful."

"I do?" Pete shrugged. "Glad for the break, I guess."

Coach nodded. He put his feet down and leaned forward, setting the paper in his hand on his desk and grabbing the ones out of Pete's hands. He reached into his desk drawer and put on his glasses.

"My eyesight's not what it used to be." Coach sighed. He grabbed a mint from the bowl at the end of his desk and then leaned back in his chair to read.

Pete was surprised that the coach was reviewing his stuff right now. Suddenly a little nervous, Pete said, "Uh, about the grades. You said you'd wait to grade mine."

"I know what I said," he said, looking up.

"It's just that I need to see if—"

"If the witch's curse is broken?" Coach finished Pete's sentence, peering over his glasses at him.

Pete opened his mouth, but no words came out. He had not given Coach any specifics about his mission. Pete looked at the mission papers. Coach had not even turned the coversheet over.

Coach Skinley lowered Pete's essay and answered his unspoken question, "Son, if you want to be a good spy, you might not want to announce what you do in the papers." He opened a drawer, pulled out a newspaper, and handed it to him.

Numbly, Pete looked at the first page. There was a bit about the school dance. Below the top article was a smaller section entitled, "Full moon troubles over?" He read the first sentence: "Negotiations with a local witch have been made. Will she honor them?"

Pete stopped reading and set the paper down. Coach said, "To be fair, I didn't know which BASA member did it until I saw your reaction just now." He winked. "Your boy can write. It's a great paper."

Pete snorted and nodded. "Very informative."

"Indeed," Coach said seriously. "You know, some of these gossip columnists turn out to be great resources."

Pete frowned, a little surprised Coach would think that about someone like Charlie, but stood quietly and watched him read his mission report. After a minute, Coach Skinley set the paper on his desk. Still leaning back casually, he lifted his hands in a question. "So what did you think?"

That caught Pete off guard. "What did I think?"

Coach Skinley took off his glasses and used them to gesture. "What did you think about all this?" He circled his glasses an inch above Pete's mission report. "It's one thing to practice fighting and picking locks in a classroom, but doing it in real life, with real people around, is different. A lot different. So what did you think?"

Pete searched around for words, but none came, just a general feeling. "Stressful," he blurted out.

Coach Skinley nodded, smiling. "Yes. It can certainly be stressful. It's not for everyone. People who are great on the mat, great in the classroom, great at everything on paper, can still make terrible spies. You have something that few of the others have."

Pete raised his eyebrows, surprised.

"You are determined and you are creative. With those two things, you can make almost anything happen." He opened his hands in question again. "So... do you want to be a spy?"

Pete nodded. "I think so." He hoped it wasn't too weak of an answer, but at the same time he didn't want to lie to his coach.

"Well, that's enough for now. You passed your missions. You are clear to continue onto next year."

Pete started. "Oh." He felt a little deflated. "Okay. Cool, thanks." That had seemed rather anticlimactic.

Coach laughed. "What? You expected a medal? You'll get a report of my critiques and recommendations when you get back from break. Other than that, it's pass-fail in the Community and so it's pass-fail here. It's best you get used to that."

Pete nodded, trying to hide his disappointment. He had at least hoped it would have helped his rankings.

Coach called out as Pete was walking out of his office, "Is it true you beat up a girl?" Pete sighed and shook his head as Coach Skinley laughed.

The break ended too quickly for Pete. November third was the first day back, but since that was the next full moon, he felt eager to see if his plan had worked. He didn't know what he would do if it didn't. It wasn't as though he could demand his money back.

Max said there was a list he could try putting the witch on that would keep her from getting any more magical work, but he wasn't sure if they would let a kid add a name to the list. "Reputations are worth a lot in the Community." He took a bite of his breakfast eggs. "But at the same time, since you don't have one of your own, they may not take your word against hers. Anyway, we don't know if we need to look into that yet. Let's see if the curse is still here, yeah?"

"Oh, what did you end up doing for your mission?" Pete asked.

"I'm going into the Historical Research branch of the Community." When Pete looked at him blankly, Max added, "I find out stuff that happened in the past. Usually, people like me are hired by politicians to dig up dirt on their opponent. I love history, so I thought I would like it. For my mission, I found out some history about the school."

Pete opened his mouth to ask what history, but Scoot cut in. "He means he loves being boring, and don't even ask what I did 'cause I'm not gonna tell you. Did you hear who got cut?"

Instantly, Charlie stopped chewing and perked up.

"I know Hanna's gone." Max ticked off on his fingers.

"She quit, like, her second day," Pete corrected.

Max nodded and continued counting. "I heard Megan got cut, and didn't Ken get cut too?"

Scoot nodded. "Ya, I heard that too, but I think it might have been a mutual thing for Ken. I think football and BASA are a lot to manage. I'm surprised Megan even made it to this semester."

"She came in too late last year to test. Coach let her pass to this semester without doing a mission."

They chatted for a while, guessing who could be the third. Scoot had never had an ounce of concern of whether she would pass into next year, but both Max and Pete shared a mutual sigh of relief that they were moving on.

Pete cleared his tray and headed for his class, eyes peeled for anything abnormal. His first hour passed without incident, and he started to feel excitement building inside him.

At first, no one else noticed how unexpectedly dull the day was going, but by the end of his second class, students started whispering. By the end of the fourth period, there was a wild excitement that not even the sternest teachers could quell. People were openly passing the Gossip Queen column around, and by the end of the day, Charlie was a hero for breaking the story.

Pete couldn't help it; he joined in on the celebration and congratulated Charlie on doing his "job" so well.

The only thing that made him nervous was knowing that Dadson might be in danger. That unease could not be shaken so easily. He found himself searching for newsletters and watching news reports from neighboring world feeds, searching for any trace that the rich and famous Dadson was anything but perfectly healthy.

A few days later, the weather took a turn for the worse. Pete, stuck inside with the rest of his classmates, endured a few last comments about his "heroism" at Halloween, but they were few and far between. The new topic to talk about was the full moon.

To top it off, Alex had started spending more time with Charlie, which meant that Pete was getting to see more of her as well. Sadly, this didn't help him much. After that one successful conversation with her on the rooftop, he didn't have much luck getting his brain to put normal sentences together when she was present. As he walked to detention that Monday—his punishment for fighting on Halloween—his face burned thinking about how much of an idiot he was around her.

Engrossed in this thoughts, his head down, he ran into something very solid.

"Ouch, oh sorry. I wasn't paying… attention." He stared at the tall stranger he had run into. "Uh, hi?"

The boy had a mean expression on his face, and within a few seconds Pete was completely surrounded by his huge, unhappy looking friends. A few cracked their knuckles, and they all looked menacing.

Pete swallowed and tried to remember his self-defense training moves that he had been practicing all year. But his mind had gone blank.

"Wait, guys," a voice somewhere behind them said. Shelly came into view. With a dawning horror, he realized these must all be her friends.

Then, completely unexpectedly, she waved them away. They grumbled, but they left Pete alone.

"Why?" Pete said.

"That's for keeping your mouth shut," she said with a grunt. "I guess you aren't as much of an annoying dweeb as I thought you were." With that, she walked ahead of him into the detention hall, leaving Pete completely dumbfounded.

He stared at her retreating back for a long while, in horrified fascination. Had he just made a friend? He wasn't sure he wanted that. He didn't think that he could survive being friends with both Shelly and Scoot.

Pete walked into the detention hall behind her, shaking his head. He spent the next hour not doing homework as he had suspected but scrubbing in between the scales of the lunch ladies, who gossiped in their eerie, slithery voices. He tried being as polite as he could, trying not to gag at the smell.

When detention was over, Pete and Shelly walked out tired, sore, and covered in grossness he didn't want to think about.

November came and went in a flash, and before Pete knew it, the ground was blanketed in snow and Christmas break was fast approaching. He would have been excited for this, but his teachers were carrying on with their classes in high gear, trying to cram as much information into their heads as possible before the break, and he was finding it more and more difficult to concentrate.

Several times a day, Pete found himself dozing off. Each time he would wake up suddenly, frightened and sweating. He was thoroughly frustrated. Charlie and Max were convinced that this was the first sign he was becoming a poltergeist, and would have none of his insistence that it was just stress. But the truth was, he was a little worried himself. On top of the midday nightmares that he couldn't remember, his brain felt like ants were crawling on it.

The need to remember was maddening. His sister needed his help. This he was certain of, but he didn't know how he was going to figure out what was going on or how he could even help her. He started seeing flashes of her more regularly, usually in the mornings. A girl with brown hair would be standing in his peripheral vision, but then disappear when he looked at her directly.

One November night, Pete was making his way through the maze in a hurry, running late. He felt rundown and tired, and he'd just woken from one of his nightmares. This was the first one he could remember. Lilly had been there, but only for a second, and then the shadows behind her formed hands that grabbed her and pulled her, screaming, back until she was a part of them. He had woken up swinging his arms wildly in a frantic attempt to pull her back to safety. He was sweaty and huffing, but thankfully he hadn't woken up his dorm mates.

Now, rushing to his BASA meeting, he couldn't get his sister or the nightmare out of his head. He wanted to tell her he was trying to help. He'd stolen his file from the school, for goodness sakes. Yet what good had that done? It had only made him into the mess he was today. He was only a fourteen-year-old boy, and he didn't know what to do.

"No! I'm a member of an elite spy group. I'll figure this out, Lilly. I promise." If anyone could figure out how to help his sister without going crazy, it had to be him. He didn't entirely believe this, but the thought made him feel better and he walked into BASA with a renewed vigor.

That night, he started planning in earnest. The trouble was that he needed to do some recon on the Department of Registered Deaths, where he could find the rest of his memory files. He needed to know where the files were kept, how to sneak them out, and, this time, how to add them to his memory without completely breaking his brain. Maybe he could contact Sam, that kid who was pulled from school by his parents.

An opportunity arose, however, with the announcement of the upcoming field trip in the final week of school. Charlie was practically quivering with excitement when Pete asked him about it.

"I know it's silly to be excited about going into town, but it's been ages, and I desperately need a new hat."

Even Scoot seem to be looking forward to the trip. Apparently, it didn't happen very often.

"Only once a semester," Max confirmed, nodding.

Blissfully, December tenth finally came, and the kids cheered as they lined up to get into buses, rented specially for the occasion. His only disappointment was that Alex would not be spending time with him during this trip. She had regretfully announced that she had promised her friends, Violet and Alice, months ago that she would go shopping with them.

"Maybe I'll see you around?" he had asked casually. She'd nodded, and he felt marginally better.

Pete watched as the white picket-fenced neighborhoods turned into happy little shops and then into the town square. People milled about, doing their shopping and errands. People on bikes chirped their bells merrily, and several mothers were gathered at the park, gossiping as their children played on the swings.

Little ducks were waddling from the nearby pond. As they walked past, the color of one of the ducks abruptly changed to a brighter color. The green was suddenly vibrant, and the bill and feet of the duck were a bright orange-yellow color.

Pete stopped walking, but in that same instant, the duck turned into its normal muted colors again. Pete frowned. He blinked and shook his head. He felt funny.

They continued exploring the town. Scoot, Max, and Charlie took him to their favorite shops. No surprise to Pete, Scoot's favorite place was a shop full of weapons. What did surprise Pete was that Charlie was the only one who bought something from the small store. Granted, it was horribly pink and very bedazzled, but still, Pete had expected Scoot to buy the longsword she was fawning over.

Max took them to a store that was so small and indistinct, Pete would have passed right by it without noticing it. "This is where I got the lockpick that I used on my mission." He held up a small set, and Pete took it curiously.

After examining the contraption, Pete set it back down and looked around. The shop turned out to be for spies and had all kinds of useful things. He found a cloak made out of shadows that helped you Shadow Walk. "Shadow Walking made a thousand times easier!" the label read. Pete tried it on and was amazed. He didn't even have to concentrate to do it. Charlie, however, had some trouble with it. He ended up stuck behind a bookshelf somehow, but seeing as it was the one and only time he had ever tried to Shadow Walk, it was still pretty impressive.

They spent an enjoyable half hour wandering around the shop before Charlie dragged them to an accessories shop. This, too, was fascinating to Pete. He perused ordinary things like earrings and hats and also less ordinary things like extra skin to cover wounds and eyeballs with different colored irises. Mix and Match! the box of eyeballs read.

Pete examined a bottle of triple-strength glue, good for attaching limbs. He considered Scoot's head with a mischievous thought. But, thinking better of it, he put the glue back. He spent nearly all of the small stipend he got for the field trip in the first shops they visited. Between all of them, Pete now owned fake fire, a walkie-talkie set, and a new set of lockpicks.

After a couple of hours, they decided to take a short break.

"Mmm, I have been dying for a caramel frappuccino for ages," Charlie said. They turned the corner and he made a fake gasp of horror. "Why so busy?" he whined.

Every patio table was full of chatting people, people on laptops, and others reading or attending to their children. Some were even standing around outside sipping on drinks and texting. They walked past a man at least nine feet tall who stood sipping coffee with, presumably, his wife, chatting amiably about a restaurant they had gone to the night before. A camera hung around his neck and she held a travel map in her hand. In spite of their size, their voices were relatively quiet, and their movements were slow and precise.

A pamphlet was half-crumpled on the ground, and Pete bent to pick it up. "Visit Purgatory with your family!" it read enthusiastically. "It's not as boring as you would think!"

"Yes, it is." Scoot read over his shoulder. She grabbed the booklet out of his hands and threw it in the trash. "Come on." She sighed. "Let's get in line."

Pete pushed open the door slowly, careful not to hit anyone. The coffee shop was standing-room only. The cafe was filled mostly with people and creatures in business attire. A few mothers or families who looked like they were on vacation filled the tables and stood in line.

"We must have hit the lunch rush." Scoot looked around in dismay. "Wanna come back in an hour or so?"

Charlie looked shocked. "No way. I can't wait that long."

The building was quite large, and the baristas worked with a focused efficiency of ones used to a rush.

"Next creature in line!" a loud, firm voice called from behind the front counter. There were three cashiers bringing people forward, one working the drive-through, and at least nine or ten others making drinks. Pete was pretty pleased to see the line moving forward. They moved in line, and a few seconds later, one of the other cashiers shouted a customer forward.

Pete watched as a man holding his head stepped forward, then backed up quickly with a yelp. Suddenly, a dark hole appeared in front of the attendant and materialized into a dense black cloud, growing bigger and bigger.

Lightning struck out of it four or five times, hitting a table and toppling it over along with the drinks. One strike carved a chunk of wood out of the ceiling, and a woman was knocked onto her backside.

Pete and his friends ducked, watching the ceiling for debris. Shouts and shocked screams erupted from several customers and a deep menacing voice filled the coffee shop. "I'LL TAKE A TALL, NON-FAT CHAI LATTE WITH NO FOAM AND EXTRA CINNAMON. PLEASE."

"One tall non-fat chai latte, no foam, and how many shots of the cinnamon dulce did you want, sir?" the barista asked in a bored voice.

There was silence from the cloud and one more fork of lightning struck out and broke a hanging light. "Well, I mean, how many does it normally come with? Listen, Lisa usually takes my order. Can you ask her?"

The customers standing in line started to grumble.

"Come on, Frank," a well-dressed man with a briefcase said. "You do this every morning. Just pick something and move on. I'm gonna be late for work, and you know Francis. She's a beast in the morning."

"Literally," his companion dressed in slacks and a button-up shirt said. "She literally turns into a warthog and bites the ankles of people who come in late."

"No one asked for your opinion, Greg. Oh, hi Lisa." The cloud's tone turned friendly as a plump smiling woman of about fifty walked to the cash register.

"Well, hello, Frank!" She gave a bright smile as she punched some buttons on the computer and picked up a cup to write his order down. "How's Maxine? Is she well?"

"She is a hell demon, a spawn of Satan."

"That's nice," the cashier said sweetly. "Glad she's doing well. Okay, have your order right up, dear."

"Thanks, Lisa."

"Next please!" she sang out.

Twenty-five minutes later, Pete, Scoot, and Max stood in front of the shop sipping their drinks and planning their next stop. They finished their drinks and enjoyed wandering around the town awhile longer, though Pete was starting to itch with nervousness that he was going to run out of time.

Finally, Charlie went off to a shop to find his hat, and Max took off alone too, saying he'd meet them later after he searched a few shops for some books and pens. This was Pete's chance, so he quickly asked Scoot if she would go to the DRD with him. She shrugged, "Sure."

He didn't know why he wanted her there. In fact, the better spy would have left her behind, but he needed her help and she was the least dramatic of all his friends.

"So, what's really going on with you?" she asked as they walked into the transit building.

The noise of the bustling people inside masked Pete's sigh. "My sister is in trouble, and I need to help her."

"Where is your sister?"

"Dunno," Pete said. "Somewhere in Life, I think."

"What's the trouble?"

"That I don't know either. I just know I have to find her."

She thought about this for a moment and then peered at him closely. "So to help your sister, you need your full memories?" Pete nodded. "And the ones you got weren't enough?" Pete nodded. "So you want to scope out the DRD to try and steal your memories back."

Pete blinked and then nodded. "How—" he began, then stopped. "I feel weird. I've felt weird since the first time I read my file. How do I stop that?"

"I dunno. I guess you just…do." Pete stared at her. Scoot was a big advocate of the "Don't be a sissy, just figure it out" mindset. He didn't say anything, and she went on. "They aren't gonna let you turn into a poltergeist even if you illegally steal your memories. If it gets bad, just let Coach know, but that's not your biggest problem."

That made his brow furrow. "What is, then?"

"That." Scoot pointed.

Pete hadn't quite been paying attention to where they were walking. They were nowhere near the room he had entered when he first died. "What? Where are we?"

In front of them was a giant room stretching the full height of the transit building, several stories tall and enclosed in glass. On the other side of the glass and stacked all the way to the glass ceiling were hundreds and hundreds of what looked like lockers. GHOSTs in pristine uniforms, fully armed, floated in and out of the lockers. There were machines along the wall and several massive mechanical arms with pincers for hands periodically moving along tracks that ran around the square encasement, occasionally stopping to unlock lockers and take out small metal objects and or put them in. He could hear the high-pitched whir as they moved and the soft clicks of the lockers as they were opened and closed.

Pete stared open-mouthed at the encasement for several moments, then blinked and looked around him. He recognized the chandelier he'd woken up under, but now he was standing on the opposite side of where he had gone when he headed to the DRD.

"I don't understand why we're here, Scoot." He pointed behind them in the direction of the Department for Registered Deaths.

"Because, stupid, this is where they keep the memories."

"What?" Panic rose inside him. How would he ever be able to help his sister if this was what he had to break into?

"Memories aren't held in the DRD; they're kept like this." Scoot crossed her arms. "There are cameras and alarms on nearly every inch of this place, at least five armed guards at all times, plus a patrol every ten minutes after hours—which, by the way, is not a real thing."

"Real thing?" Pete didn't take his eyes off the encasing.

"After hours. This is a TransPortation station, there are trains and Ports going at all hours. Granted, foot traffic significantly decreases after a certain time, but it's never entirely stopped. Plus, you have to worry about those people too." She pointed to Pete's right.

People, all holding tickets, stood in a line at a window where an attendant waited, all facing away from Pete and Scoot. "Next," called the attendant in a bored voice, and the man at the front of the line stepped forward and handed over his ticket. The attendant typed something into his computer. One of the arms inside the glass building whirred to life, whipped around to the far side of the stacks, and whipped back with a small metal object. The arm placed the retrieved object in a chute, and a split-second later, a second attendant plucked the object out of it and indicated for the man in line to have a seat in a nearby contraption. Once the man sat, the attendant lowered what looked like an old-fashioned hair dryer onto his head, then plugged in the small metal object into the side of the hair dryer-thing. The dome object above the man's head lit a bright blue for several moments and then powered down. The hair dryer was lifted up and the man walked away.

Pete swallowed. "So that's how you safely get your memories?"

"Most of them," she said.

"Hang on. How do you know all this?"

Scoot looked at Pete like he was stupid. "I've been trying to break out of this school since I first got here. I did it easily in my first semester, but I realized I don't want to spend my AfterLife without my memories. It's been a bit of a pet project of mine." She sighed. "Listen, I'll help you break in." Pete's eyes lit up, but her face made his stomach deflate again. "But you're not ready yet. I'm not ready, either. The plan is to do it next summer. I still need to train more, and so do you."

Pete looked sadly at Scoot. "I don't know if my sister will last that long."

"Well, she'll have to."

CHAPTER 22

CHRISTMAS AT THE ACADEMY

PETE SPENT THE NEXT TWO weeks training like mad in his BASA meetings. The rigorous training helped lessen his flashbacks and nightmares, and he began to see that Scoot's "just do it" attitude had some merit. Before he knew, it was the final day before winter break. The classes were all shortened, and when students were not openly chatting and joking, they had dazed, far-off looks on their faces.

Charlie had a particularly interesting debate with Mr. Shashea about whether he thought Malley O. Makey, a famous actor, would break it off with his longtime lover, Missy Hamberton. Though highly theoretical, the conversation ended with him consoling his teacher, who was in tears, patting his arm gently as his teacher wailed. "They are just so beautiful together."

The bell rang at last, and a grateful Pete, who hoped he was portraying a regretful look instead of a relieved one, waved his goodbyes.

"Merry Christmas, class!" Mr. Shashea wiped his eyes and waved. "I'm sure I'll see some of you in a few days for Christmas. Be safe."

The day passed quickly, and Pete was swept up in a rush of students running outside like escaped convicts. Nearly every kid in the school celebrated the end of term with an epic snowball fight.

Kids quickly divided themselves into teams and dove behind hastily erected forts. Even some of the teachers joined in on the fun, but by the speed and strength with which they pummeled kids in the face with snow, Pete suspected they were probably letting off steam too.

The sun was setting, which gave the vampires and werewolves playing a big advantage. Not only would they be stronger and faster in the darkness, but they would also be able to see where many of the students were running.

After getting a face full of snow a few hours later, Pete called it quits and went for dinner. He was wet and a little sore from some of the snowballs he'd been pummeled with. One thrown by a werewolf actually knocked him off his feet.

He spent a very enjoyable break with his friends and also with Alex. He didn't know how long he was going to remain at the school, now that he saw what was involved with breaking into the transit station's memory vault. He had no illusions that any attempt would likely get him caught and expelled. The thought made him very sad, but the thought of not helping his sister was more maddening than ever. Still, whenever he spent time laughing and playing games with his friends, he hoped that he would get to have a few more years with them.

In spite of the cold and having to spend most of their time in the dorms or in the empty ballroom—which had been set up like a game hall for the holidays—he was enjoying the Christmas break. The decorations adorning the school were somewhat on the pathetic side—nearly bald Christmas trees had been erected throughout the grounds; and half of the lights strung up had missing bulbs, while the other half were orange and purple, very clearly leftovers from Halloween. Still, it was enough to spread excitement through the air.

However, the break took a turn for the worse on Christmas Eve. Pete was anxious and worried all morning. He'd kept dozing off during the night, only to wake from a nightmare several minutes later. His jaw was sore from clenching it. The nightmares had all but stopped in the previous two weeks, so to have several in the last few hours was extremely frustrating.

He could tell Alex was wondering why he was acting so distant, and part of him worried that he was going to hurt her feelings, but he couldn't muster the energy to care much. Even Scoot frowned when she looked at him.

"Must be coming down with something," Pete said lamely when Charlie asked why his eyes rimmed with dark circles. Charlie raised an eyebrow at that. The dead did not come down with things. Luckily, he let it drop.

What's going on? He was having such a good time. He had not slackened on his training, not even during the break. In fact, he had increased it quite a bit since classes ended. But it was as if overnight, his brain had switched a flip and was trying to tell him something again.

That night, he and his friends sipped the last of their hot apple cider around a campfire that had been set up for the occasion.

"I'm going to grab more to drink. Uh, Alex, you want anything?" Pete stood.

"Sure." She smiled and turned to chat with one of her girlfriends.

Pete took her cup, but as walked toward the drink station, a pale shape darted past him out of the corner of his eye. A little girl sprinted past and nearly ran over him. "Whoa!" He stepped back, startled.

"Watch it!" He turned to see where she was running off to. He could hear her laughing, but the lights adorning the trees in the courtyard didn't do much to illuminate the grounds. Still, it was bright enough that he should've been able to see something. After all, the little girl had been dressed all in white.

"Where did she go?" he asked Charlie, who had walked over to join him. He turned to see Scoot and Max following too, staring at him.

"Did you get bit by something?" Charlie scanned the area nervously. "Was it a bee?" His voice was two octaves higher than usual.

"No." Pete said. "That girl just nearly ran me over. You didn't see her?"

His friends glanced at each other. "Pete," Max said cautiously. "There was no one there. No one but us. Charlie said you were having nightmares."

Pete whipped his head around to glare at Charlie, who had the grace to at least look ashamed. He had told Charlie not to tell anyone, which in hindsight was a stupid thing to do and a testament to how awful he had been feeling.

"But everyone has noticed something," Max said quickly. "Even Alex is worried about you." Pete's face heated. "You're still reading the file, aren't you."

"I don't need a lecture right now," Pete snapped. Max closed his open mouth.

"I'll be very annoyed if you become a poltergeist and haunt me." Scoot stood and filled her own cup at the nearby hot drinks stand. "I'll learn how to trap you in a cup or something if that happens." She pointed a knife at him quite unnecessarily.

"I'm not going crazy." But even to him it didn't sound convincing. He looked at them and then looked down. "There is just…something I need to remember, okay?"

As soon as he said the words out loud, it was like some sort of block released in his mind. A dam holding back floodwaters broke.

The courtyard disappeared, and suddenly the crisp air grew warm. Pete was standing in a grand living room in front of a roaring fireplace, and a beautiful woman in a brilliant red evening gown was holding his hands, spinning him around in a circle.

Her blonde hair was pinned in an elegant bun, but a lock had tumbled loose and fallen in front of her lightly lined face. Even though she was dressed for an important event, she wore only light makeup and a bit of red lipstick. Her bright green eyes needed no extra help standing out from her lovely face. She was laughing, and her brilliant white teeth reflected some of the dancing flames caged in the fireplace.

"Darling," she said in a faint accent, "doesn't our little Pete Rabbit look so handsome in your tie?"

Pete stopped spinning and looked down at his blue-and-white striped pajamas and held up the end of the white silk tie.

"Excellent knot work, son." A man a smiled. He bent to kiss a small girl with large brown eyes and shoulder-length brown hair. "Merry Christmas."

The girl was laughing too. "You should make that your detective outfit!" she squealed. She was wearing the same white gown pajamas as the girl who'd passed him in the courtyard.

The courtyard! Pete blinked rapidly, gazing around. Slowly, the snow reappeared and he was shivering, the memories of his mother and sister's laughter echoing in his ears.

His vision was blurry, and he realized a short second later the blur was because tears were gathering in his eyes. As he blinked, a couple fell down his cheeks. He didn't remembered slumping down, but he was on his knees. Quickly, he rubbed at his eyes, trying to hide the fact he had been crying.

Pete looked up at his friends, embarrassed. Instead of mockery, however, he saw concern, which somehow made it worse.

It was Scoot who broke the silence. "Let's go back to the campfire."

Pete, nodded, accepting her hand to help him up, and together his friends walked in complete silence. He had forgotten to refill Alex's cup, but it ended up being a moot point. When he approached the log where he had left her, she was gone. He looked around and saw her nearby, comforting her friend, Alice, who was sobbing. Pete couldn't hear much, but he thought he heard her say something about breaking up with someone. Alex mouthed "Sorry," and he waved his hand to indicate that it was no big deal. He felt a little relieved she hadn't witnessed his outburst.

They found nearby tree stumps set up around one of the many fire pits behind the back of the school and sat down. "Dude, you look bad," Charlie said.

Pete wanted to say something encouraging, something nonchalant, but he couldn't muster the strength. He couldn't understand what he was feeling, but there was a burning ache in his chest, and he was having a hard time swallowing the lump in his throat.

A quiet conversation started up between Scoot and Max, but Pete ignored them. He looked up at the sky to see if he could see anything in the dark snowy night.

When he had first heard that they would be visited by Saint Nick, he had laughed, thinking it was a joke. But it had turned out to be true. Here in AfterLife, it was tradition for everyone to gather outside on Christmas Eve and wait for the famous wizard who had devoted his life to helping people and then later to giving gifts.

"Not just gifts—he sometimes will grant wishes," Charlie had said excitedly.

Wishes. Pete thought about what he would wish for. He thought of his mother, and the pain tightened in his chest. He realized what he was feeling. It was…grief. He was sad. He was starting to remember them now. He remembered loving them, and he missed them with an ache that threatened to overwhelm him. As he stared at the fire, he fought back tears.

"You know what I'm going to ask for?" Charlie said, making Pete jump a little. He half-turned toward him, still trying to hide the tears forming in his eyes. "I'm going to ask for your memories. The ones you're looking for."

Pete looked into his friend's kind, understanding eyes, but he could not find the words to say thank you. They seemed to be stuck in the middle of his throat, with the lump that had been threatening to rise for the last half hour.

Still, even without words, Charlie seemed to understand Pete's gratitude and nodded. He gave Pete a quick hug, and Pete almost lost control again. He sniffed and rubbed quickly at his eyes, embarrassed.

The time passed quickly. The kids kept up their cheerful chatter around him. Pete pretended to listen to a conversation Red had started up with Charlie, but he wasn't really listening. He barely even noticed when Santa—or Nick, as he preferred to be called—made a spectacular entrance, flying wildly with a full sled led by six flying reindeer, three dogs, and a cat, of all things.

"Whoa, now!" Nick called as he made his descent. The sled barely missed the roof of the school and landed with a thud several feet away from the nearest student, knocking over several very sad looking Christmas trees.

Nick chuckled heartily, and the sound was familiar and comforting. Pete looked up from his lap and smiled when Nick picked up his cat from the snow. The cat meowed grumpily. Nick set the fluffy white cat inside the sled. "That will teach you to tease my deer and dogs, Snowflake."

Another bark of laughter shot from the chubby man, and a smile spread across Pete's face. He knew that laugh. He knew that face.

By all accounts, the man looked very much like the depictions of him in cartoons and movies. He was a tall man, with a very ample belly, thick arms, and legs hidden behind a thick red coat and pants. His pink, weather-worn face was hidden behind a thick white beard, and he wore a great big smile that creased the corners of his merry eyes.

But more than that, Pete remembered him from his past life. It was a hazy memory, but he remembered peeking from behind a pillar and watching this man setting down presents on his living room floor.

Instantly, Pete felt happier and lighter. Kids of all ages, even older than Pete, cheered and hooted at Nick's entrance. The man moved around, shaking hands and chatting with everyone before handing each student a present. The complaining cat clinging to his shoulder made Pete laugh out loud.

Pete found himself swept up in a conversation. This time Pete was actually listening, hearing stories about Christmases in the past. The merry talk lifted some of the weight off his chest.

By the time Nick had made his way to Pete's group of friends, Pete had all but forgotten the memories of his family. He listened as his friends told Nick what they wanted for Christmas. Scoot asked for several different types of weapons, as Nick raised an eyebrow. "And have you been good this year?"

"Define good. I am good at fighting," she offered. Nick chuckled, handing her a gift, and moved on. Max and Red told him what they wanted, and Nick gave them gifts that they immediately tore open.

Pete's lip quivered slightly when Charlie kept his promise and said, quietly, that he wanted the nagging memory to come to Pete.

Nick looked taken aback. "Well, that is unexpected. I got your letters with the sketches of the clothes you wanted. I had the Missus make them special."

Charlie looked heartbroken. "This is more important."

Pete opened his mouth to protest, but Nick looked directly at him and winked. "Okay, that will work. How about I get you something too, though, huh?" Charlie beamed, ecstatic and yelled with glee when he opened his present.

Nick moved to Pete, and he could smell gingerbread and eggnog coming from the man.

"What is it that you want, Pete?" He tilted his head sideways, considering. "It's been a long time, hasn't it?"

Pete nodded and smiled. "Yeah, when my sister and I were little."

"You weren't supposed to be up." Nick smiled, remembering. "Lilly was funny. She thought I was a burglar." He barked a laugh. "She's a feisty one." He thought for a moment. "I think I got her boxing gloves that year, didn't I?"

Pete nodded and then frowned when Nick repeated his question, "So, what am I bringing you this year? The memory you're looking for will come, but is there something else you wanted?"

It took Pete a moment, but finally he managed to speak in a quiet voice. "I don't want to lose my mind."

Nick looked at him knowingly, the campfire illuminating his eyes. He smiled and pinched Pete's cheek and stood up.

"Well, all right, then." He bent into his bag. Snowflake had hopped down earlier and made his way moodily through the crowd. He was now rubbing against Red's leg and looking over his shoulder at Nick to see if he was getting jealous. When the cat realized the tall man was not even looking at him, he meowed loudly and stalked off toward the maze.

Pete vaguely wondered if the man would lose his cat, then thought better of it. If he could make animals fly and Port all over the world, he could find one sullen cat.

Nick pulled out a pair of reading glasses, a pipe, and a blue-and-white striped silk tie and handed them to Pete.

Pete stared at the items and then up at Nick, who smiled and started to walk away.

Max nudged him with his elbow. "Say thank you," he hissed out of the side of his mouth.

Pete stuttered his thanks a bit too late to be polite and then sat staring, stunned at the things in his hands. He felt a growing sense of disappointment and anger flare up in him when suddenly he wasn't in the courtyard of his school anymore.

The smell of baking was coming from the kitchen, and the cooks were gossiping and clanging things as they worked. Pete ran past them, ducked low so they wouldn't catch him, going straight to his father's study. He grabbed Dad's glasses and pipe off the desk and stuck them in his pajama pocket.

He looked around to make sure Dad wasn't around, even though he knew Mom and Dad were away on one of his many work trips, and then looked to where Dad's tie was hanging with a shirt and suit jacket. Pete grabbed it, grinning. It was his favorite, one that he always stole to practice tying his knots.

He ran out past the kitchen and through the servant's door in the back while putting on the tie. As he sprinted through the garden, he earned a hiss from the gardener, who liked his gardens undisturbed.

His sister was waiting for him in their secret garden, just behind a hedge of bushes. He had been sick for weeks, and it felt good to be able to run again. His nurse had taken the day off to deal with some stuff with her daughter. Was her daughter having a baby? Pete couldn't remember. All he knew was that she would have never allowed him out of the house, so he took full advantage, loving the burn his lungs felt from the effort.

Behind the hedge, he handed his sister the pipe. She giggled and put it in her mouth. Then she put her hands on her hips and mimicked an adult man's voice. "Now, go to bed, young man."

Pete laughed and put on the glasses, though they blurred his vision. He knew it was childish to play like this with his little sister, but it was fun to do something other than lying in bed feeling like a dead person.

They grinned and messed around with their dad's things for a few minutes until they heard a strange noise coming from nearby—unfamiliar voices.

Just like that, they switched into detective mode. That had been the whole point of the pipe and glasses. Suddenly, Pete thought about Grandfather's ridiculous hunting cap and inwardly cursed himself for not remembering it. It would've completed his Sherlock Holmes look perfectly.

Together, he and his sister crept along the hedges to the edge of the house, toward the strange voices. The gardener had moved some roses to the far end of the property and was a small speck in the distance. Pete could see two figures arguing around the corner of his house. Excellent. He smiled at his sister—finally a real mystery to solve.

They moved closer, and Pete realized he had seen them before. One man was about six feet tall and thick around the chest and midsection, with dark hair and eyes. The other was shorter and older, with graying hair, but was very fit for a middle-aged man. The pair worked for Pete's father's business partner.

"What are they doing here?"

His sister shrugged. "I've never seen them here without Dad before."

When they reached the end of the hedges, he waved for her to stay put, handing her a walkie-talkie. "Stay here."

She looked mutinous, but for once she listened, bending down and out of sight.

"Tell me when they move," he mouthed to her, and she nodded reluctantly. "Tell me right away." She rolled her eyes and nodded. They had learned a shortened Morse code, and it would come in handy now. Well, really they had just made up their own, because neither could figure out where to learn the real one.

Pete darted to the side of the three-story mansion, out of view of the men but within earshot of their conversation.

"And how are we supposed to do that?" One of the men asked in a harsh whisper. "We'll stand out. It shouldn't be us—we need a professional."

"We can't risk them blabbing," the other countered. "And it needs to be soon. This weekend, he said."

"It's too risky. We need a better plan."

"Okay, I'm all ears," the other hissed back.

Their voices slowly grew louder. His walkie-talkie crackled sharply. Lilly was obviously letting him know that the men were heading his way.

He looked around wildly for a place to hide. He had found a flaw in his foolproof walkie-talkie Morse code plan. The speaker continued to crackle in a rhythmic way like firecrackers in a church.

The crunching of the men's footsteps quickened, and Pete turned to run. Before he made it a few steps, however, someone grabbed the back of his pajama shirt and jerked him backward.

He gagged as he flew through the air. He hit the ground hard, gasping, and the hands holding onto him dragged him backward to the side of the house. "Help—!" he started to scream, but his voice was muffled by a thick hand.

He was facing his sister now, her head poking out of the bushes, and she looked terrified and furious. He squeezed the walkie-talkie, quickly telling her to hide.

"He heard us planning to kill them," said one of the men. "We have to do it now."

The shorter, older man glared at his partner in annoyance. "Well, you idiot, he did hear *that*, for sure." He indicated for the man to go on, and Pete felt the hand covering his mouth rise up to cover his nose.

Pete began to panic in earnest now. He kicked out and punched out at the man. He had never been big or athletic, but months of being sick had made him even weaker, and the man actually looked amused at his feeble attempts.

"Only a man like Green would have such a pathetic offspring. I'd feel bad, but honestly, I think we are doing your folks a favor, boy," the older man said with mock sincerity.

Pete kicked and thrashed, but his vision began to funnel inward. With his last dying seconds, he finally heard the words that he had been trying to remember since he had died that late September evening.

"We'll have to wait a few months now to kill the other little brat. It'll look too suspicious. We can do it on Christmas and get rid of the whole family at once."

CHAPTER 23

CRAZY PLANS ARE FOR CRAZY CHILDREN ONLY

Pete didn't remember jumping up and running to the dorm room. But here he was.

His friends burst through the doorway. "Pete, what's going on?"

"They're going to kill my sister!" He was pacing back and forth, trying to figure out what to do.

For some reason, Alex was with them, and she looked like she was about to cry. She was hugging Charlie, whose face was pale with worry.

"My sister and my mom and my dad." Pete grabbed his hair. "It was what I was trying to remember. They're in danger!"

"I don't want to sound cold," Max said cautiously, "and I am not saying I won't help you do whatever it is you want to do, but it doesn't…. In the end, they'll end up in AfterLife. Here."

Pete started shaking his head. Max didn't know what it felt like. He didn't know what it felt like to feel responsible for someone. "They don't belong here. Not here. Not yet." He thought of his little sister, the way she giggled as she put that pipe in her mouth to make him laugh. "Not her."

Now that he was getting some of his memories of Life back, he knew he couldn't let her come over. Not yet.

"Listen," Max said quickly, as though Pete were about to sprint away, "I didn't tell you this because we weren't supposed to talk about our missions, but I did a study on Lizzy."

"Lizzy?" Pete still paced.

"Elizabeth Battinsworth," Max said. "The poltergeist."

Pete looked up.

"Her story is a lot like yours. She tried to help her family too. She got her memories early, and it drove her mad. She saved her family, but they still died later—just like everyone does in the end. And guess what? She's still crazy today."

"Listen." Pete's voice was voice. "That won't happen to me. Nick gave me this memory. I"—he searched for the words—"I can tell that my mind is…fixed."

Max started to say something, but Pete interrupted. "You don't get it. I'm supposed to help her. I just know it."

"How, though?" Max asked. "How do you help them? They're in a different World, three dimensions and at least twelve Portal stops away."

"I know how to Travel," Pete stated, but Scoot shook her head. She had been quiet up until this point.

"Not that far," she said. "That's what the Teleporting machines were built for. Long travel across dimensions like that is impossible without their help."

"There is a hotline for a GHOST recon team to send a message," Charlie suggested.

"We don't have time for that," Scoot said. "It's supposed to happen tomorrow, right?" Pete nodded and started pacing again.

"Listen, I can't explain this rationally," he said to Max, "but I need to do this. I can't ask you to help me—"

"We're helping," Scoot said simply and Max nodded, albeit, a few long moments after Scoot.

Alex nodded too, and so did Charlie.

"I'm in," Alex said. "So what do we do? Can we get a message back to your parents or something? I've heard of seances where this sort of thing is supposed to work."

"We do know a witch…" Charlie added.

Pete shook his head. His few memories of his father did not suggest that he would be open to receiving messages from his dead son.

"I have to go there," Pete said.

"We have to go there," Scoot corrected.

"We can't get a Portal to Life," Max said, thinking hard. "How else can we get there?"

"Why can't we get a Portal?" Charlie asked. "There are GHOST reconnaissance teams that go every Christmas."

They all looked at him, surprised. He shrugged. "What? I dated one once, and he told me."

They stared at him some more. "Okay, fine. I watched it on a show once, but that guard we met said it was true." Charlie rolled his eyes.

Max nodded. "Right. GHOSTs can go, but the tourist cards are pretty rare. It's mostly professionals, you know—GHOSTs or Reapers or the occasional vampire, but the other normals like us can't get a pass. They are rare and expensive—and the waiting lists are huge."

"Maybe for the legal way," Scoot countered.

"There are illegal ways to do it?" Pete asked. "Like, breaking in?"

Scoot shook her head. "No, breaking in is super-complicated. They have crazy security, even here in Purgatory, and even though I've been learning the equations and stuff, I don't know how to operate a Portal machine. What I meant is: there are illegal, unregistered Portal machines."

Pete felt a bit breathless. Could this actually work? "Where can we find those?"

"They're easy enough to find," Max said, "but they're still expensive. Do you have a ton of money lying around?"

Pete's heart sunk again. "Well, my parents have money."

"But that can't carry over, you know that, Green," Scoot said. "Come on, aren't you in a class that teaches about the different currency here?"

Alex spoke up. "My dad has money, but we could just use his business pass."

They looked at her, and Max raised an eyebrow. "Is he...wait, I thought he was in the transportation bus in...oh." He smiled sheepishly.

Alex nodded. "Yeah, he transports building supplies. But his company also does repairs and maintenance on the Portal machines."

"Can you get the passes tonight?" Pete asked, suddenly hopeful.

She nodded. "It's not a physical card. Well, I guess it can be sometimes, but not for my dad. With his type of business, he has so many constituents that he has an access code he gives his employees who deliver for him. I, uh, borrowed the code once or twice."

Scoot slapped her on the back. "My kinda girl." Alex grinned, looking embarrassed. "You've been to Life before?" Scoot asked.

Alex shook her head. "That's a more heavily guarded Jump. I wasn't sure if I had the right access code for that one. I was too chicken to test it out 'cause I thought I'd get caught." She looked at Pete. "But for this, I'd say it's worth it to try."

"It's heavily guarded," Max said seriously, "because Life is dangerous for the dead. People who go can get stuck, and we don't...do well there. Don't worry, I'm coming with you," he said quickly when Pete opened his mouth to argue, "but I just want everyone to know, what we are going to do is very dangerous."

Pete looked at Alex and grabbed her hand without thinking. He looked her in the eyes. "Are you sure you're okay with this?"

She looked a little flustered and nodded. "I'm sure."

He squeezed her hand . "Thank you." He added all the sincerity and appreciation he could muster.

Dropping her hand, he turned away and grabbed his mission-ready go-pack from under his bed. It was as if a light switch went on in everyone's mind, except Charlie's. His friends darted in all directions, grabbing supplies, with directions to meet at the gate in five minutes' time. Alex and Scoot sprinted off to their dorms to grab their things, while Charlie spun around in circles, flapping his hands.

"What do I need? What do I need?" he asked.

Pete huffed impatiently as he ran outside. "Charlie, stop! Just come on!"

Pete was surprised to see Scoot already there, but the minutes seemed to drag on before the rest joined. They were on time, but Pete was impatient to leave.

Charlie appeared last, looking absolutely ridiculous in his black leather pants, black silk shirt that opened at the chest, black biker gloves, and black scarf, with, by far the worst part, black eyeliner around his eyesockets.

Scoot's mouth was gaping, and it was an odd thing to see her so taken off-guard.

Pete was the first to snort with laughter. "I'm sorry, Charlie, but you can't go. It's just too dangerous."

Charlie looked confused. "If you think I will let my friends go into harm's way—" Charlie began, doing his hip flourish again.

"But what if there are snakes?" Pete asked reasonably. "I lived next to the woods. I remember them being all over there." That stopped Charlie in his tracks.

"How…how big are they?" he asked quietly.

"How big would be okay?" Pete asked, curious.

Charlie just stood there shaking his head. Pete raised his hands. "Listen, we need someone—no. We need you to stay and make up a story about where we are. No one can gossip like you. I need you to use that superpower to help us here in AfterLife."

Charlie looked immensely relieved. Pete turned to the others. "You should stay too. I know what the risks are here. I can… I can do this alone." He hadn't even finished speaking before Max shook his head, and Scoot punched him hard in the arm.

Pete winced and rubbed his arm.

"We're coming, and that's that," Max said firmly, and Alex nodded her agreement. Max had a hard and determined look on his face that Pete had not seen before. "Besides, there are so many possibilities," Max said in a lighter tone. "I mean, there's so much to learn by going back. I just…I just don't want Charlie writing the story of how you became the newest poltergeist, okay?"

Pete smiled gratefully. "I know. But I don't think we have to worry. I feel…better."

"What did you ask from Santa?" Max asked a few minutes later as they ran down the dirt road in front of the school, having said goodbye to Charlie.

"Nick, you mean?" Pete smirked. "I asked for my sanity."

"And illegally Porting to the most dangerous place for an unliving soul is your idea of sane, huh?"

Pete grinned. "Well, when you put it that way…"

Charlie had called them a cab. The cabbie refused to pick them up at the school, but met them at the end of the dirt road near the bus stop. Ten minutes later, they were at the town center, walking nervously into the nearly deserted transit station.

It felt like a different place when it was so empty. Their footsteps echoed, and the place seemed even more massive, even more intimidating. Pete wasn't sure where they were going and chastised himself for not thinking to ask one of his friends when they were outside and their voices wouldn't carry throughout the entire building. But Scoot and Alex seemed to know the way, so he just followed them.

They reached the chandelier before they ran into a guard. The man squinted at them suspiciously, but the girls walked with such confident focus that he went on without comment. When they had to decide between the east and west tracks, Scoot's confident steps faltered.

"This way," Alex said quietly, "to the after-hours tracks." She pointed to a sign that led them to the far end and then left through one of the marble archways.

They followed the signs until they reached a door that said After Hour Ports printed into the glass of the door. A paper sign to the right of the door read "As of October of this year, no oversized loads allowed in this portal station. Sorry for the inconvenience."

Just inside the unlocked door, they paused and looked around the station. To the right was a smaller plexiglass room with a speaker circle at about head height. The rest of the station looked like a sterile metal room. Fluorescent lights and industrial exhaust vents were placed sporadically across the ceiling.

There were tubes running in and out of the walls along with wires and what looked like small computers. To their left was a short bench, with some odd-looking equipment and bodysuits were hanging on wall hooks.

Pete looked around in wonder as Scoot knocked impatiently on the plexiglass of the Porter's station. In spite of his anxiety for his family, he was briefly distracted by the novelty of the Portal.

"Is this it?" Pete asked.

He'd thought there would be some machine he stepped into and then was zapped or something. This was just an empty room. An expensive, high-tech looking room, but still, more or less, empty of anything he would've called a Portal.

Before anyone could answer, a grumpy-looking man, middle-aged and balding with a generous bulge in his midsection, walked out of the plexiglass station. He wore a blue jumpsuit that said Portal Agent in stitching but had no name tag.

He eyed them with suspicion. "Yeah?"

"Hello." Pete forced himself to concentrate on not letting his wardrobe slip back into the pinstriped pajamas. He started to sweat from the effort. "We are here to Port to, uh…"

"Earth, "Alex said promptly. "Life, Quadrant…" She looked at Pete. "Where is the specific location again? New England, but where exactly?"

Pete told the man the name of the town and the street of his parent's house.

The man raised an eyebrow. Scoot stood, unsmiling, moving only her eyes as she tracked the man. Max, quieter than usual, did not look worried exactly, but he didn't look enthusiastic either.

"Earth?" The agent's voice dripped with sarcasm. "You want to go to a Life Quadrant. A bunch of kids in the middle of the night?"

Pete opened his mouth to speak but was beat to the punch by Alex.

"Excuse me?" She had an icy-calm tone Pete had never heard before—and hoped to never be on the receiving end of. She straightened her back and adopted a posture that could only be described as regal. No wonder she and Charlie are friends.

Pete hid a small smile behind a scratch of his brow.

The Portal Agent only raised an eyebrow again, a smile starting at one corner of his mouth and spreading to the other. He looked like he expected a bunch of his friends to jump out of the shadows at any moment and tell him this was all a prank.

"As I have a T-9 Level 1 clearance code. My age"—Alex said the last word as almost a snarl—"is none of your concern."

"It's my concern if you are not eighteen. Then you have that code illegally, and I can have you arrested."

Pete swallowed hard—he was definitely sweating now—but Alex casually pulled out an ID and held it right in the man's face. "Do I need to make a phone call and have your supervisor explain to you the procedures of clearing—"

"Yeah, yeah. Keep your hat on, prissy." He didn't seem to appreciate a teenager telling him how to do his job. He turned around to push a few buttons on the wall by his plexiglass station. He flipped a switch and lights began powering on all around the station. Machines and equipment lining the walls began whirring to life. He walked to what looked like a metal cabinet and opened a panel to reveal a monitor and a pull-out keyboard tray. He yanked it out with an angry grunt and began pecking severely at the keyboard.

"Where's your equipment?" the man asked, impatiently.

"Equipment? Oh, we're picking it up." Alex was clearly improvising.

"You...you're picking it up?" He smiled slightly and shrugged. "All right, Miss Prissy. Let's have the code then."

She gave it to him, and he said, "That's a business code."

Her eyes darted quickly. "Yeah, and?"

He chuckled. "No reason." He gave a smile Pete did not like. The man looked like a sadist might as he was watching someone walk off a ledge they didn't see coming.

Max must've thought so too because he went quiet and his frown deepened a little.

The man pulled a two-way radio off a stand. Pete stiffened, wondering if he was going to call security, but the man barked some coordinates into it and returned the radio to its latch.

The opposite wall in front of them started shaking and then began to move apart, revealing a massive, cylinder-shaped machine with a chamber the size of a large room inside.

The Portal Agent looked downright jolly as he gestured for them to enter the Porting chamber.

"Um." Alex was finally catching on to the man's strange behavior. "Thank you?"

They stepped inside the big machine. It was all steel with tubes and wires running every which way. Pete remembered Alex saying that companies used Portals to transport large equipment and even animals from time to time. Everything looked high tech.

"Why with all this high tech are we barely able to get a working computer?" he asked Scoot to help get his mind off his nerves.

She looked at him with a small, annoyed frown. "That's Purgatory for you. It doesn't have good internet or any other technology by design. People in Purgatory don't like change, and the internet brings change."

The Portal Agent continued to click on buttons and moved around the chamber pulling levers and things.

Alex bit her lip. "They didn't do all this the last time I Ported."

The man left the chamber, went back to his stand, and picked up the two-way radio. They could see him through a window, grinning wickedly as his voice came over the speakers inside the chamber. "Well, I tried. If you get stuck, you get stuck," he said cheerfully.

Pete did not like anything about that smile, and he could tell by Alex's slightly wavering voice that she didn't either. "What does that mean?" she asked.

"Normally, there is a protocol and a guide given to first-time, Earth-Life Ports, but this access code has been used multiple times, so I trust that you're very familiar with the safety protocols," the man replied.

He pulled the radio away from his mouth, but Pete could see him laughing on the other side of the glass. His voice came back on. "Strange that you would leave the Portal gear you need on Earth-Life quadrant 5 when the log says you have never been there before. But," he said in a falsely cheerful voice, "I'm sure experienced Travelers such as yourselves have it well under control."

His smile widened, and he pushed a few buttons, and a cover came over the outside of their glass tube, blocking their view of the room outside. Still, the man's voice came over the intercom. "Also, normally I would explain where to go and what places to avoid. Life is very dangerous for unseasoned travelers, but I am sure none of you will turn out like the unlucky ones who leave an eye behind because they wandered into an area with the wrong air pressure."

The mic clicked off, and Pete watched with growing apprehension as the outer doors lowered, blocking out the man laughing silently from the other side of the heavy-duty Plexiglass.

CHAPTER 24

I'LL BE HOME FOR CHRISTMAS

PETE HEARD THE OUTER DOOR click shut, and they were plunged into darkness for a few minutes before lights flicked on inside the chamber, casting them in an eerie glow. As a loud, whirring noise sounded, the chamber started to shudder.

Max pointed at seats with seatbelts, and they hurried to sit down and click them into place. That guy hadn't even told them to strap in. Pete's anger rose, but not more than his fear.

Alex grabbed his hand as the shudder turned into a violent shake, so powerful that it felt like his body was being pulled apart. He gritted his teeth. His vision darkened, and he closed his eyes, as his eyeballs felt like they were trying to jump out of his head. Alex screamed next to him—and then, suddenly, the vicious shaking stopped.

Beside him, Max turned away to be sick. Pete couldn't blame him, but it earned a disgusted look from Scoot. A few moments later, the hatch door opened, and a different Portal Agent stepped into the chamber, his eyes round with shock.

"You didn't use Jumping gear coming that far?" He hurried over to check on Max, who still looked a bit green-faced. "You guys are lucky you didn't pop an eardrum or something. Is your hair falling out?" They all ran their hands through their hair to check, Alex a bit more quickly than the others.

"Why didn't you wear gear?" The agent gestured for them to follow him out of the chamber.

"We didn't have it," Pete said weakly.

"Well, sure. Few people carry all that with them. Why didn't you get the Port gear from the agent before you jumped?"

They stared at him, and Alex pursed her mouth in a way that suggested she would ask the agent when she got back.

The man frowned. "Well, you'll have gear for your way back. Y'all know where you are headed?"

Pete gave him the address, and the man handed them a map.

"You're close—within walking distance. Closest and safest way is through the woods." He pointed at the map and drew a line upward. "The bad areas are circled here on this map. It's tough to breathe in those spots, and it's dangerous for the brain, right? But in general, it's safe around water, nature, or cemeteries." He showed them a few spots on the map. "Not all, mind you, but most. And if a lotta people were killed in an area, then it's usually okay for a deadie to go there, but you run a higher risk of running into an unregistered poltergeist. There seems to be more of them these days, and with budget cuts, they haven't had enough Retrieval Teams to collect 'em all, so mind ya step, 'kay?"

The man looked like he wanted to keep chatting, so Pete thanked him quickly—they were running out of time. The agent looked understanding, if not a little disappointed. It didn't look like a whole lot of visitors came through his port. He went to sit alone in at a desk in the small station, barely big enough to fit the Portal machine in. When they exited the station, they realized that one room was the entire building. From the outside, it looked like a rundown shack in the middle of the woods. They could hear the occasional car pass on a road that was a few feet away on the other side of the building.

Pete, by habit, looked at the watch he had taken from his go bag and blinked in surprise when he saw it working. "The time...this can't be right. It says it's only five p.m." He could still see the light from the sun shining through some of the trees.

"Time is funny when you move from AfterLife to Life," Max said. "It doesn't translate the same. Same with any Portal jump. They have their own solar system and sun to base their days off. Some places don't see light for months."

Pete nodded. "Well, that's good. I thought we would be too late, but this gives us more time." He pointed. "This way."

After about five minutes of walking, Pete stopped referring to the map and walked based on memory. He knew this place, these woods. He and his sister used to run through here when he wasn't sick in bed.

"Max struggled to keep pace with Pete, who was all but running, "Have you given any thought to what we are going to do when we get there?"

"I need to talk to my dad."

"Okay, but we're not technically living so he won't be able to see us."

Pete shook his head. "I'm not great at this stuff." He had barely covered the concepts in his BASA training. GHOST work was high-level stuff. He didn't know what he was going to do.

"We'll just have to wing it." He started to jog.

Panic rose in his stomach. What if he got there and he still couldn't do anything to save his sister and parents?

Max said, "I've studied some of the concepts and so has Scoot. She even tried practicing some of it. We might be able to do something, but I just don't know, Pete. This might be a bit out of our league."

Pete didn't know when he started sprinting, but soon he and his friends were running through the woods. Suddenly, they all came to a halt to catch their breath. "There it is," he said.

He'd spotted the hedges surrounding his parents' property. The trees thinned as they came to the massive green lawn. The hedges where he and his sister often played detective were a good forty or fifty feet ahead of them. The three-story brick mansion stood behind the lawn, snow covering most of its roof. The vines on the side of the house had browned for the winter.

Looking at the house, he realized why he had felt so comfortable at the school so quickly. Max let out a whistle, and Scoot stared at the house and then at Pete.

"Your parents own this? Or they work and live here?" she asked.

"Owned," Pete said. "I think…I think that was why I was killed."

"For the house?" Alex was shivering. Pete took off his jacket and offered it to her.

"No. For the money. I don't understand why exactly, but I think my murder has something to do with my dad's business. That's why he's in trouble—why my family is. I think…" He waved his hands. "It doesn't matter."

"Yes, it does," Max said. "It matters."

Pete had told them all the details he could remember when they were waiting for the cab.

"If those guys who did you in were not working for themselves," Max continued, "then the one they were working for could just send others and we'll have done all this for nothing. Before we leave here tonight, we need to understand who they are and why they are doing this in order to save your family for sure."

Pete nodded, finally feeling the chill. Goosebumps spread up his arms, and he started for the house. "So what do we know about how this place works—Life, I mean—for people like us?"

"Hmm..." Scoot said. "It's not a direct Port." Pete looked over his shoulder at her and she elaborated. "Meaning we're not suddenly alive now just because we are in a place that we used to live. We're halfway there. We are in between living and dead, so to speak. I didn't memorize all the science behind it."

"We don't need the science behind it. We need to know what we can do with that information. Max, you said they won't be able to see us? Not at all?" Pete asked.

"Uh, kinda," Max answered. "See, it's complicated—we have to emit enough energy. Some people have tools for that, but I don't know what they are called or where to find them."

"So how do we emit energy if we don't have any tools?"

"My uncle did it a lot," Alex said. "He was a famous GHOST. Well, he was famous back home. He could do all kinds of stuff, and he used to show some of it to me and my sisters. He said it had nothing to do with how smart you are and everything to do with the breath and the mind. And focus, he said."

Pete nodded. "That sounds like all the Other Skills. They all use focus and breathing techniques and things like that. Maybe we can figure it out. We'll have to figure it out."

"There are things we can do to make it easier though." Max's brow furrowed in thought. "There are objects or things that the dead can channel through."

"What? Like an Ouija board?" Scoot asked.

Max shook his head. "Those are unreliable and usually have a poltergeist attached to them."

"Okay, like what, then?" Pete was getting frustrated.

"Water, or things that hold water. Mirrors, sometimes, or some old objects could work."

"Like an old book? Anything old?" Pete quickened his pace.

"Yeah, but like really, really old. And it can be tricky. A book is good because we can figure out how to point to a word and spell out a message, but other old things just kinda end up creeping out the people you are trying to reach out to."

"I think I know just the thing!" Pete started running. He grabbed the back door handle, twisting it to push in, but the knob stayed firm. Instead, his momentum sent him right through the door. Off-balance, he stumbled forward and fell on his face. His friends, who had run straight through, grabbed his arms and pulled him up.

"What part of great energy and focus and breathing did you not understand, Green?" Alex pulled him forward.

"I...I..." Pete was stunned. Somehow through all the explaining and debating and worrying, it did not sink in. It wasn't until the moment that he was lying on his face that it registered that he truly did not belong there.

This was no longer his home. The realization was so shattering it left him dazed.

Scoot seemed to sense his mood and didn't continue the teasing. "Come on, Pete," she said in a gentler tone. "Where do we go?"

"Um...I...we...here, this way."

The kitchens were filled with the chattering gossip of the cooks.

He wanted to hug a few of them. Martha had always snuck him sweets, even when he had been sick, and Angelica had sung songs while she cooked, and he would sit and listen and sometimes sing along. Trenton would do cool tricks with his knife when he sliced an apple for a snack for him.

As Pete walked by, he peered in wistfully. Past the kitchens and the staircase to the servant's quarters, they found a row of windows that overlooked the grounds. He saw Mr. Olsen, the grumpy gardener, working on a bush.

He breathed in the smell of pipe smoke and coffee and indicated his friends should follow, as he quickened his pace towards his father's office. On habit, he went to grab the door handle and stumbled again, though not as bad this time. Alex, Scoot, and Max followed him inside.

His father was sitting, unshaven, with a few fingers of whiskey in a glass. His eyes were red-rimmed, like he had been crying. Pete stared at him, forgetting everything for a minute. He couldn't remember his father ever looking like this before. He seemed broken.

A gentle pressure on Peter's shoulder brought him back. He blinked back tears in his eyes and nodded. He couldn't afford to get distracted. His family's lives depended on it. Looking around, Pete spotted the book on the desk lying where it always was, under his father's reading glasses.

He grabbed for his great-grandfather's journal and cursed when his fingers went through it.

"Hang on a sec." Scoot grabbed his arm.

"We may not have a second!" Pete didn't know where the anger had flared up from, but Scoot looked unfazed.

"Stop being an idiot. You spend all your energy moving a book, then what? What are you going to say to him?"

Pete looked at her and shrugged, arms wide. "Uh, I...I could say 'Danger. Someone's trying to kill you.'"

"Okay. That's a start, but who is and how? What will saying that accomplish besides freaking him out? We're trying to save him, not put him in a mental hospital."

Pete nodded then shook his head. His shoulders slumped "I don't know what to do."

"I have an idea," Max said, and Pete turned to him hopefully. Max swallowed. "Let's first look around and see if the danger is here. You definitely heard what you heard, but what you heard was months ago. They may have other plans. I think it is more important to tell your family who killed you as opposed to warning them about themselves. I mean, we should still tell them that, but you need to tell them what happened to you first."

Pete nodded slowly and Max continued. "I was thinking about that after we came inside the house. We might not have the time or the resources to find out exactly why you were killed, but if we tell your dad that those two men hired by your dad's partner killed you, I think he can investigate the rest. He might even understand why it happened, but either way, he will lose trust in his partner and protect himself and his family against him in the future. I think that's the smarter plan."

"Okay. So, we look around really quickly and then go back to the book plan?" Pete asked.

"Yeah. If there is immediate danger, we can give a specific warning, but if not, we'll go with that," Max said.

"I like it," Scoot said. "Everyone split up and meet back in here in ten minutes."

Everyone nodded. Pete squeezed Alex's hand briefly before running upstairs. They all fanned out, with Scoot taking the outside perimeter, Max taking the ground floor, Alex taking the stairs with him but continuing up one more story to try to get onto the roof. Pete told her where the access point was, then darted down the hall. He could hear her retreating footsteps moving upstairs.

He ran straight to his sister's room. He didn't think there would be any particular danger there yet, but he wanted—no, he needed to see her, to know she was safe.

She was usually outdoors as much as possible, but Christmas was typically the exception. Pete had a rush of memories of them spending Christmas Eves inside planning how they would sneak off after dark to watch Nick—though he knew him at the time as Santa—putting out their presents.

He pushed through her door. Her room appeared empty except for the bed, where it looked like she was curled up. But a few steps forward, he saw it was only her covers that were bunched up. She wasn't here. Stifling his disappointment, he checked her closet on the way out and ran through all the other rooms on that floor, including the closets and bathrooms, leaving his parents' room for last.

Everywhere was empty of people, except for Mr. Meeps, their ancient cat. The cat looked up and meowed at him when he ran into the closet, which startled Pete. The cat's eyes tracked his movements, and he got a spark of hope.

Could the cat see him? Was it a normal thing for cats to see ghosts, or was he doing something to make himself visible?

He took a deep breath and entered his parent's room. The sound of soft crying reached his ears, and a lump rose in his throat. He had been so caught up with his family's safety he had forgotten this was the first Christmas after his death.

He found his mother across the bedroom in the connecting bathroom, sitting on the floor holding one of his old toys. Her head was down and her shoulders were shaking.

He stood there, staring at her, unable to move. Her hair was tied back in a messy bun, and she was in an oversized T-shirt and pajama bottoms, just like all the Christmases in the past. He wanted so badly to run and hug her and tell her that he was okay. That there was no need to cry.

"How do I make you see me?" he asked her, out loud.

"Pete?" a voice said behind him, and he jumped, looking back. Lilly's head poked out from underneath his parents' bed, where she'd apparently been hiding from their mother. She was wearing her old detective outfit.

There was a gasp from the bathroom. Pete turned back and his mother was staring with red-rimmed eyes into the mirror—directly at him!

CHAPTER 25

WHY FOURTEEN-YEAR-OLDS ARE NOT GHOSTS

"Oh my god!" she said in a quivery yell, getting up so quickly that she overturned the chair. "Peter?" She looked around wildly. "Peter!"

"Mom?" Lilly's voice gave away her confusion and fear.

"Did you see him?" Mom asked frantically. "Oh my god, I'm losing my mind."

They couldn't see him anymore. He concentrated all his efforts and shouted, "Mom! Mom!"

His mother jerked back and covered her mouth as a scream came out. "Pete? Pete! My Peter Rabbit. Is that you? Edwin! Edwin, come here!"

Pete could've cried from relief and joy that she could see him. He heard Dad yelling from downstairs and then his footsteps as he ran up and into the room. The door banged open, making Lilly jump and start crying. Dad ran to her, hugging her and then pulled her to his wife. He grabbed his wife's arms. "What? What is it? Are you hurt?"

He looked terrified, but his wife was sobbing and smiling. "I saw him. I saw our baby! Edwin, Pete's here!"

The look Edwin Green gave his wife wrenched all the joy from Pete's heart. It was the look of someone who feared he had just lost someone else when he thought he could lose no more. Pete had made things worse. He tried to focus, but he was feeling dizzy and lightheaded.

"Baby. Show him. Show your father!"

"I'm trying, Mom," he said desperately.

"You haven't been getting much sleep," Edwin started, but Evelyn cut him off with an angry grunt.

"Don't start that with me."

Pete was taken aback, and by the look of it, so was Mr. Green. Pete had never heard his mother speak like that to anyone, let alone her husband. He remembered always gagging because they seemed to do nothing but cuddle and kiss. The memory made him both embarrassed and a little nauseated.

He closed his eyes and let his worries fall away. He tuned out the sounds of the argument starting in the room. He let go of the aches he'd acquired from Teleporting all the way here. He let go of the exhaustion behind his eyes and the headache that was forming. Slowly, his body slipped into that in between state that would enable him to Jump or Shadow Walk. But this time, he did neither.

"Dad." Pete opened his eyes and stared directly into his father's shocked eyes.

"Pete?" The bleakness in Dad's voice threatened to break Pete's concentration. "Baby?" The crack in his voice expressed how broken the man felt.

"Dad," Pete repeated, "you're in danger."

"I can't hear you, son. I can see you talking but…I…how is this possible?" His mother was holding her mouth, sobbing, but Lilly suddenly turned and sprinted out of the room.

Pete would have been disappointed, had he not seen that determined look on her face. It was the look she always got when she had a masterful plan.

He smiled, knowing that she was figuring out a way to help him communicate with them. And he was right. She ran back into the room a few moments later, nearly knocking over their father in her haste.

"Dad! Move!" she demanded, startling him. He turned automatically, no doubt to lecture her on the importance of politeness, but she ignored him, impatiently dropping her alphabet blocks on the floor.

"Oh," he said, stunned again. "Good… good thinking, Lilly Pad."

He looked dazed and lost. He sat down on the floor of his bedroom slowly, something Pete had never seen his father do.

"Point at them, sweetheart, and we'll write it down," Mom said. "Lilly, honey, can you get us a—oh." Her eyebrows rose, impressed at the sight of her impatient-looking daughter, already poised to write on her detective's pad.

Pete wasted no more time. He could feel the connection slipping and could tell his image was no longer as strong as before when his family gasped and started looking around wildly. Pete sat in front of them and focused. Once he felt himself gain control again, he began pointing.

D-A-N-G-E-R

"Danger? What? Why? Who?" His father started firing questions.

"What's going on, baby?" said his mother. "Is that why you are here? Are you in danger, sweetie?"

Pete sighed. This is going to be difficult.

His nine-year-old sister—wait, he had missed a birthday. His ten-year-old sister seemed to be the only level-headed person in the room. She gave her parents a dirty look and said what Pete could not.

"Too many questions. We need to be efficient. Look, he's slipping away." His parents looked devastated, but she ignored them.

"Time for yes or no questions." She pulled out the Y block and the N block, and her father outright grabbed her head and planted a big kiss on her forehead.

"*Gaagh*. Gross, Dad," she complained.

Edwin leaned forward to ask a question, but once again, his daughter beat him to it.

"Let me. Pete. Were you murdered?" She stared intently at him. His parents gasped.

"Sweetheart. He was sick…" Mom began, but froze with her mouth open when he pointed to the Y.

Pete knew then that Lilly had seen what happened to him the night of his death, but his parents must not have believed her.

"Who?" Edwin said with a ferocity that startled Pete. He winked out and back again.

"Yes or no, dad," Lilly repeated. "Was it dad's guys from work?'

Pete pointed to Y.

"Told you," she said, huffily.

"Which guys?" Edwin said desperately.

"I don't remember their names," Lilly said.

Pete pointed to the blocks and spelled out, "T-I-N-G—"

"Tingsley," Pete's father finished without inflection in his voice. Pete flickered again, and he pointed to the Y.

"Pete!" a voice to his right shouted.

Pete jumped and turned to see Alex, sweaty and worried. "We have a problem!"

"Pete? Pete! Baby, what is it? Are you in danger, sweetie? Tell Mommy. Tell me!" His mother was on her feet.

Pete pointed at the N, but he looked right at Lilly, and she asked the question he needed her to ask.

"Are we in danger?"

He nodded and pointed to Y.

"It's them?" his mother asked. "They're back, aren't they?"

Pete nodded. He looked at Alex, who nodded confirmation.

His mother ran to the window, then to the house phone next to their bed on the nightstand. "I can't see anyone in the yard, but…" Her voice trailed off and she looked at the phone. "It's dead."

His father's face hardened. He stood up and pulled a cell phone out of his pocket. He punched in 9-1-1 and cursed a moment later. "There's no signal."

"Where are they? What are they doing?" Pete asked Alex.

Alex bit her lip, clearly worried. "Max said they were rigging the electrical panels. He thinks they are going to make it look like an accidental fire. Max and Scoot are trying to stop them, but I came here to help you get them out in case it doesn't work."

Pete tried to stand and almost toppled over. She caught him. He knew he must be invisible to his family again, judging by the way they were looking around again.

"You were talking to them," Alex said, stunned. "How?"

"It's like you said. Concentration and breathing. It kinda feels like the Shadow Walking that I did…I did the other…phew, I'm tired." He held his head. The room was spinning.

"Hold it together." Alex grabbed his shoulders.

The spinning slowed. He seemed to get a second wind and inhaled to collect himself. "I think I'm good."

"Pete! Pete, where did you go?" asked his mother.

"Honey," Edwin said, "we have to focus. We are in danger. I am not going to let them hurt anyone else. Alan will pay for what he did to this family."

Pete tried to show himself again to tell his family to move, but he found he didn't need to. His dad was already shuffling them all down the stairs. Pete followed quickly, along with Alex.

"Maria!" Dad suddenly called out. It was the maid, tidying up on the floor below them. She looked up, startled.

"Yes, Mr. Green?"

"Get as much of the staff as you can and get out," he said swiftly. "Try not to be seen, and go to the neighbors and call for help. Tell them two men are attacking us." Maria jumped, crossed herself, and ran towards the kitchen.

"Should we go with them?" Pete's mother asked.

"I don't know if that's wise. They're not looking for them, so I think they will be fine. But…"

"But they may pick us off if we try to leave," Lilly said.

Mom gasped. "Honestly, child, where did you learn all this? I need to pay more attention to the shows you watch."

"I don't know where they are," Edwin continued. "But, yes, they may have guns, and outdoors is pretty exposed. Let's get to my office."

They darted down the stairs to the first floor, turning the corner to run into the office, but they all stopped abruptly at the sight of the tall man blocking their path.

"Good evening, Mr. Green."

Pete, who had run a little ahead of his parents, stared with rising anger at the man who had killed him. Kenton Tinsley was a few inches over six feet, with broad shoulders, a trim beard, and a polite smile. A fake smile.

Pete heard footsteps and turned to see another man, shorter and older but very lean. Gregory Kraig was much more rugged than his counterpart.

"G'd evenin' folks," he said with a smile that was far from polite and bordered on indecent when his eyes passed over Mrs. Green.

"Ew." Alex said it with such revulsion that it snapped Pete out of his staring. His eyes narrowed at the two men and clenched his hands into fists at his sides.

"You here to kill us like you killed my boy?" Dad's voice carried a stony anger that was so unlike him.

"Now, now, now." Kenton stepped forward. "Why would you say that? We just wanted to wish you a Merry Christm—"

But the words snagged in his throat, his eyes widened, and he gaped open-mouthed as Pete materialized in front of him.

"What the—" blubbered Kenton.

Pete felt more energy than he ever had since his first day in AfterLife. Adrenaline and rage were rushing through his body—he felt like a storm, crackling with power.

"What the hell?" Kenton repeated. "You're dead." His face went from blank to confused to angry—then to a calm that made Pete's stomach turn. Something must have shown on his face because Kenton chuckled and exchanged a look with Kraig, and they turned back to him, both of them smiling.

"Well, what do you know. We was just saying how much we missed you," Kraig said.

Pete blanched, panic rising in him. He'd thought this would be easy. He'd thought he would just scare them and be done with it. Had he gone through all of this just to watch his family die?

No. No way. He wouldn't let them.

The two men dropped all pretenses. Kraig pulled out a gun and Kenton pulled out a long knife with a serrated edge. Pete fought against his fear and stepped forward with a hard-set jaw, and Kenton flinched a little.

"Whatcha gonna do?" Kenton laughed. His voice shook ever so slightly, and his hand holding the knife flinched, but he stood his ground.

"Leave them alone," Pete said in a clear voice.

"Or you'll do what?" Kraig asked mildly. He smiled sweetly. "I regret killing you first." Mom whimpered behind Pete. "I liked you the least, you know? Your father is a genius and your sister seemed to inherit his brains. Your mother is, well…"There was that filthy smile again. Hate spiked in Pete's chest. "But you, you were always worthless. Yet, somehow you were going to inherit the family fortune."

Edwin growled, and Pete glanced back to see Mom clutching Lilly. Kraig looked at Pete with an odd expression. "Even before boss gave the okay, I tried to get rid of you. I just couldn't stand to see you. I tried to make it look natural." He smiled wider, and Pete could actually smell the man's sweat. "I tried poisoning you. I had an old family recipe that fooled doctors and morticians for years, but still." He shook his head, and hissed his next words in frustration. "Still, you lived on. And then finally, we manage to kill you. And now you're back." He spread his arms wide. "Welcome back, son." His voice changed to a deadly calm. "I was just thinking this morning how sad I was that you wouldn't get to watch them die, but damn if I didn't get my Christmas miracle." He raised the gun.

Pete moved directly in front of Kraig, and the man laughed. "Seriously? What do you think you're going to do?"

That was a very good question. Pete was having a lot of trouble being here in Life. He hadn't noticed right away, but it was difficult to breathe here. Everything required so much concentration to do, and likely any bullets this man shot would go right through him. His mind was racing for an idea, but nothing was coming. Maybe Kraig was right. Maybe Pete was worthless.

And that was enough to spark something. He saw the tiniest chink in the armor.

"You've made a lot of enemies," Pete said softly. "You think that I'm alone here?" He forced a laugh.

Out of the corner of his eye he noticed Alex running off, and knew that she was going to find their friends.

"Maybe I'm worthless." Pete shrugged casually, pretending to be unconcerned. "But think about everybody you've harmed."

The man's eyes flicked around the room quickly. His expression stayed the same, but Pete noticed the man sweating. Kenton, who had been quiet this whole time, shifted uneasily beside Kraig.

"You think that I'm here for my family?" Pete forced another laugh. "You're mistaken. I'm here for you, my friends." He made his voice match the deadly calm Kraig had used on him. The one that made his skin crawl and stomach knot up. He smiled as casually and sweetly as he could. He wanted the man to believe him.

He hadn't noticed Alex return, but suddenly she was back and Max and Scoot were with her.

Scoot, seeing what Pete was doing, made herself visible. "Hi, Mister." She smiled and pulled off her head. "Wanna play with me?"

Kenton jumped, cursing under his breath.

Max, who had sprinted to the other side of Kraig for effect, made himself visible—with quite a bit more effort, Pete could tell. "You'll like it where we are. Would you like to see?"

For the first time since Pete had known him, Max showed his death face. Blood, ghostly in texture and color, welled from a massive wound on his head. It fell down his face, neck, and arms. Max grinned. "You'll like it."

Kraig took a step back, his grip on the gun shaking. He swung it back and forth from each of the ghosts, not sure which to shoot first. He landed on Pete, which was unfortunate, because Lilly was behind him.

The gun blasted and Mom screamed. Pete felt himself slip away from the sight of the living.

"You killed him!" Kenton cackled. "You did it again." Emboldened by the sight of Pete disappearing, he stepped forward, raising his knife.

Lilly! Was she all right? Pete managed to get his bearings and quickly looked behind him. His mother had yanked Lilly out of the way just in time. He let out a terrified breath. All three of his family were crouched, gripping each other, too stunned to run. And even if they ran, the bullets could fly just as far.

But Pete wasn't about to let that happen. The four dead children shared a look, turned their narrowed eyes back to the men—and let loose mayhem.

Pete reappeared and rushed at Kenton, who staggered back, wildly raising his hands, cursing loudly. "You didn't kill him!" he shouted.

Scoot did something Pete had never seen or heard of before. She closed her eyes and squatted low, then lifted one foot up and stomped down hard like a sumo wrestler. The entire room shook. Pictures fell off the walls, decorations toppled over, and the chandelier rattled and swung back and forth, and Mom screamed again.

Max squinted in concentration and pulled open the drawers and doors on the hallway cabinet, and Alex whispered something to Scoot, who ran to the kitchen and returned a handful of knives. Pete was nervous that she was going to kill the men, something Pete was sure would land them in prison, but she flung them expertly all around their attackers instead, making it look like she barely missed them every time. Kenton and Kraig both let out shrieks and yells, hopping frantically to avoid them. Kraig dropped his gun, but Kenton kept swinging his knife wildly in the thin air.

Pete turned and shouted to his parents and Lilly. "Go! Get out!" His parents, who had been shocked into terrified silence, unwrapped themselves from each other and ran towards the front door with their daughter.

Pete let himself vanish again, and Scoot and Max did the same. Scoot slumped to the floor when she did, and Alex ran over to help her stand.

"What the bloody hell?" Kenton yelled to the room. Kraig had backed up against his partner.

Kenton shook his head and started whimpering. "No. No. No. No. This can't be happening. You aren't real!" he shouted to the room." You're…you're not here." He was blubbering like a child, but he cursed loudly.

"I am here." Pete knew his voice carried perfectly. "And I am real." He popped back into view.

"Are you worried the rest of the people you killed will come for you?" Pete asked sweetly. "Because you should be." Kenton was sobbing now, and Kraig was ghostly pale. "Tell Alan that Peter Green says hello." The name sounded strange on his tongue, as Pete had only ever called their boss by his surname. "And I will come back with a lot more friends if he puts a finger on my family EVER AGAIN!"

His voice boomed out, and the walls rattled even more violently than they had when Scoot had stomped. Scoot looked startled—but not nearly as scared as Kenton. His hands were up, and he was shaking with fear.

"Yes! Yes! I'm sorry. We're sorry," he sobbed.

Kraig was cursing. "We've gotta get outta here!" He was backing toward the open door, close to bolting and leaving his partner. Pete did not want him running in the same direction as his family, so he swiftly jumped to the other side of the door. Kraig let out a scream that was much higher pitched than Pete would have expected from the man.

"Not this way," Pete said firmly. Kraig tripped as he backed away from Pete. He and Kenton scrambled back the way they had come, out the back door and around the side of the mansion.

Minutes later, Pete sat with his family and watched the red and blue lights racing up the street.

"Don't tell the police you saw me, okay?"

"Son, we aren't idiots." His smirked.

Dad eyes still portrayed a deep anger that would not easily go away. Mom was crying again. She hugged Lilly tightly, who, in spite of her toughness, had been truly shaken by the appearance of the two men.

Pete knew he only had a short while with them. He was in shock that he was still able to speak with his family after the inordinate amount of energy he had spent.

He looked at his crying mother. "I'm fine, Mom." He tried to portray all the sincerity he could into the look he was giving her. "I'm happy. I'm safe, and I even have friends here." She smiled at this and nodded.

He knew in his heart that he was telling the truth. In spite of the recent sadness he had felt, he really was happy. He finally understood what Max had been trying to explain to him. This was only a temporary goodbye. Right now, they needed to be where they were, and he needed to be where he was. He would see them again before he knew it, and he told them as much. He told them about meeting Santa, at which Lilly looked thrilled. He told them about his friends and his school. He even told them about his new girlfriend, making Alex smile.

He told them that he wasn't sure what he wanted to do yet for a career, but he had lots of choices. To that, his father instinctively started giving suggestions. "Have you considered Wall Street, son?" Mom placed a hand on his shoulder, and Pete laughed out loud.

When the sirens reached the mansion, Pete felt a gentle squeeze on his own shoulder. "We have to go." Max looked truly regretful.

Pete nodded, noting the strain in Max's eyes. Now that he was looking for it, he noticed the same in all his friends' faces and could feel the same achy strain in his own. They needed to get back to where they belonged.

He nodded again and turned to his family. "I have to go."

"Are you going to come back?" Mom asked, hopefully.

"I don't think so, Mom." He winced at the look of loss in his mother's eyes.

"I'll be there in the end for you if I can," he said to his family. "Live a good, long life. Be happy, and I'll promise to do the same. Okay?"

His mother nodded, tears flowing freely down her cheeks again. She squeezed Lilly, who stared at Pete, looking all the more like the brown-eyed, lost girl he had seen in his mind all year.

"Hey." He remembered something he wanted to ask. "Why was I wearing pajamas and a tie? When I…you know."

Lilly giggled. "That was my idea. We needed detective uniforms. You grew out of your old ones, and Mom and Dad wouldn't get you new ones since they thought you were too old to play the game, so I made up these pretend uniforms. You wore PJs and a tie, and I wore my long johns and a hat." She smiled and a memory of him dancing around the room in pajamas while she rolled on the ground laughing popped into his mind.

Pete smiled and nodded. "I remember now."

He looked at her, an overwhelming sense of loss tugging on his chest. He waved again and slowly turned to leave, knowing whatever the consequences were, he'd done the right thing.

CHAPTER 26

TEA WITH THE BAT

THE WAY BACK WAS A blur. Pete barely remembered moving through the woods. "Oh my," the Portal Agent said when he saw them. "Did you guys get attacked? I have to know if I need to send a team to get a rogue poltergeist."

They shook their heads. He seemed to sense that they had no energy to speak and rushed them into the Portal chamber without any more questions. He gave them goggles, wrapped them in what looked like bulletproof vests, and latched each vest to the machine. He tapped a button on the vests and instantly they began inflating and deflating. They looked like they were breathing. The machine closed and whirred to life.

The process was significantly quicker and smoother going back. Had Pete not been so exhausted, he would have had another flare of rage for the first Portal Agent.

But he didn't even have the energy to get angry when said Portal Agent barked a laugh at the sight of them. Though Pete did conjure enough energy to look amused when Max held Scoot back from attacking him. The agent's smile faltered slightly when he saw a flash of metal.

They heard the fading voice of the agent as they walked outside, dragging Scoot with them.

"Was that a knife? HEY—I'm talking to y—" His voice cut off when they slammed the door.

They all collapsed outside, huffing air. Pete hadn't noticed because he had been so panicked for his family, but the air in Life had not been enough. It had been thin and insignificant. He lay back on the grass, gulping in breath after breath, staring up at the night sky.

"We're home." He smiled, letting the tears fall freely down his face.

His friends lay down on the grass beside him, and he felt Alex and, more surprisingly, Scoot each take one of his hands. He sensed rather than saw Scoot take Max's as well. They lay for a long time on the grass, staring at the stars in the sky and the lazy clouds floating slowly overhead. He let his tears fall, quietly crying.

"We're home," he whispered again with a cracked voice.

Pete did not know how many times he was going to have to learn this same lesson. By the time they got back to Mrs. Battinsworth's Academy, every single person in the school knew where they had been and what they had done.

He sighed, as Charlie stuttered a hysterical apology. His friend was standing nervously at the end of Pete's cot in Nurse Gray's office. The nurse had made Charlie promise that he wouldn't get Pete all hyped up. Charlie had agreed, and then proceeded to start sobbing and pacing up and down the room explaining what had happened.

For once, it didn't sound like it had been his fault. "Saint" Nick was a bit more all-seeing than Pete had anticipated and had given the headmistress a heads-up—but not enough of one to stop Pete from going, Pete noted.

It was she and Coach who had picked them up in front of the TransPortation office, instead of the taxi they were planning on calling.

Pete and Scoot ended up in the nurse's office. Max and Alex had been mostly okay: a few bruises, but not suffering the same level of exhaustion as Pete and Scoot. Pete had been the worst, staying a full day longer than his friends. He suspected that was, in part, to make sure he would not turn into a poltergeist.

When he was released, he was instructed to go straight to Mrs. Battinsworth's office, but he decided to take a detour. He knew what was coming, and he didn't want to face it just yet. He knew he was going to get kicked out. He would have to leave like Sam and Alexandria and Dadson had been forced to do.

Pete sighed, his feet crunching on the snow that had not yet melted. The mild winter days were back, and the morning sun had melted most of the snow not hidden in shadows. But the maze had a lot of shadows, so snow lingered here, and he crunched his way to the kissing place.

He sat alone on the bench, smelling the faint muddiness of the earth and roses that surrounded him. He listened vaguely to the muffled sounds of his classmates enjoying their time off.

He was still sad, but it was a different sadness from the one a couple of days before. It felt less like a weight on his chest and more like a tinge of regret. He wiped away chilly tears.

He closed his eyes for a full minute, and when he opened them, a calm spread over him. As much as he had loved his family and his home, he had a new home and a new family.

"It's good that you realize that," a voice said, making Pete jump. He looked around but didn't see anyone.

"What?" he said.

"That you have a home and you have a family." It was Max, crunching his way around the corner. Pete blanched. He didn't think that he had said that out loud.

"I might lose you guys too though." Pete looked sadly at his friend. "I kinda messed that part up."

Max gave Pete a soft smile. "Only for a short while. Scoot, Charlie, and I are all older than you. We were always going to be separated for a short time when we graduated. It's always been part of the unspoken plan. But we—or at least I—had always planned on meeting up after."

Pete forced a smile too and nodded. They sat there in silence for a long while. Finally, he made himself go to the headmistress's office, walking much like a man walking to the gallows.

In the waiting lounge, he walked around and admired the artwork hanging on the walls, to distract himself. He was surprised to notice that they told a story. There was a scene from a troll war that he had learned about from his AfterLife 202 professor. There was also the depiction of the first time a Portal was used as common transportation.

He had forgotten reading about the significance of that day. Later, they would develop the inter-Portal financial system that they used in AfterLife today. He was surprised by how much he had learned and grown in the last few months.

His skin prickled, and he turned around suddenly. Mrs. Battinsworth studied him from her substantial height. She was in an ankle-length, long-sleeved gray dress, buttoned to her neck, and her hair was pulled into her typical bun though it looked a bit looser today. She wore elbow-length black gloves. She pulled one off and held it in her hand for a moment, still looking at him and saying nothing. Pete looked back at her, and instead of the stern disciplinarian, he saw the shadow of the sad mother who had lost her daughter to insanity.

Strangely, that, of all things, made him the most certain that he was leaving the school. He studied his shoes and slumped his shoulders.

"I'm getting kicked out," he said in a quiet voice. "Aren't I?"

She didn't say anything for a long while and then nodded toward the fireplace. "Come have tea with me." She pulled down on a candlestick and, like the old cliché, the fireplace spun slowly around.

Pete stepped onto the spinning portion and walked into the hidden room beyond. He gasped, completely thrown by what he saw. They were in a beautiful atrium composed almost entirely of windows. Each pane of glass was framed in white wood. There were plants everywhere. The tile was black and white checkered, and there was a small table with two cushy chairs, to which she led him.

Pete followed her past shelves full of books though they were walking a little too quickly for him to catch most of the titles.

"Those are from Living authors. That is, they were all written when the author was still alive." She invited Pete to sit, and then she rang a small bell. Pete studied the books and wondered how she had gotten them.

The fireplace moved again and her secretary, Sally Delerie, winked at Pete as she carried a tray burdened with a pot of hot water, two cups with saucers, and some little sandwiches on a plate.

She set the table up and asked Pete what his preference of tea was. He didn't really care but said Earl Grey because that had been his father's favorite tea.

When the secretary left, Mrs. Battinsworth looked at Pete with a small frown. "My daughter was a little older than you when she came here."

Pete looked up in surprise.

"I made this school to protect children against the dangers in AfterLife. You, going where you went... I shudder when I think what could have happened." She shut her eyes hard. When she opened them, she gazed at him sadly. "In that regard, I failed you."

Pete just stared, tea and sandwiches forgotten.

"I am an old woman. I have forgotten many things, but the pain of losing someone? That sticks with a person." She sipped her tea, her eyes distant and unfocused. "I am sorry about your family. It brings me relief that you were able to help them. I am even more relieved that you are safe. That is a rare thing, to do what you did, go where you did, the way you did, and make it back with your sanity. My Lizzie…" She swallowed visibly.

Pete stayed stock still. He couldn't believe she was telling him all this.

"My daughter was not so fortunate. You may have heard. Purgatory is a strange place, with strange magic. It was meant to be a temporary place, a lovely place to wait for those you love to come to you. Sometimes, there are those who get stuck, those who like the predictability of it, the unchanging nature of it. And then, there are those, like my Lizzie, whose soul gets altered.

"Purgatory has a strange magic. We don't understand it. Scientists have trouble studying it. Maybe with the advancements they are having in medicine, one day she can be cured." She fiddled with her spoon and then set it down, seeming to find herself again. Setting her shoulders, she met Pete's gaze. "People go mad when they have all of their memories and they stay. There have been exceptions, but they are rare—and as a result, we never let a child stay if they have all their memories. The risk is too great."

Pete held her gaze, but he could feel a lump rising in his throat. He had known it, had known this would happen since he plopped down from exhaustion on the grassy lawn of the TransPortation office. But hearing it out loud felt like a punch in the stomach. He let out a shaky breath.

"You will be allowed to say goodbye to your friends, and then we will have to move you." She looked at him. "I'm sorry, Pete," she added in a sincere voice. They looked at each other for a moment. They did not speak for a long while.

What would he say if he could speak? He couldn't be mad at her. He had broken into her files and stolen his own. He had ignored her warnings. He had not asked for help when he started getting the nightmares. This was his fault, through and through.

He didn't regret what he had been able to do for his family. Still, this was his home.

"Where…" He cleared his throat. "Where will I go?"

"You will live with your great-great uncle," she answered.

"My…my uncle? I have family here?" Pete asked, confused. "I thought I was supposed to live with family right when I got here."

"We couldn't find any record of you having a family. We wouldn't have found any, had it not been for Nick." She pursed her lips disapprovingly. "You picked a lucky day to break all the rules. We would have had to transport you to another orphanage, but he located your uncle for us. He has agreed to house you."

Then, something clunked into his memory. His file had spoken of an uncle unwilling or unable to house him. Had this been the same one?

The tone she used made Pete curious. "What's my uncle like?"

She shrugged. "He is a decent man in many ways." She paused. "And an indecent man in as many others." She sighed and held her hands as though to say, Here are all the cards. "He is a War Lord."

Pete stared. "A what?"

"He is one of the highest members of the Community," she replied.

CHAPTER 27

EPILOGUE

PETE SAT ALONE ON A train. He was on the last leg of a very long trip. He peered out the window. The landscape was fascinating. Purgatory had been as much like Life as was possible. But this—he frowned at the strange-looking trees. Their branches grew into the earth, but the trunks grew from floating clumps of grass that hovered a few feet above the ground. Flowers the size of full-grown men had sprouted everywhere. An animal that looked like a striped monkey ran on all fours and leaped into the air to catch a bright purple bird that had been hiding on a like-colored flower.

Pete looked away, grimacing, as the monkey-thing ate its prey. "Egh. Ouch."

This place felt alien. Like he was on another planet altogether. And technically, he was. The thought made him think of Alex, who had said that her family lived not too far from where he was going.

She had cried when he told them. Pete had felt like crying too. He had liked her for so many months, and she had been his girlfriend for ten whole minutes before he had to go. But he'd had to break it off, knowing it was impractical to date long-distance when they were both so young.

He had held her and kissed her, a moment that had been ruined slightly by the screaming dodo birds that had fallen off a nearby tree.

Pete remembered sighing and then turning to say goodbye to all his friends one by one. He was surprised, but pleased, by how many people had come to see him off. Mr. Johnson led the wolves and the Ware Team over to shake Pete's hand. The boys from his dorm had also come to say goodbye. Pete hugged some of the Gossip Queens, shook the hands of his other teachers, Coach Skinley and then, most shockingly, Shelly of all people, had walked up to him. She had punched him hard on the arm, threatened to hunt him down if he did anything to get himself into trouble, and then stalked off. Pete hadn't been sure if he had just been given a farewell or a threat.

Shrugging uncertainly, he'd stood looking at Scoot, whose eyes were red-rimmed; Charlie, who had tears streaming down his chubby cheeks; and Max, who was pretending to straighten his shirt, unable to speak.

"You guys were an amazing family." It was all Pete could manage to say, but it was enough.

He pushed back a tear as he thought about that moment, looking out his window once again. The sun was setting and he knew he was getting closer.

He had learned very little about his uncle from Mrs. Battinsworth. She had said that he was a very secretive and suspicious person. She'd admitted that it had taken over an hour to convince him she wasn't a spy and another two hours to convince him that Pete was also not a spy.

The train slowed to a stop an hour later. The sun couldn't seem to make up its mind and was dancing in the multicolored sky, darkness waiting in anticipation in the distance, night creeping in slowly to reclaim the sky.

The doors opened, and he walked out onto a deserted train platform. Pete wasn't sure if he had gotten off at the right place. He was about to get back on the train to ask someone for help when the doors shut and the train's pistons screamed as it started moving again.

The beginnings of panic swirled through Pete. There didn't seem to be anything around for miles and miles. They had moved away from the lush green surroundings and had been crossing a desert landscape for the past hour. Pete didn't have any more water with him and only had a small snack in his backpack.

The train cleared the platform he was standing on, kicking up dust. He coughed, looking at the back of the retreating train, waving the dust out of his face.

"Well, well, well," a deep gravely voice said from the other side of the tracks, "you must be Pete."

Pete squinted at the silhouette of the man who'd spoken. When he stepped forward, he could see a man just under six feet tall, with pale skin, a long white beard, short white hair, and an eyepatch. The other eye, brown and twinkling with a mean glint, surveyed Pete.

The man was flanked by two massive creatures. Both creatures were dressed in attire appropriate at a cattle ranch. One had the head of a bull, and the other a squid. The scene seemed so odd, like something out of a cartoon, but Pete had no desire to laugh. Both creatures had glittering, intelligent eyes, and Pete suspected there was a very good reason that they were trusted to be his uncle's right and left hand.

Pete nodded at the man with the eyepatch, saying nothing. He thought that was the best move. His skin was prickling, and he didn't like the feeling he was getting, like he had just stepped into enemy territory.

"Well, Peter Green," the man with the eyepatch said, "my supposed grand-nephew." He spat on the dirt ground, and a tiny cloud of dust was disturbed when he moved.

"Your actions have the Community very curious." He smiled unpleasantly. "Very curious, indeed."

ABOUT THE AUTHOR

Angelina Allsop lives with her husband, Bryce, and their very old and very fat bulldog, Roree, in San Tan Valley, Arizona, where she enjoys being outside on rainy days, reading, and, of course, writing about all the adventures that happen in her head.

Peter Green and the Unliving Academy is her first book. She has never been to AfterLife but supposes she will visit one day and see the friends and family who visited before her.

Thank you for exploring AfterLife with me. Be sure to follow Pete and his friends as his adventures continue in the sequels coming soon. Join my VIP mailing lists for news, free books, and giveaways at **www.aaallsop.com**

Thanks for joining in the fun!

Delightfully yours,

Angelina Allsop

CONNECT WITH ANGELINA ALLSOP

Website
www.aaallsop.com

Twitter
www.twitter.com/AllsopBooks

Facebook Page
www.facebook.com/aaallsop

Facebook Group
business.facebook.com/groups/1124229267679757

Pinterest
www.pinterest.com/aaallsopbooks

GET BOOK DISCOUNTS AND DEALS

Get discounts and special deals on our bestselling books at
www.TCKpublishing.com/bookdeals

ONE LAST THING...

If you enjoyed this book, I'd be very grateful if you'd post a short review on Amazon. Your support really does make a difference, and I read all the reviews personally so I can get your feedback and make this book even better.

Thanks again for your support!

Proof

Made in the USA
Columbia, SC
10 July 2018